LIFE AMONG SEAHORSES

LIFE AMONG SEAHORSES

CORMAC LIN

ISBN: 978-1-7352171-1-6 (Paperback)
ISBN: 978-1-7352171-0-9 (Hardcover)

Library of Congress Control Number: 2020940697

Any references to historical events, real people, or real places are used fictitiously. Names, characters, and places are products of the author's imagination.

Background cover image by Blaque X from Pexels.
Book design by Allison Chernutan.

Printed in the United States of America.

First printing edition 2020.

Fractured Mirror Publishing
Knoxville, Tennessee

www.fracturedmirrorpublishing.com

LIFE AMONG SEAHORSES

NEWS ARTICLES FROM THE PAST

DO YOU WANT A SON?

According to Dr. Robert Mastiff, one pill is all it takes! BY JONATHAN ADAMS

JULY 20, 2050 Have you always wanted a son, but keep getting daughters? Well, according to one pharmaceutical corporation, the solution is here! Yesterday, Dr. Robert Mastiff of Mastiff Pharmaceuticals announced the successful creation of the XYTablet, the first pill guaranteed to kill the X chromosome in a man's semen, promising you a son with little or no side effects. The pill, taken as a water dissolvent, is flavorless to most men and is guaranteed to work for approximately one year. Currently, XYTablet is being tested with the US Food and Drug Administration with no planned release date. However, representatives of Mastiff Pharmaceuticals have stated they hope to start selling in the North American market during the first quarter of 2051, and the company plans to expand the drug to the international market soon after. The drug is especially expected to be successful in Asia, where traditional Confucian ideology has continuously supported sons over daughters. In market news, stocks for Mastiff Pharmaceuticals rose 15% after the announcement of XYTablet.

Are the effects of XYTablet permanent? BY BRUCE STEVENS

JANUARY 15, 2055 It has been nearly five years since the release of XYTablet on the market, and now, consumers and scientists are all asking the same question: Are the effects of XYTablet permanent? Consumers of XYTablet claim that their body can no longer produce X chromosome, even well past the expected expiration of approximately one year. Scientists working for different government departments representing the United States are currently studying the long-term effects of the family reproductive drug, while a Senate committee has been created to ask if any legal action should be taken against Mastiff Pharmaceuticals. Since the release of XYTablet, the US has seen a decrease of female births by about 15%. However, across the ocean in the People's Republic of China, a decrease of female births by at least 40% over the last few years has been reported, potentially changing the landscape of the population and culture of the country over a very short period of time.

CHINA'S DISAPPEARING FEMALE POPULATION
What can be done about it?

AUTHORED BY MING-HUA LANG

APRIL 7, 2081 The People's Republic of China may still have the world's largest population, but does it have enough females? Just three decades after XYTablet exploded in the market, China is facing a gender imbalance unlike any analyst has predicted. Influenced by the Confucian ideology of filial piety and continuing the family name, this tasteless drug was easily dropped into drinks of ignorant newlyweds by parents or grandparents, causing an exponential rise in birth of sons, with families unaware or ignoring the long-term consequences of their actions on the nation. Though the government banned XYTablet five years ago and has increased awareness in understanding the result of the drug on the country, the family planning drug still thrives on the underground market. The effects of the drug have been catastrophic, with a current approximate 70 to 30 ratio of men to women under the age of thirty according to the census since XYTablet was first released. The government of China has tried to deal with the increasing male population by supporting a growth in military recruitment and other so called "masculine work." In addition, new laws and policies have increased the difficulty of emigrating abroad to prevent the rise of fleeing nationals. The government has also banned marriage of female Chinese nationals to foreigners, and in some cases, issued court-mandated divorce for Chinese women who have married Westerners.

Both local and international scientists have been working to create a solution for populations affected by the XYTablet, but hopes are not currently high.

"Men born from XYTablets unable to create X chromosome" confirmed by Mastiff Pharmaceuticals

BY AUSTIN SANCHEZ

MARCH 2, 2088 Nearly four decades after the best-selling family reproductive drug in human history was released, and banned in nearly every country in the world, representatives of Mastiff Pharmaceuticals have confirmed what many consumers and scientists have long feared.

"We regret to announce that any male born via the use of XYTablet is indeed unable to create the X chromosome needed to procreate female children," said Dr. John Mastiff, current CEO of Mastiff Pharmaceuticals, "and we are currently working to find a cure for my grandfather's infamous family planning drug."

With the current controversial company now approaching bankruptcy, analysts believe there is little hope that a cure for the drug will come from the company itself. The company, however, has been more transparent in releasing the chemical formula and other information about XYTablet to outside sources in hopes of finding a cure.

China has been most strongly impacted by the drug, with less than 30% of its population being biologically female. The United Nations is closely working with China and other nations impacted to solve this gender imbalance and the crisis it has caused.

BIRTH OF THE "TEST TUBE GENERATION" BY ALISON STINSON

MAY 30, 2098   Many countries, especially in Asia, have turned to so-called "test tube babies" in order to maintain the current population, as the dwindling rate of women means many countries no longer have the female population needed to provide consistent growth. In addition, the population of men able to create the X chromosome has decreased, leading many governments to collect eggs and viable sperm to maintain population growth, and the developments in test tube technology means that growing babies in an artificial setting is no longer a problem. Test tube babies are then given to prospective parents within the community and country to be raised. It is believed that within this decade, many regions around the globe will have all new births done through artificial means.

Although XYTablet has been globally illegal for over a decade, scientists believe it will take many more years before some form of gender balance can be achieved. Despite round-the-clock work by many nations and corporations, a cure has yet to be discovered.

Mandatory "sex change" laws announced, hoping to balance China's gender imbalance

ARTICLE BY *JOSEPH PARTRIDGE*. ADDITIONAL INFORMATION PROVIDED BY *DAVID SHI*.

OCTOBER 15, 2107   Just two weeks after the People's Congress of the People's Republic of China announced their controversial new "Women's Protection Act" which allows the government to legally remove Chinese women from their homes, by force if necessary, and relocate them into specialized camps for their protection. The Chinese government has announced another law that will clearly enter even more controversy and discussions on the global stage. Mandatory sex changes will be required for half the population to build a society that is equally male and female.

According to the government, the plan is simple: take half of the population of males and give them a sex change to make them female. New developments in breast implants and artificial vaginas mean that this process is cheap, effective and relatively harmless, noted at least one doctor speaking on the floor. "Most of the newer models will look and feel just like their natural counterparts," said Dr. Li Wenshan, an expert on gender reassignment. "I am sure most men will be unable to feel the difference." He added that "the new Chinese 'females' will be given training and re-education to uphold the dying culture and traditional roles of Chinese women."

According to current plans, candidates who will be given sex changes will be chosen by lottery, though those willing to pay a high fee or considered important members of society will be exempt. Those refusing to participate will be considered traitors to the nation and punished to the fullest extent of the law.

"Male and female roles are inheritably important and different," said one congress member. "In order to maintain a healthy society, we must have both." The law was passed unanimously in the People's Congress, and the first batch of sex changes are expected within two months.

Although some citizens noted in private that this law is discriminatory towards the lower classes, as they are unable to withdraw from the lottery, no protests or voices against the law are expected. This is due to the outlawing of large public gatherings that are not sponsored by the government thanks to the 2070 Shanghai incident and the crackdown that followed soon after.

Understanding the "nan-nu": The new Chinese "woman"

BY STEPHEN SMITHERS — *MARCH 8, 2114*

Even though Li Ran talks, looks and acts like a woman, including performing womanly duties like cooking and cleaning, once, she was a man. Li Ran is a "nan-nu," a Chinese term translated literally as "male female." Today, nan-nu, like Li Ran, have taken over the role of the traditional Chinese females; they get married to men, they cook and clean, they take care of the children, and most importantly, they serve and satisfy their husbands.

Nan-nu usually have their male genitalia removed around 10 years old, though some lose it closer to puberty, and in rare cases, after. Once chosen, nan-nu are given training on the proper roles of a woman and taught to be the most supportive wife for her future husband, including performing bedroom duties. This training is also important to prepare a person to go through the proper psychological and cultural development, as people who resist the process or don't fit in the social role are often severely punished.

Most nan-nu, like Li Ran, come from rural villages and are chosen through the lottery, though some members of the lower class are willing to give up a child to become nan-nu as an opportunity to climb the social ladder. In addition, some families are experimenting with the idea of raising male children immediately as nan-nu upon birth, though they do not receive their gender change until later. Since few, if any, nan-nu come from higher class backgrounds, and decisions on who becomes a nan-nu are not based on an individual choice, many critics, especially from abroad, have noted that the process is not only unethical, but also discriminatory.

The government of China has enforced a strict ideology defining the roles of "men" and "women" in order to maintain peace in society, as well as created a "separate, but equal" guideline. Most men do not support nan-nu working, though some receive government sponsored jobs to train the next generation of nan-nu.

It is important to note that between 10 to 20 percent of China's population are still biological females, though many hide their identities as the government has strict laws involving the rights of biological females. The risk, if discovered, is being removed from their homes for what the government calls "mandated protection."

Fifth year in Chinese Civil War, casualties continue to rise, no end in sight

BY VINCENT MAO

JANUARY 17, 2130 — Opposition forces destroyed what was left of the once great capital of Beijing this morning, ending the three-year siege, according to local sources. Most of the remaining citizens were unable to flee the city as it was burned and bombed to the ground. Even more tragic, the Chinese Semen Procreation Bank was confirmed to have been lost with the city, destroying China's biggest collection of semen not impacted by the XYTablet, as there was no way to transport the specimens during the siege.

Now in its fifth year, the Chinese Civil War appears to have no end, and with no strong leaders rising above the chaos to reunite the country, the future for this once great nation appears bleak. Though many countries around the globe have tried to propose peace treaties, no clear resolution has been found.

With the fall of Beijing, most of the country's northern territory including the areas of Inner Mongolia and Manchuria now appear uninhabitable to humans and other species due to the use of nuclear, chemical and biological warfare.

The Chinese Civil War was triggered by social unrest, starvation, and other national problems, which some people blame on the creation of the XYTablet. Whatever the cause behind the violence, this is by far the deadliest and most expensive war in human history.

THE PEOPLE'S REPUBLIC OF CENTRAL CHINA

WHAT TO KNOW ABOUT THIS NEW NATION *BY PETER CHENG*

AUGUST 31, 2136 It has been referred to as the "deadliest and most expensive war in human history," and it has destroyed much of what was once known as The People's Republic of China. But, like a phoenix rising from the ashes, the newest nation of the world, The People's Republic of Central China, officially became globally recognized after a treaty signed earlier this year divided the remaining habitable lands of China into much smaller nations.

Born from the previous central provinces of China, including Shaanxi, Hunan, and Hubei, this new landlocked nation is made up of areas that were less affected by the civil war due to their geographic location and mountainous terrain.

It is too early to tell how the government plans to deal with many of the remaining consequences of the nearly ten-year war, but what is obvious is that many challenges await this newborn nation.

People's Republic of Central China to close its border from foreigners to protect "blood purity, sovereignty and cultural dignity" By HAOTING CHAO

APRIL 4, 2142 "If the People's Republic of Central China is to survive, our blood purity, sovereignty and cultural dignity must be preserved and protected," said President Qin Jiaban today at the Capital. "From this moment forth, all foreigners, mixed raced populations and non-Han locals must be expelled from the borders. We must work on protecting our own nation," he said, leading to wide applause from the audience. "We will become the last remaining refuge of the pure and noble Han Chinese."

Since its creation, the PRCC has been affected by numerous catastrophic issues including dealing with the consequences of war, an approximate 5-10% biological female population, economic problems and environmental issues that have caused unrest within the new nation. Foreign analysts say that for officials, blaming the issues on foreigners is a popular method to stir up support and gain temporary unity. In addition, many Chinese citizens do not receive the education or information needed to understand such complex issues and only receive their news from government sources.

The PRCC military has already been sighted in the mountainous regions close to the northern border, where numerous ethnic minorities have continuously lived for many generations; the PRCC does not recognize them as "Chinese." It is widely believed that the government will use military force if the communities do not leave voluntarily within the next few days.

"We must remember that the cause of our problems, the XYTablet, was not a creation of the Chinese people, but instead by foreign dogs hoping to weaken our great culture," said a member of the audience. "The United States was fearful of China's growth and created this drug for the sole purpose of destroying our great nation. I strongly support President Qin in kicking out the blood traitors and foreign scum."

It is important to note that not all foreigners have been expelled from the PRCC as the country maintains diplomatic relationship with a few nations. However, opportunities for travel to and within the country are extremely limited and strict due to the nation's isolationist policies.

IN 2176.
THE PEOPLE'S REPUBLIC OF
CENTRAL CHINA IS A LAND
WITHOUT BIOLOGICAL WOMEN

1.
A FAMILY IS BORN FROM A HUSBAND AND A WIFE

THE YOUNG WOMAN WAS PARADED through town, locked in a rusted metallic cage, clearly made for a different species. Her silky hair covered her face, now hiding the dried bloody streaks that could only come after days of crying.

The crowd around her was silent. They had witnessed similar events before, but they were becoming rarer and rarer with time. Each of them realized that this was not only the last time they would see this young woman, but perhaps the last time they would see a biological Chinese woman.

Though this woman would have never noticed, nearly thirty feet away, hidden in the shadows of a crowd of much taller and older men, ten-year-old Wang Yi could see her perfectly. She was unlike anything he had ever seen, and it left an instant reaction flowing through his body unlike anything he felt before. Despite being only ten years of age, he knew at that moment, that this instant attraction and the woman it came from, would be something he would never see or feel again. He would never forget the way she looked, her hair streaming down like the waterfall painted in his father's favorite scroll, her body, and her chest, ample like the buns he ate every morning, her natural beauty overshadowed in his mind by the pain she was going through. As she was paraded through town and taken away, chained to her cage, somehow, he understood. For the rest of his life he would never forget this sight, this beauty, and he would be forever haunted by it. There was something about her that seemed to call to him. Though he could not touch her, he instinctively reached forward, wanting to have that fleeting touch, curious about the gentleness of a woman's body.

Suddenly, twenty-four-year-old Wang Yi woke up, hardened in pain, his groin aching for a release. It was not his first time having this dream. It was not the first time that his body screamed for a satisfaction that could never be fulfilled. The hot summer air exacerbated his heavy breathing, adding to the pool of sweat already pouring out of his body. His sudden shift in movement woke up Li Ling, his twenty-four-year-old "wife" of ten months lying in bed next to him. Ling looked around, yawning, surprised to be awoken, before seeing the erection of his partner.

"Here," said Ling, pushing his long hair out of his face and yawning. "Let me take care of that." Shifting his body to the bottom of the bed, he opened his mouth, wrapping it around his partner's erection. Yi, closing his eyes, gasped loudly as he felt Ling's warmth around his groin, slowly relaxing his body and thrusting himself into Ling's mouth, instantly enjoying the familiar state of pleasure; his breath quickened as he thrusted his pelvis forward.

In the midst of his pleasure, Yi opened his eyes and began to watch Ling and noticed his naked body. Instantly, reality awoke in his mind, destroying his fantasy. The curved feminine breasts replaced by a flat masculine chest, that "thing" dangling between Ling's legs, triggering flashes of guilt and anger throughout his body. He felt disgust entering his mind as he jerked his body away.

"What did I tell you about sleeping nude in bed with me?" Yi asked angrily, throwing the sheets at Ling's body. "Come on, quickly, cover yourself up!"

"But, it's so…so hot," said Ling, his left hand still holding on to Yi's penis. "Come on, let me take care of you, and then I will get dressed." His bright grin shone through the darkness of the summer night.

Yi felt disgust and shame rise through his body. This was not how it was supposed to be. This was not how nature meant it. Yi wanted the woman of his dreams, not the "woman" lying beside him. He felt the helplessness and anger flow through him as he spoke coolly, "It's bad enough that we have to sleep together now that we are married, but can't you just respect me enough to keep your clothes on. You know how I feel about…about seeing…"

He couldn't get the words out. "Look, just…"

"I am sorry, I will go get dressed," said Ling quickly. "Umm… do you want me to finish?" he added, trying to sound cheerful.

"Look, just go put something on. I am tired. I am going back to sleep." Yi rolled over and pretended to quickly fall asleep. He heard Ling crawl out of bed and heard the shuffling of clothes as Ling got dressed. He knew he had hurt Ling's feeling; he knew Ling only wanted to comfort him, but he just couldn't.

Ling was already cooking breakfast when Yi awoke. As he walked out of the bedroom into the kitchen of their simple, modern two-bedroom apartment, he thought about his actions from the night before. He knew he was short with Ling. He knew he needed to figure out a way to apologize to his once best friend and now wife. Instead, he sat quietly, as Ling served him his usual breakfast of millet congee, a few fried eggs, and soy milk, and watched him as he flipped between the pages of his newspaper, careful to appear lost within the text of the pages.

It wasn't that Ling was ugly by any standard definition. He wasn't overtly masculine or feminine, and, culturally speaking, he was seen as quite cute. He looked rather young, maintaining a baby face that he kept clean and smooth. Though he wasn't very muscular, he had no body fat, and he had a stomach that vertically lined up with his chest. In nan-nu terms, he had an airplane field. His hair was long as would be customary for a person of his assigned gender, and though it didn't make him look more like a woman, it did make it less likely that one would think he was a man. Despite everything that had happened in his life and their life together, Ling still maintained an aura of innocence; a sense of kindness and wholeheartedness that most would have lost by now. It was those qualities that kept Yi straddling between the line of like and dislike. It would have been better if he had a reason for treating Ling so badly.

Yi stared at Ling's face; it had changed so little. He still had that same innocent look. It was this innocence that started their friendship in the first place, that innocence that led to a friendship he wanted to protect. From that first day, when Yi met Ling in elementary school, there was a quality about Ling he didn't want to change. As the boys grew older, and began learning about their respective roles that were chosen for their lives, the desire for protection grew stronger, and Yi ultimately saw it as his responsibility to be a part in the decisions that would affect his friend, and more importantly, protect him from harm.

"You're not listening, are you?"

Yi jumped in his seat, having suddenly heard Ling's voice ring out. "Excuse me?" Yi asked, pretending to be concentrating on his newspaper.

"I want to get the surgery. I want to have my penis removed. I want to have breast implants. I want to become a complete woman," Ling said defiantly.

"No," replied Yi, returning to his morning meal and his newspaper. "Anyway, you are too old. It would never look good. It is better you stay the way you are."

"I can take hormone pills. I can do the exercise. I am already registered as a nan-nu, so why won't you let me become one?" pleaded Ling. "Come on, we both know it's the right thing to do."

"I don't want to talk about this. Can't I just eat my breakfast in peace?"

"I...I just...I just want you to like me. I just want you to be happy. Why won't you let me make you happy?"

"Look, you do make me happy," Yi said wearily. He looked at Ling, before gasping out the words slowly. "I have said this before. It's not you; it's me."

"I know you will like me more if I have the right parts. Why won't you just let me get the surgery?" begged Ling.

"Because I am not going to turn you into some sort of she-male freak, okay?" snapped Yi. He saw the tears form in Ling's eyes and felt unusually guilty. "Look, I've got to get to work; let's talk about this when I get back."

Ling nodded, standing there quietly. Not knowing what to do, Yi reluctantly gave Ling a quick hug and awkwardly stroked his hair before he walked out the door.

The city of Xincheng was no longer in the same state of glory as when the People's Republic of Central China was first born. But as the capital of the Zhongjiang province, it was by far the nicest city in the region. Economic hardships, impacts of global warming, and pollution had taken a toll on the city that was barely thirty years old. Inexperience and fast workmanship followed by lack of upkeep meant most of buildings looked older than they were and had already begun slowly deteriorating. The propaganda billboards decorating the city, promoting its splendor, had withered under time and weather. Dust storms from the north coated the city with fine, ashy sand that was impossible to remove. Some of the poorer residents of the city still collected scraps from the outskirts of town, left over from the ten-year Civil War, to sell for their basic survival. For Yi, however, this being the only city he had ever lived in, there was no finer place on Earth.

Flowing through the middle of Xincheng was the once mighty Yangtze River. Though, between the dams in the west and the pollution, the glory of the river had been destroyed long ago, and today it was a place best avoided. The smell of rotting life permeated the surrounding riverbeds, while garbage from the west made it a sewer that flowed through the city. Chemicals spills from both past and present gave the water's surface a rainbow gleam that sparkled with poison and oils. The remaining life that somehow managed to survive in the river, the few fish here and there, a couple of water plants, and the build up of algae, looked mutated and feeble.

The city was divided into four districts, based mostly on social status, with the river flowing northwards, from west to east, dividing it in half. Most people stayed in the district they lived in, never interacting with people not from their social class.

Yi lived in the northeast district, Shucheng District, home to the wealthier merchants, educators, and the minor government officials. This was also where most schools were located and was the district with the most personal shopping. Most people in the city were unable to afford to live here and only passed through when necessary.

However, being the top high school, Yi's work was situated close to his childhood home in the Zhengfu District, the south-eastern district. The government and financial quarters of the district were located on the other side of the river. The least populated, it was also where the wealthiest, most educated, and the leaders of the city resided, and where the best of the city could be found. While Yi's salary and family wealth paid him enough to live in this district, he had no interest in living so close to his family. Using the excuse that it would make the family look humbler and in touch with the people, something that could be beneficial in the future if he were to run for office, he had persuaded his father to allow him to live in Shucheng.

Towards the west lay the Shenyi District, by far the largest in both size and population, where most of the city resided and worked. It was bigger than the other three districts combined, taking up both sides of the river. Despite its size and population, it was the district that Yi was the least familiar with, and he only went if he had to visit Ling's parents.

The last district, the Shoushu District, was also the smallest and squeezed into the southwestern corner of the city. Considered to be the Forbidden District, it was home to the surgeons, the outcasts of society that played the important role of guaranteeing enough women for the city. Shoushu was also believed to be the most dangerous district, where the least amount of governing happened.

Yi grew up in the Zhengfu District. His Grandfather, Honorable Father of the City, Wang Fuqing, was a great general during the war and had become the first governor of the province. Upon his passing, Yi's father was "elected" to the same position, though he was the only candidate that could be chosen. Yi knew that he was expected to follow in the family footsteps, but politics were of no interest to him. His current job as a teacher, though admirable in society, was not building towards the career his father had destined for him and was one of their many common points of contention.

Under a faded and eroded billboard stating "Save China's Biological Woman. Report all Biological Females to the Department of Female Affairs," Yi waited for the bus. The painted woman on the poster was not as beautiful as the one of his dreams and probably never existed outside the artist's imagination. Yet, Yi still spent countless mornings at the stop wondering what her body felt like, what her voice sounded like, and building a fantasy of the home life he knew he deserved. Upon the bus's arrival, Yi headed to Xincheng #1 High School, beginning the same daily routine he had participated in for the last four years.

Yi was the youngest teacher at Xincheng #1 High School, and though he was a competent teacher, well-liked by his students and peers, he knew that like every other teacher in the school, the position was given to him because of connections over qualifications. However, as Yi was also an alumnus of the school, he usually felt a strong loyalty to the school, as well as a connection to the other students, that differed from the other teachers.

He used this loyalty as justification for many aspects of his life, including not going home after work and dismissing his father's pressure to switch jobs.

Yi taught a course that was a combination of ethics, history, and political ideology. His background, as the son of the governor, meant he was the perfect teacher to mold the future of the country. The parents and students obeyed and admired him for his connections and perceived power. Along with his colleague, Teacher Long, the two teachers ran the Social Political Science department of the school. It was acknowledged by the school as being one of their strongest and flagship programs. Though Long was older by nearly two decades and had been working at the school back when Yi was a student there, Yi had been promoted to head teacher upon being hired, which, once again he understood, was only due to the circumstance of his birth.

By the time the citizens of the PRCC reached high school, their respective sex had been selected by the government, and they had begun to receive their education accordingly. Only citizens who were assigned as being male could receive an education in subjects such as math and science in a high school. Citizens who were assigned as nan-nu were sent to training schools to learn household skills, such as cooking, cleaning, and sewing.

As Xincheng #1 was the best high school in the city, only graduates of schools like Xincheng #1 usually made their way to higher education and good jobs. The students and teachers at Xincheng #1 High School were very law abiding, hard-working, and, most importantly, patriotic, as everyone knew that stepping out of line could lead to expulsion or more severe punishments. The fear of losing this rare opportunity was enough initiative to keep most in line.

Every morning, after greeting the 2-foot by 3-foot photo of Supreme Leader Qin Jiaban (deceased 2157) and the photo of his son Supreme President Qin Jiabao, a slightly smaller photo to show respect, the students gathered in the courtyard for flag raising and military training. The morning activities concluded with a speech about the bravery of the country's compatriots or a story of a recent or historic success of the nation. The speeches, highly regulated and overly simulated, reminded the students of the importance of loyalty to the nation and placing national ideology before their own. Upon conclusion of the morning activities, the students headed up to their respective classes and the start of the school day.

"Continuing from yesterday, who can tell me about the state of our great nation after the invention of XYTablet?" Yi asked his students as he walked into class, dropping his books upon the front podium. "Anyone?"

"Sir, the status of our great nation was greatly weakened by the XYTablet," replied one student in the front.

"Yes. Western advertising greatly increased the popularity of the XYTablet in China. Some of our ancestors had been confused by ideas of gender superiority. Western countries, with the help of the Mastiff Pharmaceutical Company took advantage of that." He walked around the classroom, slapping his meter stick on the desks of students distracted by other thoughts. "Moving forward, what did our great government do to try to stop the rise of the phenomenon? Yuehan?"

Yuehan jumped as his name was called. "Sir, they warned the people against it."

"Can we go into a little more detail? I would expect more from a renowned businessman's son." Yi couldn't help smirking as the rest of his students snickered.

Yuehan thought for a moment. "Sir, I suppose they did everything they could to warn the people, but the power of the Western Countries was too strong, and our great government could do little about it."

"Yes," said Yi. He paused for dramatic effect before continuing somberly. "Unfortunately, the poison of the Western Countries hurt our great nation." He paused for a moment again, before continuing. "Despite the work of our great scientists, an antidote could not be found." He spoke directly to the class, as he usually did when presenting important points. "Much like how the British used opium to bring down the Qing Dynasty almost 300 years ago, the Americans used XYTablet as an attempt to weaken our great nation."

Looking directly at Yuehan, he continued. "Tell me Yuehan, what did our great government do to solve this problem?"

"Well, they implemented the Gender Balancing legislation," Yuehan quickly replied.

"Ok, and why did they do that? Anyone?" He looked around the classroom at the blank faces and sighed loudly.

"The problem is, like all people, we have the biological need to breed, and without a proper outlet to release this desire, our people became weak and unruly," Yi told the class, regurgitating what he had been taught. "In addition, I think it is important that we always remember, each gender has its proper roles in society, and when these roles are not fulfilled, chaos occurs. As men, the stronger gender, we are the heads of our households. We make the decisions that keep our society and families running. But we need women to balance things out. They raise the children, clean the house, and cook everyday basic meals so that men are able to do their jobs. It would be ridiculous to expect a man to do a woman's job and a woman to do a man's job."

"But," interrupted Yuehan, "aren't nan-nu originally men? Shouldn't that mean they can't do a woman's job properly?" In the background, some classmates giggled.

"To a certain point, you are correct," agreed Yi. "That is why the government started training and creating women. Remember, though originally not female, all nan-nu have been fixed and trained so they think and act like traditional Chinese women. They are more or less the same thing." He smiled, as if trying to reassure his students or prove a point.

"Except, they can't have children!" interrupted a student in the back of the classroom, giggling. When Yi didn't immediately shut him down, the other students joined in, laughing quickly.

"Alright," chuckled Yi, calming the students down. "You are right. There are some differences. But they are minor. Besides, the government has collected enough eggs to keep our great nation thriving."

The students were quiet for a moment before Yuehan broke the silence. "But I don't understand, Teacher, why not import women from other countries?"

"Hmm, can anyone answer Yuehan's question?" Yi asked the students.

"Our great leaders realized that weakening the blood purity of our great people was just as detrimental to our society and culture," Daxing replied.

"Excellent. Just as destructive to our nation's culture and purity was the weakening through influence from Western countries. Food from the United States of America made us fat, religious ideologies from Europe poisoned the culture of our country, and, most detrimental, some of our countrymen chose to mix races and create half-breed mutts, destroying the structure of our society. It was only through gender balancing, the creation of the Women's Protection Act, and the expulsion of foreigners, race traitors, and cultural traitors that our country could be saved. Unfortunately, as you know, by the time this happened, the damage had already been done."

"What about the men though?" asked Yuehan.

"I don't understand the meaning of your question," Yi replied.

"I mean," Yuehan thought for a second, "there must be men out there who can still create the X chromosome. Why not use them to repopulate the country?"

"Unfortunately," sighed Yi, "most of the men unaffected by XYTablet and the semen gathered from those men were destroyed during the Chinese Civil War. If there have been any men still able to create X chromosome sperm, it would be their legal duty to donate to the government but alas, none have done so since the birth of our great nation, as far as I know."

The students were quiet, thoughtful for a moment, before Yuehan once again interrupted and asked, "Have you seen an actual woman, Teacher? A biological woman, I mean?"

Yi hesitated for a moment, thinking back to his dream from the middle of the night. "I did once, when I was young."

The students expressed an interest and curiosity that was rather unusual for the class. Yi could hear them mumble about this information amongst themselves.

"What was she like?"

Yi thought for a moment, afraid of showing any emotion. "Nothing different than what our great gender reassignment doctors create, I suppose," he said finally.

"Sir, one day, I want to find a real woman, not a nan-nu," a student in the back said proudly.

The other students snickered around the classroom.

Yi frowned. "That would be impossible. There are simply not any biological females around, and you wouldn't want to repeat the problems in the past by diluting our culture's blood purity, would you?"

"Are there any biological women left in the country?" asked Yuehan.

Yi decided the best answer to give was the official one. "Our glorious government rounded up all biological women in this country for their protection. All biological women left in the PRCC currently live in special government facilities where they are well protected and provide the great service of donating their eggs to our glorious nation.

"Do other countries have the gender imbalance of our country?" Jiangwen suddenly interrupted from the back of the room.

"Of course, they do. Why wouldn't they?" Yi said quickly. He paused, replaying the question in his head. He had never thought about this before.

"Why don't you think other countries developed nan-nu, like

our great nation?" asked Jiangwen.

"I wouldn't know that answer. Perhaps it is because other countries lack the intelligence to develop the technological innovations like our glorious nation. But I have no interest in leaving our country to find out."

"What is outside of our border, Teacher?" asked Jiangwen.

"Wasteland. The great war destroyed much of the outer regions," Yi said indifferently.

"Aren't you curious though, Teacher, what it is like to see other places?" Daxing asked.

Yi looked directly to the class and said simply, "Our great leaders already give us so much, and we should all be so grateful. Our government and country are simply the best in the world; there can be no comparison. I don't see how I could find any other satisfaction elsewhere."

Yi was sitting in the office grading papers and wrapping up his daily duties when Teacher Long came in. He looked tired and had an interesting expression on his face.

"I heard your lesson today while I was hall monitoring," he said, putting his papers on to his desk adjacent to Yi. "It was quite impressive—the student interactions, I mean."

"Thank you. I try my best to teach everything I know to my students," replied Yi, not looking up from his work.

"I am just curious," said Long, keeping his voice neutral, "how much of this bullshit we are forced to regurgitate do you actually believe in?"

"What do you mean?" asked Yi slowly and suspiciously. He glanced around quickly to see if anyone else was walking in the halls, listening.

"I mean, all this garbage we teach," Long said, letting out a heavy sigh. "You don't believe that Western foreigners purposely introduced XYtablet to weaken our country and start the Civil War? You don't believe that mixed race children and minorities brought the downfall of the motherland, do you?" He added, trying to open up a discussion. "I mean, all this stuff about fixing genders, and stuff like that, do you think it's the right way to go?"

Yi didn't know what to say. Was this a test of his patriotism? Was this a trap to take away his job? What was happening? He thought for a moment before finally saying, "It is not up to us teachers to think about material and share our opinion. Our great government and the Ministry of Education have created the most righteous and accurate curriculum it can, and we should work our hardest to enforce their beliefs."

"Spoken like a true governor's son," replied Long, his face emotionless.

2.

FAMILY IS THE BASIS OF SECURITY. WITHOUT FAMILY THERE CAN BE NO COUNTRY.

A COPY OF *THE PRCC DAILY*, the only legally published newspaper in the country, was lying on the desk in his office when 59-year-old Governor Wang Jiangjun walked in the door. Picking it up, he smiled as he read the headline, ignoring his assistant, Su Xiaoming, bringing him his daily green tea and Chinese biscuits.

Lao Minghuan, son of Judge Lao, caught in illegal, despicable homosexual orgy behind public office

BY SU LANTAO — The Sources from the police station have reported that Lao Minghuan, son of Judge Lao Ming, was caught performing homosexual acts on a number of men behind a very public building a few nights ago. Even more shocking, sources have stated that not only do they not know the number of men Lao Minghuan was trying to seduce in this illegal homosexual orgy, but that Judge Lao was directly involved in covering up his son's incident.

"The citizens of Xincheng are shocked about this blatant act of corruption that has happened in our public office," said one citizen. "In addition, with this kind of incident, we must wonder about the moral decency of Judge Lao if he raised such a child. We should all call for the immediate resignation of Judge Lao."

Judge Lao is perhaps best known for the traitorous act of suggesting mercy to the infamous "Rebels of Shannxi," a group of citizens who attacked the City of Chengqing during the famine of 2154. Judge Lao suggested as the people were hungry, and unable to get the food rations they were promised, that it was understandable that the people were frustrated and thus deserved leniency. Luckily, our honorable Governor Wang understood the foolishness of Judge Lao's ideology and swiftly executed justice.

In the meantime, Lao Minghuan has been swiftly arrested by the government and will be receiving his surgery before being sent to the People's Court for a trial of indecency.

"If Minghuan wants to be a woman," said the Chief of Police Deng Jingcha, "then I see no reason why we are stopping him from being a woman." He added, "In addition, he must be punished under the law for committing these indecent acts. Punishments for the sickness of homosexuality, as all patriotic citizens are aware, is up to five years at the Re-Education Labor Camp after gender reassignment to cure their retched disease."

An appropriate punishment has yet to be discussed for Judge Lao for attempting to cover up such a heinous crime, but there are some who believe that the death penalty should be given for not only allowing his son to commit these disgusting acts, but also covering them up.

Governor Wang grinned as he set the newspaper back on his desk. He thought back to a few days ago when he walked into a most peculiar conversation between his assistant, Xiaoming, and another member of his staff. The two were whispering quietly, and upon his entering, the other staff member, looking uncomfortably nervous, quickly left.

"What was that about?" asked Governor Wang, pretending to be uninterested in the situation.

"What do you mean, sir?" Xiaoming answered casually, as sweat coated the back of his neck.

"Don't play dumb with me," Governor Wang sneered. Pausing as if he were making an important speech, he looked directly at Xiaoming, before speaking both clearly and precisely. "You know, I can easily replace a stray dog like you with another stray dog. You ought to think more carefully about where your loyalties lie. Those who are loyal to me may see themselves with better future benefits. Those who are not will continue just being useless street rats."

"Oh, I see. Well, it was just some gossip, sir." Xiaoming hesitated, before continuing. "Apparently, the police arrested Lao Minghuan, you know, the son of honorable Judge Lao. It appears he was seen kissing a man through the window of his home and was turned in by his neighbors."

"By Judge Lao, you mean the same judge who tried to overturn my policy on the execution of the Rebels?" asked Governor Wang thoughtfully.

"Yes, sir," replied Xiaoming. As if suddenly realizing the situation, he quickly added, "Also, he was the teacher to both of your children, sir. Judge Lao is highly respected by both his peers and his community, not only as a fair and thoughtful judge, but for his commitment to teaching and understanding of national law and passing the information to the next generation."

The Governor ignored him. "Didn't the People's Court argue that he did no wrong by questioning my actions?"

"They did, sir."

"Hmm…mistaken once again…" The Governor paused. "I guess it is once again my responsibility to fix this mistake. Tell me, Xiaoming, don't you have a friend who works for *The PRCC Daily*?"

"Yes, sir. My cousin."

"Even better. Then, I expect you have already told him this story, and he is currently printing it for tomorrow's headlines. Be sure to stress what a serious crime this is."

"Excuse me, sir?" asked Xiaoming "You want me to report this to *The PRCC Daily*?"

"I don't understand the confusion," the Governor said, shrugging as he began his work.

"But, but, Judge Lao doesn't have another son, sir. Doing so would end the great Lao family name."

"I guess the next time the so called 'great Lao family' should do better," Governor Wang said indifferently, "then to raise sexual deviants in their family."

Though he was pleased with the removal of one of his political rivals, a small part of Governor Wang's mind worried about his fate if another rival was to learn about his family skeletons currently hanging in the closet. Governor Wang's first son, Wang Yi, was a disappointment in two ways. One, he held no political ambitions; instead, to Governor Wang's disappointment, he wouldn't budge from his job as a teacher, putting the family's dynastic ambitions in jeopardy. Even more disgraceful, and potentially more damaging, was that though he was registered as married to a woman, he knew that his son's wife had yet to receive the surgery needed for the proper transformation.

Governor Wang's second son was working as a proper government official, albeit still in a lower position, and was married to proper woman—a nice, obedient one from the city who did as she was told and supported her husband. However, he was a lost puppy always aiming to please, and Governor Wang knew that he had no leadership ability. His rise in power would bring a failure of governance, and worse, shame and embarrassment to the family. More importantly, his family's political dynasty would appear stronger to those who might overthrow him if his first son were in power.

Governor Wang drank his tea slowly, toasting himself for his successful ploy in the removal of Judge Lao. Yet, he reminded himself, that as of this moment he couldn't think too far ahead. He needed to take the proper steps to guarantee the continuation of his family and its power within the country. This problem had gone on long enough; Judge Lao's son destroyed his career. Wang needed to keep his children from destroying his.

The first and third Thursday of every month was family dinner night. It was never discussed, but Governor Wang always walked into the large dining room at precisely 6:30 p.m. and expected to see his wife, children, and their wives to be there. Walking into the family dining room, Governor Wang sat down and looked around at the variety of dishes on the table. Looking at his wife, Cai Guihua, he angrily announced, "I thought I told you I wanted enoki mushrooms with beef tonight. Perhaps, it is my old age, and I am blind, but I don't see any enoki mushrooms on the table."

"I am sorry, sir," replied his wife, quietly, her head down, "they were sold out."

"Hmm…what time did you get to the market this morning?"

"Seven, sir"

"Then I would expect you to arrive at six next time," the Governor said loudly, as if this were the most obvious thing in the world.

"No, I meant that they weren't being sold. They aren't in season, sir," said Guihua quickly.

"Let me get this straight. Are you accusing the Vice Governor of being a liar? Because I know he told me he had them for dinner just two nights ago," the Governor asked sarcastically, raising his eyebrows.

"No, sir."

When Governor Wang said nothing, Guihua quickly added, "I will look harder next time, sir."

Governor Wang sat silently for a moment, taking a few bites before turning towards to his eldest son Yi. "I see you are still ruining your life by teaching?"

"I think many would consider teaching an honorable career," Yi replied.

"Indeed?" Governor Wang thought for a moment, before looking across the table at Ling. "Tell me, son." He paused, as if trying to savor the next words coming out of his mouth. "Are you a faggot?"

"Excuse me?" replied Yi, putting down his chopsticks. "Excuse me, sir," he quickly corrected himself.

"Faggot, fairy, fruit, homo, whatever disgusting thing you want to call it."

"No, sir, I am not gay," Yi replied simply. He knew what was coming. They had been having the same conversation for a while now.

"I would like to believe you, son," sighed Governor Wang, drinking his maotai liquor while staring at Ling. "But, perhaps, you can inform me why my so-called daughter-in-law is still a son-in-law."

In the background, Yi's younger brother, Wang Mengqin, snickered rather loudly, as if wishing to add in a comment or two. His wife Baihe quickly followed suit, giggling into her sleeve. Governor Wang ignored them.

"You don't think I can't tell that your so-called wife has taped his unwanted penis to his legs?" asked Governor Wang loathingly.

Yi said nothing, continuing to eat his meal slowly.

"I remember when you told me your plans to marry this thing, oh what was it, five or six years ago. Back when it was young and should have gotten things taken care of," Governor Wang said, raising his voice and standing up. "First you told me you would do the surgery as soon as you got engaged because you wanted to be there when it happened, and then you changed it to when you got married. WELL, NOW YOU HAVE BEEN MARRIED FOR ALMOST A YEAR, and the problem still isn't FIXED!"

"Now, now," said Guihua, pulling on her husband's arm, "you know the doctor told you not to raise your voice, sir."

"DO YOU KNOW how many strings I had to pull to arrange this illegal marriage?" Governor Wang continued, ignoring his wife and slamming his fists on the table. "DO YOU KNOW what would happen to my political career if you were caught? DO YOU REMEMBER you told me that you would fix it a long time ago?" He stopped, breathing deeply. "Instead, once again, you have Ling show up in a training vagina, his balls taped between his legs, and expect me to believe he is a woman." He smashed his fists upon the table in anger. "What did I do wrong to deserve this? What did I do to deserve a FAGGOT for a son?"

"Now father," Mengqin interrupted slyly, "it's not your fault that Yi has turned out to be a sexual deviant. I, on the other hand, would like to point out that I—"

"LOOK!" Yi said loudly, ignoring his brother. He hesitated, "The thing is…"

"No, I am sick of your excuses. You told me you would solve this problem. You told me you would make her a complete woman! Looking beyond the illegality of this marriage," the Governor raised his voice even louder than before, "I will repeat myself again. I will not have some faggoty, fruity son in this family. IF YOU CONTINUE DOWN THIS PATH, WE MIGHT AS WELL JUST TAKE A KNIFE AND—"

"Sorry, sir," interrupted Ling, "it's not—"

"Control that thing," snapped Governor Wang. "It is bad enough we have to let it sit at the table."

"Honey, sir," pleaded Guihua, reaching for her husband again, begging, "You know the doctor told you not to get angry."

The governor dismissed her, continuing talking to Yi, "Back to my point. Then why don't you explain to me, if you aren't a faggot, why won't you fix this problem?"

"Because…" Yi hesitated, trying to hold in his frustration.

"Because what?" sneered the Governor.

"Because…"

"Because WHAT?"

"Because…Because…Because…"

"Speak up, son. I want to hear your reason," the Governor said loudly.

"Because…" The frustration in Yi snapped. "BECAUSE I DON'T WANT TO BE MARRIED TO SOME PLASTIC SURGERY SHE-MALE FREAK!"

The severity of his own voice shocked him as the table turned quiet. No one ever raised their voice at the Governor's table except the Governor himself.

"Excuse me?" asked the Governor.

"I don't want to be married to some freak! This isn't the way life should be!" replied Yi angrily. "Look at us, married to some idea, some creature, that we have altered, we have created. I don't want to sleep with a fake woman. I want a real woman."

"Are you suggesting your mother here is some sort of freak?" Governor Wang pointed at Guihua.

"First of all, she isn't my mother; I wasn't born from her; I came from a tube, like we all did. So yeah, I guess my actual mother is some sort of freak considering she is a BIRTHING MACHINE."

Guihua gasped, bursting into tears. Knowing she wouldn't be receiving any comfort from anyone at the table, she ran out of the room with her bottle of maotai liquor to drown her sadness.

"Now, look at this, you made your mother cry." Governor Wang smiled rather inappropriately. "Well, what are you waiting for? Go grab her and bring her back!"

Yi walked out of the dining room and went upstairs, feeling a mixture of anger and shock. He had never exploded at his father, and he had never been so rude to his mother. He had never expressed those private thoughts so openly, but he knew he meant what he said. After all, he had been thinking about them for such a long time. It was not his destiny to stayed married to a nan-nu, as he could never love a man or a nan-nu. The only way he could find love was if he found a woman, a biological woman, and as that was never going to happen, he would never find love. As for his so-called marriage with Ling, he married Ling to protect Ling. He didn't want Ling to become a nan-nu because he didn't want his childhood friend to get hurt, but he didn't want to be with Ling. The marital services that Ling performed on him, that was for Ling to show his appreciation, and it was his marital duty. It was just about pleasure and satisfying his urges. Sure, Ling was good at what he did, but that had nothing to do with love or their relationship. He smashed his hands against the wall in anger. He didn't understand why things had to be so complicated.

Finding Guihua was not difficult, as he knew he would find her inside of her private room on the second floor. He felt uncomfortable as he shut the door behind him, watching her drink her maotai on the balcony and sobbing into her sleeves.

Yi rarely entered his mother's private room, even as a child. For his family social class, it was traditional for a lady to have her own space to do her "lady stuff." The room was not large and was designed in a very traditional Chinese style rarely seen. A tatami floor covered a raised section that could be used for resting or a temporary bed. Wooden shelves on the walls held some of her prized possessions: random assortments collected throughout her life and gifts from the Governor.

"Look…Mother," Yi said, feeling exacerbated as he walked towards her before.

"No, you made your point. You're right, you know. I am not really your mother," Guihua sighed, still sobbing. "I am just some freak that raised you."

"No. Sorry, I just meant…"

"No, no, no, you made your point perfectly clear," she sighed, looking at the full shining moon above her. "You think…I am a monster." She shuddered, obviously drunk. "Do you know what it is like to raise two children and know that one of them thinks you are a monster?"

Yi said nothing. He didn't know what he should say.

"I-I-I didn't, I didn't—" she choked out her words with great effort. "I didn't want this life, you know…" She burst into tears, sobbing into the arms of her dress as Yi sat down and hugged her, attempting to comfort her in some way. "They just came… came for me…one day, and told me…that…"

Suddenly and sloppily, she twisted her body out of Yi's body, and pointed at the flowered ceramic vase, her bao, sitting on the shelf. "I asked them to preserve it for me, just like the eunuchs of the Forbidden City of old. When I die, if they are buried with me, perhaps we can be united in afterlife," she slurred sadly, and suddenly started singing.

Once, twas child of Mars
Now, tis child of Venus,
Taken away, like the stars
My penis, oh my penis

There, on the high shelf
Sitting there, covered in dust.
Must resist, I tell myself
To reconnect, my only lust

It's all I think about
In health and in sickness
I just want to shout
About my penis, penis, penis

She finished, wiping her tears with a drooping sleeve. "You know, you have always been so different, yet you have a good heart. You speak what you believe in. That's why I have always been proud of you. You think for yourself, and you are independent and strong. I know you mean well, even if you don't always show it." Wrapping herself around Yi, she hugged him tightly. "Look, my son, whatever you think of me, just know I love you. I guess I love you in a way only a mother can." Smiling somberly, she spoke quietly, "Now, come on, let's get cleaned up before your father gets any angrier…"

Yi and his mother walked back into the dining room as everyone else finished up their meal. The Governor smirked arrogantly as they sat down. Yi tried to ignore the pleasure brimming across his father's face that was only shown when someone else was humiliated or in pain.

"Well, now that everyone is back," Mengqin said suddenly, standing up proudly. "Father, Mother, Brother, I have some great news. I didn't want to tell anyone, but I applied for a Form 88." He looked at Yi, adding in, "That's to apply for a child by the way. You know, to form a proper family. Just thought you should know." Mengqin ended his sentence with a confident smirk, proudly looking around.

Yi ignored him.

"And?" Governor Wang said excitedly.

"It got approved!" Mengqin beamed. "I sent off my DNA, and we are going to have a baby soon."

"Oh! Praise the heavens, my son, congratulations!" gasped Guihua, stumbling over to hug her youngest son tightly. Streams of tears once again flowed down her face as she asked, "Do you know when you are expecting?"

"I sent in my sample three months ago," Mengqin explained happily. "The fertilization was successful. I guess we are just waiting for the delivery…also my eggs came from—"

"Ahem," Governor Wang interrupted, grinning menacingly.

"So, Yi, aren't you going to congratulate your brother on starting a new family?"

"Yeah, congratulations," said Yi bitterly. "Congratulations on your son."

It was nearly midnight when Yi and Ling got home. They stumbled into the house tired, both slightly drunk from celebrating over his brother's news. Yi giggled stupidly as Ling helped change him into his night clothes and brought him to bed.

"We never finished our breakfast conversation from a few days ago," Ling said casually as he started collecting Yi's dirty clothes.

"Excuse me?" asked Yi, starting to sober up.

"Even your dad agrees with me. I need to get the surgery," Ling said defiantly.

"I don't care what my father says. My father isn't responsible for everything," Yi said, his voice rising.

"It would be good for your father's career you know. It could be good for our life," Ling pleaded.

Yi scowled. He didn't understand why Ling kept bringing this up. He didn't understand why Ling was so whiny. "Look, why is this so important to you?" Yi asked, trying to hide his annoyance.

"I want…I want to make you happy."

Yi scoffed, slowing crawling into bed. "If you really wanted to make me happy, you would stop bringing this up."

"I see the way you look at me," Ling said shamefully, shuddering. "You hate me; you blame me for the problems in your life."

"Look, I have said this before. I don't hate you. It's not you. It's me." Yi replied.

"Why can't we work things out?" Ling pleaded. "Let us sit down and talk about this."

"I just want to go to bed."

"We can't keep avoiding this problem you know!" Ling said angrily, reaching over and grabbing Yi's arm. "Let us talk about this! How can I make you happy?"

Perhaps it was the alcohol, or the pressure from his parents, or his sexual frustration, or the sound of Ling's whiny voice, or perhaps it was a combination of everything, but at that moment, Yi just couldn't take it anymore. He raised up his hand and swung it, backslapping Ling in the face. He heard Ling gasp in pain and shock as he rolled off the bed.

"I...I..." Yi sobered up immediately. He didn't know what to say. He had never hit another human being like this before. He watched as Ling covered his face in surprise, speechless, cowering on the floor. "I-I-I'm...I am...I am," Yi paused, the shock inhibiting his speech. "I am going to sleep on the couch tonight." He finished and averted looking at Ling, grabbed his feather comforter off the bed, and headed to the living room, leaving Ling lying on the floor.

As Yi lay down on the couch, he heard Ling pull himself off the floor, sobbing quietly while he crawled into bed. He sighed, burrowing himself in the crevice of the couch, and curled up, trying to get some sleep.

3.

IF IT IS TO SURVIVE, A SOCIETY MUST HAVE BOTH MEN AND WOMEN

The Shoushu district, home of the gender reassignment doctors, was located on the southeastern corner of Xincheng. It was here parents would take their children to get altered at the right age. The gender reassignment doctors of Shoushu were respected for their skill but culturally kept as outcasts from society. Superstition surrounded the lives of these surgeons who did all the dirty work. Many in the city of Xincheng believed it was bad luck to know one personally and worse still if you had any sort of relationship with them.

Rumors spread about the community, not only about their skills, but also that they were untrustworthy. If you didn't heed their advice, they would go out of their way to harm you with their strange skills. As normal citizens avoided the district unless in need of surgical services, the district became a safe haven for crime and illegal activities. The larger cultural stereotypes also impacted the government, meaning the areas received little policing and governing, which only continued to build upon the isolation.

The reality of what was happening was much simpler. Understanding the work performed by surgeons would have required acknowledging deeper cultural and social issues. Most families just didn't want to be involved in such dirty work and face the reality of the circumstances happening to their loved ones. It was easier just to collectively outcast the people doing the brutal deed behind creating another generation of "women." The surgeons of Shoushu, unable to integrate with rest of the city, accepted the isolation. Though many were able to make large quantities of money through their skillset, they understood the only recognized interaction with people from other districts was when their skills, passed down from generation to generation, were needed. It was best to keep their money, and themselves, only in Shoushu district.

For Yi, however, Shoushu District housed one of his only friends, Liang Qiang. Though Yi would never admit it, Qiang was perhaps the only true friend he had. He had first come to the district as a teenager when his father had to travel to all districts throughout the city. Like most other citizens, Governor Wang looked down upon the gender reassignment doctors with bias, but as a politician, he saw it as his responsibility to keep the surgeons minimally happy to prevent rebellion. Qiang's father was the most esteemed surgeon of Xincheng and perhaps the only one his father could talk to without total disgust and contempt, given that he had performed the surgeries of the wives of most government officials. During one of these meetings, Yi met Qiang in the backroom and started talking. Unwittingly and perhaps because of teenage rebellion, as he knew his father would never approve of them talking, the two became friends.

Yet, this was a friendship that came to serve him well. With Shoushu District being less governed than the general city, this was often a good place to express ideas without the spying eyes of noisy neighbors. Qiang, living outside of Yi's proper friend circle, provided Yi with an outlet to talk about things his other friends would never speak of, such as his complicated relationship with Ling and difficulties with his father. In addition, as the two grew closer, Yi had been surprised to learn that not only was Qiang was a confident, intelligent, and extremely talented doctor, but he was also a homosexual. Later, he had been equally surprised when Qiang started what sounded like a very loving relationship with another man named Zhuang. It was Qiang's confidence and non-judgmental worldview that allowed Yi to feel more comfortable about sharing some household details with Qiang. Just as important, his sexuality provided Yi with leverage in case Qiang was to ever betray his secrets. All these factors made Qiang Yi's perfect confidant, and therefore, whenever Yi's problems occurred, he would naturally visit Qiang's doctor's office after work, often talking for hours in one of the many examination rooms.

"Okay, let me get this straight. You hit him?" Qiang said, slightly surprised, as he filled in the final pages of his doctor's log, summarizing his daily work. "Hmm, I never really saw you as the violent type…"

Yi said nothing as he sat on the examination table, fidgeting his legs and twisting his fingers.

"Have you hit him before?" asked Qiang thoughtfully as he closed the final folder.

"NO!" Yi replied, stunned. He thought for a moment. "I mean, I don't think I have ever hit another person before."

"Hmmm…" Qiang said staring uncomfortably into the distance, sitting in his chair. Then, suddenly breaking the silence, he continued, "I assume you apologized and made up."

Suddenly Yi felt nervous, as if he was being criticized, so he sat there saying nothing, shame reddening his face.

"Wait, so you haven't apologized…?" Qiang asked, confused and shocked.

Yi thought for a moment before finally speaking, "I…I…I don't know what to say."

"How about," Qiang said, perhaps too sarcastically, "'I am sorry for slapping you in the face. You mean a lot to me, and I didn't want to hurt you.'"

"Umm…hmm, that seems a little too much. It's not like I—"

"Too much? An apology is too much?" interrupted Qiang.

"I mean, look, it's complicated," Yi said, defensively.

"You backhanded someone across the face, hurting that person, physically, and emotionally, I might add, and now you aren't sure if you should apologize. Yep, it's so complicated," Qiang replied sarcastically.

"Yes! No. I mean, I don't know…okay?" Yi continued, burying his face into his hands, "I mean, I know I should apologize, but I don't know what to say, and it all happened so fast."

"I guess you should tell me what happened. I can't deny, I am a little shocked at the idea of you hitting someone," Qiang said, "especially Ling."

"We were coming back from my father's, and you know how he is, so I was already annoyed and slightly angry. Then, Ling had to bring up how he wanted to have his reassignment surgery. I was a little drunk, and I guess the pressure caused me to just snap," Yi said uncomfortably. "I mean, it all happened so fast. One minute we were talking, and the next minute, I was above him as he withered on the floor."

"So why don't you just let him have the reassignment surgery?" asked Qiang. "I mean, you keep saying you aren't gay…so why not transform him into something you're attracted to?"

"I don't know," Yi paused, thinking. "I guess, I just think it's, you know, morally wrong." He paused, arranging the words in his mind. "Anyway, like I said, it's not like I am attracted to him, I am just protective of him. For most of my childhood he was my best friend." He stopped for a moment. "I made a promise to him once to protect him at all costs. I guess that's why I married him. I wanted to protect him."

"Well, then why not marry another nan-nu?" asked Qiang. "There are other ways to protect him, you know."

"It just seems so morally wrong," Yi said. He stood up and began pacing nervously around the room. "We have talked about this before. I can't be the only person who feels this way.

That going around, changing genders, none of this is natural? I mean, don't you ever just think, 'Why I am doing this?' That there has to be another solution."

"You ask if I, who does this as my job and my profession, think changing genders is morally wrong?" replied Qiang, cocking his eyebrows.

Yi paused, thinking for a moment. "Okay," he said as his mind settled on his question. "Let's just say I wanted to change Ling into a nan-nu. What would that process entail?"

"What do you mean?" Qiang replied slowly, slightly surprised. They had never talked about his job. In any case, it wasn't considered proper conversation to talk about gender alteration.

"I mean the whole process," Yi said. There was an odd determination in his voice. "What do you do to alter the gender of a person?"

Qiang chuckled. "Well, I don't alter the gender. I alter the sex. I can only change the outside, and well, with hormones, I guess I can regulate the inside."

"You know what I mean."

"Ha. Why the sudden curiosity?" Qiang asked, not hiding the suspicion in his voice. "You have never asked in the past."

"I guess...I just need to know," Yi said simply.

"I'm assuming you are talking about the bottom half, and not the top half?" Qiang asked quietly. "The top half is easier."

"The bottom half. I have heard about the top half. Isn't just like silicone stuffing?" Yi replied quickly.

"Okay, well it starts with hormone therapy, to prepare the body. After an amount of time, the patient comes in and we remove the testicles. Following that procedure, we can choose to remove the penis and form a vagina by making an incision. Or, we can invert the penis to form a vagina while giving the new vagina some sensitivity. That takes care of the lower half, and for the top section, breast implants. Of course, once the procedure is done, a nan-nu needs to use a dilator to keep the vagina open, because the body treats it as a wound, and it will close up if she doesn't use the dilator. Additionally, she needs be on hormone therapy for the rest of her life," Qiang explained. "I guess that's the basic procedure. Surgery takes a few hours, a few months for healing, and then my role is complete. Sometimes, the client asks for more than the basic model. I mean, the more money I get, the more time I will spend, and the more realistic I can shape the body. I can do different things, but that would also take a lot more time."

"More realistic?" asked Yi, feeling slightly sick.

"Well, you must have noticed, some nan-nu look better than others." Qiang shrugged. "I can do a lot of different things; bigger breasts, smaller breasts, wider hips, larger butt, shape and size of the labia. You know, a little sculpting here and a little sculpting there, whatever the future husband wants."

Yi said nothing. The two sat there before Qiang finally broke the silence. "Well, before you judge, 98% of my customers are pretty satisfied with what I create, and apparently it feels just like a real vagina."

"How would they know?" snapped Yi, perhaps louder than he planned. "There aren't any real women left."

Qiang just shrugged. "I guess there are documents, and people who do talk about it. I suppose some of my older customers could remember, if they had that experience. Or maybe some of them have slept with the foreign women in the Capital."

"I don't see how it could," Yi said defiantly. "Look, it's just not right. I don't think there is any possibility it can feel like the real thing."

"Hey, to be honest, I don't think it matters to most in this country," Qiang said quietly. "People need to find a way to have sex. Most, apparently, want to have sex with a vagina. It doesn't matter if it is natural or artificial."

"I think," said Yi, "that perhaps people in this country need to accept that they will never have real sex."

"I don't see what you mean. For example, you do have sex with Ling."

"I mean…not in the technical sense. I am a man, I have needs, and I do stuff with him, but I don't think it should be called sex," Yi replied, slightly embarrassed.

"Meaning…?" asked Qiang, hesitant about the direction of the conversation.

"I guess what I am saying is I don't think it should be considered sex if it is not you know, penis to vagina. A real vagina, not like you said earlier, an inverted penis," Yi said simply. "Like with Ling. Well, you know, he uses his mouth a lot, and sometimes, you know, I…I…you know…use him from behind. But I don't think any of that is really sex."

"Well, I disagree," Qiang said. "I think sex is any time two people connect in that special, physical way, and that includes vaginal, anal, oral, or whatever. If you don't consider what you do sex, then what would you call it?"

Yi thought for a moment but said nothing.

"Since we are on the topic of sex, and since we are talking about you and Ling," Qiang began. "I have some small questions. What do you do to make sure Ling is happy?" he asked curiously. "Do you kiss? Hug? Anything? Maybe give him a little oral pleasure?"

"NO," Yi replied loudly and then added quickly, "I mean, we kissed at our wedding because we had to. But other than if I must, to save face and stuff, and keep people from questioning, like during my wedding, why would I? I am not gay."

There was an awkward silence. "So…like I have been saying, you just use him," Qiang said simply. "He is just your sex toy."

"No, I don't see it like that. It's his responsibility to keep me happy. It's the least he could do after everything I do for him."

"And what do you do for him," asked Qiang.

Yi felt annoyed and defensive. "That's a dumb question. I give him a home, I work, I provide him with everything he needs to survive. Without me, he would have nothing. Without me, he would be back in his old village. Him giving me sex, or whatever we want to call it, it's the minimum he can do. After all, we are married."

"In that case, do you do anything to make sure that he is happy? Do you make sure he has the same satisfaction as you do?" questioned Qiang.

"No. Like I said, I am not gay, so why would I?" Yi said. Looking at Qiang's annoyed face, he added quickly, "Look, usually he goes in the bathroom afterwards and takes care of himself. Judging by how long he is in there for, he probably likes it. Therefore, I am not just using him."

"But you don't ask if he 'likes it'," Qiang said while mimicking quotations in the air. "You just assume he does. Therefore, my argument still stands. You are just using him. He is just an outlet for you to take care of your needs."

"I don't know why I have to keep repeating this, but I am not gay, OKAY?" Yi said, raising his voice. "If I had a woman, I would never need a man like Ling."

"I don't know. You do sleep with a man. You do let a man pleasure you. Have you tried experimenting a little? You shouldn't judge until you've, how should we put it, expanded your horizons?" laughed Qiang. "I mean, don't you ever just look down at his penis and just want to lick it?"

"No, because like I said," Yi replied frustrated and annoyed, "I am not a fucking faggot like you." He immediately regretted his words.

Qiang frowned. "Well, that hurt."

Suddenly, the shame and regret he felt the night he hit Ling returned. He thought for a moment, before stating loudly, "I am sorry. I didn't mean it like that." When Qiang said nothing, he quickly added, "Come on, you know me, I fully support you and Zhuang. You know I don't have problems with the gays."

"Yeah, it does sure sounds like that," Qiang said without emotion. He paused. "Look, it's getting late. I don't think I have time for drinks tonight. Why don't you let yourself out?"

Yi got up, not looking at Qiang directly, opened the door and prepared to leave. Standing in the doorway he repeated,

"I am sorry."

"Yeah, yeah," said Qiang, not hiding his anger. "I get it, so if you'll excuse me, I've got work to do."

"I am sorry," Yi repeated. "I really am. I didn't mean it in that way. You know how much…I…respect you. I just lost control of my emotions." He sighed, watching Qiang. Leaning against the doorframe, talking to no one in particular, he continued. "It's just difficult, you know? Living this life. Not ever getting what you really, truly want. Having everyone judge you for each move you make."

He pushed his head in his arms. "Do you know how much pressure I feel? Do you to know what it is like to have all these expectations and never be able to fulfill them all?"

"Nope," replied Qiang, "because you are the only person in the world with needs, wants, and expectations. You are the only one who—"

"No, no, I mean…" interrupted Yi. "It's just different. You have no idea how difficult it is to be me."

"Yep, I don't know how difficult is to be you," snapped Qiang, "Spoiled rich kid has a perfect life laid out in front of him but chooses not to take it. Lives with a person who cares for him yet treats him like shit. Tell me how difficult that is."

"You just don't get it," Yi said, sliding down the wall and landing on the floor. He put his head in his hands, tearing up. "You get to live outside of society. You get to be with a person you love. You get to live the life you want, and not be judged. I have to—"

"Excuse me?" Qiang interrupted loudly. "You do realize that the reason I am living 'outside of society' as you would call it, is because I am not allowed in your society."

Yi hung his head, not saying anything.

"Take a look at yourself," Qiang, continued bitterly, "given everything you want in life and yet complaining it is not enough. Coming from the most powerful family in the city and yet doing nothing to benefit others. Having opportunities to make your own decisions, but blaming others for your choices. Hitting someone across the face, but you see yourself as the victim. Why don't we switch places for a change, and I'll be the rich kid with all the power?"

"You don't get it," said Yi, still sitting on the floor, looking up at the ceiling. "You don't get what I mean…"

"You are right. I don't get what you mean," Qiang said harshly, choking up. "You think I enjoy knowing that no one wants to know me except when they need my services, that I am an outcast from society? You think I enjoy knowing that I am in an illegal relationship with the man I love? A relationship that could get us both killed if we were caught?"

The harshness and the tears surprised Yi. It suddenly occurred to him he never thought much about the experiences of others. He had always taken Qiang's confidence and perhaps, happiness, for granted, but to see him in this position made him feel oddly uncomfortable.

"You asked earlier if I thought changing genders, committing these surgeries, chopping off testicles, and building artificial vaginas was morally wrong?" Qiang said between tears. "Of course it is morally wrong. This whole society, how we operate, how we have isolated ourselves from the rest of the world, how we have valued differences over similarities, all of this is morally wrong." Yi didn't know what to say as Qiang continued. "I am not the guy that wants to physically harm others, creating lifelong psychological and physical damage for them. Yet, here I am, doing it every day, sometimes to more than one person per day."

"I-I-I didn't…"

"You think I like the situation I am in? I didn't get a choice to be here anymore than you." Qiang wiped the tears off his face. "But, at least I am not a coward, Yi. I know who I am, and I make the best of my situation. It may be illegal, but I love Zhuang, and Zhuang loves me. You, too, have a person who at least cares about you, if not more, and if you care about him as you said you do, you need to fix your mistakes. You need to treat him with the respect he deserves."

"I know. I know what I need to do," said Yi exasperated, slowly standing up and preparing to leave. "It's just so hard."

Qiang stared blankly at the wall, sighing, "Look, I get it. Your life is difficult, and you're frustrated. But you know what? All of our lives are. At least, you are the governor's son. You get it better than the rest of us ever will. But the rest of us, us common folk, all we can do is make the best of it, to accept those who care about us, and work with that."

4.

COOKING, CLEANING, AND PARENTING ARE THE CORNERSTONES OF A WOMAN'S LIFE

Yi had been sleeping on the sofa for a few nights now. He had also been purposely coming home late after work, preferring to spend the evenings out and about than face Ling. Ling could feel Yi looking away every time he looked at him, and other than a few words here and there, the two didn't speak to each other. Ling knew Yi felt some guilt over the incident, but he also knew Yi didn't know how to handle it. Therefore, Ling concluded he had to break the silence and change the situation. He decided that today he would take the extra time to prepare an extra special dinner for Yi. Yi merely nodded when Ling double checked if he would be back for dinner, not saying a word as he swiftly walked out the door. Ling sighed and began his day.

As always, he started by cleaning Yi's apartment. Though they could afford an *ayi*—a house cleaner—Yi had seen it as unsafe to keep one around with Ling's sexual organ issues, which meant Ling had to do all the chores himself. The two-bedroom apartment, though located in an average and inconspicuous neighborhood, was remodeled and better furnished than the other apartments, reflecting Yi's social background. In the past, Ling had stayed in the second bedroom though after a short while, because of the fear of being caught by others, they bought a large bed that both shared, and the second bedroom had been converted into an office that no one used. The living room, where Yi spent most his time, was furnished and decorated in a style only someone of high social background could afford: wooden furniture, a rather large TV, and even a small imported bookstand that was a gift from a family friend.

The kitchen, where Ling spent most of his time, was extremely modern for residents in the PRCC and included rarities such as an oven instead of just the usual gas stove. The nooks and crannies of the apartment were decorated with random items that were uncommonly seen or expensive to the common citizen: statues, glassware, and assorted souvenirs from other countries that the Governor or his friends had given them throughout the years. Yi preferred the house clean, and the house remained in a state of spotlessness as Ling believed it was one of the few things he could do to thank Yi for bringing home the money and giving him a place to live. Every day, working from room to room, he made sure that everything shined with that extra glisten to make his husband happy, polishing and cleaning every corner of the house.

After the morning chores, Ling began his daily preparation of looking like a proper woman before heading out. Looking in the mirror, he examined the black eye that his husband gave him just a couple of nights ago. It was starting to heal, but Ling knew he would have to be extra careful with his makeup if he was to hide the damage and avoid the potential shame of the neighbors finding out. He hopped into the shower, carefully shaving and removing each hair from his neck down, before washing himself with feminine smelling soap, shampoo, and conditioner. After drying himself off and moisturizing his skin to keep it smooth and soft, he carefully taped his testicles and penis to the side of his leg and put on his special underwear which was designed to hide his male organs and create a feminine look. Just to be safe, however, Ling always wore a puffy and free flowing skirt when leaving the apartment. After examining himself carefully in the mirror, he put on his bra, inserted his fake silicone breasts, and latched everything together with a corset, completing the build of his female body. He didn't wear much jewelry, just his wedding ring as would be culturally expected and a small feminine watch, as he found it more convenient then using his cellphone to look at the time.

Ling considered himself lucky that he didn't have much facial hair and had such a boyish face. It made the morning makeup application much easier. Covering up a black eye, however, was not as easy, and it had taken him quite a while before he could layer on a concealer that wouldn't be too obvious yet hide the visibility of the altercation with his husband. Once finished, he took another look in the mirror, tied his long hair into a half pony, and adjusted his dress before walking out the door. He walked down the street, caught the bus, and decided to go to his parents' place. It had been a while since his last visit, and he was starting to feel slightly unfilial for not seeing them more.

Ling's parents lived in a two-story home with a functional flat rooftop that was an engagement present from Yi. They had converted the first floor into a small noodle shop to make money, while living on the second floor and using the roof to hang clothes and for storage. The place itself wasn't large, located in Shengyi District, and not even a particularly good part of the district. Coming from the countryside, however, the two parents could not have moved to the city without connections and therefore felt obligated and loyal to Yi for helping them out. Though business was often sluggish, they made enough to survive, and most customers enjoyed the simple noodle dishes they offered.

Ling's parents were wrapping up from the morning rush when Ling walked in. His mother, Wupo, and his father, Nongfu, said nothing as Ling sat down and waited for them. Soon Wupo walked over, bringing a bowl of noodles for her son, and sitting down in front of him. "You have been busy," she began. "I assumed you forgot about us and how we brought you in the world. We haven't seen or heard from you in a while. Nearly three months."

"Yes, it's been a busy couple of months," Ling replied. He never had much to say to his parents. "How is business?"

"Usual. Your father and I have been very busy," Wupo said as she mixed shallots, peppers, and garlic into Ling's soup.

"That's good," Ling said quietly. Taking the noodles away from her, he began to eat after blowing on the hot broth to cool it down.

"I see you have yet to get your surgery," Wupo said, looking at his body. She looked around making sure that no customers were listening. "I had assumed that the reason you haven't seen us all this time was because you were finally doing your operation." She sighed, not hiding her disgust and disappointment. "I guess I was wrong."

Ling said nothing, focusing all his attention on sipping the broth of the salty noodles.

"With all this time, I don't understand why you haven't done it already," Wupo glared at him angrily. "How much longer are you planning to wait? I don't want to say this, but your father is becoming quite embarrassed. Look at him; he doesn't even want to talk to you anymore."

Ling didn't know what to say. He thought about Yi's reactions just a few nights ago. He couldn't tell the truth to his parents. There was no way they would support and empathize with him, so he just continued eating his noodles.

"What happened to your eye?" asked Wupo suspiciously, interrupting his thoughts.

"Oh, umm," Ling thought for a moment. "I fell. I fell down the stairs," he added with confidence.

"No, that can't be. Don't be ridiculous." Wupo stared closely at his eye, carefully observing him. "Did someone hit you?"

Ling felt his face turning red. "Umm, yeah. Yi and I got into a fight a few nights ago." Quickly, he added, "It was an accident though."

"Hmmm," Wupo began. "That's odd, I never thought of Yi as the physically violent type. He is always so polite and quiet."

"Yeah," agreed Ling. "He isn't the physically violent type. This is the first time he has ever hit me. I don't think he has ever hit a person before. Like I said, it was an accident."

"There are no accidents when a man hits a woman," Wupo said quietly. "I am sure whatever reasons he had for hitting you, you deserved it."

Ling looked at her but said nothing.

"Yi has done so much for you and our family," Wupo said simply. "He befriended you as a kid, and he has married you, even though you refuse to do your womanly duty and become a woman for him. I don't blame him for striking you," she whispered angrily. "I don't see how you can live with the shame you must be bringing on him and his family."

After leaving his parent's restaurant, Ling decided to take the bus to Zhengfu District and stop by the only import supermarket in Xincheng. Perhaps it was a consequence of his upbringing or societal pressures, but Ling knew that Yi would be too stubborn, or perhaps too ashamed, to apologize. He thought back to one of the many educational and important statements he had to memorize in high school: "The closest path to a man's heart is food." If he could find the right ingredients and create the perfect meal, this uncomfortable situation could end.

The closest bus stop was about two blocks away from the supermarket, but Ling chose to get off a stop earlier, walking past his and Yi's elementary school: Xincheng #1 Elementary School. Listening to break bells ringing and seeing the children running between the halls, Ling thought back to the first day they met.

Even as a child, Ling not only understood how fortunate he was to have been selected to receive his education at Xincheng #1 Elementary School but also the reasoning behind it. He had come from a farmer's family that could barely afford two meals a day. His parents were of low education, and he was the perfect poster child to show that under the PRCC every person had equal opportunity under the government. He remembered being extremely nervous on his first day. His parents, having borrowed money from his neighbors, had bought him a brand new uniform. It was the most expensive clothing anyone in his family had ever worn. He sat quietly at his desk. Naturally, his parents had suggested that he avoid the other scholarship kids and reminded him to befriend someone of a higher social class, but as a first grader, he didn't quite grasp why his parents thought that was important. He supposed it meant not befriending his current desk mate, who came for the same village as him. For the first few weeks Ling was shy and alone, preferring to stay in and read during breaks instead of playing outside with the other children.

He couldn't understand why then, but there was another classmate who seemed to be unable to make any friends, only this child clearly wasn't poor. It wasn't until later that Ling understood that because of Yi's family background, the other children's parents simply weren't sure what kind of relationship they wanted the children to build. If things between the two children were positive, then it would bring great honor and benefits to the family. But if they didn't go well, Governor Wang had a reputation for being fond of revenge. For most parents, it just wasn't a risk to partake in, and they encouraged their children to stay away from Yi.

Then, one afternoon, Yi walked up to Ling and said, "Hello."

"Hello," replied Ling shyly.

"How come I have never seen you outside of school?" Yi asked suspiciously.

"Huh?"

"Jin's parents come over about once a month, and I see Jun'ren at my private lessons, Nan-Nan is my neighbor and... well..." Yi rambled on for a while before asking, "How come I never see you?"

"Oh, umm, my parents, they live in the countryside..." said

Ling shamefully.

"You are one of the scholarship kids?" asked Yi, surprised.

"Yeah."

Yi smiled. "My father says that kids like you are special, that you prove how great our society is. That in our country we are all equal."

"Really?" asked Ling, perking up.

"Yeah," Yi giggled. "But I know he is lying. He says in private you all are a waste of money and resources for the school."

"Oh," Ling frowned, not knowing what to say.

"But you seem fine to me. You wanna play?" Yi said, grinning, throwing his cards on the table.

And from there a friendship blossomed. As a child, he never thought that a simple card game would design his future.

Ling was nine years old when he learned that his days as a boy were over. He had been living at the boarding school for two years, only seeing his family during the holidays, and he was excited when he learned his parents were coming to town to take him to dinner. To his surprise, his mother came alone and took him to one of the better restaurants.

That night, over a rare meal of beef, which was a rather expensive meat, Ling learned that at the end of fifth grade, he would be changing schools to learn how to be a proper lady and wife and eventually become a woman. Even though he was unsure what was about to happen, he felt, somewhere, that this was not a good thing.

"But I don't understand, Mother," Ling said, tearing up. "Why are you doing this?"

"Ling, you have to understand. This is a great honor. Our government has chosen you, to make you special," Wupo said, telling him the common reason that most parents told their children.

"What is going to happen?" Ling asked. "Will I still be able to see Yi at school?"

"No," Wupo said, frowning. "You will have to change schools. Then when the day comes, you will have a surgery, and the doctor will give you special parts, and you will then learn how to do a mother's job. How to take care of a man one day."

"But…I don't want to be a woman," said Ling, now crying loudly. "I don't want to have surgery."

"That isn't for you to choose." Wupo said. "This is a great honor for you and our family. The government has agreed to send you to the best nan-nu school in the city. Plus, with your education, you will be able to find a better man, unlike me." She didn't hide the envy in her voice.

"But I want to stay in my school." Ling continued crying, "I want to learn more. I want to play with Yi."

"You will learn more. You will learn how to please a man. The most noble of duties, I might add."

"Can't Yi transfer schools with me?" asked Ling.

"Ling, Yi is on a different path. It wouldn't be fair to lead him from his path. Would it?" She straightened herself up, making it clear that the discussion was over. "I remember, the day when I became a nan-nu. I remember what an honor it was. Now it's time for you to carry on that honor."

Ling was rather depressed at school the next day, something his best friend quickly noticed.

"Are you alright?" Yi finally asked as they packed up their bags at the end of the day.

"No. I am transferring schools," said Ling.

"Really?" asked Yi. "When?"

"In two years."

"Oh, wow. That's a long time from now," Yi chuckled. "I don't see what the problem is. Two years is like forever. Come on, you want to come over to my house this afternoon to play cards?"

Ling didn't know how to express himself. His mother had told him last night it was not proper to bring the topic up to his friend. But he couldn't hide this information from his best friend, so he just said what was on his mind. "They…they are making me a girl. I am transferring schools because they are making me a girl."

"What?"

"They are going to make me a girl," Ling said. "I don't know why? But I don't want to be a girl."

Yi thought for a moment, his face twisted in confusion. "I know how we can solve this problem. Come over this afternoon. Let me talk to my father," he said confidently. "My father is the new Governor. If there is anyone who can solve this problem, it's my father."

Ling had only been to Yi's house a few times prior to that day. The outside of the building looked like any other building in Zhengfu District. However, it was built with better quality materials than the rest of city to reflect pride and spirit, while still being humble enough to symbolize equality. The black iron gate was maintained at all times by two guards, who smiled at the gawking and curious passersby. Inside, however, was a different story. Instead of reflecting the equal struggle that *The PRCC Daily* said that all government officials suffered along with its citizens, it was filled with riches that very few could afford. Marble slabs lined the walls, solid wood furniture built from the few remaining forests furnished every room, and the antiques, remnants of the Civil War, gave the house an experience rivaling few in the country.

"DAD, DAD, DAD, DAD, DAAADDDD!" screamed Yi as he ran into the house, throwing his bag and jacket on the floor for the household ayi to take care of.

"Don't you know I am busy, Yi?" called the Governor from his office upstairs. "I have told you not to make a ruckus when you come from school."

"Dad, I need your help!" Yi said running up the stairs, leaving Ling to follow him. "You can't let them take Ling away!"

"What do you mean?" asked the Governor, stepping out of

his office.

"They want Ling to change schools. They want to make Ling a girl," Yi said quickly. He wrapped his arm around Ling. "Please, Dad, you can't let them do this. He is my best friend."

"Look, son," sighed the Governor. He looked at Ling with shame and disappointment. His son's best friend should not be a country peasant. "Let's have a quick talk, inside my office." He pointed at Ling. "You there, you can wait outside. We will be done in a moment."

Sitting outside of the door, Ling could hear the gist of the conversation. The Governor explained quite clearly that society needed both men and women, and that to put it simply, Ling had been chosen to be a woman and that was that. Ling had to accept the fate that was chosen for him, just like Yi did, too. He reminded Yi that he was of a different class, a different kind of person, so that it was only logical and understandable that his destiny was different from Ling. To have them stray from their fate would be going against the natural order and the country. After about ten minutes of talking, Yi walked out, closed the door behind him and stared at it.

"What was that about?" asked Ling curiously, pretending not to have overheard.

Yi said nothing, his back still towards Ling. Suddenly, he turned around, his face forcing a large grin. "You don't have to lie you know; I know this door is thin. I have stood outside and listened many times."

Ling said nothing, as tears started floating in his eyes.

"Now, now," said Yi still grinning, taking his friend around the corner, away from his father's office. "You don't have to cry." Hugging Ling tightly, he whispered into his ear. "I will protect you, from now to forever. I will protect you, so don't you cry."

Yi kept his word and whenever possible, protection he did provide, though Ling couldn't help wondering if it had been the right decision. It was Yi who, behind the scenes, kept creating reasons to delay his surgery, arguing that the two would eventually be married, and he would want to be part of it. It was Yi who decided they would get married, and it was Yi who was becoming more and more frustrated with this decision. Ling knew his mother was right; Yi had made a lot of sacrifices for him. Looking at his watch, he realized he needed to stop reminiscing and headed directly to the import supermarket.

Yi no longer lived in the same luxury that he did as a child. After graduating from the top university, he had rejected the pressure and expectation of entering a high positioned government job and instead decided to become a teacher. Ling felt this too was partially his fault, as he was not a proper woman. It would have been too risky for Yi to work in the public eye. Yi always vehemently denied that Ling was the reason he didn't work in government, yet like many other problems, he would refuse to discuss it further whenever Ling spoke to him about it. Today, it wasn't as if they currently lived badly by current standards, but it was rare for the two of them to do something more luxurious. The country's isolation policies and economic difficulties had made anything coming from the outside world extraordinarily expensive. The import market wasn't large, but it offered better meats, better fruits, and some hard to get items like higher quality milk, bread, and canned goods. Foods that Yi would have eaten everyday as the governor's son but could no longer afford on a teacher's salary.

Ling bowed to the familiar security guard as he walked in. There were no explicit rules banning the common people from entering the supermarket, yet it was clear that this was a place for exclusive members, and the guard was there to deter anyone who didn't quite belong. Ling became especially excited when he noticed that they had watermelons, as the fruit was not in season. It was Yi's favorite fruit, and though it would be heavy to carry home, he knew it would be the perfect dessert to put a smile on his face. Checking the time, Ling immediately noticed how late it was and did his shopping briskly before heading home.

Walking along the dike by the river, Ling smiled to himself. He could not hide the joy coming out of him. He felt oddly confident. He had all the ingredients to make a perfect dinner. Tonight would be different. Tonight, he would fix things. Even though things were different now, they used to be good friends. Tonight, things would be fixed. The words repeated over and over in his mind.

A motorcycle appeared out of nowhere, driving fast and nearly hitting Ling. In a swift motion, he leaped out of the way and accidentally dropped his bags as he dodged the incoming vehicle. He cried out as the watermelon popped out of his bag and began rolling down the side of the dike before splashing into the river.

Ling couldn't believe his bad luck, but he felt a slight sense of relief when he looked over the edge. The watermelon did not appear to break from the fall. It bobbled about two meters from shore, drifting among floating trash in the oily river. If he could find a way to grab it, he knew that the hard shell of the watermelon would have protected the meat inside.

Walking down to the bank around the river, he searched the shore frantically for anything at all that could be used to pull the watermelon back to shore. With any luck, he could find a long stick, a pole, or an old oar that had drifted from upstream. As he searched, he watched the watermelon float among the soft currents, pushing through the garbage and oil, before finally tangling in some brown reeds underneath the bridge. It stopped, just bobbing in the water.

Ling looked around. There was nothing he could use to reach the watermelon from shore. However, he noticed as he looked down, the water didn't appear too deep here. It was, at most, waist deep and the watermelon was only a few meters away. Looking around and seeing no one, Ling accepted that the only way he could rescue his precious watermelon was to enter the river and retrieve it himself. Slowly, he stripped off his dress and lowered himself into the water. The sound of him of splashing awoke the slight cry of something alive, that echoed under the bridge. Surprised, he quickly looked around for the source of the noise.

Downstream from him, he saw the silhouette of a basket, floating in the surrounding debris, hidden by the shadows of the towering bridge above. Concluding it to be the source of the cry, he grabbed his watermelon, waded towards the basket, and dragged both the basket and watermelon to shore. From the outside, it looked like a normal bamboo basket with a lid, one would you find being used by any nan-nu in a supermarket. He could see slightly soggy blankets sticking out of the sides. Hesitantly, he opened the lid, unsure what he would find outside.

He didn't know what he was expecting to find, but it certainly wasn't what he found. For inside was a baby, probably no more than a few months old, wrapped in a white cloth. It burped and cried as Ling looked down at it. Ling looked around. There were still no other people in sight up or down the riverbank.

Ling hesitated. There was no way Yi was going to be happy with this decision. But somehow, he felt it was the right decision to be made. Leaving the watermelon behind, Ling took the baby out of the basket, wrapping him up so no one could see him, and quickly began his walk home.

5.

OUR CHILDREN ARE OUR NATION'S FUTURE. SUPPORT YOUR CHILD, SUPPORT YOUR COUNTRY.

Yi UNDERSTOOD LING'S INTENTIONS WHEN he asked if he would be home for dinner. Although Ling had kept it casual, Yi was familiar with Ling's speaking style and mannerisms enough to understand that tonight would be Ling's attempt to normalize things between them. In his heart, even before speaking to Qiang, Yi felt he had done something wrong. But years of education and his parents influence had taught him that men were almost never wrong, and that men should never apologize, especially to a woman. Even if Ling wasn't 100% a woman, or as much a woman as he could be, Yi felt uncomfortable with the idea of directly apologizing to Ling. Besides, he reminded himself, the incident only happened because of Ling irritating him. In addition, he had always been taught that there was nothing wrong with a man hitting a woman every once in a while, especially if she deserved it. It was only hitting her too hard or too often that was wrong, and he had only hit Ling once since they got married. He felt proud he could logically justify his actions.

Yet, Yi still felt it was somewhat his responsibility to return things to the way they were before the incident. After class, and before heading home, he decided to stop by at a department store to look for a small present for Ling. It was difficult to find a gift for Ling; he wasn't comfortable buying him dresses or jewelry like other husbands would buy for their wives, and small gifts like chocolate and flowers were too romantic and felt insincere. Finally, after about twenty minutes of searching, he found the perfect gift, but it would have to be delivered later in the week. He supposed he could just give Ling the receipt as symbolism.

Yi found it unusual to see Ling, tears in his eyes, sitting on the couch instead of in the kitchen or waiting to serve him dinner when he walked into the apartment. Even more unusual, he appeared to be holding something in his arms. Something wrapped in blankets.

"What are you doing?" Yi asked suspiciously, as he dropped his bags on the ground. "Why aren't you cooking? Where is our dinner? What do you have in your arms?"

Ling looked at him, his face pale, before whispering somberly, "We have a problem."

"What did you do?" Yi asked angrily. He rushed over to the couch and sat down next to Ling.

Carefully, Ling opened up the blankets in his arms, exposing the sleeping baby. He was still in shock. He had spent the early part of the evening with it, feeding it some milk powder he normally used for Yi's breakfast, and finding new, clean blankets to wrap the child in.

Yi gasped in surprise. "Is that what I think it is? How did you get that? Where did you get that?"

Ling nodded, feeling unable to say anything.

"Who does it belong to?" Yi asked horrified. "You can't just go around, taking people's children and bringing them home. Why didn't you bring it to the police? To a doctor or something?"

"I don't know. I found it all wrapped up. In the river. I didn't know what to do. There was nobody around. I couldn't see anyone who could be the parents." He looked up at Yi's shocked face, with tears in his eyes. "Please don't be angry with me. I was only trying to help."

Yi sighed, sitting down next to Ling, pausing before awkwardly wrapping his arm gently around Ling's shoulder. "I am not angry with you." He looked down at the baby. He was surprised how cute it looked. He hadn't seen a baby up close in a long time. "But you know, this is probably someone's child. Someone is probably freaking out right now about a lost baby. We have to turn him into the police."

"I know." Ling shuddered, trying to gather his words. "But... but there is something strange about the baby. There is something I have to show you."

"What do you mean?"

Ling said nothing, instead slowly and carefully he unwrapped the baby, exposing the naked body for Yi to see. Ling was correct, there was something odd about the body. He thought for a moment. It did look kind of strange, but he couldn't quite figure out why. It was as if something was missing. Suddenly, it dawned on him. He gasped in realization.

"Ling," Yi said in shock. "Where is this baby's penis?"

"She doesn't have one."

"She?" The word slowly flowed through Yi's brain. He gasped. "You mean this child...is a girl?"

"As far as I can tell...yes..." Ling quietly replied as he wrapped up the baby. "That is my only conclusion so far. I have been thinking about it all evening."

"Then it must be a nan-nu," Yi said quickly. "That's the only possibility."

"I don't think so." Ling looked around nervously. He couldn't hide the fear in his voice. "I examined her carefully when I bathed her earlier, to wash the pollution off her body. She doesn't have any scars, any traces of surgery. I think it is a biological girl."

"How is this possible?" Yi asked, his brain straining for an explanation.

"I don't know."

The two men sat quietly, looking at the baby between them. The situation seemed so much more serious now. "We have to tell someone," Yi finally said, breaking the silence.

"Who?"

"I don't know. My father, the government, the police, somebody, I don't know. Basically anyone."

"No!" shouted Ling loudly. He froze for a moment, as if surprised by the volume of his own voice, before whispering. "Please, we can't tell your father, the government, the police, or just anyone. If this child was really a biological girl, do you know what they would do to her? Please, Yi, we have to help her," he finished, his eyes pleading.

"Ok. Let us be logical about this…" Yi thought for a moment. "We need all the facts, and for that to happen, we need a doctor, and for that to happen, we need a doctor we can trust."

Quickly, he picked up his cellphone and called the only person he felt could help him. Glancing at the time, he suddenly became aware of how late it was. Despite their last meeting not ending well, Yi was confident he would answer.

His cellphone rang about six times before Qiang answered, his voice annoyed. "Do you know how late it is? I am busy now. What do you want?"

"Please, it's an emergency!" begged Yi into the phone. "Can you meet us at your clinic?"

"Don't you have your own doctor you can go to?" groaned Qiang. "You know I am not your normal physician, right?"

"You're the only one who can help me," Yi said desperately.

"Right…" Qiang paused. "Guess what, I am busy now. I am at home, about to sit down for dinner. I'll call you tomorrow."

"Don't hang up!" yelled Yi into the phone. He paused for a moment, when he spoke again his voice was pleading. "Look, I know you are mad at me, and you probably have every right to be." From the corner of eye, he spotted Ling's confused expression, but he ignored it. "But, I have a situation right now that only you can solve. I don't know who else to turn to. You have to help me, Qiang."

"Okay, what is this about?" Qiang said. "You know if you have finally decided to give Ling his surgery, we can wait till tomorrow. You don't need to do it this exact moment."

"What? No, this is something…different. Look, Qiang, I am begging you, this is serious. An absolute emergency. Can you please be there in ten minutes? Ling and I are about to jump into a taxi," Yi said quickly. "I will explain when I get there."

"Yi," Qiang sighed. "I am not angry with you. But it has been a long day, and I am exhausted. I just want to relax, take a bath. Can this wait till tomorrow?"

"No!"

There was a moment of silence, before Qiang gave in. "Fine. I will be there in ten. But once again, I am warning you, Yi, this had better be important."

Yi and Ling were already waiting at the front door when Qiang arrived. He noticed a small basket in Ling's arms. Qiang took a good look at Ling as he paid for his taxi. It was rare for him to see Ling, and he immediately noticed how much skinner he had gotten. Qiang had always found him a rather handsome man. He had cute boyish looks, and it was obvious he would age well. And, he added in his mind, as he checked out Ling's dress, due to some of his more androgynous features, not only was he a handsome man, but he would also make a beautiful woman. Someone like Ling deserved better than Yi, he thought as he took out his keys and unlocked the clinic door, beckoning both of them inside.

"Okay, what is this about?" asked Qiang while locking door behind him. "Zhuang promised me a good time tonight, and we are both pretty pissed right now. This better be important."

"Can we go into the examination room?" Yi asked quickly.

"Sure, follow me."

Once they entered the room, Qiang turned to them. "What is going on? If this is about Ling needing surgery…as I said, it can wait till tomorrow"

"It's not," Yi interrupted. He hesitated for a moment, pointing at Ling. "It's easier to just show you…"

Qiang watched curiously as Ling took a bundle of blankets out of the basket and carefully began to unwrap it, exposing a baby's face.

"Wait!" Qiang said stepping back. "Is that a baby? Why are you bringing me a baby?"

"Look, we had to bring it to you."

"I don't understand. Doesn't your family have a pediatrician?" asked Qiang. "I don't think I need to say this, but I specialize in gender surgeries, not babies."

"Exactly," Yi said as he took the naked baby out of Ling's arms and handed it to Qiang. "Take a look, do you notice anything…odd?"

Qiang gasped in surprised as he looked at the naked baby, speechless. "This isn't possible. At least, I don't think it is possible. I can tell you from my experience it would be impossible to build an artificial vagina on a child this age. This just isn't possible."

"We don't think it's a nan-nu," Ling said quietly. "Well, I don't think it's a nan-nu. I think it's a biological female."

"How did you guys get a baby?" Qiang asked. "I don't remember you telling me you were applying to be a father, Yi."

"I didn't," replied Yi. "I came home from work, and there she was, in the living room, with Ling."

"I found it…err…her. I found her in the river," Ling whispered. "I was coming back from shopping and—"

"In the river?" Qiang interrupted, horrified.

"Yeah…" Ling felt nervous as both men stared at him. "I was walking by the river, and I heard this noise, so I jumped in. And I found this basket, and then, she was in the basket. And there was no one around, so I took her home."

The three men stood around in silence, staring at the baby sleeping.

"I see," Qiang finally said. "First of all, let's get a better idea about her health and maybe her background. Let me do some tests; maybe we can learn more? She doesn't have to be a biological girl. There could be another, simpler explanation. It could be a boy with ambiguous genitalia, or maybe it is a nan-nu. Let's not jump to conclusions until…"

"What kind of tests?" asked Ling nervously, picking up the baby and wrapping her in his arms. "I don't want to hurt her. She is just…you know, so…so small."

Qiang hesitated, looking at Ling's concerned face. "I am not trying to hurt her, but I need to draw some blood, do some DNA tests, and so on. This is the only the way we can get clear and definite answers. But, don't worry, nothing I do will hurt her. Although, if you can, I will need you to hold her still as I draw her blood."

He looked towards Yi as he prepared the necessary medical equipment. "Don't worry, this won't take that long. I can do everything in my lab. I realize how much you want to get out of here."

Ling held the baby close, playing with its little hands as they sat, waiting for the results to arrive. Yi couldn't help but notice what a natural parental figure Ling was and the bond that was growing between the baby and Ling in just the last few hours. Yi had never given much thought about having children. He never saw himself truly being in a marriage, and therefore children didn't seem like much of a possibility. Although he knew his parents would take offense to his decision of not having children, they already disapproved of everything else in his life. However, as the child slept, cradled comfortably, sucking on Ling's thumb, Yi had to admit to himself that if he ever did have a child, Ling would be the person he would want caring for that child.

"You should not get so attached," said Yi suddenly, unable to bear his own thoughts. "Once we find the baby's parents, we are going to have to return it."

Ling said nothing, just looked up and smiled before continuing to rock the child.

"Look…" Yi said quietly. "I need to tell you something now."

"Okay," replied Ling.

Yi watched Ling carefully. He was too busy concentrating on the baby to provide Yi with his full attention. Yi didn't know why, but it annoyed him. "I said," Yi said, raising his voice, "I need to talk to you."

"I am listening," Ling said, still playing with the baby.

"First of all," Yi began. He walked over to Ling, took out his wallet, and pulled out a receipt. "I got you a small present."

Ling looked up, feeling slightly surprised, reaching up and grabbing the receipt. "What is it?"

"This is just the receipt. The gift will be delivered in a few days."

Ling read the receipt carefully. "You got me a new vacuum cleaner?"

"I know how much you have wanted one. Besides, this will help you clean faster and better in the house. It is the latest model. This way, you can focus more time on your other responsibilities."

Ling didn't know how to respond, but in an odd way, he felt genuinely touched by the thought and gesture. Smiling, he stuck the receipt into his pocket.

"Also," Yi continued, taking a deep breath and continuing. "I hope we can avoid something like what happened a few nights ago from happening again. But…you shouldn't have pushed me so hard and made me so angry. However, I do want you to know that I forgive you. I forgive you for pushing me so hard and making me so angry."

"What?" Ling asked confused.

"You shouldn't have made me so angry, Ling. It's not right for someone like you to question the husband. In the future, I hope you won't make me so angry, and this way things won't be awkward and uncomfortable between us. But the important thing is I forgive you," Yi finished, smiling awkwardly. "I hope after we go home tonight, things will go back to normal."

Ling didn't know what to say. He looked back down, frowning, and continued playing with the baby.

"Excuse me," said Qiang, suddenly walking into waiting room. "The results are ready."

"Good." Yi jumped up, feeling relieved. "What can you tell us?"

"Well, the child is indeed female." Qiang looked intently at Yi's face before continuing. "But, other than that, I really don't have any concrete information. I guess I can also conclude it was a natural birth, as her DNA does not match anyone on record."

"How is that possible?" Yi asked her quickly. "Did you test her for a race? Is she Han Chinese? Maybe she is a foreigner? A minority?"

"As I have said many times already to you Yi, race is not a biological factor. It is something we have created. We are not that different from each other." Yi looked as though he disagreed, but Qiang ignored him and continued. "However, we can use DNA to compare with people in different regions. Though she does not match any person registered, her DNA shows similarities to people of this region."

"But, how is that possible? Every single person in this country is registered."

"Perhaps that is what the government thinks. However, we all know that out west, especially with some of the poorer villages in the more mountainous regions, the government hadn't been as detailed in registering. It is entirely possible that some of these survivors may be female, hiding their gender in fear of the government. Furthermore, there may be some men out there who are still able to create the X chromosome. We have all heard rumors, and the government has made mistakes in the past." Remembering how patriotic Yi could be, he quickly added, "That being said, keep in mind that based on where she was found, the survival rate of a baby drifting downstream, I think it is logical to conclude this child was born in our country."

"Like I said earlier, maybe it's a foreigner, or minority, or maybe a half-blood," Yi said stubbornly. "There is no way that child is pure Han Chinese. I think you forget how thorough our government was. I mean is."

"I think the chances of foreigners, minorities, or half-bloods in this country are even less likely. Remember, the government has removed anyone they suspect of not being pure Han Chinese. Do you remember how they started to expel people for having brown or dyed hair? Don't you think it would be much easier for a biological Chinese woman to cut her hair and pretend to be a man, or just pretended to be a nan-nu?"

"If there was a biological Chinese woman out there, she could just come out to the government, and she would be protected according to law," said Yi. "There would be no reason for her to hide."

"I understand you are the Governor's son, and you want to believe that," said Qiang, "but, let us stop pretending. You and I both know in our heart that isn't what happens." Qiang took a deep breath. "May I remind you, once again, that a baby can only float downstream for so long and be alive, much less healthy. This baby looks East Asian; therefore, she is most likely Han Chinese. The question of how the baby got here is not what is important. What is important is the next step."

"Exactly. What happens now?" asked Ling, looking up from the baby for the first time. "Since we can't find her biological parents? What happens to the baby?"

Qiang said nothing, looking at Yi to make the final decision.

"We have to turn her in to the government," Yi said finally. "For the good of the country, she could become some sort of beacon. A symbol of hope."

"Are you sure you want to do that?" asked Qiang, "Like I said earlier…let's not pretend here. Do you know what the government would do to her? Have you heard the rumors of what happened to the remaining biological females in this country? They were harvested for their eggs, Yi. Harvested like they were livestock."

Yi thought for a moment. "It's what's good for the country," he said finally.

"But, is it what's good for her?" asked Qiang. "She is only a few months old. Three months at the most. Do you really want to put her through that misery until she is able to reproduce? And, I don't even want to mention the horrors that are bound to happen once she can reproduce."

Yi looked over at Ling holding the baby tight. He never really understood why people said babies were adorable until he met this one, and despite only spending a few hours together, it was clear she and Ling had bonded. The baby looked relaxed and happy in Ling's arms.

"Please, Yi," begged Ling. "Please keep her safe. I don't ask for much. But please keep her safe."

"I suppose there is another option. If don't want to keep her, and you do want to protect her," Qiang said quietly. "You could always take her to the Capital and smuggle her into one of the embassies. Someone from another country could take her. Other countries don't have the gender imbalance we do. They don't have the laws we do. They would keep her safe."

Yi took a good look at the baby as Ling passed her into his arms. She was so cute and innocent. He reminded himself of what he had been taught his whole life, the right choice should be so easy right now, to turn her in the government and be done with her. Tomorrow, he and Ling could pretend this never happened. They could even be celebrated as heroes for discovering another biological woman. His father would finally be proud of him for bringing this honor to his family.

Yet, as the baby twitched her mouth in her sleep, he couldn't help remembering the woman that continued to haunt his dreams: the cage, her tears of blood, the fact that she probably no longer existed. He knew what happened to biological women. Could he allow the same fate to happen to her?

With a heavy sigh, he realized what decision had to be made.

It did not matter what the law or his father would say. He could not allow harm to come to this child. He and Ling had to be responsible for her life. In a hollow voice, he spoke clearly and carefully.

"We will keep her, and we will raise her, and we will keep her safe. She is innocent, and…turning her in…we know what will happen. But, this—this is our secret." He emphasized the last sentence, as he turned to Qiang. "We need to have clear rules to protect her. You will be her doctor. You will register her in the national archives, and you will register her as my son. We will raise her as my son, and we will never, ever talk about her true sex." He paused for a moment, hesitant and scared of the words about to come out of his mouth. "I don't want anyone to underestimate the risk we are taking here. I don't think I have to tell anyone here the severity and the illegality of what we are doing. If we were ever caught…well, I don't even want to think about what would happen."

TWO YEARS LATER

6.

GRANDPARENTS AND GRANDSON! WHAT A SPECIAL RELATIONSHIP!

TWO-YEAR-OLD HANBING CRAWLED ON THE floor, slowly picked herself up, walked over, grabbed her new teddy bear, and brought herself over to Yi, settling herself in his lap. Stroking her short hair, he had to admit that things were working out better than he had feared. It had been two years since the day Ling had found her by the river, and today the three of them were having a small party to celebrate her Arrival Day. It had become customary to celebrate the day of the child's arrival in the family instead of the day of birth in the PRCC. As Yi watched Ling in the kitchen cutting up a watermelon, which had become a symbol of the family's prosperity, after their small celebratory dinner, he couldn't stop thinking about how lucky he was. He remembered the first day he brought Hanbing to his family.

Guihua was the only person in Yi's family that had been pleased with the news when Yi brought over his new baby to the Governor's Manor for the first time, two days after the child had been registered. Between both Yi's and Qiang's connections, the registration of her into the national database had gone smoothly, with no suspicious questions asked about the child's origins or, more importantly, her sex. With Qiang registered as the child's only physician, and all medical examinations going solely through him, they were all confident that no one would find about the baby's secret. As Guihua marveled above the resting child in Ling's arm, the Governor turned towards Yi, his face surprised.

"What do you mean you had a baby?" said the Governor confused. "I mean, I didn't even know you were planning to have a son."

"Well," Yi replied casually, "I wanted it to be a surprise."

"Do you really think this is the best time to be having a son?" the Governor asked. He looked towards Ling, not hiding the disgust in his voice. "Especially with the problem in your house. Do you really trust that thing with your son? My grandson?"

"Ling has gone through all the proper training like every nan-nu. He is registered as a woman in our glorious country. Visually, if you didn't know better, you would think he is a nan-nu. I see no reason why Ling can't take care of my child," Yi said. "It's not like Ling is going to be naked in front of the child."

"You really think it's healthy to allow a household like yours to have a baby?"

"What's done is done," Yi stated. "This child is mine, and I intend to raise him as mine. If you want to get to know your grandson, I guess you'll have to accept it."

The Governor said nothing for a moment, thinking. "This doesn't change my opinion about your 'relationship' you know." He looked at everyone in room, before announcing loudly, "I still expect Ling to get the job done. I will not accept a faggot as my son, and I especially do not accept a pair of faggots as the parents of my first grandson."

"That is not important right now. I brought my child over to celebrate, and we should be celebrating my first child, and your first grandson, right now." Yi added quickly, "I mean, isn't getting a grandson what you always wanted?"

Before the Governor could answer, Guihua interrupted. "Have you chosen a name?"

"We were thinking of Hanbing," said Ling standing in the corner, cuddling the baby.

The Governor ignored Ling and looked towards his son. "Yes, have you thought of a name?"

"Yes, sir." Yi said, repeating after Ling. "We were thinking of Hanbing."

"Hmm, so Han for masculine, and Bing for military?" asked the Governor. Yi nodded. The Governor smiled for the first time during the night. "I like it. The next generation of this family needs a masculine-named child." He took Hanbing out of Ling's arms. "Well, aren't you a big baby?" he said, smiling, and playing with the baby's fingers. "I guess this means you are going to be a strong man! My manly little Hanbing!"

Yi's brother, Mengqin, could hardly hide his contempt. "So," he snarled, "you heard that I got approved for a child, so you decided to get one first?"

"It isn't a competition, Brother," said Yi.

"Sure, it isn't," Mengqin said and then mumbled something offensive under his breath.

"I wanted it to be a surprise! That's why I didn't say anything to the family," Yi lied.

Mengqin ignored him and mumbled again before saying louder, "I am sure this has nothing to do with becoming Father's favorite again."

"Look," Yi began, "isn't this a good thing? Now your son and my child can grow up together. This way they will be brothers from a young age. This will only strengthen our family's bond together."

"Whatever," dismissed Mengqin. He fidgeted his fingers, as he often did when he was uncomfortable, and refused to look at Yi directly.

"I had hoped," Yi said out loud, "that by having our children at the same time, they could bond and be even closer. They will not just be brothers but also best friends. After all, what is more important than family?"

The issue of the child's gender was ever present for Yi and Ling. There had been close calls, and both of them were careful that Hanbing was always under one of their supervision, careful never to let Hanbing alone with any other adult. Guihua was especially surprised and disappointed that Yi and Ling refused to allow her to participate in what she called "normal grandmotherly duties" such as babysitting the child alone or chores like cleaning or bathing her grandchild. Yi even threated to ban her from seeing Hanbing when Guihua tried to clean up her grandchild after a particularly messy dinner one night. The extended family was baffled by Yi and Ling's odd insistence of doing everything by themselves, not even hiring a nanny to come help them, but ultimately they dismissed it as another weird and stubborn characteristic trait of Yi's. Thankfully, Guihua was able to help with Qinghuang, Mengqin's son, who arrived six months after Hanbing. Mengqin, like other men, found it below him to be helping with childcare.

The Governor was also furious when he learned that Hanbing was not going to the family's traditional physician and was instead getting all healthcare from Qiang.

"Instead of going to the doctor you grew up with, one of the best doctors in the country," the Governor yelled over the dinner, "you are telling me that my grandson is seeing some... some third class freak instead of our family doctor. Someone, who I must add, has been watching over this family since before you were even born."

"This doctor has been a close friend of mine, and when he asked me, I felt I couldn't say no," Yi replied, keeping his voice calm. "Qiang is very well respected by his peers, and since he is my friend, I can trust him to take care of Hanbing like his own."

"He isn't even a proper doctor; he does sex changes! His job isn't suitable for children," the Governor yelled. "Haven't I told you I didn't want you running around with freaks like him? It just isn't proper. As if you weren't failing enough in life," he added bitterly.

"My decision has been made," Yi said firmly. "I am the father of this child, and I want my child examined by someone I personally know and trust." Before the Governor could say anything, he repeated firmly, "Hanbing is my child. I know what is best for my child, and my word is final."

Yi sat on the couch, watching his child curled up in his lap resting peacefully. He realized that he felt a connection to her that he didn't share with anyone else. Yes, the last two years had been frantic, but he couldn't have ever imagined the joys that fatherhood could bring. To the surprise of others, and even himself, Yi had dedicated himself to being a hands-on father and doing as much as he could. He and Ling had even bonded more tightly over the shared responsibility, fighting less and feeling more comfortable in all aspects of their shared life. Yi wondered if, perhaps, this was what true love felt like. No matter what this feeling was called, he accepted that there was a peace and harmony brought into the household by this new addition, and the last two years, overall, had been wonderful. He couldn't stop smiling as Ling placed the watermelon in front of them.

The next day was the extended family celebration. After a quick breakfast and Ling's daily preparation, they brought Hanbing to visit Ling's parents. It was unusual for them to visit, and though Ling's parents loved her, they too, agreed that not visiting often was the right decision as Hanbing was not only of a different social class but also didn't belong to their family. Still, they valued the limited visits and spoiled their grandchild in simple ways. Today, they had prepared the traditional longevity noodles to be eaten on one's Arrival Day. Ling's father, Nongfu, had spent much of the morning rolling and cooking the single strand of one-meter noodle, careful not to break it in the process.

"Eat, eat!" Nongfu gushed, setting the bowl containing a single strand of noodle in front of his grandchild. "Remember to eat as much as you can without breaking the noodle! The more you eat, the longer you'll live!"

Ling stood around, beaming and taking pictures of their child. It was hard for him to hide the tears forming in his eyes.

Yi stood to at the back of the wall, next to Wupo. They had not seen each other for nearly a year but had little to say to another.

"I hope my 'daughter' is treating your child with the love and respect he deserves," Wupo said suddenly, staring at a very happy child stuffing her face. "Such a handsome child of such high prestige deserves only the best."

"Ling is a great mother," Yi said smiling. "Hanbing loves Ling very much."

"Good." She smiled, before adding quietly, "I am sorry that she refuses to get the surgery. I keep telling her to, but I don't know why she keeps refusing. I am sorry about the shame she is bringing upon your family."

Yi kept his face neutral, careful not to show too much of the thoughts going through his head. "As long as Ling does a good job raising Hanbing, I am happy. My happiness lies with my child."

Wupo smiled. "I know she will, I know she will. But, just remember, if she ever steps out of her place, like I have said before, don't hesitate to put her back to where she belongs. My 'daughter' can be quite the rebellious one."

Yi smiled at her in a way he could only hope looked understanding before leaving her and joining Ling and his father in the celebration of their child.

Despite being a time of economic hardship for the nation and it being only a small family affair, the Governor had gone all out in preparing an Arrival Day celebration that he thought worthy of his grandson. The best food available in the season had been prepared. Presents and exotic foods from abroad had been imported. He even hired a small theater group just to entertain Hanbing and her cousin Qinghuang. He was especially proud of the large stainless-steel toy tank he had specially ordered for his grandson from Eastern Europe. After dinner, the men of the family gathered in the living room to sit down and talk, while the women helped clean up and serve tea. Hanbing sat on the floor, busy playing with the wrapping paper instead of opening presents.

"When are you going to let my grandson start hanging out with other children his age?" asked the Governor. "You know many of my underlings have children now, and from what I gather when they are gossiping instead of working, they all get together for play dates. It is time for him to hang out with boys his age. I am not saying he should hang out with the children of our staff. We all know Hanbing is above them in every way. However, I don't think it would hurt to hang out with children of other government officials. I recall your friend Chen has a child. Maybe the two of them should start hanging out. It's never too early to start building proper connections. I keep thinking, if I had raised you with the proper people when you were younger, we wouldn't have ended up with it over there, and you would have married a proper woman."

"Chen lives in the Capital now, not Xincheng. But, that is not the point, I think he is still a little young," Yi said as Ling poured him tea. "I have decided that I want to wait a little longer before we start bringing him out and having him meet other children." He sipped his tea slowly. "Besides, he has Qinghuang right now, and I think building a proper family relationship is more important than introducing him to strangers who might just be using him to get to his grandfather. Don't you agree, sir?"

Before the Governor could respond, Mengqin's wife, Baihe, interrupted. "Excuse me, sir, sorry to interrupt you like this, but if you want him to know people..." She looked to Mengqin, who nodded in approval. "I recently brought Qinghuang to join a small family group run by some very elite people. We started going last week..." She looked around at the men sitting around her, smirking at Ling, before adding quietly. "Oh, I meant to tell you all about it on another day."

"See!" the Governor said. "Even Qinghuang is going out, and he is six months younger!" He looked at Baihe with a rare eagerness and interest. "Tell me more about this family group, who are these very elite people? I want to make sure that my grandchildren are only getting the best."

"Sir, I can assure you, Mengqin and I only give Qinghuang the best," beamed Baihe. "This group, it's very formal. All the ladies there are wives of successful businessmen, generals, politicians—that class of people. So you can tell, obviously, it's only for the best of the best. It's very elite and the maximum membership is only, like, seven or eight people. All the children are between the ages of two and four, so age-wise it's perfect. The children get a chance to play with each other, while us ladies sit around and learn about being ladies. It's very exclusive as you obviously realize. We were only able to get in because Mengqin and I recently hosted General Lihong for dinner. After dinner, his wife, Meigui invited us to…"

"Oh," said the Governor, surprised, looking at Mengqin, "you have been hosting General Lihong."

"Indeed, sir," Mengqin said arrogantly and turned to Yi. "Just a reminder, General Lihong served with our honorable grandfather and is highly respected for his role in stopping the Eastern Rebellion." When he noticed Yi ignoring him, he continued, glaring angrily in his direction. "But, I digress. We have hosted General Lihong more than once. We have had some very important discussions about the future of our glorious country, and I believe he really does trust my knowledge and advice. You might say we are becoming close confidants. Besides, I might add, someone in this family has to show some interest in continuing our honorable role in government. After all, it would be detrimental to not only our family, but to our country, if one of us did not continue all the hard work you and grandfather put in to make Xincheng a better place."

Baihe giggled proudly. "Like I was saying, the General's wife, Meigui, runs a small group for children of our elite background. It happens nearly every Saturday, during the weekend, so we can give our husbands a chance to relax. This way the children can play together and make friends that are worthy of one another.

I am sure if you are interested, I can bring Hanbing next week. I agree with what you said earlier, sir. It's never too early for your grandchildren to start making connections. Wouldn't you all agree?"

"Sure," Ling said quietly, feeling uncomfortable. "Just let me know which day, and Hanbing and I will be ready."

Baihe frowned, not saying anything before gently putting down her tea. "Actually, if it is not too inconvenient, perhaps it is best if I bring Hanbing by myself. I would hate to distract you from your daily—"

"Don't worry," Yi interrupted, understanding Baihe's implication. "No one other than this family knows about Ling's secret. When Ling is out in public, no one has ever suspected anything different. Anyway, as Hanbing's father, I will not allow my child to go out alone with you."

Guihua interrupted the awkward silence that followed Yi's statement. "You know we are all here to celebrate Hanbing's arrival day. Why don't we talk about this later? Hanbing, dear, why don't you show us all of your new toys?"

It took Hanbing multiple trips to carry all her new toys over, before carefully setting them in the front of the family. She looked around, unsure of which one she should play with.

"Hanbing, do you want to play with your new tank?" asked the Governor proudly, pushing the brand new, stainless steel tank in front of his grandchild. "Granddaddy bought this especially for you. See all the cool things it can do!" he said as he moved the different parts of the tank.

"No, I want that!" said Hanbing pointing at the army solider that came with the tank. "I don't want to play with tank. I want to play with the doll."

"Excuse me?" asked the Governor angrily. "You want to play with what? The what?" The whole room went quiet rather quickly.

"Doll?" Hanbing replied, confused.

"He meant action figure," Ling said quickly, jumping over

to protect Hanbing, and adding in quietly, "Hanbing, this is an action figure."

"You see!" the Governor raised his voice, scaring Hanbing who hid in Ling's arms. "This is what happens when…"

"Please, sir," said Ling, interrupting and speaking extremely fast. "Hanbing just made a small mistake. He doesn't know what this is called, so he called it doll because I have a doll, sir. He doesn't know it is called an action figure."

The Governor ignored Ling, turning on to Yi. "I knew this would happen. See what happens when you let a bunch of faggots raise a child?" He sighed loudly. "My first grandson, already turned into a faggot at such a young age! What is going to happen next? Start playing house with an army man, pretending he is a housewife? What will happen next!"

As if on cue, Hanbing picked up the little army action figure, looking at the gun in his hands. "Pew, pew, pew! I will kill bad guys. Pew, pew, pew! I will kill evil foreigners, just like I see on TV."

The Governor watched, his face surprised, before turning to Yi with a look of approval.

"See," said Yi, careful to hide the relief in his voice. "As we told you, it isn't that Hanbing wants to play dress up with dolls. He simply doesn't know what it is called." He watched his daughter running around pretending to shoot bad guys. "As you can see there is nothing feminine about his actions. Your grandchild…" He hesitated, not looking at Ling. "Your grandchild will be the man suitable to carry on our family name."

Yi and Ling were quiet during the taxi ride home. When they arrived home, Ling gave Hanbing a quick bath before putting her into their bed, and then stepped out to the living room where Yi sat watching TV.

"You coming to bed?" Ling asked, standing in the doorway.

"Just a moment, I want to finish the news."

Ling thought for a moment. Hanbing was asleep, and he didn't want to risk starting a fight. He reminded himself both that it was improper to speak up against his husband and how perfect the day had been. But the words left his mouth before he could control them. "So, are we just going to discipline Hanbing every time she does anything remotely feminine?"

"Excuse me?" asked Yi, turning off the television.

"Is this the plan? We are just going to pretend Hanbing is a boy and raise her like a boy?"

"We already pretend you are a girl," shrugged Yi, turning the television back on. "I don't see what the problem is."

"I am trying to have a serious conversation."

"Well, I don't think there is anything worth talking about."

"We can't just continue to pretend that everything is normal when it's not. We need to talk about this."

"Fine. What do you want to talk about?"

"Turn off the TV," Ling said in a voice louder than he expected. "I am trying to have a serious conversation here." Ling hesitated, carefully watching Yi's annoyed face as he turned off the TV, before continuing. "I feel like there is a better way of doing this. We have the first natural female found in this country in who knows how long. Perhaps the only natural female in this country, and we are just going pretend she's a boy?"

"We have talked about this before. I don't see what choice we have," Yi said, annoyed. "I am sick of talking about this. I want to watch the news." He stopped, reading Ling's falling face and decided to change the tone of his voice. "Besides, we know she isn't the only natural female in the country, someone had to give birth to her. When we found Hanbing two years ago, I told you, in order to keep her, this is what have we have to do. It's the best thing for her and the only way to protect her."

"Do you really believe that this is the best thing for Hanbing, our daughter?"

"I feel like you keep forgetting, or purposely ignoring, the severity of what would happen if someone, especially someone like my father, found out Hanbing was a biological girl." He cut Ling off, already anticipating his counter argument. "And no, I do not think that the love my father might have for his grandchild would prevent him from allowing her to get gutted like a pig for science."

Ling said nothing, allowing Yi to continue. A rare glimpse of emotion escaped him, his voice cracking as he spoke. "I love Hanbing more than anything in the world. Quite simply, I will do anything to protect her."

Ling smiled meekly. "I know you will. I am just worried, that's all." He stood up, walked over and gave Yi an awkward hug.

Yi swallowed uncomfortably as Ling hugged him. He cleared his voice with a small cough. "However, I think my father is right. You should take Hanbing out more. I think joining Baihe and the other ladies is a good idea. Also…" He hesitated. "I have been thinking. We should work on developing more independence in Hanbing. We can't continue to keep letting her sleep in our bed. I think we should start by moving her into the office. We don't use it anymore. Perhaps we should convert it into her bedroom?"

7.
A LADY IS THE HIGHEST AMBITION A WOMAN CAN ACHIEVE

IT HAD BEEN MANY YEARS since Ling had met people outside of his family and random strangers at the store or on the street. He didn't have any friends in elementary school besides Yi. During middle school and high school, students studying to become nan-nu were discouraged from becoming close friends with one another, as close friendship could become a distraction in the future when a woman's most important duty was to take care of her husband and his children. When Ling got engaged to Yi, he understood and accepted that Yi was going to be the most important person in his life, and it was disrespectful to go out and meet other people, especially considering that he hadn't had his surgery. He was, therefore, understandably nervous as he and Hanbing took a taxi to meet Baihe in Zhengfu District, where they would finally be joining the children's group. Upon arrival, Ling stepped out of the taxi, smoothed the brand new dress that he had bought just for the occasion, and walked up to rather luxurious apartment complex. Baihe greeted them with Qinghuang in her arms at the front gate.

"Hello, Hanbing," Baihe greeted them cheerfully. The cousins ran to one another as soon as she put her son to the ground. "You two will have so much fun today. I am so glad you could make it."

Turning to Ling, Baihe said coolly, "This complex has extremely good security. Normally, you would need special permission to enter, but you are lucky because they know me." She eyed Ling up and down with judgment. "Thank goodness you dressed appropriately. I thought I was going to have to teach you about fashion. Also, if you would please, try not to embarrass me today."

Ling didn't know what to say. Taking out a small mirror from his purse, he fixed his hair, tightened his dress, and followed his sister-in-law through the gate into the complex. They walked quietly through the manicured garden of small trees and hedges before entering the tallest building at the back of the complex. Finally, they rode the elevator to the sixth floor and entered a large, spacious apartment. Standing in the middle of the room was group of ladies talking quietly with one another. They went silent as Ling walked into the room.

Ling's first reaction upon seeing the group was that these were the most beautiful women he had ever seen. He could hardly believe that any of these women were ever men. They were all thin and tall, with shiny porcelain skin that glistened underneath the lighting. They had perfect bodies, ranging from their ample perky breasts to their curvy hips, down to their long sleek legs. Even their faces, so young and clearly shaped under the knife, were small and perfectly symmetrical. Their long shiny hair was styled flawlessly, with not a single strand out of place. Any semblance of their previous lives as men could not be seen on them. As they flocked over, giggling quietly, Ling couldn't help but compare his fashion with theirs. From their stiletto heels to their tight Chinese style dresses, each piece was much more beautiful and classier than his was. Clearly, this was the best money could buy. Ling suddenly felt very ugly and out of place. Although his dress was formal and the most expensive clothing he owned, he had bought it from a regular store close to his house. It was not a designer piece like they were all wearing. He hoped the other ladies would not notice.

"Baihe!" one of the women stepped forward from the group

and greeted in her honeysuckle voice. "Long time, no see. I see you have brought a friend." Her voice contradicted with her uncomfortably cold smile. She was clearly the leader of this little club.

"Yes," Baihe bowed lightly to acknowledge the woman. "My honorable Meigui. Thank you for allowing me to bring her. This is my sister-in-law, Ling. Her husband is my husband's brother and the Governor's eldest son."

"Hehehehe," one of the ladies in the background giggled. "We have the future Governess in our group now."

Ling merely smiled and nodded. "If the heavens allow it," Ling said humbly.

"Unfortunately," smirked Baihe, dismissing Ling with a wave of her hand, "her husband doesn't seem to show much interest in politics. He prefers to stay in a lowly position as a teacher. At this rate, it is more likely I will be the future Governess."

"Please, Baihe," scoffed one of the ladies from the group, "stop lying to yourself. As if the backup ever rises up to a position of—"

"Be quiet, you," said Meigui. Everyone went instantly silent. She turned towards Baihe, careful yet deliberate with her movements. "Now, now, Baihe. Be wary of the words coming out of your mouth. A lady should never insult her family, nor should she ever speak negatively of others." She turned to the group, who all gave her their full attention. "Teaching our next generation is most important. I have heard much gossip about the Governor's eldest son. Apparently, he is the head of the Political Science Department of Xincheng #1 High School. Youngest in history, if I heard right, and quite good at his job. A very respectful position indeed." She turned to Ling. "I am Meigui. I welcome you and your son to our little gathering."

She turned around, pointing from left to right at the group behind her. "And these fine ladies are Mudan, Shuilian, Hua'er, and Zhubao. As you know, we all come from the finest families in the city. Mudan's and Zhubao's husbands work in business, doing import and export work. Very prestigious as you might guess. Shuilian's husband works in government, with your father-in-law, of course, but not as high of a position. Hua'er and I are military wives. Her husband works as a colonel under my husband, who is a general." She emphasized the last sentence, as if reminding the ladies of her superiority in an indirect way. "Of course," she added, turning back towards Baihe and Ling, and taking a slight bow, "none of us come from such high, honorable positions as the Governor's daughters-in-law, and wife of the eldest son. You'll have to forgive us if we seem like just common folk."

The ladies in the group stood around nodding and giggling. They watched Meigui carefully, as if awaiting her next order.

Ling looked around at all the beautiful women surrounding him and the modernly furnished apartment. He had never been in a place quite like this apartment. It was like something he saw on TV and he felt more and more out of place as they stood there. "Your apartment is gorgeous. Thank for you inviting me and Hanbing into your home." He said politely.

Meigui smiled coldly. Behind her, Ling could see Baihe groan quietly. "This old place," Meigui chuckled. "We would never *live* in place like this. This is just an old apartment my husband and I bought so I could host these meetings. Naturally, my husband and I would be unable to live in a place so small."

"Oh, I am so sorry," Ling said quickly. He wasn't sure Meigui heard him.

"Wait. We forgot someone," Meigui said, twisting her lips, as if trying to contain a laugh. "She isn't someone of importance, but I guess what she does could be seen as necessary. Where is Fenghuang? Fenghuang, where are you?"

A plump middle-aged woman walked out of the kitchen carrying a plate of snacks with a group of children following her, her face covered in a large, genuine smile. Unlike the other woman in the group, she was dressed casually.

"And this is Fenghuang." Meigui said smirking. "Fenghuang

watches the children. You don't have to worry, despite not studying at the Capital School of Childcare and Education, she came highly recommended and helps us out during this time. This way, we honorable ladies get some time alone to talk and learn how to be better high-class women."

"What?" asked Ling confused. He felt reluctant to hand Hanbing to another woman, "We don't watch the children?"

"Oh, my goodness, no," said Meigui shocked, covering her heart with hand. "We spend plenty of time with them as it is." She reached over and grabbed Hanbing and Qinghuang's hands, handing them to Fenghuang. "This is our personal time. Think of it as a well-earned break from your motherly duties and a chance to learn other skills."

It had been years since Ling was with a group of women. The last time he had this experience, he was still in high school, and he assumed things had to be different. He followed silently and awkwardly as the ladies collected themselves and walked to a tatami room at the back of the apartment, where they all sat down comfortably around a table filled with a tea set, assorted snacks, and chopped fruits.

"Tell me, ladies!" Meigui began as she gently poured tea for everyone. "How is everyone this week?"

"Very good, Meigui," the group replied in unison. "How was your week?"

"It went well. Last week, as you all know, I visited the Capital. Let me tell you ladies, I have a surprise for you! There is a new fashion in town." The other ladies giggled gleefully in unison as Meigui took out a carved teak box, opened it carefully, and took out a white silk scarf. "This, ladies, is the Xinweijin."

"The Xinweijin?" gasped the other ladies in surprise, before once again giggling in unison.

Ling contained his laugh. It all felt rather fake and over the top. "It's just a scarf," he said quietly.

If any of the ladies heard him, they showed no signs. Meigui continued, "The Xinweijin is no ordinary piece of cloth. It's spun out of the finest silks from the western provinces. This limited piece of clothing has multiple functions…" she paused, looking at Ling, but spoke to the group, "I am sure I don't have to explain here what the purpose of this fine clothing is. I know I can count on you to all remember Rule 18 of being a proper lady."

"Yes, Meigui," said all the ladies in unison.

Ling sat there looking baffled. Meigui, noticing Ling's silence, turned towards him. "You are familiar with Rule 18," she said, staring him in his eyes.

"Ummm," Ling shifted uncomfortably in his seat. "I…"

Baihe, looking embarrassed, interrupted, "You have to understand…my sister-in-law is a very busy…she hasn't had time to read…you know with all her duties and such…"

Meigui ignored her. "Why?" she asked, surprised. "You mean you have never read *Madame Xue's Etiquette Guide for the Ladies of the Higher Social Class?*"

There was a moment of silence as the ladies stared at Ling. He felt sweat dripping from his forehead as they judged him.

"No," he said finally.

"I see," chuckled Mudan. "That explains a lot."

"Now, now," giggled Shuilian, "let's play nice."

Meigui smiled at Ling, and her teeth shone through her cold smile. "Why? You should have just said so. Remind me to bring you a copy next time. It is only the best book ever written." She turned to group, "Who here can tell Ling what is Rule 18?"

"A lady should always keep her head down. It's not only submissive and respectful, but also hides her apple," the ladies called out in unison.

"Her apple?" asked Ling, confused.

"It's often the most obvious part," Meigui said, stroking her neck, "that keeps us from becoming truly ladies."

"Oh," replied Ling.

"But as I was explaining earlier," Meigui said, "this item, the

Xinweijin, is the most talked about item in the Capital. As a group, we must all ask our husbands to get them as soon as possible. After all, we don't want to fall behind on the latest fashions of the upper class. Do we, ladies?"

"No, Meigui," said the ladies in unison. Ling uncomfortably joined in.

"Okay, ladies," Meigui said as she put away the scarf, "how are things at home? I assume all of you are making your husbands very happy."

The ladies nodded together

"How are things at home, Zhubao?" she said turning towards the other woman. "I hope you worked out your problem."

"Yes, Meigui," said Zhubao shamefully. "I have been controlling myself. I haven't done anything wrong since the last time."

The other ladies looked at her with support, although Ling was unable to tell if it was genuine. "What's Zhubao's problem?" he asked quietly and cautiously.

"Oh yes. Of course, you don't know. You are new," said Meigui. Her voice was ripe with over-the-top emotion, as she sighed dramatically. "Zhubao here likes to watch sports on TV. Her husband caught her watching a…a basketball game last week. She has been struggling with this issue for quite some time."

"What?" asked Ling, confused.

"I know," sobbed Zhubao, as she cried into the sleeves of her fox fur jacket. "But I just can't stop by myself. I just love all the sports. Baseball. Basketball. All the sports."

"What's wrong with watching sports?" asked Ling.

"Do you watch sports?" asked Mudan in disgust.

"No," replied Ling hesitantly. It was the truth; he had never been much of an athlete and watching games had always bored him.

"Exactly!" said Meigui, "It's not very lady-like." The other ladies nodded in agreement. "Naturally, and rightfully," Meigui continued, "her husband punished her for the wrongful behavior. Five lashes with a bamboo stick, isn't that correct, Zhubao?"

Zhubao cried louder. The other ladies began to cuddle around her and comfort her. Ling could see their gleeful smiles over Zhubao's shoulder as they hugged her.

"I want to make it clear, though, especially as we have a new member in our group," Meigui began, speaking over Zhubao's tears. "It is our duty to uphold the morals of being a proper Chinese lady. If you are unable to follow them and continue doing unladylike activities or do not complete all your lady duties, you will be dead to us. I don't want to remind you all what happened with Hu'die."

"What happened with Hu'die?" asked Ling.

"Normally, a lady should not talk about someone who is dead to the group. But, as you are unfamiliar with that embarrassing incident, it would be proper for me to inform you. To serve as a warning, of course," Meigui said. "Hu'die was an old member who was unable to do her wifely duties of pleasing her husband."

"What do you mean by that?" Ling asked.

"There was an incident in which Hu'die's husband wished for pleasure, and Hu'die was not in the mood. But her husband had his way, and got what he wished, which he deserves as he is the man of the household. Afterwards, Hu'die was unhappy, and accused him of hurting her, stirring up an incident in the family, and causing everyone to lose face." Meigui sighed loudly before continuing. "In reality, it was completely Hu'die's fault for not pleasuring her husband when he wanted her to. A lady who does not obey her husband is not a lady at all, especially when it comes to Rule 5. Speaking of which, Zhubao, did you please your husband to make up for your mistake?"

Zhubao wiped away her tears, regaining her voice. "I did, Meigui, I begged for his forgiveness and pleased him." She looked around at the group. "I pleased him very well."

"That's a proper lady," Meigui smiled. "Have you all been

pleasuring your husbands?"

"Yes, Meigui," the ladies replied in unison.

"And you are all following Rule 5?"

"Yes, Meigui!"

Baihe leaned over, whispering to Ling to prevent future embarrassment, "Rule 5 states that only a husband's pleasure and happiness is important, and a lady must do everything to pleasure her husband and make him happy."

"Then, tell me, how have you been pleasuring your husband?" asked Meigui curtly.

Zhubao smiled awkwardly, "In every way possible, Meigui."

"And how often?"

"Often, Meigui." Zhubao looked up at Meigui's disapproving face and quickly added, "I try to pleasure him as much as he asks. At least three times a week."

"Well," interrupted Mudan, "I pleasure my husband at least five times a week."

"That's nothing," interrupted Hua'er, "I pleasure my husband every day!"

"None of you are doing anything worth mentioning." Shuilian interrupted, a smile forming across her face. "I pleasure my husband twice every day, and I do a good job."

"What do you mean by 'good job?'" interrupted Baihe, giggling quietly. "Your husband is easy. Anyone and anything can pleasure him. Even a vacuum cleaner."

Shuilian angrily snorted, "Whatever. Look at yourself, Baihe. At least I am pleasing to the eyes. Unlike you, when my husband sees me without clothes, he can't see the scars."

Mudan jumped to Baihe's defense. "She was just making a joke. No need to get so angry and personal."

"You know that's not true," Shuilian said angrily. "She is angry at me for implying that her husband is nothing more than a backup and—"

Meigui suddenly coughed politely. All the ladies went silent. She smiled, gently wiping her mouth with a tissue. "Sorry, ladies, it appears we are out of time."

The ladies looked ruffled and annoyed but quickly settled back into their graceful positions before gathering themselves and slowly walking out of the room to collect their children.

Baihe approached Ling as all the other ladies walked out, her face slightly flustered from the morning's meeting. "Mudan and I are going to the grand opening of that new luxury shopping mall. You know, the one close to the Governor's Manor." She paused for a moment, trying to look disappointed. "I would invite you, but it's a really restricted event, and I've only got two tickets."

"It's not a problem," Ling said smiling. "I have been to plenty of shopping malls. You two go and have fun. Hanbing and I were planning to go directly home after this."

Baihe frowned, looking disappointed. "I suppose if you really want, you could come with us, and, maybe, I can get you in. It's going to be an awesome event. I would hate for you to miss such an amazing opportunity. Even if you don't get in, you could always wait outside until I come out! I think it would be very important for you to understand what great connections I have."

"No, really, it's fine. It is not a problem. Go have fun!"

"Fine then!" Baihe looked annoyed. "In that case, I will see you next time, I guess."

As the other ladies and their children gathered their belongings and left the apartment, Ling watched Fenghuang collect everything and start cleaning. After everyone had left, Ling walked up and spoke to her.

"Thank you for everything, especially for watching Hanbing," Ling said, holding Hanbing in his arms. "We are both looking forward to coming back to this meeting every week."

"Oh, it was no problem, dear. Anything for the children," Fenghuang said proudly.

"Are none of these children yours?" asked Ling looking around the apartment. He was surprised that Hanbing was the only child left.

"Oh, my heavens, no. My children are much older. They are in middle school now."

"You have more than one?" Ling asked surprised. Only families of higher social status qualified for multiple children, and Fenghuang did not look the part.

"Oh yes, we got blessed with identical twins." She smiled. "They are great teenagers, but toddlers are just my favorite. I asked Meigui if I could come and help out. I don't think she minds the free time to hang out with her friends." She let out a huge laugh, as if she had just told the world's funniest joke.

Ling smiled awkwardly. "Thank you. We both had a wonderful time. We should get going now. I guess I will see you next time."

"Okay, enjoy the rest of your day." Fenghuang eyed Ling up and down. "Although, next time, I would be more careful if I were you."

"I am sorry?" Ling asked. "Did I do something wrong?"

"Oh, dear. Do you think I can't tell that you are still a man?" Fenghuang said, laughing as she saw Ling's shocked expression. "Don't worry, your secret is safe with me. I am sure no one noticed today, but even in a group so oblivious, they might notice one day. I would advise you to probably make it less obvious. I don't think these ladies, especially Meigui, would be happy if they knew."

"Oh, umm, okay. Wait, what makes you so sure I am a man?"

"Besides your facial reaction when I told you, dear?" Fenghuang laughed. "I don't think this is the best place to talk about it. Why don't you come over to my house? I have been told I brew the most excellent tea," she added with a grin.

"Umm, well," Ling hesitated. Excluding his relatives, he hadn't been to another person's house since high school. "I am not sure that is a good idea. We are, um, quite busy today. Also, um, my husband is waiting for me."

"Please, dear. I don't bite." Fenghuang laughed as she

finished the final cleaning in the room. "Besides, I actually have met your husband. He and my husband are coworkers. I am Teacher Long's wife."

Ling was surprised that to learn from Fenghuang that she and Teacher Long lived within a twenty-minute walk from him and Yi. Ling didn't know much about Yi's colleagues as he never spoke much about work. Long was one of the few people he knew and had heard about during the few times he and Hanbing had met Yi in school. Based on the few things Yi had said here and there, Ling knew Yi respected Long as a teacher, but he distrusted him. He sat quietly in the taxi as the three of them headed to her house. Ling felt too awkward to talk and wondered not only how Fenghuang could figure out his secret, but also how Yi would feel when he told him later where he went. They said nothing as Fenghuang paid the taxi driver and then walked up the stairs to her apartment.

"Make yourself at home, dear," said Fenghuang, pointing as old worn-down couch. "I'll go boil us some water for tea. There are a few toys in that box over there if Hanbing wants to play. In the meantime, sit down and make yourself comfortable."

Ling looked around. The décor was simple and suitable for a teacher, neatly arranged. He saw the small toy box in front of the TV and sat Hanbing in front of it, where she proceeded to start taking things out of the box. He sat down on the worn-down sofa and looked around uncomfortably. He wasn't sure what made him more uncomfortable, being in a stranger's house or knowing that a stranger could see his secret. Fenghuang came out a few minutes later, carrying a porcelain foreign-style tea set and sat it gently down in front of Ling.

"Do you like this tea set?" asked Fenghuang as she took out a box of teabags. "It's imported from Europe. It's the most expensive one I own. I only use it during special events."

"Why are we using it today, and why aren't you using tea leaves?" asked Ling curiously.

"I wanted this to be a memorable occasion. You don't look like you go out much," Fenghuang said, handing Li a small cup. "Teabags are much more European, don't you think? There is sugar and powdered creamer in those little containers if you need some. So, now that we are alone, be honest, what did you think of our little social gathering."

"You could say I was a little surprised. It wasn't what I was expecting," Ling began. He hesitated, still uncomfortable, wondering if he could trust the woman in front of him. "I was told it was a chance for the children to meet, and I guess I expected it was a chance for me to see how other mothers raise their children," he said finally.

"Oh, as if these women have ever actually sat down and raised a child in their life," chuckled Fenghuang. "They have ayis, nannies, relatives, and assistants to do that for them."

"I wasn't expecting to sit around and gossip, and I certainly wasn't expecting that conversation about fashion, and you know, women lifestyles."

"These are the type of women who sign up for a parenting event, but send their assistants to take the class," Fenghuang said coolly. "All of these women have children out of social obligation and are indifferent about their child's existence. I doubt any of these women, especially Meigui, have ever done anything related to children, except maybe posing for pictures."

Ling couldn't contain himself anymore. "I must know, so are you still a man like me?" He asked quickly. "I mean, how else would you know that I am…ummm…still a man?"

"Oh, my heavens, no. Getting my penis chopped off was the best thing that ever could happen to me," Fenghuang laughed. "No, my dear, it's the way you walk, and your little mannerisms that give it away."

"What do you mean?"

"Men who become nan-nu walk differently than men who haven't. Your voice is a little lower, and you didn't tuck yourself in as neatly as you think."

"Oh no," said Ling nervously. "Do you think anyone else noticed? No one is supposed to know!"

"Oh, my heavens, no. Don't get me wrong, your long hair looks amazing, and your stuffed pushup bra is surprisingly realistic. But you don't close your legs as tightly as you could; you walk as if something is still in the way." Fenghuang chuckled loudly again. "The rest of us can cross our legs a little more comfortably than you can. You clearly still have a big secret in that dress."

Ling felt embarrassed but couldn't understand why. "Wait a moment," he asked, "earlier when you said, 'getting my penis chopped off was the best thing that ever could happen to me.' What did you mean by that? Is that a joke or do you like being a nan-nu?"

"Well, I wanted to start by talking about other topics, but I suppose since this is one of my favorite subjects to talk about…" Fenghuang put her cup of tea and the table and smiled. "Let me tell you about my background. Perhaps that will give you a better understanding."

"Okay?"

"My father was a Professor of Psychology at Qin Jiaban University, when it was still Xinzhong University. You know, before the Education Reformation Revolution," Fenghuang began. "But fortunately, though some of my father's ideologies may have been considered too liberal and too controversial by the government, he was not affected like some of his colleagues."

Ling nodded. He didn't know enough about history to understand why Fenghuang was telling him this. But he knew that Qin Jiaban University, where Yi had graduated, was the best in the country. He didn't know much about the Education Reformation Revolution, except that many professors and educators were sent to Re-Education Camps due to their dangerous and destructive philosophies.

"Judging by my father's position," continued Fenghuang, "I

was meant to live my life as a man, but I decided to become a nan-nu. Because…"

"What? You volunteered to be nan-nu?"

Fenghuang chuckled loudly. "I can see you are surprised, but let me continue my story."

"You are gay?"

"No, dear. I suppose I am gay in your thinking since I am attracted to men. At least to my husband. But…" replied Fenghuang sincerely, "what I was trying to say is that I actually identify as a transgender woman."

Ling thought for a moment. "Oh…what does that mean?"

Fenghuang paused. "I can only explain it by what it means to me. From when I was at a young age, I always felt like I should be a woman. I always felt my physical sex did not match my identified gender."

"Oh," Ling replied, still looking confused. "Why would you want to be a woman?"

"Because that's what I felt like I should be. Remember, if we followed the government's decision, due to my family's social class, I would still be a man. But I always knew in my heart, that I was meant to be female."

Ling couldn't hide his shock. "What do your parents think then?"

"I can't deny I am very lucky; I can thank the heavens for that," Fenghuang smiled. "I am sure most parents would be horrified if their child chooses to be a nan-nu, unless they're forced, I mean, *selected* by the government. I was lucky that my parents wanted me to be myself, and I am lucky that I live in a country, which ironically, allowed me to be me. I am also lucky to be married to a man who is more educated than most about this subject and has continuously supported me."

"What do you mean by all of this?" asked Ling, uncomfortable and confused. "I have never even heard of this word, transgender."

"Gender and sexuality are much more complicated than

our country, or even most people, give credit to. Even with everything that goes around here, no one ever talks about it. The complications of gender identity and sexuality, I mean."

"Huh?"

"For insistence, the best example is most nan-nu, though they would never admit it, still secretly identify as being a man," Fenghuang said. "Just because their external organs have been changed doesn't mean they see themselves as women. Most of them aren't even attracted to the men they are married to."

"Really? Are you sure about that?" Ling asked defensively. "In school, we were always taught that once we got our operation, everything would fall naturally into place. We would wake up and know that this was the life for us."

"In school, you guys are taught false information to keep the status quo. It isn't based on fact. Our sex and gender are two different concepts, just as our physical attraction isn't defined by what organs we may or may not have. Just because you cut off someone's penis and give them a vagina doesn't mean they identify as a woman, and it certainly doesn't mean they will be attracted to men." Fenghuang said. "For me, I am lucky. Since I was born, I always wanted to be a woman, and now I am one. I was also lucky that I found a man I am attracted to and love."

"Oh." Ling went silent.

"If you want to know about this topic, of gender and sexuality," Fenghuang said before sipping her tea slowly. "I have many books on the subject. They are written and translated by Chinese who live overseas. Of course, this collection is probably illegal, and it was given to me by friends of my father. It might be a little outdated, but I can let you borrow a few books, this way it will give you a basic understanding. I just find the whole concept of human gender and sexuality fascinating. It's one of my favorite things to talk about."

Ling stared at Fenghuang for a moment as he thought. "You are saying that even before your surgery you identified as a woman, and you didn't identify as a woman because of your surgery?"

"Exactly."

"But you don't look like the perfect woman. Not like Meigui and the rest of them. If you want to be a woman, why not be the perfect woman?"

Fenghuang's face fell, but she laughed as spoke. "I would like to say I am perfect in my own way. There is more to being a woman than just your outer appearance. This is about my gender identity."

Ling didn't really understand. He felt as though what was being said contradicted with his education, where it had been so perfectly laid clear. Men had boy parts and did boy work; women had girl parts and did girl work. Real men and real women both looked a certain way. It was simple and precise. There were no grey areas, it was not something you studied or thought about. It was just the way things were. He concentrated for a moment before asking, "Do you think the other woman, like Meigui, identify as transgender? After all, they do look so perfect. Is it because they identify as female?"

"I cannot speak for other people, but I don't think so," Fenghuang said finally. "I cannot speak for everyone in the group, but I don't think Meigui identifies as a woman. For her, being an ideal lady is all about power, at least what power she can get, given she is a nan-nu. I don't know much about her background; she is quite secretive about it, but I know she is from the Capital. She understands the power of people with higher status, and I know Meigui wants that, and Meigui will play her role correctly in order to get that power. For her, that meant marrying a successful general, becoming the perfect woman, visually at least, then befriending ladies of similar social status and bossing them around."

Ling thought for a moment. "I think I am a little confused here. You seem to say that Meigui likes being a lady but isn't transgender. These ideas are still new to me…but I don't really understand your meaning here."

"In this country," Fenghuang began hesitantly, "choice plays a big role. From a young age, I felt that I should be a woman. As I said earlier, this was a choice I made for myself. I would say nearly all nan-nu were chosen and not given a choice, which goes back to what I said; while from the exterior they look like women, they don't identify as women. I would argue that being forced to be a woman is different from being transgender, which to me, is when you identify as one. That being said, with Meigui, while I don't think she identifies as being a woman, that doesn't mean she doesn't accept it, and use it to her advantage."

Ling said nothing. He slowly sipped his tea and watched Hanbing build a small structure out of wooden blocks, laughing cheerfully.

"Ok, dear, my turn," Fenghuang interrupted, smiling slyly. "My turn to ask personal questions. Why aren't you a nan-nu?"

"Oh," said Ling. He shrugged his shoulders awkwardly. "Umm…my husband won't let me."

Fenghuang raised her eyebrows but said nothing, continuing to slowly sip her tea.

"Oh, he isn't gay," Ling said awkwardly, understanding what question Fenghuang was thinking, "At least he says he isn't… gay, and I believe he isn't. He just thinks this whole nan-nu thing is morally wrong."

"Most people would never admit it, but I think most people do think it's morally wrong," Fenghuang said casually. "At least he is man enough to stand for his beliefs."

"Yeah…I guess…" Ling thought for a moment. "I guess, I have never thought about it that way."

"Do you want to become a woman?" Fenghuang asked directly. "Do you think of yourself as a woman? Would you identify as being transgender?"

"No, not really. I don't think of myself as a woman." Ling felt uncomfortable again. "But, I think I should become one, and I guess I have always assumed after my surgery, I would feel more like one."

"Meaning?"

"It is my social duty. I was assigned to be woman, and I am not one. Furthermore, Yi takes a lot of abuse from his family because I am not a nan-nu. They don't know he won't let me become a nan-nu. They often yell at him, and they refuse to speak to me. I just think things would be better if I just did the surgery." Ling suddenly felt embarrassed and stood up quickly, wiping down his skirt and looking around for his belongings. "I am sorry. I said too much. I have shamed my family. I think I should get going. Thank you for the—"

Fenghuang stopped him. "Sit down. Take your time. Clearly you have much to talk about. Don't worry. This is a safe place. Let me be a friend and just listen to your thoughts," she said kindly.

Ling nervously sat down. He didn't know why, but he felt he could trust Fenghuang, despite just meeting her. He took a deep breath before speaking. "I am sorry," he said, his voice barely louder than a whisper. "I have never really talked to people outside of Yi and his family. This is my first time in a really long time being alone in someone's house. Someone who is not related to me. I don't know how I am supposed to act or what I am supposed to say. And, and, I have never talked about… personal stuff, gender stuff, bedroom stuff, with anyone before."

"I figured. Like I said earlier, this is a safe place. Nothing you say will leave this room." Fenghuang continued sipping her tea. "I think you have a lot on your mind, any person in your situation would, so let's just talk. Would that be ok with you?"

"Yeah, I think so," Ling replied cautiously.

Fenghuang smiled gently. "In that case, do you think are you gay? Or are you only with Yi because you are supposed to be with him."

Ling thought for a moment. "I don't know. I mean I have never had the option to think about women…and Yi is the only person I have been with."

"Can I assume you and Yi have sex?" Fenghuang asked

casually.

"I mean, this is a weird thing to talk about considering I just met you," Ling said awkwardly, feeling his face turning red. "But, I mean, we are married, and it is my job, so, yeah, we do."

"It's your job?"

"Well, yes, even if I am still a man. I am still his wife. I think everybody would agree it's my job to make him happy," Ling said, as if stating the obvious.

"What do you guys do?"

"Sex wise?" Ling replied, confused, as Fenghuang nodded. "The normal stuff, I think. I mean the stuff I was told to do by my sex education teacher to keep him happy. So…umm, I use my mouth a lot. He likes that…a lot. It makes him very happy if I do it at least once a day." He hesitated and giggled uncomfortably. "And…and…sometimes he uses my behind. I know he likes that a lot also. It just takes too much time, plus you know, he was taught it is dirty. I guess it is kind of is dirty, but you know, since I haven't gotten my surgery, we don't have another choice. I have to lay on my stomach though. He hates the sight of my penis."

"Do you mind the sex?"

"I don't mind at all. I mean, actually, I like it," Ling said. He paused for a moment, shocked with the realization he just admitted he enjoyed having sex with Yi. It was not something he had really thought about before or admitted out loud. He felt awkward and didn't know what to say.

Fenghuang looked at him and smiled, as if reading Ling's mind. "There is nothing wrong with enjoying sex with your husband, even if you are the one being penetrated. Biologically speaking, it does make sense. More importantly, it's good you are able to bond with him in this way. I suspect many nan-nu don't enjoy being with their husbands that way. Sometimes, it can be very uncomfortable. I think it is a good thing that you enjoy being with him. You have nothing to be ashamed of."

"Yeah. I don't mind it at all. Sometimes, if he real slow and gentle, I can even, you know…orgasm. It feels really good," Ling said thoughtfully. He paused, blushing and giggling. "I am sorry. That is too much information. I shouldn't have said that."

"Don't apologize. I say this probably too often and too openly, but people should talk about these subjects more. This is the only way we can understand what experiences are natural. Anyway, scientifically speaking, what you are saying is logical. You are a man; you probably would like prostate simulation because it's so sensitive. More importantly though, I think it shows you two have a connection," Fenghuang said logically before continuing. "But let me ask another question then, does that mean he takes care of you? Makes sure you are comfortable?"

"What do you mean?" Ling asked.

"Does he make sure you always reach orgasm like he does? Does he kiss you and make sure you enjoy it as much as he does?"

"No. I don't even think he knows I like it. I actually think it would horrify him if he knew I did," said Ling. "Like I said earlier, he isn't gay. He always tells me he doesn't want to do gay stuff. He hates the sight of my naked body. He has told me before we only do bedroom stuff because he needs a release, and that if he had a real woman, he wouldn't need me."

Fenghuang frowned, but said nothing, waiting for Ling to continue as she sipped her tea.

Ling thought deeply for a moment. "But we have kissed a few times. I don't think he remembers though because he was usually quite drunk when it happened, when he was feeling very, umm, friendly. I think he only remembers one time, if had to guess. We had to kiss at our wedding. That was…uncomfortable, very uncomfortable, for him. But we had to do it. I…don't mind it though when he kisses me. Secretly, I actually wish he would do it more. He isn't a bad kisser." Ling paused. "But, like I said, I know he isn't gay. I would never expect him to touch my… penis or any other part of my body with his hands. When he does me…we have to use lube of course. Sometimes, he is very gentle. It can almost feel romantic, I think…and afterwards… I go in the bathroom and take care of myself. Like I said, he doesn't like to see my penis because, you know, he isn't gay. I can't imagine how horrified he would be if he ever saw me orgasm."

"If I understand correctly, what you are saying is all he cares about is his pleasure, not yours."

"Well, yes, but…" Ling thought quickly, trying to correct himself from a wrong he wasn't sure he committed. "But…but, as Meigui mentioned today, it's all about Rule 5, and…and… Rule 5 states that a husband's pleasure is most important, and a lady must do everything to pleasure her husband."

"Please don't quote that bullshit book to me. We may be living in an abnormal society, but that doesn't mean we can't all treat each other equally," Fenghuang said. Her voice sounded casual but was full of anger and judgement. "The problem with that book is that it teaches a false idea that women, or in this case nan-nu, must be subservient to real men. That simply is not true. A relationship, no matter how strange and unusual, should be based foremost on respect, care, and, hopefully love."

Ling looked around the room quietly as he sipped his tea, trying to find another topic to discuss. He had never thought about any of the ideas that Fenghuang had brought up. He had never met someone who asked him so many personal questions, and asked questions so bluntly. He wasn't even sure that this was a type of topic and thoughts a person like him should have and discuss.

"Do you love him?" Fenghuang asked suddenly.

"What do you mean by that?"

"It's not a complicated question," Fenghuang shrugged. "Do you love him?"

Ling sat there in silence, looking down at his cup of tea. "I think so," he said finally. "I think I love him."

"You think so?"

"I feel…I think…I know…I am indebted to him." Ling

stopped again, trying to control the impeding words and the emotions behind them.

"Yi has done so much for me over the years. He has protected me in so many ways, even now, when I know he hates the sight of looking at me. I can feel his disappointment when he looks at me. I know he wishes I were a woman, but he wants to protect me from being a woman. He doesn't want me to go through that pain. I know my existence brings him more difficulty than he deserves. I know his parents are angry with him and ashamed of him because of me. Thanks to me, he will never have a proper wife, and enter politics like he is meant to. I know all his sacrifices are constantly tearing him apart, and I know he is struggling more than he lets on. For that, I love him. I love him for protecting me and protecting Hanbing. I know he loves Hanbing, and I know he will protect me and Hanbing. In the end, I love him for sacrificing so much for me, and I guess for all of us. I just want him, us, to be happy. I hope if I love him, I can make him happy."

Fenghuang said nothing, choosing to pour him another cup of tea. The two sat there quietly, watching Hanbing as she continued playing with blocks on the living room floor.

8.
TEACHERS ARE OUR EDUCATORS, OUR MORAL GUIDANCE, AND THE BUILDERS OF OUR FUTURES

YI WAS HAVING A DISCUSSION with Teacher Long in their shared office about some new curriculum ideas when Vice Principal Yan came in, looking unusually gleeful. This was uncomfortable to them both as they were aware Yan didn't smile unless he had information he could work to his advantage or cause another person pain.

"I suppose you to have heard the news already?" Yan said. He began grinning widely.

"What news?" asked Yi, putting down his books and preparing for the worst.

"About Teacher Jian?" He looked around at the baffled faces and beamed. "Ah, then let me be first to share with you. Jian was arrested yesterday and has been fired."

Yi could not hide his shock. Jian, the head of the Mathematics Department was a man of honor and was not the type who would do something illegal or foolish. Yi didn't know him well, having only met him at a few school gatherings, but Jian's positive reputation always preceded him. He was well-liked by both his students and the staff for his agreeable personality and traditional sense of humor.

"Why was he arrested?" asked Long calmly. He put his hand on Yi's shoulder, as if trying to relax him.

"I am glad you asked, Long." The vice principal paused, grinning sadistically as if cherishing the words about to come out of his mouth. "It has turned out that our math teacher shouldn't even be allowed in this country! He is an illegal resident."

"And why do you say that?" asked Yi.

"Last week, during the teacher reviews, there was an inquiry into Jian's background. It turns out that our math teacher is of mixed race." The vice principal smiled. Yi felt uneasy watching how much he was enjoying this moment. "His great-grandfather was a white American."

"In other words, he is one-eighth white American," Long calculated in his mind

"It appears so," Yan said. He looked around the room, as if expecting the others to celebrate with him.

"Now that he has been fired, do we have any other information? Do we know what is going to happen to him?" asked Long.

"All I know is he is on his way to the city court as we speak. At best, a lifetime in prison, sentenced to hard labor. At worst, the death penalty. Personally, I am hoping for the latter. It has been a few years since we have enjoyed a good public shaming and execution," Yan said excitedly.

"Don't you think that is a bit harsh?" interrupted Yi. "I mean…"

The vice principal paused for a moment, looking carefully at Yi, before smiling wickedly. "Excuse me, Teacher Yi, please tell me I misunderstood. Are you suggesting that this man should not be punished for his crime?"

"No, no, no," Yi thought for a moment, careful to frame his argument. "No, I am saying that the punishment should fit the crime according to our law. Teacher Jian may not have been aware of his American heritage, and therefore while expulsion from the country could be a just punishment, the death penalty is not. This crime was not committed on purpose, and therefore must be treated as such. I am just saying, in this case, he should be given leniency as he has proven himself to be an outstanding citizen."

"I am surprised you said that, especially as our Honorable Governor's son. The law is clear, Yi. All foreigners must be punished to the full extent of the law," Vice Principal Yan said. "The law, as we all should know, not only bans impure people from becoming citizens, but states that foreigners and other wanted people who did not leave the country could face the death penalty, as they damage the stability of our glorious country. Surely, you must recognize that with his impure background and his lies, Jian could have been brainwashing his students all this time, thus weakening their minds and damaging the future of our glorious nation."

Yi scoffed. "The fact remains that until Jian is proven to have been brainwashing his students and has been shown to be a threat, I don't think we should be calling for the death penalty so early."

"Excuse me, Yi?" Yan began. "I don't think—"

Long interrupted, "Sorry to interrupt, Yi, Vice Principal Yan, but…" he paused to point at the clock. "We have to go. Yi is watching my class today, for the review."

"Oh, yes, I understand. Go on then. We can continue this conversation afterwards." The vice principal smiled. "Long, I sincerely hope we don't find any shameful secrets in your life as we did with Jian."

The two teachers walked silently down the hallway. Yi thought about what he had said to the vice principal. He wasn't usually one to express his opinions in public, especially with his work superior. Disagreeing with Yan was a foolish decision, and he was sure he was going to regret it before the end of the day.

Long decided to break the silence. "I am sure you heard, but your wife met my wife, Fenghuang, recently."

"Yes, yes, Ling told me," Yi said, disinterested.

"Ling is quite a special person and a great mother," Long continued. "My wife was quite impressed by how much she cared for Hanbing and her thoughtfulness."

"Yes, yes, I know. She is good with my son," Yi replied.

"Fenghuang tells me that Ling is quite intelligent, willing to think about issues, and willing to learn. It's uncommon to meet people with these traits. I hope you value Ling for who she is. She seems like such a special person."

Yi felt a little uncomfortable. "What do you mean by that?"

Long shrugged. "Fenghuang just very rarely speaks so highly of people she meets. She is always looking for new friends to talk to, but she finds most of them so disappointing. I was surprised by how much Ling impressed her. I guess I just wanted to share that with you. I know they will start seeing each more often, perhaps we should, too. The four of us can perhaps go get dinner one night?"

He noticed Yi's discomfort and laughed, stepping forward to open the classroom door. "I was just thinking out loud. Think nothing of it. Moving forward, are you ready to give me your thoughts and review?"

Yi stood in the doorway for a moment. He thought about what Long had just said. What was he implying? He remembered what the vice principal said earlier about not wanting to find anything shameful in Long's past. He nodded, clearing his thoughts, and slowly walked in.

* * *

Ling and Hanbing were standing at the corner of a sidewalk on the border of the Shucheng and Zhengfu District, saying their goodbyes to Fenghuang. The two adults had taken Hanbing to a small local park after the Ladies' Meeting, and Fenghuang was getting ready to go home, while Ling was preparing to go dinner shopping. Ling has always enjoyed this spot in the city, as it was where the contradiction and differences between the style and design of both districts was most obvious. The modernity and cleanliness of Zhengfu stood in stark contrast to Shucheng, which had been slowing dilapidating without proper care. He always felt the most appreciative when he stood on this corner.

It reminded him, despite his difficulties, how much worse his life could have been.

Suddenly, a car of teenagers drove out of Zhengfu District, zooming down the road. They stopped in front of Ling and Fenghuang and rolled down the window.

"Hey, lady!" the teenage driver said to Fenghuang. "Your breasts are sagging. Can't you tell? How are you not embarrassed to walk out in public? Maybe it's time to get a new set." From the back of the car they could hear the others laughing. The teenager in the front passenger seat looked over at Ling. "You are a hot mom, but you could get bigger breasts. Maybe the two of you should go in together. This time ask for a larger cup size."

Everyone in the car roared with laughter, and then the car sped off. Ling and Fenghuang stood there for a moment, pondering in silence. Ling decided to speak up first. "That was..."

"Quite rude? Yes, it was," Fenghuang said, finishing Ling's sentence. "I hate these spoiled, well-connected children. They think because their parents have government positions and they are not quite legal adults that they can say and do whatever they want and not be in trouble with the law. They don't understand anything outside of their very small social bubble."

Ling watched the car drive off in the distance. "You know, I have been thinking, since Yi won't let me get a sex change, maybe I should ask to get a top surgery instead," he said quietly, staring at the open road.

"Why would you do that?" Fenghuang asked curiously.

"It's just something I have been thinking about," Ling said blankly. "You know, recently, going to all of these meetings. I am just suddenly more aware how much I am not a woman."

"That's because you are not a woman," chuckled Fenghuang.

"But, as I told you before, I was trained to be one. It may not be what I want, but it is my destiny. My role in society. Maybe, if I got this top surgery first, I can persuade Yi to let me get a complete sex change at a later date."

"But it isn't what you want," Fenghuang said quietly.

"It's not about what I want. Besides, those teens just said I am a hot mom. I just need to get bigger breasts. Anyway, it's just something that I am thinking about."

Fenghuang sighed kindly, "It is understandable that you would feel this way, especially given the meetings and what those teenagers just said. But, I don't think you need breast implants. I don't think that will make you or Yi happy."

Ling didn't know what to say. He just continued to stare out in the distance, holding Hanbing's hand.

After Fenghuang left, Ling and Hanbing walked into Zhengfu District to the international supermarket. Since Hanbing was born, he had been coming here more often as Yi and the Governor both demanded the best for the child. He was standing in an aisle, trying to decide on what to cook for dinner when suddenly he heard someone calling his name.

"Ling? Ling is that you?" called out a lady from down one of the aisles.

Ling turned around, squirming to recognize the late forty something year old woman who called out his name. "Why, Miss Hua! It has been a while." He bowed towards his old teacher and pushed his shopping cart towards her.

Of all the teachers who taught them the proper traditions and behaviors of "A Proper Chinese Lady," Miss Hua was the only one Ling remembered positively. Although she was just as traditional as her colleagues, she was the least strict, and more importantly, was one of the few who provided any emotional support to her students during their transition. Since she wasn't very attractive, having what appeared to be a botched or cheap surgery from a less qualified doctor, this and her cheery demeanor were helpful for the students who found her easier to relate to than some of the other teachers. Many students also took comfort using her as evidence that if after graduation they couldn't find a man, they could still have the backup plan of teaching the next generation. Upon graduation, Ling had maintained a friendly relationship with her, even inviting her to his wedding. However, Ling lost contact with her soon after.

"Is this Yi's child?" Hua asked, reaching in and pinching Hanbing on the cheek. "He is so handsome, looks just like his father. These are the cheeks that build the face of a handsome man. It's obvious to all what good genes he has."

"Yes, yes," said Ling nervously. He tried to hide his discomfort at Hua's directness in touching his child. They didn't usually let non-family members touch Hanbing.

"And look at these muscles!" said Hua, picking up Hanbing's little arms and feeling them. "You can already tell he is going to be so muscular. A big strong man!" She picked her up, terrifying Ling, and spoke directly to the toddler. "You are going to make everyone jealous you know. You are going to be such a manly man that all of the ladies are going to LOVE YOU." Hanbing giggled, smiling at the attention. "And that laugh, why that's the laugh of a future leader of our glorious country!" she added.

She handed Hanbing to Ling who stood breathing nervously, not knowing what to say. "He is an absolutely adorable child. You must be so proud of Yi for being able to create such a beautiful son. I hope you are doing a good job taking care of him to show how much you appreciate your husband. A boy like him only deserves the best of the best."

Ling stood there cuddling Hanbing in his arms. He could only force a smile and nod as his child giggled.

"Though I must say," Hua said, "it has been many years. I was disappointed that you would invite me to your wedding, but not to your Arrival ceremony. Did you forget about your favorite teacher?"

"Oh," Ling said. He gently sat Hanbing back in her seat. "We never had one. Yi didn't want the publicity and the drama."

"Ha, a politician who doesn't want publicity," Hua laughed. "There is no such thing!"

"Yi isn't really into politics. He prefers teaching. He is a good teacher, like you were to us."

"You can deny it all you want," Hua continued, laughing. "But, I know better. Yi will follow in his father's footsteps and become our next governor. I am so proud I was able to teach someone like you to find a man like him. Don't forget when you are First Lady that I was your teacher! I expect to be mentioned when your husband takes power. It would be quite disrespectful to forget your roots."

"How have you been?" Ling began awkwardly, trying to change the subject. "How has teaching been? How are the students these days?"

"Have you not heard?" asked Hua, grinning. "I've got good news; I am retiring soon. This year is my last year, and for the last year, I haven't done much teaching, I have only been doing advisory and trainings."

"Really? You are retiring?" asked Ling. "You always told us you would never leave. I remember how you used to tell us how honorable it was for you to pass on the customs of being a proper Chinese lady. Didn't you used to tell us you would teach forever?"

"Yes, yes," said Hua in agreement. "That was my plan, but something better has happened. I met a man, and I will be getting married soon!"

She proudly thrust her hand forward, showing off a small cheap aluminum band with a speck of glass crystal in the middle. "Isn't it beautiful?" she bragged. "He told me it was super expensive. Apparently made with the finest silver. And will you look at diamond in the middle? See how it glitters in the light!"

"Congratulations, Miss Hua. I am so happy for you," Ling said genuinely. "How did you meet him?"

"We met just a few months ago. His daughter attends our school. He was married before, but his wife passed away. But, you know how men are; they need a woman. He tells me he is very rich," Hua continued. "Teaching was nice, but a woman's proper place is serving a man. I can't be a wife and have a job at the same time. That would be simply improper. Therefore, I must quit my job to fulfil my destiny and take care of a man."

"That's so exciting, Miss Hua! What does he do?"

"He won't tell me. He isn't much of a talker, but I don't think that is important. What is important is that I am getting married. My father was so proud when I told him." Hua breathed a sigh of relief. "I never thought this day would happen. It's so exciting. That's actually why I am here. I need to buy some imported goods to impress my man, and tomorrow…" Ms. Hua leaned forward lowered her voice to a whisper and giggled excitedly. "Let's just say tonight is my last night in this flabby old body. Tomorrow I am going into Shoushu to do some touch ups. A little lift here, tightening there. I'm going to make myself exquisite for the wedding."

"Oh, Miss Hua, I am so happy for you," said Ling.

"Thank you," said Ms. Hua. She looked up and down at Ling, "You know, now that you are a mother, maybe it's time for you to take a visit to the clinic yourself. Freshen things up a little for that husband who has given you so much joy by providing you with a child to give you purpose. I have always felt your breasts have always been quite small. If I were you, I would put a little more effort in to fit the role you are supposed to have. Be that gorgeous wife for your successful husband. It's like what I have always taught you, the three priorities of a first-class lady." She held up three fingers as she said, "Please your husband, take care of his child, and look beautiful."

Ling thought back to the teenagers in the car he saw less than an hour ago, and subconsciously squeezed his breasts, as if trying to push them to be bigger. He quickly snapped back to the reality that he didn't have any, remembering he was only wearing a stuffed bra. He felt speechless and could only give Ms. Hua a simple smile.

"I am glad to see things are going well between you and Yi," said Ms. Hua while looking into Ling's shopping cart. "I must confess, I never would have expected you and Yi to get married and certainly not for things to last."

"What do you mean?"

"Men of his level don't marry village girls; they marry girls from the Capital. Classy ladies with perfect bodies. You know what I am talking about; I am sure you have met them at political events. You just never looked the part. I always assumed you would just find a businessman or a low-level government official if you were lucky."

"Yi avoids the whole political scene," Ling replied, squeezing the handle of the shopping cart. He tried not to focus on what Ms. Hua said to him: he didn't look the part. Instead, he just smiled. "He really prefers to just teach; he isn't a real fan of all that government stuff."

"I hope you aren't holding him back," Hua said darkly. "A successful man needs a proper wife to support him at all times. I don't doubt you are a good wife, but I hope you remember to always be a great wife."

"I try my best, Miss Hua. I recently joined a ladies' group with my sister-in-law. All the ladies are married to very success-ful men." He suddenly felt the urge to push the cart ahead, "But I hope this group will help me be a better wife, so everyone will be proud of me, and so I can give Yi what he deserves."

"Your sister-in-law…" Hua said, thinking fondly. "I remem-ber seeing her picture in the newspaper once, attending some event with your brother-in-law. She looks like a well-trained, classy lady. She graduated from the Capital, did she not?"

"She did, Miss Hua."

"All the best ladies come from the Capital. I know I taught you all well, but despite how wonderful our old school is, it can't compete with the Capital." Hua smiled sadly, reflecting, "It's no secret you are my most successful student. The most successful student in the history of the school actually, if you think about it, with whom you were able to marry. We have talked about you before, as an example. The students admire you so much when I tell them your story, how someone from a village can end up marrying the future governor. Now, with a handsome son, the students are going to be so jealous. Your life really is a fairy tale come true."

"Thank you, Miss Hua. I couldn't have done it without you," Ling took a bow and tried to look humble.

"I suppose my biggest disappointment with my retirement is I was only able to get about half of the women into successful marriages. So many girls these days just don't understand what it means to be a proper lady. They don't understand the honor it is to be chosen," Hua said. "Remember your classmate Lulu? Before, I always counted her as one of my successes. Remember, she married that businessman with the plastic factory? He was such a rich, successful man. Apparently, she has left him and ran back to her village because he had two other women on the side." She sighed loudly again. "Such a disappointment. It makes me feel as though I failed as a teacher. In the end, the only thing more disappointing than an unmarried woman is a divorced woman."

She paused, reached over, and stroked Hanbing's head, "But seeing you here with your handsome, strong son and knowing you are still with your husband…I am happy to know that at least some of you were successful."

Ling looked at his watch, realizing how late it was. "I am sorry, Miss Hua, it's been great seeing you, but I have to go home and cook for my family. Good luck on your marriage."

Ms. Hua's smile greatly brightened. "That's a good wife. I am so happy to see you today. To know that at least, in the end of the day, one of my students was not only able to marry our future governor, but is also using the skills I taught her to make him happy."

✳   ✳   ✳

Yi never did enjoy doing reviews of Long's class. In the beginning, he always reasoned it had to do with age. Long was over 20 years older than him and was a teacher at Xincheng #1 when Yi was a student, although he never studied in his class. Recently, however, he had to conclude that while Long was a good teacher, Yi fundamentally disagreed with how he taught the material.

"You know how the process works," Yi said to Long as he watched the last student leave the classroom. "I will give the higher ups my notes, and they will speak with you next week. I don't expect any problems."

"What do you think of my class?" asked Long as he collected his supplies. "You have watched so many, and yet you constantly refuse to give me a direct answer."

Yi stopped under the doorway and thought for a moment, "If you must know, I think you are a good teacher, and you covered the overall basic material, but you stray off the official curriculum a lot. You injected many of your own ideas into the materials, and you allow the students too much time in discussion. For example, I thought it was inappropriate to allow the students so much time wondering what life is like outside of our border, and I don't think you should have added in your opinion either."

"Why do you think that is a problem?" Long asked, wiping the blackboard clean. "I do it to not only to make the materials more interesting and relatable to the students, but also give them a chance at critical thinking. Don't you think it is important for the students to think about the information and form opinions? If my class topic is discussing other countries, don't you think the students could have a better understanding if they imagined what it would be like to live there?"

"I don't think the students need to think about the materials. They just need to understand it," Yi replied staunchly. "The official policy is to follow the lectures and the curriculum. We should only teach the facts and information given to us by our glorious government. I don't think it's our job as teachers to give our personal opinion. Our job is to teach what our great leaders gave us. After all, they know better than we do."

"Perhaps. But, don't you think as teachers we can be more than that? Of course, we must teach the official materials that our honorable leaders chose. However, I don't think it hurts the students to think about and discuss the ideas. Our students are the future leaders of the province, if not the country. I think it benefits them to start learning how to analyze information. Perhaps, it can help them introduce new ideas that will benefit all our citizens."

"It is true that a little discussion doesn't hurt anyone. We must not forget our students are still teenagers, however. This means their worldview is not fully developed, and they can be easily influenced and brainwashed. We both know that unfortunately not everyone in the city fully trusts and believes in our glorious government. Teaching them the official material is the only way to keep them on the right path. I think you forget what an important responsibility we have as teachers, especially with the topics we teach. We not only influence them but teach them what the government knows is correct. Learning about politics and our relationships with other countries properly ensures our country's future survival. Remember what we were taught as children: 'Our leaders are our leaders because they know what is best.' We do not know more than them, and therefore teaching the official material is the only correct way forward."

"I don't deny that we have a huge amount of influence over our students, Yi. I certainly hope I have a positive influence on them. I hope my teaching makes them better students. Besides, as I said, I am not straying from the material, I am merely having them think about it a little deeper."

"As I said earlier, I don't doubt you are a good teacher," Yi said. "I just think you need to be careful. Teenagers are easily manipulated, and we need make sure that they are taught to be respectful patriotic students who…" Yi subconsciously hesitated. "Never do anything morally wrong or illegal."

"I am teaching them to do what is morally right," Long said, walking past Yi in the doorway and into the hall. "It is my main goal, and I think it should be the main goal of every teacher. That's why it is important we teach them how to think."

"I just think you need to consider more about your reputation and your representation to our school, as well as our country's values and laws. Don't focus so much on what you believe is right," Yi said, following Long. "I think it is always better to follow the rules because you know the consequences if you don't. Our government knows the right way to do things, and as citizens, we should listen to them." He shuddered as he recognized the hypocrisy of this statement.

"Like I just said, I am teaching them to do what is morally right," Long repeated, this time a little louder. "It is my main goal, and I think it should be the main goal of every teacher."

Yi didn't know what else to say. It seemed better to just leave the situation alone. "Are you heading back to the office?" he asked finally.

"No. I have all my stuff with me, so I will just go directly home. I will see you tomorrow, Yi. Thank you for your review and discussion."

Yi was not surprised to find Vice Principal Yan waiting by the door of his office, though he was certainly not happy about it. He opened the door and allowed Yan to walk inside. Annoyed, he sat down at the desk and waited to hear what Yan had to say.

"I wanted to continue our conversation from earlier. I must say I was surprised by you today. I would have expected more out of you," Yan said.

"I don't understand your meaning," Yi said. "I don't think I said anything that wasn't appropriate."

"You and Long have been getting rather close, I must say," Yan said, walking around the classroom office slowly. "I am really surprised by that. You have watched his classes. You see what he says, how he teaches…"

He paused and sat down at Long's desk, looking through his classroom materials. "There are some in this school who have suggested that Teacher Long holds radical, perhaps, traitorous thoughts. We can't prove anything just yet, but I am keeping my eye on him. However, in regard to what is best for you and our school, I would hate for him to influence you through his sneaky ways, especially as you are our head political science teacher and the son of our esteemed Governor. I wondered today, based on how adamant you were, if he was manipulating you…"

"Excuse me?" Yi said, careful to control the volume of his voice. "I don't know what you are implying."

"To defend Jian like that," Yan shrugged. "It is unlike you and rather dangerous for a person in your position. You and I both know that blood traitors like his family must be expelled before they destroy our glorious nation."

"I didn't defend him. I just said he didn't deserve the death penalty," Yi replied.

"Exactly." Yan smiled slyly. "I am just saying, as the Governor's son, I would be more careful about my worldviews. I hoped that this afternoon we could take this opportunity for you to apologize and admit I was correct. This way, we could move forward. After all, between the conversation this morning and your closeness with Long, we would hate for people to think you are a radical and a traitor. Understand?"

Yi thought for a moment about how to respond. He had never been accused of being a traitor before, and it annoyed him in ways he couldn't imagine or express. He needed to say something, but he wasn't sure how he wanted to move forward. He took a deep breath. "No, I will not apologize."

"Excuse me?" Yan looked surprised. "Let's be reasonable here. You made a mistake. I am giving you an opportunity to fix it. Don't you want to take—"

"No. I didn't make a mistake. I merely pointed out your interpretation of the law wasn't correct, as you made the law much simpler than it actually is. However, I no longer see that as the problem," Yi interrupted. He felt the anger rising from the pit of his stomach, an anger he hasn't felt since before Hanbing came in this his life. "What I don't understand is how you dare believe you can come into my office, and accuse me, the son of our beloved and esteemed Governor, of being a radical traitor. Especially, and let me stress this, after everything I and my family have done for this country. Not to mention everything I have done for this department and the school. Do you really think you can just come in here and accuse me of something so terrible? And without any evidence?"

He paused, got up from his desk and slowly walked towards Yan, looking him directly in the face. "How do you think my father would feel after hearing you make such accusations? Especially after everything I have done here. Perhaps, we should start an inquiry into *your* life, to understand why you even considered making such accusations."

"Yi, let me clarify. I meant no offense, I was merely suggesting," Yan said standing up and backing away, unable to hide his nervousness, "that perhaps you could pick your words more carefully. For the good of the country, of course."

"Next time, instead of suggesting, you should think before you start going around making such accusations. Unless you want me to suggest to my father that he should look into why people are accusing his son of believing in a ridiculous ideology?" He paused and watched Yan carefully. "Unless you have something of more value to add, I suggest you leave. I need to finish my class preparation for tomorrow, so I, too, can head home. Have a good evening."

"I understand. I am sorry for questioning your loyalty," Yan said quickly and quietly. "It is clear you are an honorable and patriotic man who would never do anything illegal and has excellent morals. I am so sorry about any such misunderstanding that may have come from my behalf. I hope you have a good night, Teacher Yi."

9.

FATHER AND MOTHER MUST PLAY THE CORRECT ROLES IN CHILD CARE

LING LAY THERE ON HIS stomach, staring at the backboard of their bed on a Saturday morning as Yi penetrated him from behind. Since moving Hanbing out of the room, Yi had been using Ling for pleasure more often than before. This was Yi's favorite position as he didn't have to notice Ling's face or any of Ling's frontal features. After about five minutes of thrusting and grunting, Yi finished, leaving Ling naked on the bed, the results of the morning activities dripping out of his behind. He stared at the clock as Yi took a shower. The red digits told him it was 7:16. Hanbing usually woke up around 7:30. He still felt a bit disappointed. Although he had enjoyed more intimacy with Yi recently, he had also secretly hoped that Hanbing would be reluctant to sleep in her own room and would rather continue sleeping with her parents. But, Hanbing had not shown any signs of wanting to return to co-sleeping with her parents and instead seemed to enjoy having her own bed.

"Hey," said Yi as he walked out of the shower a few minutes later, "you can go clean up now." He threw a towel on to the bed.

Ling grabbed the towel, wrapping it around his body, careful not to expose anything that Yi wouldn't want to see but failing. Out of the corner of his eye he could see Yi frown in disgust. "You should wake Hanbing up," Ling said quickly before Yi could comment.

Yi stood there frowning. He would never admit it, but he hated how Ling's flaccid penis was longer than his erect one. "Ok, go take a shower, and I'll take care of Hanbing and breakfast," Yi said, forcing a smile.

Ling walked in about twenty minutes later as Yi was serving Hanbing breakfast. Ling had always considered himself lucky. In many households, only the wife or the nanny took care of the children, but Yi seemed determined to always put in his share in contributing to some of the responsibility.

"That was a long shower. What did you do in there?" asked Yi, grinning widely.

Ling blushed, surprised by Yi's unusual humor, as he sat down on at the table and began to feed Hanbing.

"Are you going to meet the ladies today?" asked Yi casually as he looked over his newspaper.

"No," said Ling, not looking up from feeding Hanbing, "Today's meeting was canceled because Meigui and her husband are out of town."

"Oh, I see." Yi paused. He tried to sound indifferent, "Perhaps you should invite one of the ladies out to meet up? Perhaps a cup of coffee?"

"Really?" Ling paused, confused. Hanbing was busy chewing on a piece of bread. "Why would I do that? I don't know them very well. We are more like 'meeting' friends."

"I am just saying it could be nice for you to go out and make more friends. Learn something from these fine ladies," Yi said shrugging. "I mean, think about it. You have been going to these meetings for a few weeks now. Wouldn't it be nice to connect with them on a more personal level?"

"I guess? I just don't think we have a lot in common. Don't get me wrong, they are all quite nice, I suppose. But I see them as the people I see in the meetings, not outside of the meetings. Besides, I am much too busy with Hanbing, I don't have time for a friend."

"You have hung out with Fenghuang outside the meetings," Yi noted. "You like hanging out with her. Perhaps you have more time than you think."

"I don't really see Fenghuang as part of the group. Besides, she is busy today," Ling replied, now cutting up pieces of egg for his daughter.

"That's not my point."

"Then what is your point?"

"I just think you should expand your circle of friends. You know, you joining this was about learning about how to act like a proper lady," Yi said casually. "It wouldn't hurt to learn from them."

"The problem is I am not a proper lady," Ling chuckled.

"You know what I mean. I am just saying you should hang out with more people of our social class."

"Fenghuang is of our social class. I mean, both you and Long do work together. Just be straightforward, what is this about?" asked Ling, surprised. "Do you not want me to hang out with Fenghuang?"

"Ok, fine. Now that you mention it," Yi said, raising his voice and surprising both Ling and Hanbing, who started crying. "What I am trying to say is I don't want you hanging out with Fenghuang. She is not the type of person I want you to be around."

"Oh," said Ling, shocked. He paused to comfort Hanbing by wiping her face and stroking her, holding back his own tears. "If that is what you want. Then, I guess, I will stop hanging out with her."

Yi felt rather guilty again. He didn't want to appear like a controlling husband. "Let me rephrase that. I am not saying that you should stop hanging out with Fenghuang…but, maybe cut it down a little and get to know the other ladies of the group."

Ling said nothing but looked rather saddened. "What is this all about?" he asked finally. "I am really trying to be a better wife for you, and if you don't want me to see Fenghuang I won't…

but that doesn't mean I won't miss her as a friend."

"Look, I am glad you found a friend, and I know Fenghuang is good with the other children and Hanbing," said Yi, forcing on his biggest smile, "I just think that the other ladies may be more suitable as friends and may be better for you. I just want you to be happy, you know. I think you guys have a lot more in common than you realize. Maybe if you give them a chance. Go out, talk about fashion, cooking, children, and other womanly stuff."

Ling said nothing, and instead focused on finishing feeding Hanbing before gathering up the dishes and bringing them into the kitchen.

"Fine," Yi said loudly, as he listened to Ling wash the dishes. "How about we drop this issue. How about this? Since I am free today, why don't you, Hanbing, and I go to People's Park. Hanbing has never been, and I remember you loved the park when you were young."

People's Park was the largest and most extravagant park in Xincheng and a symbol of the city's previously perceived grandeur. Yi's grandfather was one of the commissioners behind the park, and a statue of him stood near the gate to commemorate his success. While all were welcome to go, its high-ticket prices and location in the Zhengfu District made it inaccessible to all but the highest social class, though many came to its high gate to gawk and look in. The park was famous for reasons other than its exclusivity, including an extremely large and extravagant playground, advertised as the largest in the province, and numerous traditional gardens to walk through. Yi used to come to the park a lot as a child not only to play on the playground but also to celebrate his family's successes. As he grew older, this became more of a reason to avoid the park. He did, however, have fond memories of the place, including the time he came with Ling.

The two of them must not have been more than ten or eleven years old. It was one of their last times hanging out before Ling transferred schools to begin his training into becoming a nan-nu. Ling had mentioned to him that he had never been to a good park before, and Yi had begged and begged his father to take them both there. Finally, after weeks of begging, the Governor agreed, allowing the two of them to go with the household servants one weekend. In retrospect, the afternoon was unremarkable. The two boys played on the swings, slid on the slides, and chased one another through the fields—just normal ten, eleven-year-old boy stuff. Yet, Yi would never forget that smile plastered across Ling's face.

"What are you thinking about?" asked Ling, holding Hanbing's hand as they walked through the park towards the playground.

"Nothing." Yi felt his face turning red, and he looked away, mumbling in a low voice, "Nothing important, just some old memories."

"FLOWERS!" Hanbing's voice echoed out, as she pointed out the small garden in the distance, snapping Yi back into reality. "I want to go play with the flowers and then see the butterflies."

Yi felt himself turning red again, this time for entirely different reasons. He looked around, thankful that no one was nearby, before stepping down to Hanbing level. "Hanbing," he said sternly, "boys like you don't like flowers and butterflies. They like military and cars and other manly things. Not girly things like flowers and butterflies."

"But, but, but," said Hanbing, confused. "I do like flowers and butterflies. They are so pretty. I never see flowers. Can we go look at the flowers?"

Yi looked up at Ling, who said nothing and just shrugged sadly, as he thought about their fight earlier this morning. He gave it another moment, before smiling. "I understand now, Hanbing. You like nature. Can you repeat after me? I like nature!" He grinned as Hanbing nodded and repeated. "Then, let's go look at nature. Nature includes many things, including flowers and butterflies, but also trees, grass, birds, bugs, and other animals, manly animals like tigers and bears. Let's go look at nature."

Hanbing nodded again, and the three of them walked towards the garden with the two adults once again contemplating how to deal with Hanbing's little secret.

Hanbing didn't want to leave the garden, but after about thirty minutes, Yi felt it was enough. He was, however, happy to see other boys playing around the garden, though none showed as much interest as Hanbing. At least, he thought, if such an incident would occur again in the future, especially in company such as his family, it would be easier to dismiss and justify this as normal boy behavior. He just needed to think of more ways to control her female tendencies and prevent this from happening again.

The three of them arrived at the biggest playground in the province after leaving the garden. Like all children, Hanbing's eyes grew wide as she looked over the numerous slides, swing sets, and many different places to climb including rock walls, fake forts, and other sets for her to play with. As she ran towards the first thing that caught her eye, Yi handed his stuff to Ling and chased after her. He followed her as she climbed up and down on the equipment, sliding down with her and chasing her around. Her giggles were infectious, and he couldn't stop laughing with her. Up and down they went, father and child trying out everything on the playground.

Ling sat on the bench on the side, their stuff piled at his side, taking pictures with his cellphone. He was happy at what a great father Yi was, so willing to participate in their child's life. His meeting with the ladies had taught him that most fathers rarely played a role in childcare, with Baihe even confirming Mengqin was never home, and when he was, showed little interest in being with Qinghuang.

The differences between Ling and Yi seemed to work in

collaboration when it came to childcare. It wasn't just about their gender roles and social positions. There were other little things, too. Ling loved how Yi could do the things that he couldn't. He was much better at playing games with Hanbing and more imaginative when it came to storytime. It wasn't just the fun stuff. Yi was also better at getting her dressed for the day and getting her prepared when they went out. Yi could even teach her stuff that Ling never knew about.

He loved how Hanbing had bonded with both of them equally. Ling loved watching Yi play with Hanbing. He remembered how much fun he used to have with Yi when they were both children, back before things became…complicated. When Yi was happy, he was fun to be around and put all of his attention on the people he cared about. Ling couldn't stop smiling as he watched Yi push Hanbing on the swings; she laughed like there was no tomorrow.

Yet, he couldn't help feeling a twinge of jealousy. It would be inappropriate for him to join Hanbing on the playground equipment, despite him wanting to. If given the same opportunities as Yi, would he also be good at games?

What if he had been destined to live as a man in society? Would he have been the type of husband who would play with his son? If it weren't for Yi, would he still be living in his village? Would he have ever even been able to see a place like this? Would he, his wife, and their son do activities like this? Could he even imagine himself with a wife? All he knew was he desperately wished he could join Yi and Hanbing climbing, sliding, and chasing one another up and down on the playground equipment. Hanbing's loud laugh brought him back to reality, and Ling scolded himself for having such thoughts in the first place as he tried to clear his mind and resume taking more pictures. He reminded himself how fortunate he was as he cleared his mind of any other inappropriate fantasies.

About fifteen minutes later, Hanbing was exhausted, running back to her mother to get a drink of water and eat some snacks. As Yi and Hanbing munched on crackers, Ling took the opportunity to excuse himself to use the bathroom.

After using the bathroom, Ling decided to take a short walk. The back of the park included some hills and a forest which usually had less people, if any. Ling knew Yi and Hanbing would be eating for a while, joking around, and Hanbing would probably take a ten-minute rest before she would be ready to play again. He figured he could take advantage of this alone time, something he almost never had anymore, to enjoy the peace and clear his mind. He turned towards the forest. Tall, healthy trees were rare in Xincheng, and he breathed deeply, enjoying the scent of fresh air and nature.

As he reached the back of the forest, he heard laughter, and to his surprise, it was familiar laughter. Against his better nature, he decided to follow the laugher. It came from off the path, but Ling decided to push through the bushes and the trees towards the laughter. Five minutes later, he reached a small clearing, only to find what looked like a lady dressed like a man and her son playing baseball. Ling let out a small gasp as he recognized the lady's face. Zhubao. Instead of wearing the expensive silk dresses that she usually wore, she was wearing athletic pants. Her hair was tied up and shoved uncomfortably in a baseball cap.

Zhubao tossed the soft plastic baseball in the air towards her four-year-old son who hit it back towards her. "Good job," she cheered. "Now, let's finish this up. Your daddy will be worried that we have been out all day."

"More, Mommy, more," cried the son.

Zhubao chuckled. "Ok, just five more minutes."

"Yeah, Mommy, five more minutes," the child cheered back.

"And, remember, son," said Zhubao, preparing to throw the ball, "this is yours and Mommy's secret. You can't tell Daddy, you can't tell Nanny, you can't tell anyone."

"Yes, Mommy," laughed the son. "It's our secret. Throw the ball, Mommy."

The two continued to play, Zhubao laughing and her

son cheerful, both unaware of their secret audience in the background. Ling smiled to himself, unwilling to interrupt this love between a child and his mother, before noticing the time, and slipping away back in the woods, returning to his own family.

*   *   *

It had been a particularly difficult Ladies' Meeting, as Meigui had been busy berating everyone for their appearance, but Ling decided he had to do what he needed to do. After the meeting, he stood around and waited for Zhubao. He found her walking out of the bathroom and looked around to see if anyone was watching. Anxiously, he walked over to her.

"Excuse me, Zhubao," Ling asked quietly. "Can I speak with you? Privately?"

Zhubao stared at him, annoyed. "Fine, but make it quick. I have better things to do."

Ling took Zhubao into the children's room as there was no one there. They could see toys and snacks on the floor, even a used diaper in the trash can in the corner. Fenghuang had yet to clean up the room.

"What do you want? Make it fast!" Zhubao said impatiently.

"I saw you in the park last weekend," Ling said quickly and quietly. "I saw you in People's Park."

Zhubao stiffened, looking around room nervously. "I don't know what you are talking about."

"Look, Zhubao, I am not here to judge you," Ling began. "But..."

Zhubao interrupted angrily. "I wasn't in the park, but even if I were, it is none of your business what I was doing. If you have nothing else to say, I have nothing else to add."

"Zhubao, I want to talk to you about what you were doing."

"Is this some kind of threat, Ling?" Zhubao said furiously. "Because you can't prove I was there. You don't have any evidence."

"Zhubao," Ling sighed uncomfortably. "I am not here to make

any threats, but I saw you playing sports with your son and—"

"You want to blackmail me?" asked Zhubao. Her voice was high-pitched and hysterical. "Are you threatening to tell Meigui or your father-in-law what you saw? Because, like I said, you have no proof. I don't handle threats well, Ling. I don't know what kind of game you think you are playing, but—"

"Zhubao," Ling interrupted quickly. While he understood why Zhubao was acting so defensively, he couldn't stop feeling slighty hurt that she would think he was that type of person. "I don't want to blackmail you. I came to warn you. I don't want you to get hurt."

"Warn me? I don't understand what you are warning me about."

"I don't want you to get hurt, Zhubao," Ling said earnestly. "I remember our first meeting, when I heard what happened to you. I felt so bad hearing about you getting beaten. I know it isn't my business what goes on in your life, but if I saw you, someone else could have. I just wanted to warn you to be careful."

"Are you being serious right now? I don't understand what kind of game you are trying to play here, Ling," stated Zhubao suspiciously.

Ling nodded. "I am not judging you, Zhubao. I haven't told anyone what I saw. You and your son looked very happy. I was envious. But I know how traditional this group and your family is. I don't want you to get hurt, that's why I am coming to warn you."

Zhubao relaxed a little. "You haven't told anyone what you saw."

"No. It isn't their business, or mine for that matter."

Zhubao stared at Ling quizzically before speaking. "In that case," she said as her voice normalized, "thank you, Ling, for your concern, but—"

"Excuse me," a sweet voice rang out from the doorway. "What are you ladies still doing here? And why are you talking in this room?" Meigui walked in the room. "Excuse me, but what are you ladies still doing here?" She looked at them both with suspicion. "What is going on?"

"Meigui," gasped Zhubao. "Why are you still here?"

"Not that it is any of your business," Meigui answered, watching them carefully. "But, I was talking to Fenghuang. I need a new nanny. My current nanny, despite her so-called education, is doing a terrible job raising my husband's children, and Fenghuang, despite her many, many faults, at least seems to understand and knows how to raise children properly. That doesn't answer my question, however. What are you ladies doing here, and what in the world are you talking about?"

"Nothing, Meigui," stammered Ling. "I was just talking to Zhubao about…"

"About what?" Meigui said, her voice dangerously high. "I don't like it when I see ladies sneaking around and sharing gossip. So, quickly speak up! Tell me, Ling, what is going on?"

"Umm…"

"She was giving me advice," Zhubao said. Meigui turned to her. "I had asked Ling for advice. She seems like she has such a happy marriage, and I figured she must have some skills in the bedroom that I don't. Everyone here knows I have been having difficulties with my husband. I figured asking the Governor's daughter-in-law and future First Lady was a great way to learn some new skills. Since it is not a ladylike topic, I didn't want to talk about it in the group. But, I thought I could ask Ling privately."

Meigui eyed them both carefully. "I guess I can see your reasoning," Meigui said, finally looking at Zhubao. "You are right; it is not a ladylike topic. However…I can see why you would ask Ling. Ever since she joined this group, judging by her lack of fashion and the fact that her behavior is more suitable for a village bride, I have wondered myself why a governor's son would marry her and stay married to her. I, too, would assume it's because she knows how to pleasure her man better than anyone else."

She turned to Ling, eyeing him up and down. "I will say I see your sense of fashion has improved since your first visit, and I think you are finally learning some first-class ladylike behaviors. Do keep up the good work. I will see you both next week."

Meigui gave them both a smile before gracefully walking out of the room.

"As I was saying," Zhubao said a few minutes after Meigui left, "thank you for warning me, Ling. But I don't think you have anything to worry about."

"I was scared for you. I mean, I saw you playing with your son, and you looked so happy. I just don't want to see you get hurt," Ling said. "I am sorry if I gave you the wrong impression."

Zhubao looked around again. Her voice broke as she spoke. "I understand now, and you are right. You can't be careful enough. If you say the wrong thing, you will get hurt. The ladies in this group, they are my friends, but I know I can't trust them, especially with things like this. This has to be a secret."

"I know, Zhubao."

"I have already spoken to my son. He loves playing with me. But I told him if he wants to keep playing he can't ever tell anyone. Not even the ayi. And especially not his father."

"Your secret is safe with me, Zhubao. I promise I will never tell anyone. Not even my husband."

Zhubao smiled. "Thank you, Ling. I will see you next week."

Ling watched as Zhubao left the room. Fenghuang walked in as soon as she left.

"That was a very noble thing you did, Ling. Warning her," Fenghuang said. "I, too, would be scared for her. A lady playing sports in this country is a dangerous thing."

"You could hear me talking," Ling said. "In that case, could Meigui—"

Fenghuang interrupted him with a laugh. "I like you, Ling, but you aren't very observant. Look around, there are baby monitors everywhere. I use them to help keep the children safe. But don't worry." Fenghuang pulled a single earbud out of her left ear. "I am the only one who can hear what goes on in this room."

Ling smiled awkwardly. "I guess next time I know better than to choose this room for private conversations. Anyway, what is this I hear about Meigui asking you to become her new nanny?"

10.
LEARN FROM PEERS. AS LONG AS THE PEERS ARE PROPER PEERS

Yi and Ling sat around the living room watching the latest popular TV show as Hanbing played with her toy trucks and soldiers on the rug in front of them. This new historical epic was about the founding of the PRCC and starred the most popular actors and actresses of the country, with the highest budget yet for a TV show. They both enjoyed the realistic fight sequences and the emotional beats of the love story between the lead characters, with their romance being torn apart by the difficulty of war and social change.

"Don't you think she is beautiful?" Ling asked Yi casually, after watching a sequence in which the main actress walked through a flowing cherry blossom forest. "She really has a great body; I can see why she was given the 'Most Beautiful Woman of the Century' award last year. She is even more beautiful than Meigui."

Yi looked at Ling and frowned. "I don't think it is appropriate for you to be checking out other women. A person like you isn't supposed to like the way a woman looks. Surely going to all these ladies' group meetings have taught you that."

"Speaking of them," Ling said casually, "Meigui has been teaching us all about appearances and how the way we look can define what kind of ladies we are, and…I am sure you know, with the way they look, I was thinking…"

"Are you asking for new clothes again?" chuckled Yi. "Didn't you just buy that dress from that new store that opened in Zhengfu District? I guess I now understand why they say women are expensive. You know I don't have the money that the other ladies' husbands have right? I am just a teacher."

"No, no, no. I don't need another dress. The other ladies liked the dress a lot. Meigui even said I looked a lot better recently. More and more ladylike."

"That's good," Yi replied, indifferent.

"But," Ling continued casually, "I don't think a new dress makes me look more like a lady. I think I need to work on my body. You know, the dress is beautiful, but I don't think it fits my body as well as it should."

Yi paused for a moment and looked at Ling carefully. "I suppose you have gained a few pounds recently. Maybe you can invite Fenghuang over once or twice a week to watch Hanbing, and you can join a gym after you finish your chores. Better yet, have her go with you so you can keep an eye on them while you exercise."

"If I needed someone's help to watch Hanbing, I would ask your mother. You know how she always complains she doesn't see him enough. Besides, Fenghuang is my friend, not a babysitter." Ling hesitated, and spoke quietly, conscious that Hanbing was in the room. "Actually, I was thinking maybe I could get top surgery. It's much faster than bottom surgery, and it will give me a better shape..."

"Excuse me?" said Yi loudly. "You want to get surgery again?"

"It's just something I thought about recently," Ling said quickly, looking towards Hanbing, and speaking quietly. "It's quicker than doing the bottom, and it will make me more beautiful and ladylike, and the recovery is not that long."

"What about Hanbing? Who is going to watch Hanbing?" Yi said angrily.

"Like I said, the surgery doesn't take as long, and the recovery time is much shorter. It is just a few days of rest," Ling said, pleading. "The whole point of having me go to these ladies' group meetings is to have me act more ladylike. Having me get this simple surgery will make me more look ladylike. We can have Qiang do it. I am sure he will give a great price!"

"No," said Yi, quietly and angrily. "You will not be getting any surgery. Top or bottom. I have said this before."

"Why not?"

Yi sighed loudly, but continued speaking in a quiet, angry voice. "I don't know why you keep bringing this up, Ling. Do you not remember the fight we had right before Hanbing came into our lives? I have told you not to bring this up anymore." He paused. "Besides, going to these meetings is about changing your inside, not your outside."

"I understand. I won't bring it up again…by the way, I think I have made a new friend at the meetings. A friend who is not Fenghuang. An actual lady. Her name is Zhubao."

"Really?" asked Yi, his whole body perking up.

"Yes," Ling continued, "and I am thinking about inviting her out to a nearby teashop after our next meeting."

Yi smiled. "I am really happy to hear that, Ling. It is good of you to hang out more with the ladies. This is a good thing. I know it will make you happier. In fact, why don't I meet you after your next meeting, and I can pick up Hanbing, so you ladies can have more quality time together."

* * *

To Ling's relief and surprise, Zhubao agreed to hang out with Ling after the next meeting. They ignored the other ladies' baffled yet curious faces as they left the meeting and handed their children to their nannies and Yi respectfully. The ladies giggled loudly when they saw Yi, and commented how handsome he looked, and how much Hanbing looked like his father. Afterwards, Ling and Zhubao walked to a small local teashop, around the corner from where the meetings were usually held.

"I am curious," Zhubao announced as they sat down with

their respective drinks. "Why did you ask me out? You have never shown much interest in me during the meetings. We have only talked…that one time, a few weeks ago."

"Yi thinks I should spend more time with you ladies and less with Fenghuang," Ling replied truthfully. "And, I figured maybe you would give me a chance."

"He isn't wrong, you know," Zhubao said, sipping her tea. "Fenghuang is not the type of person you should be hanging out with. Meigui has told us all about the radical thoughts she and her husband have. Fenghuang even told me I shouldn't be ashamed of playing sports with my son. Which I know is wrong, but I can't stop doing it." She finished with a sigh.

Ling didn't know what to say; he just smiled supportively.

"Also," Zhubao said suddenly, "as a general rule, it's just not appropriate for us ladies to hang out with one another. As a lady, we simply don't have time for friends. Our priorities must be our husband and his child, children if we are so fortunate. These meetings are an exception because we aren't meeting as friends; we are meeting to learn from another. But, unless there is a special occasion, it's simply not appropriate for us to meet one another in public."

Ling thought for a moment and spoke quietly. "There is just so much I don't know about being a proper lady."

"Yes, we noticed," Zhubao said indifferently. "We talk about it all the time, when you aren't there."

"You also talk about it when I am there," Ling said, chuckling nervously.

Zhubao smiled. "I suppose we do. Why did you ask me out to tea today, Ling?"

"I supposed I was hoping to learn more about being a proper lady from you."

Zhubao frowned. "Unfortunately, as you know, like you, I am not very good at being a proper lady. But, I suppose there are still things I could teach you. What school in the Capital did you study at again?"

"I didn't," Ling said. For some reason, he felt embarrassed and shameful. "I studied here. In Xincheng. But, as you know, at #1 School for Proper Ladies, the best school in Xincheng. You might have heard Meigui mention it."

"Oh yes, I remember now. In that case, then how did a girl like you meet such an important, high class man like Yi?" asked Zhubao curiously.

"He was one of my elementary school classmates. He was…one of my friends, actually. I was one of the scholarship students. My family comes from a village about two hours from here. When I was selected, I mean, had the honor of being selected to become a woman, he decided then that in the future he would marry me," Ling replied.

"I see. You have known each other for a long time. That's why he chose you," Zhubao said. "He pitied you. It's not that you have some special skill that we don't. That is a relief to hear."

"How so?" Ling asked, confused.

"Like Meigui said, the last time we spoke," Zhubao said with indifference. "We have all wondered for so long why a man like Yi would choose a woman like you. We all thought you had something that we didn't, some skill we don't have, or maybe an important relative, that helped you end up with a man like him. It is a relief to hear that he only chose you because you knew each other as children. You really are just what we see. Just a normal woman. Nothing special."

"Oh, I see," Ling said. He felt embarrassed for being hurt by her words.

"I meant that as a good thing," Zhubao said, watching Ling and trying to be nice. "I don't know if you know this…" She hesitated. "Baihe gossips a lot about you guys. Especially prior to you and Yi's son joining our little group. She gossiped about Yi, and about how Yi helps watch the children, and helps clean about the house, and how you can't afford a nanny, and all these other weird things. How weird and improper you are. I am sure you know she doesn't really like you. But the thing is…like the rest of us, I think she is…for lack of a better word, jealous, and not just because your husband is the future governor as opposed to hers."

"What do you mean by that?" Ling asked, surprised.

Zhubao hesitated again. She cleared her throat before speaking. "Yi seems like a gentleman. An ideal man, in fact. It is highly inappropriate for us to admit this, but I think all of us wished, to different degrees, that our husbands were more like Yi: more than willing to help out with their child and help us out here and there. I hope you know how lucky you are that he chose you."

Ling smiled modestly. "I suppose I am lucky."

It started raining gently outside as Ling looked out the window. He was glad they had both brought their parasols. Meigui had recently instructed that they all should bring one as it would make them look more lady like and protect their skin from the sun, keeping it fair and helping to distinguish them from the countryside peasants. Turning back to Zhubao, he asked, "What about you, Zhubao? Where did you study?"

"Oh," said Zhubao, "I studied in the Capital, of course, like all the rest of the ladies."

"Did you all go the same school?"

"Oh no. I mean we all went to one of three best. Actually…I don't know where Meigui studied. She is very secretive about her past. But, I went to The Capital School of Lady Perfection. It's the best school in the country, if you didn't know. Every one of us who graduated from there have married someone of importance. It's also the alumni of Baihe, if you didn't know as well," Zhubao explained casually.

"I didn't, actually," confessed Ling. He thought for a moment. "We all know that the women who come out of the Capital are the best. I always wondered how one gets chosen to study in the Capital. After all, none of us come from an especially high social status, otherwise we would have never been chosen for this honor of becoming ladies in the first place."

Zhubao looked uncomfortable hearing the last sentence but spoke normally. "It is indeed very difficult to be chosen to study in the Capital and receive your surgery there. You simply cannot compare the quality of becoming a lady there to here." Zhubao paused for a moment and thought. "I suppose everyone gets chosen for different reasons. A lot of my classmates' families had connections to someone in the Capital, or they paid someone who helped them get in, once they knew their child was picked from the lottery, because it is the best choice for them." She smiled and giggled, remembering a fond memory. "I am different though. The people in my village, we are thought to be the most beautiful people in the country. When I was young, an official came to my village and saw how beautiful I was. He selected me because he told me I was the most beautiful one in the village. He told me that studying and getting my surgery would only enhance my beauty."

"Does the government pay for your studying like they did mine?" asked Ling curiously.

"Of course," Zhubao said. "Obviously, our glorious government paid for all of our education and our basic surgery." She looked up and down again at Ling. "For the extra things that make me different from you, extra classes and stuff, we had to find sponsors or pay for ourselves. But you know, as I went to the best school, it wasn't hard to find sponsors to support us. Today, my husband is a successful businessman. He likes to keep me looking, as he would put, young and hot," she finished, giggling.

The two of them sat around for a moment, watching the rain slowly die down. Zhubao put down her empty drink. "I suppose I should get going. I need to go home to my husband." She collected her belongings and prepared to leave.

"This was fun," Ling said nervously. "Perhaps we can do it again in the future."

Zhubao paused for a moment, thinking, and smiling softly.

"I don't think so, Ling. Don't get me wrong, you are not a bad woman. In fact, you are probably kinder than the rest of us. But, as I said earlier, it just simply isn't appropriate for a lady to have friends. We have to keep our focus on our husbands and our children. Going to the meetings is one thing, and I guess a shopping trip here or there is okay, but sitting around, talking, we just don't have time for that. Besides, Ling, you shouldn't be hanging out with people like me, or Fenghuang. We are not the same class of people as you and your husband. It could be damaging for your husband's reputation. I will see you at the next meeting," Zhubao finished with a smile and walked out of the door.

✱　✱　✱

Yi watched all the other ladies leave the apartment complex as he stood there deciding how he was to spend his afternoon alone with Hanbing. Suddenly, out of the corner of eye, he saw Teacher Long walking towards him. He wondered for a moment if he should say hi.

"Hello, Yi, what are you doing here?" Long asked cheerfully, before Yi could say anything.

"Oh, not doing much," Yi said nervously looking around. "Ling is busy this afternoon with one of the other ladies, so I came to pick up Hanbing, so she can have some free time to, you know, to do lady stuff. What about you?"

"I am here to pick up my wife, Fenghuang," Long said. "She is just wrapping up. Apparently, one of the children, not yours of course, made a big mess today. I figure I will take her out to dinner tonight to cheer her up. I am sure she will be down soon."

"Cool," Yi said awkwardly. He was unsure if he should leave or stay. He had never spoken to Teacher Long outside of school, nor did he feel particularly comfortable about doing it.

"How are things?" Long asked. "Are you ready for the big meeting next week?"

"The one discussing our upcoming curriculum and potential

class changes? I don't know," Yi replied hesitantly. "I suspect they will only continue to make our lessons stricter. As you know, our glorious leaders feel our students are too willing to speak out their ideas without understanding what they are saying. Apparently, we are making changes to help guide the students speak more patriotically and logically and more in tune with our glorious government's beliefs."

"Do you think our students speak without understanding what they are saying?" Long asked casually. "You are a department head. What is your opinion?"

"I don't see a problem in moderating what the students say," Yi said carefully. "We wouldn't want the students to get into problems by saying the wrong thing."

"According to Article 28 of our country's Constitution, 'Citizens of the People's Republic of Central China enjoy freedom of speech, of the press, of assembly, of association, of procession, and of demonstration.' Do you not think that applies to our students?" Long asked.

"Technically speaking, our students are not adults and, therefore, not given the full rights of a citizen," evaded Yi, "which renders your question inapplicable. Besides, just because our constitution can protect us does not mean we should create chaos for the purpose of chaos. We should be careful of how we act in society because it impacts all of us."

Long looked at Yi for a moment. "I remember you as a student, you know, even though you were not my student. All of us knew who you were given your father. But I remember hearing from your teachers about you. You were definitely of interest to all of us teaching."

"Why?" said Yi, unsure where Long was going with this.

"All your teachers talk about how patriotic you were and how good you were at following the ideology of our country. That you were destined to be a great governor and have a successful career in politics. Yet, here you are, working as a teacher instead of working in politics. Why do you think that is?"

Yi shrugged. "I like inspiring the next generation. In addition, it's a good way to give back to a school that has done so much for me."

"Do you know what I think?" Long said thoughtfully. "I think you didn't get into politics because you don't agree with everything that our government says or does, that you are smarter than the average person here, and know the difference between right and wrong. Since I am sure you know that, why not fight for what you believe in?"

Yi thought for a moment. "I don't think it's that simple, Teacher Long," he said finally.

"We aren't in school anymore. There is no one around," Long said, smiling. "You can tell me what you honestly think."

"That is what I think," Yi said. "I know what the Constitution says; I know our history. Our country has had its problems, but we are working on it. Our students should wait until they understand the full picture before they make comments. They need more experience to know what they are talking about."

"In other words," Long asked directly, "you really do agree with the changes being made towards our curriculum, limiting what our students can say?"

"As I have said many times, Long," Yi replied, "I think it is our job to teach the curriculum. It is not our job to interpret or question it, nor share our opinion. Even when I was a student here, that was true. I learned the material, and I used what I learned to get into a good university. Today, I teach so my students can do the same."

Long begin to speak, but Yi interrupted. "Besides, I don't think any good can come from too much discussion about any topic. I know what the constitution says, but I am also aware of the reality of the situation around us."

Long laughed. "That last thing you said, I guess that is one thing we agree with. You are a cautious man, Yi—perhaps too cautious."

"There is nothing wrong with being careful. I think you should think about that," Yi replied awkwardly. "I need to get going. I want to take my son to the park before it gets dark. I hope you have a good dinner with your wife, and I will see you on Monday."

11.
EVEN FRIENDS CAN BE ENEMIES OF THE STATE. REPORT ALL TRAITOROUS THOUGHTS TODAY.

SINCE HIS MARRIAGE TO LING nearly four years ago and the adoption of their child, Yi had more or less stopped going out to see his friends, especially friends from his days back in school. Most of his friends from school had come from well-to-do families, were currently working at well-to-do jobs, and living the well-to-do lifestyle that Yi was supposed to be living. Over the years, most of his old friends and classmates had slowly fallen out of his life, except for one: Cheng Chen, his supposed best friend, who had remained stubbornly in contact with Yi.

Yi had met Chen in middle school and the pair had become close due to the pressures from their parents. Chen's father was an important member of the provincial parliament, and a close ally of Governor Wang. Yi and Chen had then gone on to university together, with both studying politics and government. Secretly, Yi always had mixed opinions of Chen, but for the sake of face and family *guanxi*, he ignored them, even choosing Chen as his best man during his wedding to Ling.

After graduation from university, Chen moved to the Capital to get what was considered a proper job for someone of his degree and background: employment working for the national government in the Capital. His job was rather secretive, as he worked for the National Central China Intelligence Agency. For the last few years, the two had mostly remained friends over biannual phone calls, with them only meeting when Chen was back in town for work or visiting family. When Chen called Yi one afternoon, inviting him to Gao Ji Cai, the best restaurant in the city, Yi felt obligated to join as it had been over a year since their last meeting.

Gao Ji Cai was Xincheng's only restaurant for the elite, and its tables were only available for a select few, making it the perfect location for both impressing and negotiating without disturbance. Yi hadn't been there since his wedding, as his career as a teacher no longer made him the target customer for the restaurant, and socially speaking, it would have been improper for him to go unless he was invited by another. As he and Chen walked through the restaurant, Yi was not surprised at how little the restaurant had changed and how many of the customers he recognized as his dad's friends, colleagues, and partners. He was quite surprised, however, to see the waiter who greeted them at the door and brought them to their private room.

"Was that Judge Lao?" asked Yi, surprised, as they sat down at the table and the doors shut behind them.

"Yep. Despite claiming to have no interest," laughed Chen, "from what I hear, it seems our old 'esteemed professor' does attempt to keep up with the daily nuisances of government. He hasn't been able to get proper government work since his son brought so much shame onto the family through his heinous choices. This is the only place he can work and still feel… involved." Chen turned to Yi, speaking more seriously. "Honestly, I never understood how he was able to weasel out of going to a Re-Education Camp, like he rightfully deserved. But, I guess that's corruption for you—using your connections to avoid punishment."

Yi said nothing. He had never been comfortable with Judge Lao's expulsion from government, given what his father had arranged and the fact that Judge Lao was one of his old professors. He shook his head, trying to move on. "How have you been?" he asked Chen. "I heard you have been out west. Are you coming back from a big project?"

"Not bad, been very busy. A secret project actually, of the highest level, very few would know about it…maybe I'll tell you later. After a few drinks perhaps?" Chen replied hastily. Taking out a nice bottle of imported wine he had in his bag, he poured Yi a tall glass. "I know you don't drink much, but this a special occasion. I hardly see my best friend anymore."

"We have both been busy. And I look forward to hearing your stories. It's basically the only reason I still hang out with you," Yi joked, taking the glass and raising it. He did appreciate how much Chen told him, even if he knew that some of the things Chen revealed to him were illegal to tell a civilian.

"When are you going to get a real job, my brother? With your background and intelligence, you should be aiming for much more. Come join my department; we would have so much fun together," Chen said, flipping through the menu, deciding what to order. "You are more than qualified, you know, even now. Plus, with your connections, you could be one of the department leaders, like me."

"You know I really like teaching. It's suitable for me. I like the quiet life," Yi replied as Judge Lao came back into the private room. It was obvious Judge Lao recognized them both. Though he wanted to say something, Yi knew it would be best to follow his friend and proper cultural customs, so he didn't acknowledge him as Judge Lao took their order.

"He is a sneaky one," scoffed Chen when Judge Lao was out of the room. "You should be careful around him; he is like a spy now. Hoping for that one bit of information that will bring him back into government. Well, guess what, sir, if you can't even raise your son properly, how can we trust you to judge properly?"

He looked at Yi as if hoping for some sort of validation, but when Yi said nothing, he continued, "I know you think you love teaching, but you could really do something better. Come on, we could work together. Like we used to talk about, in the dorms, remember? Besides, you can't avoid politics forever. It's best you get some proper experience before you take over your father as governor."

Yi thought back to their dorm room conversations. They often worked on projects together, and he could not deny that, despite their differences, they did work well together. "As I said before, I am not interested in working for the government. Besides, my brother, Mengqin, is already working in politics. If someone in my family wants to continue the family tradition of being governor, it can be him. Also, your job is in national government. Even if I did want to be governor, working with you wouldn't be the best way for me to gain experience," he added with a chuckle.

Chen laughed, hard. "Look, we are friends, so I can be honest. I may be in the national government, and no longer involved in provincial issues, but even I know the only reason your brother hasn't been fired is because of your dad. That spineless wimpy ass kisser can't even run a department, much less a province. We need someone like you who has conviction in what he believes in."

Yi felt obligated to defend his family honor but decided to say nothing as he knew what Chen said was true. "That is not important. It is no longer my destiny to follow my father's and my grandfather's footsteps. I will continue training the next generation of politicians to guide our great nation in continuing being the greatest nation on Earth. That will be my contribution. Anyway, let's not talk about this. How have you been, brother?" He raised his glass for a toast.

Smiling, Chen raised his glass. "Then I must add, before we change the subject, even though you refuse to take your rightful destiny, your students all appear to be doing quite well and will make fine future leaders for our glorious country. One of them, Yuehan, is now working in my department. I must say I am quite impressed on how much you have taught him." As the glasses clinked, he added, "Though, I must once again add, if the student is already this good, can you imagine how good his teacher must be?"

"Actually," said Yi, smiling modestly, "something happened in school a few months ago that I wish to get a friend's opinion about."

"I can't say I am familiar with the complicated world of education," Chen laughed, "but, sure, what's happened?"

"One of my coworkers, our math teacher, recently got fired. He got fired for being mixed. His great-grandfather was apparently a white American."

"So, he is one-eighth white American?" Chen asked, as Yi nodded. "Naturally, he should get fired. He is impure and unsuitable for teaching."

Yi thought for a moment. He tried to sound casual. "I was against him being fired, you know."

"Really?" Chen replied, looking genuinely horrified.

"He is only one-eighth. It was his great-grandfather. He could have not known."

Chen looked at him, as if unable to recognize the man sitting in front of him. Yi quickly corrected himself. "I understand the dangers of mixing up the races and our blood. I am just saying, this man's action has shown him to be a good teacher, and it could be detrimental to the school and the student's education to lose a good teacher."

"I believe you aren't thinking clearly," Chen said simply, "but it is understandable, as you are thinking with your emotions. This teacher was your friend, and you want to defend him. However, if you were to think about this issue logically, you would understand that this man betrayed you. You just didn't see it at the time." Chen took a sip of his wine. "You must not forget, brother, how dangerous mixing the bloods of two races can be. Not only is it unnatural, but it creates dangerous and unbalanced thoughts. An incurable sociological and psychological disease, so to speak. This teacher must be removed from society. Who knows how his white American background might influence his thinking and biologically drive him in destroying our great nation!"

Yi looked at him for a moment, before forcing a smile. "Of course, you are right. I was letting my emotions get a hold of me." He raised his glass. "Thank you, my brother, for your clarification. Cheers!"

Judge Lao came in, bringing many expensive dishes that could not be found in any other restaurant in the city and brought the resturant its fame—stir-fried shrimp, steamed crab, and a full roasted goose—and began setting them on the table with the help of another younger waiter that Yi did not recognize. Realizing that this was not the time to talk about anything personal, Yi asked, "How is your family?"

"Meh," replied Chen. "I mean I don't see them much, but I am not happy with how my wife Jingjing is raising my son. The nanny isn't great, either. How about you?"

"Good, Ling and I have been really enjoying being parents. We took my son, Hanbing, to People's Park together a few weeks ago. It was a good time. Hanbing's first time actually; he loved it."

"You like being a parent?" said Chen, surprised. "Why wouldn't you just hire a nanny to take care of your child? It frees up so much time to do things that are actually…enjoyable. I can't imagine coming home all day after working and having to watch the child. It's good to just be able to go out and get a beer. Relax."

"I actually like being a dad," Yi shrugged, beginning to eat. "It's been a very interesting hands-on experience, and I am glad I get to participate in a lot of it."

"I forget how weird you can be sometimes," laughed Chen. "First, you tell me you like teaching, then you question our government policies about blood purity, and now you tell me you like being a hands-on parent. Are you sure you don't have some sort of illness? Or, maybe, you secretly want to be a nan-nu?"

Yi forced himself to laugh loud and hard. This was how Chen and he used to joke. Anything that was slightly different was connoted with sickness or wanting to be a woman. Somehow it didn't seem as funny as before. But whatever awkwardness he felt, to Yi's relief, Chen didn't seem to notice.

"Anyway," continued Chen, "what does confuse me, though, is that you have had a son for three years now. Yet, me, your best friend, the best man at your wedding, has yet to meet the child."

"You just have been so busy. You never come to Xincheng anymore. Who knows what you are up to?" said Yi, forcing another laugh. "It's not like I can just call you up and invite you back. I would just hate to interrupt one of your secretive missions."

"Speaking of secret missions," Chen said, winking, "after Judge Lao, I mean Waiter Lao, does his job and cleans up this mess, let's pop open another bottle of wine. Have I got a story for you!"

"Okay, what happened?" asked Yi after Judge Lao took all the dishes away and the two were sitting comfortably drinking a new bottle of imported wine and munching on a small plate of boiled peanuts and edamame.

"My last mission, as I told you before I left, was to follow up on some rumors. Big rumors." Chen began.

"Indeed? Can you spare any details?"

"Hmmm, I don't think I should say," Chen said teasing, dragging on the story a little. "But, whatever, you haven't leaked anything I have told you in the past, but keep this one a secret because it's a big one. Like, it could have been national news. Change the fate of our glorious nation type big news. I am not sure even your esteemed father knows the details yet. We have another meeting in a few days to talk about the results. That's the reason why I am back, actually."

"I see," said Yi, sipping his wine. "Should I be concerned?"

"We have been out in the western side of the province,

exploring a rumor," Chen paused to add drama. "According to the local gossip, there is one village that still has biological women, and, more importantly, they have been giving birth naturally. There are apparently at least three sisters, and their father and husbands have been protecting them. Over the last few years, this one village has been bragging to other surrounding villages about it, and finally it reached the ears of the National Intelligence."

"Really?"

"And," Chen continued dramatically, "it only gets more interesting. The rumor is, one of the sisters, a few years ago, gave birth to a daughter. However, at the time, being afraid that she was going to get caught, her family decided to toss away the baby. Apparently, she and her family thought they would be in danger if the government ever found out a daughter was born."

Yi paused for a moment trying to figure out what the proper reaction to this story was to be and how to control the amount of interest and emotion he could show. He could feel the sweat dripping down his neck as he tried to control his heartbeat. Finally, he said, trying to sound curious yet casual, "Why would she do that? I mean, don't they know it's illegal to hide as a woman and that the government only wants to protect them and care for their wellbeing?"

"I have never really understood the peasants out West; they don't really understand our civilized ways," Chen said indifferently. "Anyway, we decided to go out and investigate. We hear rumors like this all the time: foreign scum, women, mixed breeds, minorities. All hiding here and there. But this rumor has been floating around neighborhood villages for a long time, so that made it seem worth investigating."

"And to toss out a baby," Yi added, careful to control his tone. "This baby could have changed the future of our glorious nation. How dare they toss it out! How could they be so thoughtless and careless?"

"Like I said," smirked Chen. "One cannot understand the

foolishness of peasants, and it would be worthless and a wasted attempt to try."

"Finish your story, then. What did you find?" said Yi, still trying to sound curiously casual. "Are the rumors true?"

"There were reasons to believe these rumors are true. Initial investigation did suggest that there were biological females and they were giving natural birth, and perhaps one of these children could be a woman. It was decided we needed to start genetically testing everyone so that was our plan of action."

"Well, that's great news," said Yi excitedly. "Not only were you able to find biological women, but potentially find men unaffected by the XYTablet." He raised up his glass for a toast. "Congrats on a successful mission. When will you announce it to the public?"

"Hmm," said Chen, suddenly turning quiet. "The problem is the mission wasn't successful."

"Meaning?"

"The villagers, despite spending years of gossiping to nearby villages and treating this information as a sense of pride, were unusually stubborn. And, well, to our disappointment, they refused to cooperate with us and take the mandatory genetic tests," Chen said uncomfortably, as if trying to control his emotions. "That meant we had to consider other options, and none of us knew what to do."

"Meaning?" Yi repeated, this time more somberly.

"You are going to be proud of Yuehan for this one," said Chen, smiling oddly. "He really understands politics and laws. He reminded us all in our time of weakness about the dangers of disobedience and that disobedience leads to rebellion. He reminded us what needs to be done when people don't listen to government officials."

"Oh, no," Yi said in a voice barely louder than a whisper, suddenly understanding the direction of story.

"Anyway," continued Chen, struggling to find the conviction in his voice. "Me, Yuehan, and the rest of our team—we rounded up everyone in the village, and anyone who didn't agree to work with us, we shot in the head and sent their body to the lab to be examined." As Yi said nothing, he continued. "After this, well, they started to cooperate, but it was too late. We can't risk having people disapproving our esteemed government. We can't risk a potential rebellion. We shot every single one of them—men, women, children—and wrapped each one up in a body bag and sent it to the lab."

Yi didn't know what to say, though he could feel his stomach rolling in turmoil. He tried to control his emotions towards these villagers he never met, villagers who could potentially be Hanbing's biological parents. As he knew that Chen would see him as weak if he showed any emotion, he could only whisper out one emotionless word: "Why?"

"Come on," said Chen, looking blankly out into the room. "You understand how dangerous rumors can be; you know the dangers of disobedience. These rumors about biological women out there are already detrimental towards our great nation, but a whole village disobeying our esteemed government over these women? If we accept the acts of disobedience, that could lead to chaos, and chaos would destroy everything our great leaders have spent years and sacrificed so much in building. As your student, Yuehan, so wisely reminded us that day, it is our duty to protect our great country from rebellion and acts that could lead to its destruction."

The two sat there in silence, each lost in their contemplation, each trying to act as if they were unaffected by the story that was just told. "Chen, are you doing alright?" Yi asked finally in a quiet voice.

For a brief moment, Yi thought he saw the shadow of fear and sadness behind Chen's eyes. Chen froze and forced a smile as he responded. "Yeah. I mean, why wouldn't I be? I did what was best for our glorious country."

"Then, in this group of villagers," Yi asked, "did you find any biological women or any men unaffected by the XYTablet?"

"I just got the lab reports back right before I met you, actually," said Chen. He paused, looking around the room. "There were no biological women, and doesn't appear to be any men who could breed women. Whoever they were trying to protect, if anyone at all, was not in the village that day."

Yi swallowed all of his emotions, forcing himself back to a level of minor curiosity and indifference. Speaking carefully, he asked, "Just wondering, what would the government have done, if biological women or men capable of creating X chromosome were found?"

"What do you mean?" asked Chen, raising his eyebrows.

"I mean, I know the facts," Yi said quickly. He tried to phrase his sentences as intellectual curiosity. "I understand how the government policy is to protect its people and, more importantly, these biological women. But, you know, as a teacher of politics, and having close friends and family in government, you hear these rumors, which…" he added quickly, "we know are over-exaggerated gossip spread by people with nothing better to do."

Chen looked uncomfortable for a brief second before showing a bright smile. "Of course, the rumors are exaggerated. We would take them in. The government has created special housing for them. For their protection, of course. I mean, would we take some eggs from them? Of course, but it is for the best of the country…"

"Of course," Yi replied. "What about the other rumors? You know of real biological females, working as prostitutes in the Capital?"

"There are real biological female prostitutes in the city, that is true. However, I doubt any of them are Chinese. Maybe a lesser Asian race like Japanese or Korean, or mixed and impure."

"If there are biological females in the city," asked Yi, "why don't you think more men try to sleep with them? Isn't it in our biological urges to try to procreate?"

"I think most real men would rather sleep with a nan-nu with an artificial vagina, then stick their penis in a dirty foreigner's vagina," Chen replied with a mixture of pride and horror. "But…" Chen shuddered briefly and uncomfortably, "it is getting complicated. We are running out of eggs, you know. Even with the best of technology at our hands, we can't preserve the eggs forever. I don't know that the public understands how serious it is. Think about it—when was the last time a biological woman was found in this country? Ten, fifteen years ago? The government had to make some…decisions, for the betterment of this country of course, and some of these women…well…things got complicated."

"The government knows best," said Yi. "It is not our duty to question it. But, I mean, from your understanding, are there still even biological Chinese women left in the country? I mean, my students ask all the time, and of course I give the official and correct answer, but…"

Chen looked uncomfortable. Finally, he spoke. "I mean, between you and me, and speaking unofficially, I am sure you know that the government had to make some choices, and well, not all those choices worked out as we hoped. From my answer, probably not. If there were, it would be above my pay grade to know where they are being housed. But, I mean, even if there were women left within government control, it doesn't change the fact we still only have enough eggs for at least another generation or two. I mean, biological women age, and we need genetic diversity. But, that's why we investigate every rumor. Statistically speaking, there has to be some biological women out there who have yet to be found."

"What do you think I should say then," asked Yi, "when my students claim to have seen biological women or know of biological women?"

Chen smiled stiffly. "Come on, you know the answer to that. I would remind them that it is our patriotic, nay, our moral duty to report any biological women we see out there to our glorious government. For the good of the biological women and the country. Any person who doesn't do that is nothing short of a traitor to our glorious nation and should be treated as such."

"Well said," Yi replied. He shuddered internally as he picked up his glass of wine, and gave Chen a toast, before finishing it up with one final gulp.

12.
SURGEONS. IMPORTANT BUT UNNATURAL. CANNOT FIT THE USUAL SOCIETY

"So, how is my favorite social experiment coming along?" Qiang asked happily as he put Hanbing on the table to begin her bi-annual physical.

"It's good. Things are going very well at home," Ling replied timidly. "We celebrated her third Arrival Day last week. Hanbing was very happy, got a lot of toys and attention. Overall, I guess things are going quite well."

"I would assume so," Qiang said sarcastically, as he began checking over Hanbing. "Yi has been so busy he no longer comes over to say hi. My life has been so dull without his unintentionally offensive comments."

"Oh," Ling wasn't sure how to reply. "I mean, he has been quite busy. He is quite the doting father. Between work and Hanbing, he doesn't really have time for anything, or anyone, else."

"Or…" said Qiang with a straight face. "Now that he is a father, and he is happy to be a father, and I am sure his family is happy that he is a father, he is 100% fulfilled, and I no longer serve a purpose in his life because he has nothing to complain about."

Ling looked around uncomfortably, trying to figure out a reply, but couldn't and said nothing.

"I am only joking around; I know he is busy," Qiang said as he laid a hand on Hanbing's back and took out his stethoscope to listen to her heart.

"I must say, I am happy to hear," said Qiang quietly, as if testing the atmosphere of the room, "that you refer to Yi as quite the doting father. Very happy to hear that, in fact."

"What do you mean by that?" Ling replied cautiously.

"I am sure you are aware that most men don't participate in childcare," Qiang said causally, as he put away his stethoscope and turned Hanbing on her back. "I like Yi a lot, but you and I both know that he is often torn between doing what he believes is right and what society says is right."

Ling didn't quite know how to reply and watched Qiang carefully as he continued Hanbing's physical. "I know most men are not involved in childcare. I have been going to a ladies' group for about a year now. It's a group of ladies who meet up once a week, ladies of the most elite background."

"Oh really? I assume these ladies don't know that you still have male genitalia then. What is that like?"

"Umm, well, I can't tell them about my biggest secret," Ling said awkwardly, "but besides that, it's nice, I guess. We aren't very close, but I have learned a lot about how to be a better traditional Chinese lady. It makes me a better wife to Yi. He has been very impressed with some of the new clothes I have bought and some of the snacks I have learned to make. They really understand how to live a first-class lifestyle, which I know Yi misses sometimes. Now that he is a teacher, he misses out on some of the privileges of being the son of our esteemed governor."

"Compared to most residents of this city, you and Yi live a more comfortable life, but I can understand it lacks the luxury of his childhood. So, what are these other women like? I know you just said you aren't very close, but surely you have made a friend?"

"I don't really get along with the ladies. But I have befriended the nanny of the group, Fenghuang. Her husband is actually Yi's colleague."

"I see…" Qiang took a moment to exam Hanbing's ears,

before continuing. "How does Yi feel about that?"

"Oh, well, he doesn't exactly approve. He thinks I should hang out with the ladies more, the ladies in the group, I mean. He feels I should try to be more like them. That they are the right type of women I should be hanging out with."

"Who are some of these ladies? Would I know any of them?" Qiang asked. "You know my clientele are mostly the wealthiest of this city."

"I don't think so. I don't really know any of their backgrounds well. I mean, a lady isn't supposed to talk about her life outside of her husband, or her life before being a lady. But I know they are all from the Capital, like my sister-in-law, Baihe. They have a much better education than I do, with a much higher level of class, which is why Yi wanted me to start attending these meetings in the first place." Ling suddenly noticed Qiang staring at him as if questioning him. Feeling awkward, he continued. "Anyway, it's not that many of us: my sister-in-law Baihe, a few businessman wives, government wives, those type of people. Oh, it's run by a lady named Meigui."

"Meigui?" Qiang asked, surprised. "As in the wife of General Lihong?"

"Oh, you know who she is?" Ling asked. It was his turn to be surprised.

"Yeah…" Qiang trailed off, as if in deep thought, leaving Ling confused. Then, just as suddenly, he perked back up. "You know, just now, when I asked you about the ladies in your group, I was just trying to make small talk. I didn't really expect you to give me any names. But yeah, I know Meigui. I was one of her surgeons, actually."

Ling looked baffled. "How is that possible? Meigui is only a few years older than me, than us?"

"That's why I said one of her surgeons," Qiang said quietly. "She was my father's case. She was the first case I worked on under his supervision actually."

"Your father's case?" asked Ling.

Qiang chuckled for a moment. "You know being a sex change surgeon is a family business, right? No one wants to get into this industry. Not with all the social stigma attached, and not to mention what the job is actually about. And when your family works as surgeons, it's really hard to find another job. People don't want to be involved with people like me, other than, you know, for the surgery. Anyway, I have been in an operating room since I was around 10, slowly learning the skill. My father was actually quite famous in this city for his operations. He was one of the best. That's why he got to meet Governor Wang; that's how I met Yi."

"Oh, I guess Yi never really talks about you, like how you two met and stuff." Ling paused, awkwardly, before speaking really quickly, "I mean he is a very private guy; I don't really know any of his friends. I have only heard of a few of them. Prior to Hanbing, I didn't really know who you were."

"I know. I would have been surprised if you knew about mine and Yi's history," Qiang said, laughing.

"But back to an earlier question, your first surgery was Meigui?" Ling asked quietly. "It really is a small world. What was like that?"

"Are you asking me about the process of surgery?" Qiang asked humorously. "Or some details of her surgery.?"

"No, no. Nothing like that. That would inappropriate," Ling said uncomfortably. "I think I was just surprised that you know Meigui and remember her."

"She was my first case, and Meigui's case was rather special actually…"

"Really? What do you mean by that?"

Qiang sighed for a moment. "I am breaking patient confidentiality by telling you this story, but…" He paused for a moment. "I know you won't tell anyone else. I have never told anyone this story, and I won't lie, I think about Meigui's case a lot. Now that you bring it up…it really makes me think…"

"Wow, what happened?" Ling asked curiously, holding

Hanbing. "I mean, I must say you did a very good job. Meigui is probably the most beautiful lady I have ever seen. I have never seen a biological woman before, but I can't imagine them being more beautiful than Meigui."

"Do you remember the story of Kun Guangrong, son of Kun Rong?" asked Qiang. "You might not, actually. It happened when you would have still been in middle school."

"Kun Guangrong..." Ling repeated the name in his head, thinking deeply. "Wait, the son of the Vice Premier who was murdered by his father's political enemies? I remember that case. Wasn't he kidnapped and brutally murdered?"

"Yes," Qiang said grimly. "Kun Guangrong was our vice premier's son. As the story goes, his father made some enemies, and they abducted eighteen-year-old Kun Guangrong and murdered him. Being such a prominent member of society, it was a huge story. It was such a serious case, you might have remembered, that when the abductors were arrested, they were executed on live TV."

"Yes. I remember now. Even though I was in Woman's School, we still had a day of mourning. They called it a loss to our future. But how does that deal with Meigui?"

"Because..." Qiang hesitated. "Well, because Kun Guangrong wasn't murdered; he was castrated. The abductors felt that it would be more humiliating to his father that way. And to make sure that there was no way his penis and testicles could be reattached, his captors smashed them and sent them to his father."

"Wait, really? How do you know this?"

"Yes," Qiang grimaced. "Because after Kun Guangrong was found, and his castration discovered, he was brought out of the Capital to Xincheng, where he became my father's client. After much discussion, it was decided that Kun Guangrong would become a woman as too much damage had been done to the genital area. That day, Kun Guangrong died, and Meigui was born."

"No way…" Ling replied, shocked. He reached over and hugged Hanbing closely, suddenly feeling the urge to protect her.

"Yes, and to his father, Kun Rong, the loss of face, having his son changed to his daughter, was equal to him being dead. Therefore, he chose to announce that Kun Guangrong was dead. Which, in some ways, he was. The only thing else he did for his child was to arrange for her to marry into a wealthy family. But of course, naturally, he couldn't attend the wedding. It would have made it obvious who she was," Qiang finished sadly.

"I have noticed that Meigui…she is different from the rest of us ladies. She is much more outspoken…she is so much more confident; she is much more ambitious. It's like she is a natural leader."

"Yeah. I would think she is more confident and ambitious. She didn't have the same education that you did. She was told that one day she would lead the country and that all got taken away. But anyway, now that you know this story, you are the only person alive, outside of her family, other than me, who knows her past," Qiang said somberly.

"What do you mean?"

"Six months after the surgery was complete, my father passed away, leaving me the only one who knows her story. Patient confidentiality meant I couldn't tell anyone else, so until today I didn't."

"Oh no…" said Ling, assuming the worse. "Did they, I mean, Kun Rong come after your father?"

"No," Qiang chuckled. "Scared you, didn't I? My father died of lung cancer. Like many people in this career, he was a smoker to deal with the stress. He didn't live a healthy life. After he died, I inherited this clinic, and I just built upon his reputation."

"How do you think General Lihong feels all about this?" Ling asked suddenly.

"What do you mean?" Qiang asked, confused.

"Meigui knows more about being a proper lady than anyone I know. She is also one of the most beautiful ladies I have ever seen…" Ling began thoughtfully. "But, now that I know her background, it is just so sad. She lost her opportunity to be who she was meant to be, to be a man. How do you think General Lihong feels that his wife was almost a man?"

"I don't understand your question. Every woman in this country, except Hanbing here, was once a man."

"Yes, but Meigui wasn't chosen to be a woman like the rest of us were. She was ready to enter society as a man. She graduated high school as a man."

"But you just said that Meigui knows more about being a proper than lady than anyone I know. I guess I am confused on what your point is," Qiang said, exasperated.

"I just think it is weird knowing that his wife wasn't meant to be a woman and didn't become a woman till much later."

"Well you also said she is one of the most beautiful ladies you ever seen—which, by the way, I should thank you for saying, considering I did her surgery," Qiang said, chuckling. "But I still don't understand your point."

"I just think it would be weird for General Lihong to know all of this."

"Is it any more weird than your and Yi's relationship?" Qiang asked quietly.

Ling didn't know how to reply. He stood there silently thinking for a moment and holding on to Hanbing.

"I have only met General Lihong a few times, and I can't say I know him well," Qiang interrupted Ling's thoughts, "but every six months, I visit their house to do touch-ups on Meigui. That's how she stays so beautiful. However, from my feeling, I think Lihong likes the more dominating aspects of Meigui. I think he knows how smart Meigui is, and I think he uses that to his advantage. In many ways, they are the perfect political couple. He provides the face, and she supports and advises him."

Ling and Qiang stood in silence for a few moments as Qiang

finished Hanbing's physical. Finally, Qiang spoke. "For an approximately three-year-old baby, Hanbing is very healthy for her age. You guys should be proud of your parenting skills."

"Thank you," said Ling humbly. "It can be hard doing it with just the two of us. You understand how we can't hire nannies or even have our family help us. Everything involving Hanbing has to be done by either one of us."

Both men stood around the examination room looking uncomfortably at each other, not sure what to say as Ling prepared Hanbing to leave. "Umm, thank you," Ling said quickly. "For everything, as always, and thank you for sharing your story. I promise I won't tell anyone."

He was almost out the door when Qiang suddenly spoke up. "Actually…there is another thing I want to talk to you about. Something different," Qiang began hesitantly, trying to figure how to phrase his words. "I have asked Yi before, but I am not sure…I was wondering, how should I put this? I have been wanting to invite Yi, you, and Hanbing of course, for dinner at my house one night. I know Yi would probably be uncomfortable…but I have always wanted to have you both over. I think it would be fun."

Ling thought about it for a moment. Of course Yi would be uncomfortable, and Ling knew he would likely say no. Yet, he still replied politely, "Thank you for the invite. I will talk to Yi about it. Perhaps we can work something out."

It took some major convincing on Ling's part, but after a few weeks of discussion, Yi and Ling were sitting in a black taxi arranged by Qiang, who had promised Yi multiple times that the driver was trustworthy. Although Yi did not have the fame of his father and was rarely recognized outside of his immediate circle, he knew the political and social repercussions and the huge loss of face it would bring the family if the Governor's eldest son was seen hanging out at the house of a surgeon in the Shoushu District.

In addition, though he would never admit it, Yi believed the bias that most of the city and the country felt towards surgeons. Their job was dangerous and not for proper discussion, and their district of living tended to attract the worst of society. It simply was not proper for someone of his social class to be there.

He had already taken a great risk in being friends with Qiang, and Qiang should have just respected that and not put him and Ling in this awkward situation, Yi thought to himself during the car ride over. Since the adoption of Hanbing, Qiang simply was not needed as a friend in the same way as before. But as Ling had reminded him, Qiang knew most of their biggest secrets and visiting him, if anything, was a sign of respect to someone who could easily make their life quite difficult if he wanted to. While deep in his heart Yi knew Qiang was not the type of person who would betray him, it was hard for him to trust anyone given the circumstances.

Yi was not surprised at the poverty of Qiang's neighborhood. The apartment building, if you could call it that, was located in an abandoned factory, built forty years ago. The surroundings were dilapidated, garbage flowed in the streets, and the smell of excrement and pollution mixed in the air burned his nose. Yi could not believe anyone would choose to live in such an area, until his subconscious guilt fully reminded him that for some people there was no other choice.

The driver opened the door and let Yi, Ling, and Hanbing out. "Your friend lives on the top floor," he began simply. "I will wait for you downstairs. You should be okay to go up by yourself. It is safer than it looks."

The three of them walked up the old metal stairs of the abandoned factory, careful not to make too much noise and alert the neighbors of their presence. Yi carried Hanbing tightly to protect her, seeing no one, but hearing the hushed lives of Qiang's neighbor's behind closed doors. The hallways were dirty, covered with dust and litter everywhere, and it appeared to them that each of the old rooms of the factory had been converted into apartments. Finally, after walking in uncomfortable silence, they reached the top floor, and knocked on an old grey metal door.

Qiang opened the door with a huge smile on his face, "Come in, come in. Make yourself feel welcome." Pointing towards the small shoe storage by the entrance, he said, "Take off your shoes. Slippers are on the bottom shelf."

Yi could hardly hide his surprise as his mind consciously recognized the contradiction between the inside of the apartment and outside of the building. The overall design was reflective of its factory days, with its large windows, high wooden beams, and a large central room that once probably housed different pieces of equipment. Looking around, he could see hallways that led off towards smaller rooms, probably what used to be offices. But rather than the filthy remnants of old machinery and the smells he was expecting, the interior of the apartment had been remodeled and well decorated with the original brick walls cleaned of their smoky stains and lacquered for protection. Stylish furniture of a unique yet modern style, different from what Yi was used to, decorated the apartment. Paintings of an anonymous artist hung on the wall. The floors, no longer grimy as one would expect from a factory, shone with a thin wax coating. The overall feeling of the apartment reminded Yi of some of his father's richer friends, albeit with strange furniture and an odd, personal style.

"Not what you were expecting, huh?" Qiang nudged Yi, laughing. "I told you before, I have high standards, and I like to live a good life. Welcome to my humble home."

A tall muscular man in his late 30s with a slight limp walked out of what Yi assumed to be the kitchen, wearing a navy apron. "Welcome," he said, holding out his arm. "I am Zhuang, Qiang's partner. Welcome to our home."

"This is a really lovely place," Ling said, interrupting Yi's awe. "Thank you for having us."

From another room, a fat long-haired calico cat came out,

trotting towards the guests and sniffing curiously. "Kitty," gasped Hanbing, struggling out of Yi's arms to play with the cat.

"That's Mew Mew," chuckled Zhuang, as Hanbing started petting the cat. "Don't worry, she's super friendly. She is basically our spoiled daughter."

"Hanbing has never pet a cat before," said Yi. It was true. Animals were a luxury item that few could afford, and excluding the diseased strays that roamed poorer neighborhoods, an uncommon sight in the city.

"Why don't you let her play with the cat, then. Her toys are in the box next to the sofa," said Qiang, smiling, "and I'll take you to our table. Zhuang has been cooking all afternoon for us."

As Ling followed Hanbing and Mew Mew, Qiang led Yi into the dining room next to a rather large rooftop balcony. Outside, Yi could see there was a sizable garden with a variety of plants and vegetables. A wooden table sat in the center of the room. In the corner was a metal cage inside which sat a gray bird on a perch.

"I thought about us eating outside," interrupted Qiang, watching Yi, "but I think the air pollution is a little higher than normal, and it lacks privacy."

"You guys grow your own vegetables?" asked Yi, surprised.

"Zhuang does. He used to be in the People's Army, so he is used to growing his own food. I can't really take credit for most of the work in the house."

"What's with the bird?" asked Yi. "You seem to have a lot of animals here."

"Just two, unless you count my boyfriend," Zhuang's cheerful voice interrupted them as he walked in carrying a tray of assorted dishes. "He is a falcon; I rescued him." He began laying out the dishes on the table. "We should start eating. Before the food gets cold."

Like gracious hosts, Zhuang and Qiang had prepared more food than could be eaten. The four adults and one child sat around the table and began eating the different home-cooked dishes. Yi was surprised at how much effort had been put into the cooking. Looking across the table, he could see bok choy, eggplant, and even some meat dishes spread in front of them. As he used his chopsticks and slowly brought pieces of different food to his mouth, he soon found himself pleasantly surprised. The taste was light but flavorful, the vegetables crisp, and the meat fresh. He wasn't going to admit it, but he had assumed that the food—coming from the district they were visiting and the fact it was cooked by two men who were not professional chefs—was going to be terrible, if not inedible. He had even had Ling prepare an extra dinner in case they needed it once they went home.

"This food is surprisingly delicious," said Yi. "I don't think I have ever tasted bok choy that is as crisp as this."

"That's what happens when you grow a lot of your own food. I was in the People's Army most of my adult life," Zhuang explained. "You have to learn how to take care of yourself so you can take care of the country. We used to help farmers out during the famine. That's where I learned how to farm and cook. There are many traditional ways to grow vegetables that are no longer practiced, and I try to use some of those techniques on my little farm on the rooftop."

Yi wasn't surprised. Mandatory army service was required for most men in the PRCC, though some men, like him and Qiang, were excused due to social reasons. "How long were you in the army? Did you just do your mandatory service, or did you stay longer?"

"Oh, I was going to do it for life, but I was only in it about twelve years, before retiring."

"Why did you leave?" asked Ling curiously before suddenly feeling embarrassed for asking such a personal question.

"Knee injury, and both my parents passed away," Zhuang replied. He looked over at Ling and chuckled at his embarrassed blush. "Don't worry, you can ask me anything. My mother passed away from illness when I was young, and when my father passed away because of old age, I decided to retire. Plus, my leg got injured during a training in my tenth year of service so I was unfortunately limited on what I could do for our motherland. When I learned that my father passed, I retired to take care of the farm, but there wasn't much left. I still own the land though. That's actually how I found You'sun over there," he added, pointing at the falcon in the cage. "My family lived in the mountains up north, and on my way home, I found him pushed out of the nest. When some birds of prey have two chicks, sometimes the parents or the sibling will try to get rid of the weaker one, especially if they both can't get enough to food to survive. His wing is permanently damaged from the fall, so he can't fly. I guess I related to that because of my leg. So…I kept him, slowly raised him, and now he lives with us. He and Mew Mew don't get along very well, but other than that, he seems happy. Sometimes I take him out to the garden, so he can walk around and enjoy the fresh air," he added, pointing outside.

"How did you two meet?" asked Ling curiously. Yi looked at him disapprovingly for asking such personal questions.

Zhuang chuckled, looking at Yi. "I told you, you can ask us anything." Turning to Qiang, he asked, "You want to explain, babe?"

"Nah, you go ahead." Qiang smiled, looking carefully at Yi.

Zhuang chuckled again. "I was retired from the People's Army, and I was crippled so there wasn't much I could do on a farm in the mountains. I decided to come to the city to find some work and maybe get married. The thing is, though, I always knew I liked men, which is probably why I stayed in the army for so long." He paused to laugh at his own personal joke. "I was living in the Capital as part of my military training, but after I retired, it was too expensive. I have always preferred cities, and Xincheng seemed liked a good choice for a restart in life, being a provincial capital and all. Like most migrant workers, I was trying to get a job in Shoushu, and I was doing random jobs, carrying furniture, basic service stuff, but it was hard because of my leg. Anyway, during one of these random jobs, I was assigned to help with some supply delivery and that's when I met Qiang, and it just sort of spun out from there." He smiled brightly as he glanced over at his partner. "I like to say Qiang is my reward for my hard years of service."

"What do you do now? For work?" asked Yi.

"I don't have a paying job. It's kind of hard to get one because of my injury," said Zhuang. "I am lucky enough that Qiang makes enough to support the both of us. He is quite good at what he does." He beamed proudly. "In the meantime, I take care of the animals, I grow our vegetables, I made a lot of this furniture—"

"Zhuang is really good at making and designing stuff," interrupted Qiang with a hint of nervousness in his voice.

"—I also try to paint a lot, keep the house clean, and I cook. It's important for me to help us build the comfortable life that we both want," Zhuang finished.

"Oh," said Yi, "you are the woman in the relationship. You are like his wife. His woman."

"Haha, except in the bedroom, then we take turns," Zhuang said, not missing a beat. "But—"

Qiang interrupted again, speaking calmly, as if he was prepared. "No, Yi, Zhuang is not my woman. And he is not my wife, definitely not my wife in the standards of this country. Zhuang and I are equals. Zhuang likes to do things like design furniture, paint, farm in our little balcony, and watch the animals, and I am lucky enough that I work in a job in which I can support the both of us. But Zhuang doesn't do any of this because I force him, or because he has to. He does this because this is the life we have chosen for ourselves."

Yi said nothing and decided to continue eating. "This food really is delicious," he said finally, ignoring the fact that everyone was staring at him. "I am really impressed by the texture and spices you used. Like I said earlier, this bok choy dish is amazing.

Thank you for inviting us over for dinner."

Zhuang smiled. "Thank you. There is plenty of food, so don't stop until you are full."

After dinner, Ling offered to help Zhuang clean up while Hanbing went to play with Mew Mew some more. Yi decided to take a look around the apartment. He was continuously surprised by how modern it looked and how much the apartment reflected the life of his friend. Instead of expensive paintings and ornaments displayed only to present wealth like most apartments he had visited, the walls were covered with personal pictures and Zhuang's paintings. As he looked at the pictures on the wall, he suddenly realized how respected Qiang was. Many of the people whom he had operated on were the wives of famous celebrities. There was even a picture of the two of them with someone who looked like an older Caucasian female, which was shocking given the low number of foreigners, and even lower number of foreigners of European ethnicity in the country.

As he walked from room to room, he noticed that everything, from furniture to decorations, had a very distinctive Qiang or Zhuang voice. He had never been in such an intimate and personal place before. There was nothing fictitious about how the apartment felt, and looking at all of this was starting to make him feel very uncomfortable. Yi decided to take a break and go onto the balcony to get some fresh air and a moment to think.

The garden on the balcony, like the rest of the house, was very well cared for. Yi had never grown a plant in his life, but he knew, based on the few farms he had visited with his father as a child, that this was something different. Most of the farms had been poorly run, based on the designs of government officials who knew nothing of farming and botany and yet adamantly believed that their ideas would yield the most crops. He marveled at the plant boxes, growing different leafy greens, and smelt the combination of compost mixed with polluted air drifting around him.

Walking towards the edge of the balcony, he looked out into the Shoushu District. He couldn't see much, but he could hear the sounds of stray dogs barking. Qiang came out, bringing a couple glasses of water and handing one to him. The two stood in silence, enjoying the atmosphere.

"You have a great place," Yi said finally. "Thank you for inviting me out. I am not going to lie, I was really uncomfortable coming here, and I am sorry if I made you uncomfortable."

"Like I said earlier, I can't take most of the credit," Qiang said, smiling. "Zhuang really has made this place our home. This garden, all the furniture, the redesign of this place—it's all Zhuang's handiwork."

"Yeah, he seems like a really great guy. Also, a really good cook."

Qiang smiled. "Thank you for saying that. I am glad you approve."

"I have never seen a house like this; this is really different. I am glad you can find your happiness here."

"You know, as a surgeon in this culture, your culture, it means I would not be accepted if I tried to move out of this district," Qiang began. "The unfairness and hypocrisy frustrate me at times, this knowledge that I cannot participate in the larger society like others. However, I cannot deny that living in Shoushu gives us a certain privacy and allows us to build a life we want. It gives us a freedom that the other parts of the city don't have. Here, Zhuang and I can live a life that would be harder to hide in another district, and we certainly would not have as large of a home." He smiled at Yi, who seemed baffled by his statement. "But of course, even here, we play it safe. Only a few people know that Zhuang and I aren't just roommates. We even keep a separate bedroom furnished in case people ever ask, or worse, visit. But the thing is, as this is Shoushu, no one will ever ask. The government doesn't care what happens here as long as I keep doing my job."

Yi said nothing, so Qiang continued. "As I have said, everything I have here is only possible because I am not allowed to participate in society like you can. But this struggle and annoyance has made us stronger and allowed us to grow and develop in our own ways. Zhuang makes our furniture because many stores outside of the district don't want to deal with my dirty money, so we take what we can buy and improve it. We only have this big place because it's in an area that no one wants to live in. It is like what I've always told you. We can only take what we have and make the best of it."

Yi thought for a moment but didn't know how to respond. "You know what," he said finally, sounding slightly frustrated. "That's what bugs me so much. Your house, your life, it's so happy. How can you be so happy?" He looked at Qiang who said nothing but smiled and shrugged. "You are excluded from society, and yet you are probably one of the only people I know who is actually…happy."

Qiang smiled. "Like I said, being excluded from society is what allows me, *us*, to have this life." He paused for a moment looking out at the haze over the city. "Actually, what I should be saying is happiness comes from within. If you want to be happy, then you have to choose to do the things that make you happy. I guess that is what I do; I live the life I want to live so I can be happy." Qiang paused, staring out over the city. "You and I are lucky, you know. We have much better lives than most of the citizens in this country. While we may be trapped by society, we should still understand our positions in life, and make the choices to live better, more honest lives. Because unlike most other people, we have some opportunity to do that, and we should take advantage of it."

The two men stood there for a moment, silent, listening to the sounds of the night. A man and woman were fighting in the distance, and some trash cans were being rummaged through by beggars or stray dogs. "I am sorry I haven't been visiting as much," Yi said finally in a rather quiet voice.

"You know, I have said this before, but I'm not the one you

should ever apologize to."

"I really have been trying to treat him better, especially since Hanbing came into our life," Yi said after comprehending Qiang's words. "I think having a child is exactly what we needed. Being a father has made me a better person. I think in the last three years we have both become happier. He is a good mother."

"I am glad to hear that." Qiang smiled as they both looked off the balcony into the distance.

Ling could hear Yi and Qiang walk out to the balcony garden as he and Zhuang washed the dishes and wrapped up the leftovers from dinner. Ling couldn't believe how spacious the kitchen was, and how modern the equipment was. Many of these cooking utensils he had never even used before, but he was familiar with them through discussions during the lady's meeting. Out of the corner of his eye, he could see Hanbing playing with Mew Mew in the living room, a toy mouse in her hand. He had been hesitant to leave her alone with the cat, but she seemed to be enjoying herself. Behind him, he felt Zhuang walk over, towel in hand, and began drying the dishes and putting them away.

"Thank you for helping with the dishes," Ling said quietly, trying to break the silence.

Zhang paused, looking slightly flabbergasted. "Why are you thanking me?" he asked, chuckling. "It is I who should be thanking you. This is my house, you are my guest, and yet here are you are offering to help me do my chores."

Ling felt himself turn red with embarrassment. "It's just that I've never seen a man in the kitchen at home before. It's a little weird for me."

"You are a man, and you are in a kitchen," Zhang said casually.

"No, I mean like a real man. Like you," Ling explained.

"Yi doesn't help out around the house?" Zhuang asked. He immediately regretted asking the question. He knew most relationships were different than his and Qiang's, and he knew Yi's and Ling's relationship was very different than theirs.

"He helps out with other stuff," Ling replied, taking no notice of Zhuang's sudden discomfort. "But he says that the kitchen is a woman's territory. He doesn't cook or clean."

Zhuang didn't know what to say. Reaching around Ling, he continued to grab dishes and put different things away properly in the cupboard.

"You are very different from any man I ever met," said Ling suddenly, awkwardly. "Not that I have met many men before. That would be inappropriate…" he added quickly.

"What do you mean by that?"

"You are just different. And your relationship with Qiang," Ling said, "it's also so different. That's why Yi asked you so many questions during dinner. He…I…we have just never seen two people like you and Qiang. I am sorry if he was being rude. He wasn't trying to be, but you guys are just so different." He felt obligated to defend his husband.

Zhuang chuckled again. "It is because we are equals. It's rare in this country, so it seems confusing. But I would like to think it is the right way to do things."

"I think you really freaked him out with the bedroom comment," Ling said, trying to make a joke. "The whole 'except in the bedroom' thing."

"Hey, if you don't mix things up a bit, it's gets really boring. Plus, it keeps the intimacy strong," Zhuang smiled. "I am really lucky that Qiang and I fit together well in almost every aspect of our relationship. That doesn't mean we aren't constantly working on it though."

"What do you mean, 'mix things up'?" asked Ling, confused.

Zhuang paused for a moment. He was hesitant to continue down this road. Given what he knew about Yi and Ling's relationship, he wasn't sure he wanted to develop a friendship with Ling. He would never tell Ling this, but Qiang's friendship with Yi had been the cause of a couple arguments. He just couldn't believe that someone as intelligent as his partner would hang out with someone as spoiled and insensitive as Yi. But, as Qiang always told him, there was an inner goodness to Yi, and he felt he could influence Yi to be a better person.

"Well, you know," Zhuang said finally, "even if you choose to keep the same role each time, which you know Qiang and I don't, you can still experiment with different positions. It makes the relationship more enjoyable for both parties."

"Different positions?"

"There are lots of ways to have sex," Zhuang said, smiling. "Plus, like I said, I think mixing things up increases intimacy."

"Intimacy?"

"Sex should be very intimate and pleasurable to both partners," Zhuang said casually as he wiped the counters. "If both parties aren't enjoying it equally, it just isn't very fair."

Ling didn't know what to say. He had his first two conversations about sex and relationships with two different people happen within the last year, and both seemed to imply he should be getting more than he was getting. It felt different this time as Qiang and Zhuang had the same organs still as him and Yi. He smiled awkwardly at Zhuang. "What else do you want me to help you out with?"

As it was getting cold out on the balcony, Yi and Qiang gathered their glasses and walked back into the apartment. They could hear Zhuang and Ling laughing and joking in the kitchen as they finished cleaning. Walking into the living room, they found Hanbing fast asleep on the couch with Mew Mew curled around her, snuggling her tightly.

"I told you she was a friendly cat, though if I didn't know better, I would guess they had grown up together," smiled Qiang, watching the two sleep. "I think you are going to have to come back again in the future. I know Hanbing will want to." He wrapped his arm around Yi in a friendly sort of way and grinned. "I am really glad you came over tonight. You know, despite what you say sometimes, I do consider you a close friend."

13.
OUR GLORIOUS CAPITAL REPRESENTS OUR GLORIOUS NATION

YI LOOKED OUT THE TRAIN window at the barren farmland outside as Hanbing slept on his lap. Across from him, Ling was curled up on two seats taking a nap. The family was taking a trip up to the Capital for an important annual political conference where Governor Wang would be speaking and Mengqin would be attending. As it was summer vacation, the Governor had invited everyone in the family so that this could be like a little family vacation. It was also going to be Hanbing's first time outside of Xincheng, and Yi was excited to show her a little more of the PRCC. He was relieved to have a private room on the train; it would be the last time for the next three days in which the three of them would get any privacy. This morning and the last few days had not gone well.

Since the arrival of Hanbing, Governor Wang had mostly ignored Ling's problem as it was obvious that Ling was a great mother towards Hanbing. Combined with no one at the Ladies' Meeting ever noticing, the issue had been mostly dropped in the family and just seen as another skeleton in the closet. A few days prior to the family leaving, Yi had received an angry phone call from his father.

"Are you planning to take Ling on this trip?" yelled the Governor over the phone.

"Umm, yes…" Yi answered, confused. "It is a family vacation, isn't it? What it this about?"

"You told me he was going to get his surgery. You have been telling me that since you two were engaged," the Governor said angrily. "You realize what will happen if someone catches on in the Capital. This is the Capital, not Xincheng. People there will notice, and they will care."

"No one in Xincheng other than our family knows about Ling's secret," Yi said calmly, not wanting to get into another fight over this issue. "Also, the only reason Ling didn't get his surgery in the last three years is because a child needs his mother. We have talked about this before, sir."

The Governor scoffed loudly. "I am just warning you. Our family's face and my honorable career is on the line. It's already embarrassing enough that my eldest son is nothing but a common teacher. If someone finds out Ling's secret, then—"

"No one is going to find out, sir," Yi replied calmly. "Ling has been going to meetings with other ladies for over a year now, and no one has ever suspected a thing. Ling will be a proper wife, worthy of being your daughter-in-law."

Yi, Ling, and Hanbing were waiting outside of the diplomatic part of the station for the Governor and Guihua to arrive, as Mengqin, Baihe, and Qinghuang were inside resting. Traveling with the Governor was always difficult due to security reasons, but it was still seen as customary and good for publicity if the elder son was standing there doing his filial duties of helping out his father. The three of them were dressed their best, with Yi and Hanbing wearing expensive suits and Ling dressed in a long, floral gown. Around them, security guards and a few reporters stood waiting to take a few pictures of the Governor arriving and boarding the train. After waiting around fifteen minutes, the Governor and Guihua arrived in a black limousine. Yi stepped forward, opening the door for his father and mother. Governor Wang stepped forward, waved at the reporters, and the family entered the station.

"Grandma, Grandma," Hanbing said excitedly and earnestly. "I love your dress, Grandma; you look so beautiful. I love those beautiful pink flowers; they are my favorite."

"Thank you, dear," Guihua smiled, reaching over to hug her grandchild.

Governor Wang smiled as a few reporters chuckled and took pictures and walked inside the private room where the rest of the family was waiting.

Once the reporters had left and the family was still in the exclusive waiting room, Governor Wang turned to Yi. "What was that about?" he whispered angrily, careful not to raise his voice too much as most of his security team was still around.

"What was what about?" Yi whispered back.

"Your son, my grandson, just complimented Guihua on her dress, said he likes the flowers," the Governor said angrily. "Do you know how embarrassing that was?"

"Excuse me?"

"What kind of a boy talks about dresses? See, I knew this would happen, you two are turning my first grandchild into a wimpy faggot."

"Hanbing said a dress looked nice," Yi said indifferently. "Please don't make a big deal out of this."

"You don't see Qinghuang complimenting Guihua on her clothes," scoffed the Governor. "I don't think he ever notices things like dresses."

"That's because Qinghuang has no manners," shrugged Yi. "Hanbing, on the other hand, has manners. He knows it is polite to compliment a lady. Perhaps you should be talking to Mengqin on how to raise his son to be polite."

The Governor scowled trying to think of what to say, but his assistant, Xiaoming, standing behind him, interrupted in Yi's defense before he could speak. "I wouldn't overthink it, sir. All the reporters thought it was super cute. It humanizes your family, sir. Yi is right; Hanbing was just being polite."

"No one asked for your opinion," the Governor snapped. "That being said, if the reporters liked it, then make sure they publicize it. I want everyone to know what a great family man I am. In fact, now that I think about it maybe, Hanbing and I should take a couple more pictures together. That will look good for the front page."

"Yes, sir," replied Xiaoming.

Yi looked in from the train window and watched Ling sleep, thinking back to an uncomfortable moment a few nights ago. They were in bed, and Yi was penetrating him from behind. Yi was really enjoying it, and Ling was breathing hard, his face buried in the pillow. Suddenly, Ling moaned something under his breath.

"What?" asked Yi, confused. Ling had never spoken before when they did stuff like this.

"Kiss me, bite me," moaned Ling. "Kiss me, bite me on my shoulder. Push it in me harder. Use me in all the ways you please."

"What?" asked Yi, shocked. He pulled himself out. "You want me to kiss you?"

Ling flinched as he heard the disgust in Yi's voice. "Not on the lips, like on my neck or something," Ling said quickly. "But I thought maybe we could do things a little differently? Make things a little more, you know, intimate." He turned over on his back, careful to cover himself, while looking at Yi with pleading eyes.

"Did Fenghuang put you up to this?" asked Yi suspiciously, backing away. "Is this what you talk about when—"

"No, no," Ling interrupted nervously. "We don't talk about personal lives. I heard about it when…" He paused for a second, he was never good at thinking on his feet. "When some of the ladies were talking, and I just thought, you know, we should mix things up a little. Make things a little different."

Yi didn't appear to believe him. "A group of high-class ladies would never talk about stuff in the bedroom," he said questionably.

"That's what Meigui told us," Ling replied quickly. "I know it was wrong. I am just trying to add a little spice, you know. Try out new things?"

"I like things how they are, thank you very much," Yi said with finality, getting out of bed.

"Where are you going?" asked Ling. "Don't you want to finish?"

"Not in the mood anymore," Yi replied, sounding annoyed. "I am going to use the bathroom; you go to sleep."

As Yi watched Ling sleep, he realized that he was glad they were leaving Xincheng for a few days. Perhaps if Ling saw how proper people acted in the city, he would develop a better connection with the lady group, and then perhaps he would be more willing to hang out with those who were more suitable for him. He wasn't feeling comfortable with how much Ling was changing since Fenghuang came into Ling's life.

Hanbing twitched in his lap, bringing Yi back to the present. Looking at his cellphone, he noticed that there were about two hours left on the train ride. Perhaps he too should get some rest before they arrived. Patting Hanbing on the head, he noted how handsome she looked dressed in a suit and how good Ling looked in a dress. Laughing silently at the irony of their life, he took another look out the window before drifting off for a short nap.

The Capital of the People's Republic of Central China was the largest city in the country and yet was one of the least understood cities in the world. Its modernity compared to the rest of the country made it the pride of the nation. Built upon the ashes of a previous great city that was destroyed during the Civil War, it was located downstream on the Yangtze River from Xincheng. Near the city was once an infamous hydroelectric dam, one of the largest in the world, that was supposed to provide surplus amount of energy, but instead had a much more detrimental effect of destroying the biodiversity of the river, flooding out ancient cities, and never managing to provide as much energy as promised. Though the dam was no longer used as anything more than a tourist spot, it served as a reminder of the old country, both of its glory and its problems, which still affected the people in the city today.

The citizens of the Capital were especially proud to live there, as it meant they survived through a difficult patriotic vetting process and were selectively chosen to inhabit its greatness. Everything in the Capital represented the best the nation had to offer. It was also the only city in the country that allowed non-PRCC citizens to work and visit; the government and its peoples worked hard to present a worldview that was inaccurate to the reality of the rest of the country. Buildings and streets were kept spotlessly clean, trees carefully manicured, and storefronts fully stocked even in times of famine, as it was more important to display a perfect image than an accurate one. Even the citizens, at least the ones who walked about in public, had to be perfect representations of mankind and ideal beauty. The nan-nu of the city were perfectly designed, with proportional body shapes sculpted by the best surgeons, accentuating their beauty and femininity, while the men, whether through natural or artificial means, all had muscular bodies, with strong pectoral muscles, iron thighs, and just the right amount of bulge to stress their virility and masculinity. No matter the gender, their porcelain faces were always perfectly symmetrical with each hair flawlessly styled to keep any strays from falling out of place.

Yi had come here often as a child, mostly for grand political conferences, which his father saw as future training. He had always found the Capital to be an odd place. Everyone was so formal, so polite, and dressed in a specific style. As a child, he had found it rather disconcerting that everyone would choose to make almost exactly the same choices. It wasn't until he was older that he understood that they had no choice.

"Are you sure you don't want to come with us?" the Governor asked in the lobby of Golden Surplus Galore, the best hotel in the city, after they had arrived and the women were upstairs unpacking. "You know, despite not being a member of our esteemed government, I can bring you to the conference as a guest."

"No, he would rather spend the day with the ladies," Mengqin said. "Let him go have fun with the girls. It's not like he has a future here."

Yi ignored him, speaking directly to the Governor. "I want to introduce my son to the Capital, help him really understand our great nation and its importance. I remember the many trips you took me on as a child, and I really valued that time we spent alone together. I want to give my son the same experiences so he to can be a wise future leader." He looked directly at Mengqin but continued talking to the Governor. "I know you didn't have the same amount of time and commitment with Mengqin, and I want to make sure that I give Hanbing that opportunity, to make sure he turns out to be a better man."

The Governor gave a slight smile, enjoying the flattery. "I suppose that is important. I am glad to hear that our trips had such a strong impact on your life. Now that I think about it, someone should keep the women and children safe. You don't really know what kind of trouble women can get into in a large city when they are alone, and I suppose family is more trust-worthy than a bodyguard. However, I would like you to attend at least one event. I don't want you teaching forever. If you really valued those trips, then you know what I want from you."

"Yes, sir," Yi replied. His corner lip smirked so that only Mengqin could see. "I will attend at least one event, and I will make you proud."

The Governor had organized a driver to take the family around while he and Mengqin attended the conference, making things easier for the rest of the family. As the trip was short, the family had decided to pack the three days with as much as possible, giving the children a trip of a lifetime and educating them with a better understanding of their glorious nation. After leaving the hotel, the driver took them around the city, pointing out the important areas of business and politics. They drove by the parliament building, where Yi explained the basic politics to the two children who showed little interest due to age. They were, however, excited to learn that's where their grandfather, father, and uncle were working.

They drove through the embassy area, located on the edge of the Yangtze River that flowed through the city, where Yi pointed out the few embassies of nations that still held diplomatic relations with the PRCC. He wondered for a brief moment what it would be like to see another country and realized how little he knew about the larger world outside of his city. Even as a university student, when studying international relations, there was never a huge focus about understanding the other countries in the world. The children gawked out the window as they noticed people with different colored hair and skin. They were especially surprised to see blonde hair and even darker skin tones.

The next morning, the family went to the tomb of great leader Qin Jiaban, father and eternal president of the country. Looking at his embalmed body resting under the giant mausoleum, they taught the children the proper ways to pay respect to great leaders of the country. Yi taught the children the history of the nation and how the wrongdoings of other countries had destroyed them and all the detriments that had been imposed on to their great people. Visiting the National Museum afterwards only continued to engrain the history into the children's minds, to remind them of the glory of their nation and how they overcame the most difficult struggles.

Late that afternoon, the Governor took the children behind the scenes to the offices of major political leaders and taught them about the importance of patriotism, loyalty, and filial piety.

Yi even participated in a few political events that evening to make his father happy and annoy his brother.

Soon after, Baihe and Ling took the children shopping, buying the latest fashions for themselves and the ladies back home. Shopping in the embassy area allowed them to see foreign fashions and buy rare imported goods not seen in the rest of the country. They even had the opportunity to interact with a few foreign biological ladies, who they had their children take pictures with to show off back home. The children, meanwhile, were amazed at the toy store, which offered brands and games they had never seen before.

Baihe, Guihua, Yi, Ling, and the two children decided to spend their last day in the Capital in the PRCC Zoo and Aquarium. It was the only legal one in the country and would be fun for the children. Yi knew how much Hanbing liked animals, while Qinghuang had never seen many animals in the first place. Together, the group of them walked through the cement cages filled with different exotic species, many of which were now extinct in the country due to unstainable practices and environmental disasters. The animals, malnourished from years of tourists feeding them junk food despite it being against the rules, looked dreary lying there in their cement compounds, with only a few sticks for decoration, and a feeding station. However, the family enjoyed seeing creatures they had never seen before, not knowing any better, nor giving much thought to the animals' circumstances. The children enjoyed seeing the large mammals, flabbergasted by their size. After feeding some waterfowl in the zoo's central pond, something the children especially enjoyed and the adults enjoyed taking pictures of, the family set off for the small aquarium in the back of the park.

Walking through the dark, dimly lit halls, Yi was amazed at how much lived underwater. He had never seen the ocean before, and besides the Yangtze River that flowed through Xincheng, which didn't have much life left in it, he hadn't seen another large body of water. He had never seen so many different species of fish before and felt foolish for assuming all fish were just variations of silver and gray. As they walked through its halls, looking at the different tanks, Yi came to the realization that he had never really thought about how biologically diverse the world was, and he had never thought about what nature actually looked like outside of a textbook. Standing in the dim hall, he suddenly stopped as he became acutely aware of how little about the world he knew. Not just about nature, but the world outside of Xincheng. It made him think back to some of his conversations he had with Teacher Long, and how he never actually thought about things more than what he was taught. He always spoke as if he was an expert in every topic, and he understood the reasons behind every decision, but did he? He didn't understand why seeing a few fish was causing him this identity crisis, but it was.

"What's this? What's this?" called Hanbing towards her father, looking in a column shaped tank filled with peculiar sea creatures. "Baba, what's this?"

Yi quickly walked over, peering into the tank. Inside were a few small gray, skeletal creatures with oddly large bellies and long noses, floating vertically, with their tails wrapped around thin strands of seaweed. They had tiny fins, which flapped as they hovered in the water. They didn't look like any animal he had ever seen before.

The aquarium guide, who had heard Hanbing calling, came walking over from behind them. "Good eye, young man," he said peering in the tank with them. "That is one of our most special collections. A very rare collection indeed. These peculiar looking creatures are called seahorses."

"I didn't know that there were horses in the sea," said Hanbing, looking perplexed. "I have only seen normal horses, donkeys, and zebras before. I just saw zebras in the zoo. They are like horses, but with stripes!"

The guide chuckled. "Seahorses aren't related to horses, donkeys, or zebras. They are a type of fish." He pointed in the tank, "See their heads? They are shaped like horses, so we call them seahorses. Seahorses are very special, as you can tell, because they look very different from all other creatures in the ocean."

"Whoa," said Hanbing. "Baba, that's so cool."

"Yep," said the guide, smiling. "Want to learn something else that is cool about seahorses?"

"Okay," said Hanbing shyly, latching on to Yi's arms.

"With seahorses, unlike other animals, the father gives birth. You see the mother seahorse lays her eggs into the father's pouch, and then the father gives birth to the baby."

"Okay…" said Hanbing, not understanding the science.

"I think he is a little too young for this," said Yi sternly. "He is only four."

The guide continued, smilingly slightly, and ignoring Yi. "Some foreign countries say the citizens of this country are like the seahorse because we are in a country in which men are providing babies. Some foreign countries say living here is the human equivalent of life among seahorses."

"Yep," Yi said, covering his child's ears, "he is definitely too young for this. Thank you for your time."

The aquarium guide, shrugged, smiled, and walked off, leaving Yi covering his child's ears while looking at seahorses.

14.

ALL CITIZENS MUST UNDERSTAND THEIR PROPER PLACE AND PROPER ROLES

YI SAT IN THE GOVERNOR'S living room watching Hanbing play with her cousin. The family had just finished celebrating Qinghuang's fourth Arrival Day. He could sense Mengqin's anger during dinner because Hanbing had received more presents than Qinghuang did from the grandparents on Hanbing's last Arrival celebration. However, the two children didn't seem to notice the rivalry and were currently enjoy playing with a military themed building set that Qinghuang received.

Ever since they were children, Yi and his brother had a rocky relationship. Having two children was rare in the PRCC due to the limit of eggs, and most families could barely afford having one child, let alone two. Yi still remembered the first time it was mentioned he would be getting a younger brother. It was one of his first memories.

"Daddy," he said one day to the Governor and Guihua when he was a little over two years old. He had just read a very exciting picture book about a boy and his dog. "Can I have a puppy?"

"A puppy," gasped the Governor. "Why would I want a flea-ridden mutt running around here?"

"Because I am lonely. Nobody plays with me." It was true. Yi was raised by multiple nannies, but none of them were very interested in playing with the child.

Guihua was more sympathetic. "Come on, sir," she said

gently to the Governor, taking a sip of her maotai. "Let him have some company. He needs someone to play with."

Because of that discussion, the Governor decided to get another child. It was a good decision, he thought. An alternative in case Yi was bad at education or if some accident were to befall him. An extra guarantee to maintain the family power in government.

However, despite any fears the Govenor may have had, Yi thrived in school and in many ways grew up to be the perfect heir to the government and the family's power. Therefore, being the elder son, the Governor spent what little attention he had for his children on Yi, treating Menqin as the unwanted spare. The brothers were also encouraged to be competitive with one another, which the Governor saw as important training for the future. Being older, and receiving more attention from his parents, Yi tended to do better than his younger brother. Indeed, nothing Mengqin did appeared to impress the Governor, causing more and more resentment between the two of them. When Yi decided not to enter governmental work, to the disappointment of the Governor, and instead become a teacher, Mengqin used it as his moment of glory and applied for a government position. However, lacking the natural talent and the confidence to do his job well, he soon found himself being shifted to smaller, unimportant positions, while Yi, although working in a lesser profession, appeared to excel at his job. Indeed, to Mengqin, it felt like Yi always took the moments of glory away from him. Yi even adopted a child before Mengqin, right after Mengqin announced it, which he took as more proof of his brother always sabotaging him.

In his heart, Yi had always hoped the closeness of their two children would bring him and his brother together, but Mengqin appeared to take his adoption of Hanbing as evidence of the final betrayal. However, despite their unpleasant history, he did not prevent the two cousins from getting close. The two brothers consciously maintained a cordial relationship in front of the children and hid the unspoken rivalry behind closed doors.

"Yi!" said the Governor, walking in the living room and looking angry. Behind him, Mengqin followed, smirking, and Yi knew immediately that there was something going on. "Your brother just informed me that Hanbing hasn't been going to preschool, and from the sound of it, isn't even going to be going. Yet Qinghuang, who is ten months younger, has been going to preschool. Are you planning to raise an idiot for my grandson? Is it not bad enough he is being raised by faggots?"

"I decided that it would be best for Hanbing if he continues his education at home," Yi said calmly, glaring at his brother. He immediately regretted letting that information slip to him. "We will send him directly to elementary school when he is six years old.

"Let him stay at home? Like a wife?" the Governor said angrily. "Why won't you let him go to school like a normal boy?"

There was a very obvious reason why they were holding Hanbing home for an additional two years. She was still too young to understand the complexities of her differences and still needed help every once in a while when using the bathroom. Not to mention a lot of the activities in preschool, especially when related to physical education, still involved teachers getting up close with the students. It just wasn't a risk worth taking. But as there was no way to tell the truth, Yi decided to dismiss the reason. "That is not important. What is important is that Hanbing is my child, and I don't want to send him to a preschool. Ling is a stay-at-home mother, and I prefer my child being raised by family and not by strangers."

"I could buy that excuse when Hanbing was a baby," the Governor scoffed. "I allowed it to slide when you chose not to hire a nanny or let Guihua here take care of your child, and your whole 'I want to do it myself' bullshit. But this is different. It's time to let the child go to school, meet other children his age, and end this codependency."

"It is not your decision," Yi said, standing his ground. "Han-bing is my child. I will decide what is best for him. Besides,

Hanbing already sees children his age weekly."

"See," the Governor said, practically yelling as Baihe and Ling came into the room to remove the children from the situation. "This is what happens what you let a couple of faggots raise children. They can't let them live and develop a normal life. They become overbearing and controlling."

"All Hanbing would be doing in preschool is learning to draw and color. By keeping him at home, I can make sure Hanbing is learning things like math, science, and language, so he is more competitive in the future," Yi said. "I want Hanbing to be the best in his class."

"I don't like it," the Governor said, grinding his teeth. "You will send Hanbing to preschool, and you will send him to the same preschool as Qinghuang. It's the best in city."

"It may be the best in the city for connections," scoffed Yi, "but it is certainly not the best for education. All Hanbing would be doing is drawing all day. If he is learning at home, at least he can learn educational stuff, like reading, writing, and math. I want my son to be smarter than the rest."

"Excuse me," yelled the Governor. "How dare you insult your alumnus. Every man in the family has attended that preschool, and Hanbing will too. My word is final."

"Now, now," said Guihua running over hugging her husband and rubbing him on the chest, "let's not fight anymore. Remember what the doctor said about your health? About not raising your voice? I'll talk to our son, maybe I can reason with him." She turned to Yi. "Let's talk, son. Follow me. We'll talk in my private room."

Yi followed Guihua into her private room and sat down on one of the pillows thrown on the floor. She closed the doors behind her and locked them. From her shelf, she took out her hormone pills, opened a bottle of baijiu, and drank them down. Then to his surprise, she opened a box and took out some silk clothing, turning the music on her cellphone and putting it next to the teddy bear on the shelf, and began dancing tossing her clothing around sporadically yet precisely. Yi stared at her confused.

"Your father records everything that happens in this room. He thinks I don't know," Guihua whispered, sitting down next to her son. "I pretend I am dancing to cover up all the cameras, and the music will hide our conversation. This way when he looks at the recordings later, he won't be able to hear us." She paused, looking around nervously. "We only have a few minutes before security comes up and wonders what is really going on. Let's make this fast. I know."

"Wait? What? What's going on?" Yi asked, now extremely confused. "What do you know?"

"I know why you won't let Hanbing start preschool," Guihua said, sighing. "I have known for a while, and I kept hoping you would talk to me…but you haven't, so let's just get it out there."

"Umm…yeah, you know because I just explained that I don't want Hanbing to start preschool because I want to teach him for a few more years, and—"

"Look!" interrupted Guihua. "We don't have much time. Security is going to wonder why the cameras are covered and why I am blasting music." She paused, taking a deep breath and another swig of baijiu. "I am just going to get straight to the point. I have known for a few years now. I know that Hanbing is a girl."

Yi's confusion turned to shock. His immediate reaction was wondering what sort of trap this was. "I don't know what you mean," he said finally.

"You are my son, and I understand why you are keeping this a secret, given the circumstances, but you don't have to, you know… You can trust me," Guihua pleaded.

Yi said nothing, looking at the tatami floor in front of him.

Guihua, realizing there was no way to get her son to talk naturally, continued, "I've known since she was a baby, maybe right after her first Arrival Day celebration. One day she was at our apartment and…" She looked at him again, before continuing. "I know what you're thinking, but it isn't Ling's fault. Ling fell asleep, and Hanbing needed a diaper change, and rather than wake Ling up, I just decided to do it. When I took off her pants, I saw. I knew. It all made sense about why you were doing what you were doing."

Yi said continued standing there in silence. Guihua leaned against him, rubbing his back. "I kept hoping you would tell me. Tell your mother. I understand why you didn't. But there was never a way to bring it up."

Yi took a deep breath. "Does Father know?"

"If he knew," said Guihua, "would Hanbing still be around? Would we be talking privately in this room?" She held him close. "I understand why you kept this a secret. But I have been keeping this secret for a long time also, and I wish you would trust me."

Yi, not knowing what to say, just sat there, contemplating, listening to the patriotic pop music in the background.

"Does Hanbing know?" asked Guihua, breaking his thoughts.

"Does Hanbing know what?"

"Does Hanbing know that she is not a boy?" Guihua asked, as if this was the most obvious question. "Does Hanbing know she is different from the other boys out there?"

Yi took another deep breath before blurting everything out in one breath. "Hanbing does not know she is a girl. She thinks she is a boy because we tell her she is a boy. She does not know the difference between boys and girls yet. She can sort of see some differences between a man and woman based on what they do. Like she believes that boys have short hair and girls have long hair, and that boys work and girls clean. Simple stuff like that. But other than that, no. Hanbing does not know she is different and actually female."

"Oh." Guihua paused for a moment, thinking about words clearly before talking super fast. "In that case, what do you plan to do? Just raise her as a boy? How did you get her in the first place? She is clearly not your child; you can't create an X chromosome."

"Ling found her," Yi said, breathing heavily. He was unsure how he felt about this whole situation unfolding, and how much he was willing to share with Guihua, but he felt a huge weight lift off his shoulders as he spoke. "Ling found her in the river one day and took her home. When we realized she was a girl, we searched but couldn't find any information on the genetic database of where she came from and who her biological parents were, so we decided to keep her." He stopped, realizing how fast he was talking and took another deep breath before continuing. "We have decided the best thing right now for her is to raise her as a boy. We don't want to risk anyone, especially father, figuring out she is a girl. Therefore, we will continue to raise her as a boy."

Guihua thought for a moment. "How long do you think you can keep this façade up?"

"We will keep it up as long as it is necessary. I love Hanbing, and I promised Ling I would keep her safe for as long as I can."

"You realize it's not that easy."

"What do you mean?"

Guihua sighed. "I am sure you realized this by now, but as she is not a boy, sooner or later she will figure out she is different. What will you do when she realizes that and is angry at you for hiding such an important part of her identity from her?"

Yi looked at her, confounded and upset. "Hanbing is my child. I will protect her for as long as I live. I will keep her safe. I don't think you understand what I am willing to do for her."

"Actually, I do," Guihua took another swig of baijiu, standing up and turning to look at the wall. "I see the way you look at me, Yi, and I know you don't understand it. I may not be what you wanted, but I am your mother. Of course, I understand. I would do the same for you. I would do the same for your brother." Tears flowed from her eyes. "I love you as much as you love Hanbing. I have always loved you as much as a mother could. I am just sorry I am not the person you wanted me to be." Taking a final swig of her drink, she wiped her tears. "I just don't want you to ever forget. I will always be here for you. Just like I know you will always be there for Hanbing."

Yi felt awkward and somewhat guilty. He took another breath. "I know it's not your fault, Mother. I love you, too." Saying those words felt uncomfortable, but he smiled meekly before continuing. "I will try to show that better in the future. I appreciate everything you have done for me."

Suddenly, there was a knock on the door. "Governess," came a concerned voice on the other side, "Governess, are you alright?"

Guihua gave Yi a final hug and look at him directly in eyes before kissing him on the cheek and opening the door. "Yes, I am. Just talking to my son and showing him the new dance I recently learned. He is really proud of me for taking all these dancing courses. He says it's good for me to exercise and keep fit. Is there a problem?"

The Head of Security stuck his head in, staring at the mess and Yi, checking things out. "Just haven't heard from you in a while. Your husband wanted to make sure everything was okay."

Guihua smiled. "Isn't that sweet of him? He knows I came to my room to speak to his son. You can let him know that I was showing his son the dances I have been practicing recently. Tell him that I just started talking to him about sending his grandson to preschool. Trying to understand better why he wouldn't listen to his father and explaining to him why he should. Reminding him the importance of filial piety." She turned to Yi and winked. "We decided to listen to some music to cheer things up a little, and like I said, I wanted to show his son the dances I have been learning. But you can let my husband know that I appreciate him caring, and we will be out in a moment."

"I'll let him know, Governess," said the Head of Security before walking off.

"Isn't he sweet?" said Guihua to Yi loudly, smiling falsely. She gave him another big hug. "You are my son, and I am so proud of you. I will always love you no matter what you do." She walked out of the room heading back to the living room. "Come along now, we need to get back to your father."

TWO
YEARS
LATER

15.

CHILDREN MUST BE REMINDED THAT MEN AND WOMEN ARE DIFFERENT

LING STOOD OUTSIDE OF XINCHENG #1 Elementary School waiting to pick up Hanbing. The October weather was brisk, and he pulled his woolen shawl closer to him as his long hair flowed in the wind. Behind him, he could see Baihe waiting impatiently in the car with Qinghuang. Though Xincheng #1 Elementary School was only a fifteen- to twenty-minute walk from their apartment, the Governor had demanded that both children be picked up for their safety, despite the driving time being thirty to forty minutes due to traffic. Despite usually hating the car rides, today Ling was grateful. The cold weather had come unusually early this year, bringing forth the start of extreme pollution caused by coal heating. He couldn't believe how fast time had gone; Hanbing was already entering first grade and thankfully transitioning well, making lots of friends and doing well in her classes.

Hanbing walked slowly out of the school alone, kicking the gravel with her tiny feet, immediately catching Ling's attention. Shocked not to see her with her best friend, Nan Zihan, he rushed over to see what was wrong, "Hi, honey, what's wrong?" When she didn't reply, he asked her, "Where is Nan Zihan today? Why aren't you guys walking out together?"

"We got in a fight," Hanbing said sadly. "We didn't want to play the same games, and he got mad at me."

"Oh no," Ling said with concern. "I am sorry to hear that,

sweetie."

Hanbing didn't speak for a moment, silently walking to the car holding her mother's hand. As they reached the car, Hanbing looked at her mother, worried. "Mama, am I weird? I think I am different from my classmates. Very different."

Ling froze, shocked, thinking about how to reply. Finally, he said with false cheerfulness, "No, you aren't different, but why don't we talk about this when we get home."

Though Baihe and Ling lived in separate directions, the Governor demanded they only take one car so the children could play together. Baihe lived closer to the school than Ling did, but the driver always took Ling home first, as Hanbing was the son of Yi, the eldest son.

Qinghuang and Hanbing, thankfully, had a better relationship than their parents did. Baihe and Ling usually pretended to enjoy each other's company in front of the children, though never spoke much past small talk. Today, Ling sat quietly, thinking about his conversation just a few minutes ago with Hanbing. He needed answers, and he wanted them fast.

Going against the Governor's wishes, Yi had chosen not to send Hanbing to preschool and kindergarten. Instead, Hanbing had learned from a curriculum created by Yi covering the basic skills she needed know concerning basic math, science, and language. Ling was especially ecstatic to continue having time to spend with Hanbing and thoroughly enjoyed teaching her. Hanbing took to the material well and quickly excelled at learning the materials her parents had provided. Even the Governor, once he realized that Hanbing was learning much more than she would at a preschool or kindergarten, stopped complaining, despite his continual insistence that the school he had chosen was the best in the province.

However, there was no avoiding elementary school and beyond. Yi had no interest in homeschooling. By not using gender specific words, like boy and girl, they had trained Hanbing to fit into school without allowing her to know that she was different. Using a custom-made funnel, they had taught her to pee standing up. By teaching her privacy and respect for her body, they had made it clear that no other person should ever see her naked, under any circumstances. Exploiting cultural norms, they taught her not to ask questions about other people's bodies or judge how they look. They had taught her to develop an interest in things they felt boys her age would be drawn to: military, fighting, cars, and sports. Most importantly, thanks to Yi's social background and his father, even if someone did suspect the impossible or found her odd, it would never be brought up because no one would want to question the Governor's eldest grandchild. Therefore, after all this teaching and training, it baffled Ling that Hanbing would think she was weird or different from her classmates, as he and Yi had worked so hard to make sure that she would not stick out from the rest of her classmates.

Ling decided to wait patiently until Hanbing was finished with her afternoon snack of milk and fresh fruit before continuing the conversation. "Tell me, Hanbing," he said nonchalantly as he took the plates back into the kitchen, "why do you think you are weird? How are you different from your classmates?"

Hanbing looked up from the box of construction toys she was building on the living room floor. "I don't know," she said quietly. "I just know I am."

"What do you mean by that, sweetie?" Ling asked, standing in the doorway, watching his child play.

Hanbing thought for a second, "We like different things. I like being clean, and they like being dirty. Also, I am smarter than them. I study hard, and all they like to do is play.

"The reason you are smarter is because we taught you a lot when you were younger, sweetie," said Ling calmly. "That doesn't make you different. You like being clean is because you know better. You know being dirty is not healthy or hygienic." He sat down next to her. "Besides, everybody thinks they are weird, but nobody really is."

"Also, I don't really like the toys they like. I don't really like games they like to play. I just like different things."

"Such as?" asked Ling patiently. "What do you like that they don't?"

"I don't know. I just know that we don't like the same things. I am just weird. That's all," said Hanbing, crossing her arms angrily. "I know I am weird. I know I am different. You don't understand. You just don't get it."

"Sweetie, you aren't weird," Ling said. "You are exactly like everyone else, and I love you for that. You are as normal as normal can be."

"Also…." Hanbing paused, looking embarrassed. "Some of the other boys…when they go pee…they pull down their pants…they don't use a funnel thingy like I do." Hanbing turned super red and giggled. "Also, their privates look different than my privates."

Ling froze, frowning. He raised his voice to enough to let her know he was angry. "What did I tell you about your privates, Hanbing? And what did I tell you about looking at other people's privates?"

Hanbing gulped, knowing she that was in trouble. "That they are private, and I must never show mine or look at others."

"Exactly." Ling raised his voice enough to sound angry and hide the escalating fear building inside him. "Please explain to me, Hanbing, why are you looking at other people's privates and seeing if they are different?"

"It was an accident," Hanbing said in a small voice. "I'm sorry."

"I don't want to you to ever look at other people's privates again. Do you understand me?" said Ling, reaching over and hugging his child. "Privates are private and should never be looked at."

"Okay," said Hanbing, as she relaxed into Ling. "But why are their privates different?" she asked innocently.

Ling thought on his feet before speaking in an awkward, but gentle, baby voice. "Well, sweetie, it's just like our faces. Everybody's face is different. Trust me, your privates are the same as everyone else. Just slightly different." He spoke more seriously again, looking at Hanbing directly in the eyes, "However, it is very wrong, Hanbing, to look at people's privates, just like it's very wrong to ever let anyone see yours. I don't want to hear about this ever happening again. Your father will be very mad when I tell him."

"Don't tell Baba. Please," said Hanbing nervously. "I promise I won't do it again."

"I won't this time. But I need you to promise me that this will never happen again," Ling said sternly.

Yi came home about thirty minutes later as Hanbing was watching TV and Ling was finishing cooking. "How was your day?" he asked as he walked in the door, tossed keys on the shelf and picked up his daughter.

Ling walked out of the kitchen and took a deep breath. He had been thinking about his talk with Hanbing all afternoon. "It was good. Listen, there is something I need to do tonight. Can you watch Hanbing? Dinner is finished and all you have to do is serve it. I will back in a couple of hours." Without waiting for a reply, he grabbed his keys, purse, and cellphone, pulled on his jacket, and swiftly walked out the door before Yi could say anything.

Qiang was finishing his paperwork, preparing to go home, when he heard a knock on the door. He groaned. All he wanted to do was go home and see Zhuang. It had been a busy day. His reputation for building the most natural looking and beautiful artificial vaginas had only improved over the last few years, and it was said he was the best outside of the Capital. October was seen as the most auspicious time to marry, so he had been quite busy for the last few months, not only with new sex changes, but also altering and fixing the finished work of other doctors.

He opened the door, surprised to see who was on the other side. "Ling," he said in shock. "What are doing here?"

"I needed to talk to someone. Immediately," Ling said nervously, as his eyes darted around the clinic. "It's about Hanbing. Can I come in?"

"Sure." Qiang looked out in the hallway. "Umm…where is Hanbing? Is Yi bringing her in?"

"Actually," said Ling awkwardly, as he sat down on the examination table. "I came alone. I needed to talk to someone about some stuff. I have some questions I wanted to ask. Maybe you can help me?"

"Okay?" asked Qiang, closing the door behind him and locking it. "What do you want to talk about?"

"Today…" began Ling, "after school, Hanbing asked me if she was different from the rest of the children. She told me she thought she was weird."

"I don't see the problem. All children think they are weird. Peer pressure is difficult, even when you are at that age. I am sure you remember from your childhood."

"Yes, that's what I told her," he paused for a moment. "But then, she told me more. For example, she noticed in the bathroom that some people, you know, have something down there that she doesn't."

Qiang tried not to chuckle. "Hanbing doesn't know the difference between men and women still, huh?"

"We can't exactly tell her. I mean we have given her a basic answer, like girls have long hair, and boys have short hair," Ling said, feeling exasperated. "But I just worry now about what we are doing. We are not being honest with her. I mean, what effects will this have on her life? Will she be, like, psychologically damaged?"

"She lives here in this country. Of course, she will be psychologically damaged," Qiang replied with a controlled straight face. "Don't worry. That's why she'll have no problem fitting in."

"I don't think you understand how serious this is," Ling said, visibly freaking out a little. "First, she tells me she feels different. Then she notices she is different. Who knows what will happen next? Sooner or later she is going to know. I mean, what are we doing here? Will this little experiment ever work?"

"First of all, relax," Qiang said calmly. "Look, the chances of your experiment of raising a girl as a boy never had much of a chance to succeed." He looked at Ling who appeared to want to interrupt. "But as we discussed that night six years ago…what choice did you have?"

"You could have raised her!" Ling said, hyperventilating. "You already live a secret gay life in Shoushu District, and as you often say, the government doesn't care about Shoushu. You could have kept her a secret."

"Putting aside that it would have been illegal for me to raise her, single unmarried people can't adopt children, and by law I am unmarried," Qiang said calmly, "I would never have been able to give her the quality of life you and Yi are able to provide for her. Besides, keeping her in a family who is well connected with the government is a form of protection. It means people are less likely to ask questions. I know you don't feel that way right now, but the decision we made the night you found her was not only the most viable solution, but it also happened to be the best situation. Unless, which I believe you guys vetoed that night, you wanted to try to smuggle her out of the country. Now take a deep breath and calm down."

Ling took a deep breath. "It was really difficult for me, you know. I still remember when my parents told me they were going to take me out of school, that I was going to learn to become a girl. It really affected me. What if this affects her in the same way it affected me?"

"Let's first get this straight, it's not really a fair situation to compare," Qiang said truthfully. "You aren't telling her you are going to do an invasive surgery to change her genitals. You are merely telling her the truth of who she really is. Secondly, of course it will affect her. Although it was necessary, you guys did lie to her. However, how she is affected by this lie, that is what you have control over. But Hanbing is a very well managed and bright child. I think she will be able to handle it."

Ling stood there staring at the pictures of doctored vaginas on the wall. "Okay. What happens now? Do we just continue this lie? I mean how much longer will we be continuing this lie?"

Qiang chuckled. "Even if she knows the truth, she will still have to hide who she is. Like I said, there is no other choice. Unless you want the government to take her and send her off to who knows where."

"What do we do when she starts noticing? She is going to start noticing more and more that she is different. I mean, at least physically. Sooner or later she is going to hit puberty, and that brings…differences?"

"Would you like me to turn her into a boy?" said Qiang shrugging. He laughed at Ling's horrified face. "Just joking, of course. But you still have a few years before puberty hits. That being said, sooner or later, you realize that you and Yi are going to have to tell her."

Ling paused, thinking. "It's not an easy conversation. We are basically admitting we have lied to her. That's not an easy conversation to have with a six-year-old."

"Who said you have to do it now?"

"I am just sick of all these secrets. All the hiding. All I want is Hanbing to be herself and be happy. I am afraid the way we are raising her will lead to problems in the future."

"She is being herself, and she is happy. She is just being herself and happy under the circumstances. Like all of us are. We all have our secrets. We all need to change ourselves to some degree to fit into society. Everyone, even children, understand that," Qiang said simply. "Besides, you can never truly change who she is. Nature and nurture both take parts in developing a person. You can nurture her, but you can't change her nature."

"What do you mean by that?" asked Ling hesitantly.

"People are who they are," Qiang replied. "We can give them

new identities, raise them a certain way, and pretend we can mold them, but people aren't puppets that we can control. Hanbing is going to realize that he is actually a she, no matter how you try to hide it. All you can do is explain to her why you guys made the choices you did and support her as parents."

Yi was pacing around the living room when Ling came back to the apartment. "I put Hanbing to bed an hour ago," he said furiously, careful not to raise his voice to avoid waking their child. "Where the hell have you been?"

Ling took a deep breath, "Hanbing said something to me after school today that made me worried, and I figure you probably didn't want to talk to about it, so I went to see Qiang and asked for his opinion."

"You went to see Qiang?" Yi asked shocked. "Alone? How could you betray me like that and see another man?"

"Yes…" said Ling slowly, "I wanted to ask some questions about Hanbing."

"Hanbing isn't Qiang's child. Shouldn't you be talking to me?" Yi snapped. "And since when did you and Qiang start having alone time together?"

Ling took another deep breath. This wasn't how he wanted to approach the conversation. "This is the first time I have seen Qiang alone. The reason I went to see Qiang is I wanted another opinion before talking with you. I was going to talk to you about it when I got back."

"Okay. You are back now. Talk."

"Hanbing told me today she felt different from her other classmates…and then…." Ling looked down, averting his eyes. "Then she told me…she noticed that other children…had a… penis."

"Excuse me?" said Yi sharply.

"I didn't know what to do! Because I was panicking, I wanted to go talk to Qiang as I know she is growing up, and I wanted advice. She told me she is noticing different things and figuring things out. I wanted to know from Qiang that if perhaps we should be finding a way to raise her…differently."

"You are questioning the way we raise her?" asked Yi, raising his voice again. "We had this conversation on the first day we got her. We have this conversation like every two years. Why are you bringing this up again?"

"I am just afraid we are going to damage her psychologically. We aren't letting her be her natural self."

"She is a biological woman living in this country. She could be damaged way worse psychologically and physically," snapped Yi. "We had this talk on the first day we decided on the adoption. We have talked about this before. We both know what has to be done. It is what it is. I don't understand why you keep bringing it up!"

"I know," said Ling meekly, "I just think—"

"If you already know," Yi interrupted loudly, "then why are we talking about it?"

Before Ling could reply, a small voice spoke from the other side of the room, "Mama, Baba, why are you fighting?" said Hanbing, rubbing her eyes and yawning.

Ling ran over, picking her up and hugging her, "Oh sweetie, did we wake you up? Baba and I weren't fighting; we were just having a discussion." He looked over at Yi who nodded but said nothing.

"Is this about what I said today?" Hanbing said tearing up. "I am sorry, Mama, Baba. I am sorry I am weird."

Yi walked over, rubbing the short hair on her head. "No, honey, this is not anything that you did. Like your Mama said, we are just having a small talk. Why don't you get back to sleep, honey? I'll see you in the morning."

"Okay, good night, Baba. I love you," said Hanbing yawning as Ling carried her into her bedroom.

"I don't want you to think I am foolish," Yi said a few minutes later, lying in bed as Ling walked in from tucking Hanbing in. "I think about this a lot. About what we are doing. About how it affects Hanbing." He sighed as Ling crawled into bed and laid next to him. "I understand that we will eventually have to tell her the truth. But this is not the time." He surprised himself by reaching over and holding Ling's hand and slightly caressing it. "I do know, though, when time does come to tell her, we will do a good job, and we will do it together."

16.
STRAYS FROM SOCIETY MUST BE RE-EDUCATED TO SAVE THE COUNTRY

BAIHE, LING, AND THE REST of the ladies were standing around the apartment chatting, waiting for Meigui to arrive. It was unusual for her to be late, but none of them thought much of it. Mudan had just bought a new dress made of the finest silk, and everyone stood around admiring it. While Ling had been coming to these weekly get-togethers for many years now, he still felt like an outsider, though he was now excellent at hiding it. From the corner of his eye, he watched Fenghuang play with the other children in the other room. She looked somber today, and Ling thought to himself that he would ask about it once the meeting was over. Going against Yi's wishes, Ling still found himself connecting more with Fenghuang than any other person in the group, but he limited himself to seeing her outside of the group setting to only once every two to three months. Perhaps it was time to arrange another little tea party and catch up.

Ling was so busy thinking to himself that he didn't hear or see Meigui coming, looking absolutely furious. "Ladies," she snapped. "What are you all standing out here for? Quickly, let's go to the tearoom. Quickly, ladies."

The other ladies mumbled amongst themselves, wondering what was happening, as Ling followed suit walking into the tearoom and sitting down. Meigui sat down last and cleared her throat loudly. "I am sure you all noticed that Zhubao is not here with us here today."

The ladies whispered among themselves in hushed voices, before Shuilian asked quietly, "Where is Zhubao today? Is she sick? Should we send her a bouquet of flowers or a get-well card?"

"Zhubao is no longer a member of our group," Meigui said, sipping her tea. "And you are all forbidden to talk to her." She waited a moment for the ladies to talk among themselves before continuing. "It turns out our 'friend' Zhubao…" Meigui made sure everyone saw her exaggerated quotation marks, "has been secretly doing manly activities, like playing sports with her son for the last few years."

The ladies all gasped in horror. Hua'er made her usual exaggerated gesture, waving her hands in front of her face as she pretended to faint.

"That's the reaction I was looking for," smiled Meigui as she nodded towards Hua'er with approval. "Anyway, Zhubao is out, and to preserve the dignity and honor of our little group, you are never to speak with her again, and you are to never bring her back up. She is dead to us. Also, this goes to show if—"

"Excuse me," interrupted Ling timidly, raising his hand. Baihe glared at him, embarrassed. "How did you hear about this? What is going to happen to Zhubao?"

Meigui looked irritated. "I told you we are not to ever speak of her again. She is a traitor to our ways and is dead to us. But if you must know, I found out from her husband, who found out from her son. Apparently, he got mad at his mother and decided to do the right thing. He told his father that he and Zhubao have been sneaking off during the last few years to go play sports in the park. In fact, often they went right after these meetings," she scoffed loudly and looked around at the group. "As for what is going to happen to her? I am happy to report she is getting what she deserved. Zhubao is being sent to a Woman's Re-Education Training School where hopefully, this time, someone will train her how to be a proper lady, instead of the wannabe she is. Maybe this time she will actually learn to follow the honorable culture of a Chinese lady."

The other ladies giggled for an appropriate amount of time before Meigui cleared her throat and continued. "You ladies all remember from a few years back, we tried to help her. We tried to teach her the errors of her ways, but apparently, she never listened. Moving on, as I was saying. We are an exclusive and honorary group of ladies who not only want the best for our children but also to be the best, proper ladies for our husbands." She paused, looking at everyone around her seriously. "If any of you have any secrets that do not fit the ideal female ideology that we hold so dearly, then, say something now, so we can help you…or face the wrath and consequences."

The ladies mumbled to themselves, no one speaking out loud. Baihe looked over at Ling, staring at him directly, as if daring him to say something, before taking a sip of her tea, and looking back at Meigui.

"No one has anything to say?" Meigui said quietly. "Well then, I hope you are all as honorable as I think you ladies are. Let's drop this topic and move on to happier things, shall we?"

The rest of the meeting, although awkward and uncomfortable, went very well. Mudan continued the previous discussion of her new dress, and the ladies very happily spent the rest of the time pondering new fashion styles. More than usual, Ling had a hard time concentrating. He couldn't stop thinking about what would happen to Zhubao and if he should have done more in the past.

At the end of the meeting, as always, Ling waited for everyone to leave, before grabbing Hanbing and talking to Fenghuang. He couldn't help noticing that her usual simple makeup was smeared, as if she had been crying. "Hey," he began hesitantly. "Are you alright? You look a bit upset…"

Fenghuang smiled, unusually nervous instead of her usual cheerful self. "I am fine. Just trying to clean up and go."

"I see…" Feeling uncomfortable, Ling ventured a guess. He didn't realize that Zhubao and Fenghuang were close, but then again, it would be improper to talk about everyone's relationship to one another. "I heard about the news. Don't worry, I am sure everything will be fine."

Fenghuang gasped in shock. "How did you hear? Did Yi tell you?"

"No," replied Ling surprised. "Meigui just did. We spent the first half of the meeting talking about it."

"Oh no, Meigui knows," she said, tearing up and flustering. "Oh no, this is so very bad."

"Yeah," Ling replied solemnly. "Apparently, we are all banned from talking to Zhubao now. I guess, that is that."

"Oh, wait," Fenghuang awkwardly perked up. "You are talking about Zhubao…oh yeah…I heard about that. It's so sad, her son turning her in. I really hope the best for her…." She trailed off, as if thinking about something else.

"Wait, you weren't talking about Zhubao?" asked Ling, now thoroughly confused.

"No…" Fenghuang paused, holding back her tears, before leaping forward and hugging Ling within her arms, sobbing. "We…we…can't…we can't talk about it here…but…they took Long from me…they took…they took my husband. My husband is gone."

It was an awkward taxi ride to Fenghuang's apartment with neither of them saying anything. The silence was only broken by Ling texting Yi, informing him that he wasn't going to be back until later, and Hanbing's random noises as she tried to endure the car ride quietly as best as a child could.

Fenghuang's apartment was messy, as if a small physical altercation had recently occurred. Ling stood there nervously as Hanbing pulled out the toys she had previous played with on their prior visits, and Fenghuang prepared her tea. Ling could see her shaking and hear the tea set rattling in the background but said nothing as they both sat down. Fenghuang, still shaking, poured them both a cup.

"Can you tell me what happened?" asked Ling, reaching over and helping Fenghuang steady her hand.

"Long…he," Fenghuang held the tea cup, her hand shook so much that tea was spilling over the edges, "he was fired on Friday…and…when he came home to tell me…members of the Cultural Protection Ministry came over…they said he had…been teaching…revolutionary…material…" She looked around the room, as if still in shock by the state of it. "They ripped apart… the…apartment, looking for examples…of revolutionary propaganda, and then they took him."

"Took him where?" asked Ling.

Fenghuang took a letter out of her dress; it had become crumbled over multiple readings. "I got this this morning, before I went to watch the children. She handed it over to Ling, who scanned it. "He was found guilty of corrupting the minds of the future generation. They are sentencing him to hard labor and re-education. Two-year sentence, with potential early release depending on behavior."

Ling finished scanning the letter, handing it back to Fenghuang. "So…so what is going to happen to you? And your children? Are you…" Ling didn't know how to finish the sentence, as families of people who were found guilty of revolutionary crimes were often equally punished.

"They decided we weren't guilty," Fenghuang said, taking out another letter. "Apparently my husband confessed to all charges to save us. Plus, with the children in boarding school, and them not finding what they were looking for, the authorities were more easily convinced that…this was a work issue." She sobbed loudly, wiping her eyes with her sleeves.

"What about your books? The books on gender studies. The ones you showed me years ago, that you thought were illegal. Did they find those?" Ling asked cautiously.

"No, if they did…well, I might not be here. I do a good job keeping them hidden, and they were not careful when looking around. Mostly, they just ripped things off our shelves."

Ling sat there quietly, looking around at the mess. He didn't know what to say or to do. Suddenly, surprising even himself, he jumped up and leaned over, giving her a big hug. "Now, now," he whispered, "it is going to be alright." He didn't believe the words he was saying but said them anyway. "Do you know what you are going to do now?"

Fenghuang stopped crying, and Ling slowly backed away. "I guess…I am going to have to move. I have spoken to my parents. They said I can move back to my hometown. My father is retired now, and his job at the university guaranteed him a comfortable place and a decent living stipend. I can help take care of them. They are quite old. Until, you know, this cools down, and I figure out the next step for me, for us. My children, they are covered. They can continue to stay in boarding school."

"Why do you have to move? Why not just stay here? This is your home," asked Ling.

"This apartment," said Fenghuang, looking around and thinking about the life she had built. "It's provided by the school. Now that my husband no longer teaches there, they will kick me out, especially because of that vile vice principal. And, it's not like I can go out and work. Finding a job would be impossible. And any savings we have must be used to pay for the twins' education."

Ling said nothing and instead looked over, watching Hanbing playing with the toys by herself on the floor. He didn't really understand how to react. Fenghuang was the only true friend he had. He felt himself tearing up. Fenghuang reached over, putting her hand on his shoulder, "Look, you are going to be alright, and don't worry about me. I am also going to be alright."

Ling wiped his tears, looking back over. "I feel so embarrassed. You are going through this big thing, and I am the one crying."

Fenghuang smiled gently for the first time. "It's isn't wrong to show people that you care about them." She gave him a big hug. "Now listen, I know things are not easy for you, but you are going to be fine. You are a stronger person than you think."

"What do you mean by that?"

"You are still hiding your true gender, and it takes a strong person to continue doing what you do. Plus, you remained friends with me for all these years." Ling looked at her, baffled, but Fenghuang merely laughed and continued. "Come on, I am not stupid. I know what those ladies, and even what Yi must think of me. I am sure you have been warned or told not to hang out with me, probably multiple times. But you didn't listen to them. You continued to make time for me. Even if we didn't always hang out, you still spoke with me after every meeting, in front of all the other ladies in the group."

"That's because we are friends," Ling said, sniffing.

"Exactly, Ling. We are friends," smiled Fenghuang. "It's natural for you to feel this way about me leaving your life. And since this may be our last time hanging out together for a very long time, let's make the best of it. Why don't you and I wipe off our tears, smile, and celebrate our time together."

Yi was sitting on the couch watching TV and eating takeout when Ling and Hanbing walked in the door. "Hey," he said, looking up from his meal. "I didn't know when you two would be back, so I ordered takeout. There are more dishes in the kitchen if you are hungry."

Ling said nothing and began setting his things down as Hanbing ran over to join her father on the couch. "What's wrong?" asked Yi, putting down his food and turning off the television.

"Hanbing," Ling said in a calm, angry voice. "Why don't you go play in your room for a while. Baba and I need to talk." He waited till his daughter left before continuing, "Why didn't you tell me about Long?"

Yi sat there for a moment, as if trying to think up an excuse before setting on the truth. "I didn't want you to worry."

"You know that they are sending him to a Re-Education

Camp," Ling said, and when Yi said nothing in response and nodded, he continued, "What are you going to do about it?"

"Nothing," Yi said, before turning the TV back on and resuming his dinner.

"You weren't the one who reported him, were you?" Ling asked, afraid to know the answer. "Is that why you want to do nothing?"

"What? No!" Yi said in surprise. "No. No. No. I did not report Long to anyone. Have I been worried that Long could get in trouble for what he was teaching? Yes. But, did I think he would be fired or arrested? No. This is as a big of a shock to me as it is to you."

"In that case, your friend and coworker got arrested and will be sent to be Re-Education Labor Camp. Yet, you want to do nothing," Ling said, sounding disappointed.

"Okay, fine," Yi said, in an almost jeering and dismissive sort of way. "What do you want me to do?"

"I don't know. Protest, talk to the school, ask your dad or something?" Ling said emotionally, stumbling around the room. "The point is Long is not a revolutionary. He is a good man, and we need to help him."

"Ask my dad?" Yi laughed. "Are you thinking clearly? Do you not realize what kind of man he is? If he wasn't the one to sign off this order, then he certainly supports it."

"I know…but…we have to do something," said Ling vehemently.

"No." Yi sat his food down and looked at Ling seriously. "We don't do anything."

"Excuse me?"

"Look, I am sorry I didn't tell you," Yi began, "but your reaction is exactly why I didn't tell you. You are thinking about this emotionally, not logically. It is unfortunate that Long got sent off, but he wasn't careful. Like I said, I warned him that this could happen, and he didn't listen."

"But…but…but," stammered Ling.

"If I get involved in this, then I put all of us at risk," Yi said simply. "Arguing with Vice Principal Yan and whoever else is involved with this decision will only cause them to attack me. I don't need to remind you that looking into our lives can cause a lot more problems that put our family, the three of us, in danger. I will not risk that for a coworker, even if it is someone I respect and saw as a friend."

Ling could not think of a reply. Shrugging disapprovingly, he went to go grab the takeout and called Hanbing out of her room before the three of them sat down together, turned on the TV, and continued dinner in silence.

17.
CONFUSED IDENTITIES CREATE CONFUSED CITIZENS; CONFUSED CITIZENS DESTROY OUR GREAT NATION

It was a sunny Friday afternoon. Hanbing sat at the dining room table of Qiang and Zhuang's apar ment, working on her homework. Mew Mew sat on her lap. Across from her, Zhuang was reading the newspaper. Hanbing had always enjoyed coming here because of Mew Mew, the falcon, the little vegetable garden that Zhuang let her pick vegetables from, as well as the little snacks Zhuang always baked for her when she came. Her favorite thing, however, was definitely the cat, Mew Mew. She couldn't explain why, but Hanbing felt a connection to that calico cat that she did not feel with anyone else. Now in the second grade, she had often requested her parents send her here instead of taking her to her grandparents after school on days they were too busy to watch her. Usually, she felt relaxed and cheerful there, always trying to finish her homework early so she could play with the cat or pick vegetables with Zhuang on the balcony. Today, however, she was nervous, chewing gently on her pencil. There was a topic she wished to talk with Zhuang about but didn't know how to begin.

"Uncle Zhuang? Excuse me, Uncle Zhuang?" Hanbing called out quietly and timidly. "Can I ask you a question?"

"Sure," said Zhuang looking up from the newspaper, "what do you need, sweetie? You got a problem with your homework?'

"Umm…yes… a homework question," said Hanbing, trying to work up the nerve to ask the question she really wanted to ask. "A math problem. It is a story question. If there were 48 violent foreigners trying to murder happy Chinese children, and 13 evil foreigners trying to rape innocent Chinese women, but a beautiful Chinese missile blew up 27 wicked foreigners, how many more revolting foreigners would the honorable and brave Chinese warriors have to kill?"

Zhuang looked at Hanbing for a moment, confused. "Hanbing, that is just a basic math question. I know you know how to solve that question. Why are you asking me this?"

Hanbing looked embarrassed and spoke quietly. "Actually, Uncle Zhuang, that is not the question I want to ask you. But the question I want to ask you…has nothing to do with my homework…and I am afraid to…"

"Hanbing, there is nothing to be frightened of. You can ask me anything," Zhuang said kindly.

Hanbing took a deep breath. "Ok, then…are you and Uncle Qiang faggots?"

"Excuse me?" said Zhuang. He was too confused to be offended.

"You and Uncle Qiang, you guys are together, right? Like the way my mom and my dad are?" asked Hanbing.

"Yes," said Zhuang, deciding to be honest and unsure where this conversation was going. "Uncle Qiang and I are together like your parents are."

"My grandfather told me that if two men like each other like the way my mom and dad do," Hanbing said nervously, "they are called faggots, and they are the worst of society and will ruin our glorious nation."

Zhuang took a deep breath. He knew Hanbing meant no offense, but he was still offended. He quickly reminded himself that Hanbing was barely seven years old and that her worldview was a reflection of her family, who he knew was not accepting. Also, young children were not at the age where they could think about things articulately.

"But…" continued Hanbing, unaware of how much she was

shocking and offending Zhuang. "I know you and Qiang are good people, and my grandfather is wrong on this idea. You guys are the best uncles I can have, even if we aren't related." She paused as Zhuang took a deep breath of relief. "I like you guys. That's why I want to talk to you…I have been thinking… and…well…I think I am also a faggot…" She began to tear up as she said her final sentence.

"First of all," said Zhuang; this wasn't the direction he expected the conversation to head towards. "Let's change the word we use to describe two men who are dating. How about we just use the word gay instead. Why do you think you are gay, Hanbing?"

Hanbing began to cry nervously. "In school, we have been talking about relationships, and girls, and how boys should be with girls. Well…I don't like girls; I don't think I want a girlfriend. There is this boy in my class, and I like him a lot, and I think I like boys, and…I am a boy. So that makes me a…gay?"

Zhuang paused for a moment, trying to figure out to how to approach this topic without angering her parents. Finally, he just asked. "Hanbing, do you know the difference between a boy and a girl?"

"Yes…" said Hanbing hesitantly, noticing how Zhuang was watching her carefully. "Boys have short hair, and girls have long hair…and their body shape is different…and…and." She paused, thinking hard, "and…and…and they do different jobs, like boys go out and work and make money, and girls stay at home, to clean and cook and watch the kids."

Zhuang stared at Hanbing for a moment. Yes, he was well aware of the complexity of surrounding Hanbing's true gender identity and the lies her parents told, but he never expected to talk to her about it, and definitely not to him. He simply didn't know what to say, which meant he said what all people would say in his situation. "Hanbing, I think you should talk to your parents about this. I am not the right person to speak to."

"But…but…what if my parents don't understand," Hanbing replied, scared and tearing up again. "I don't think they hate…

gays, like my grandfather does, but…"

"Hanbing," Zhuang said solemnly, "your parents understand more than you think. Do not worry. They will not get angry with you. But you need to tell them this as soon as possible." He reached over with a napkin and wiped off her tears. "Now quickly finish your homework; I've got some eggplants and tomatoes that are ripe and I need help picking them," he finished with a smile.

Yi looked around the hall outside of Hanbing's classroom at Xincheng #1 Elementary School. He always had mixed feelings about coming back to his alumnus school. He sat in the chair twitching nervously, with Ling next to him. It was time for another parent-teacher conference. In addition to dreading the meeting, he was also uncomfortable about leaving Hanbing at Qiang and Zhuang's house. It wasn't that they weren't responsible, but he wasn't sure if it was safe to allow his child to be in such a dangerous neighborhood with people living such an alternative lifestyle. Yet, ever since that dinner many years ago, Hanbing always begged to go over, to see the cat or to pick fruits and vegetables, and he liked making her happy. His parents, especially Guihua, were not too happy at being demoted from Hanbing's favorite babysitters, but Yi had justified it by explaining that Zhuang was a very masculine ex-military friend who had served his country well and received many honors, which the Governor approved of immensely.

Hanbing's teacher, Teacher Ben, was a sixty-year-old man and the head teacher for the second grade who had been working at the school for far too long now. Yi remembered that he had already been teaching at the school for some time when he and Ling were in second grade, though neither of them were in his class. After finishing a conference with another classmate's parents, he called Yi and Ling in the classroom.

"Hello," Teacher Ben rasped, waving them to sit in the chairs in front of his desk. He took out Hanbing's grade and coughed.

"You would be pleased to know that Hanbing is doing very well in school."

"Glad to hear that," Yi said. Next to him, Ling merely smiled and nodded. It was inappropriate for him to talk during this meeting, yet he had to be there for emotional support and an acknowledgement of him as caregiver.

"As you can see" continued Teacher Ben gruffly, "he has the top grades in nearly every class and is doing quite well academically. Of course, I would expect nothing less from your honorable family," he added with a slight bow.

"Thank you very much," Yi replied. Ling leaned over, whispered something in his ear, and he nodded and continued. "Do you have any concerns about Hanbing's education?"

"Education…" said Teacher Ben. He hesitated for a half second. "No, I have no concern about his education. He is a fine student, reflective of his background. Like I said, top student in almost every class."

"Hmmm…" Yi said. "Remember I am a teacher. If you have a problem with my son, you can always talk to me about it."

"Umm…" Teacher Ben said, sweating a little. "Umm…and I mean this with no disrespect, Teacher Yi, but Hanbing is very different from the rest of the students."

"How so?"

"How do I put this? It feels like he is faking a lot. Like when trying to fit in. I mean, Hanbing has many friends as you know, and he is well liked by his classmates for his intelligence. He is also a nice boy, has a gentle soul, and wants to help out. But, for a lot of social things, it feels like he is acting, pretending to enjoy things. Like he doesn't like the same things that they do," Teacher Ben replied with much hesitation. "Don't get me wrong. He is alright at sports, not the best, not the worst. But activities like sports don't seem to interest him very much. It's like he doesn't like the things we would expect a boy his age to like."

"I didn't like sports as a child, either, Teacher Ben," said Yi sternly. "What are you trying to say here?"

"Oh, I didn't mean any offense," Teacher Ben said quickly. "Like I said, Hanbing is a very bright boy. Probably one of the best students I have ever had," he added nervously. "But, there is something peculiar about him, something different, that I have never seen in any of my students. Maybe it's just a phase or his personality."

"I can assure you there is nothing peculiar about my son," Yi said, raising his voice just slightly. "Perhaps you are just not used to students of Hanbing's level and background. I seem to recall from my childhood years that you didn't always get the best students. Perhaps this new promotion as head teacher is not fitting for you."

Teacher Ben gulped. "It must be my misunderstanding, sir. Like I said in the very beginning, Hanbing is an excellent student. Top marks in all his classes."

Yi was furious as the two of them walked out of the classroom. How dare this teacher suggest Hanbing was peculiar or different. He had spent all his energy to make sure, with the exception of being an excellent student perhaps, that Hanbing was the most normal boy in school. He and Hanbing had spent hours talking about what was appropriate to like and what was appropriate not to like. What in the world could this teacher be seeing that would make him think that Hanbing was anything but 100% normal?

"Umm…" interrupted Ling, "I just got a text from Zhuang. It's about Hanbing. You aren't going to like this."

"What?" scowled Yi. "What happened?"

"Here." Ling gave his phone to Yi. "It is best you read it yourself."

Hi Ling (and Yi if you read this) I need to speak with you about something that happened this afternoon. Hanbing asked me if she was gay because she liked boys. She said she knows boys who like boys are gay.

It was followed by another text.

I know this is complicated. But Qiang and I believe it may be time to start talking to her about her true biological sex. If you want support, I can cook a big dinner and we can all talk about it tonight after we eat. Let me know, and if we can help in any way.

"Well," asked Ling. "What do you want to do about this? You know we can't keep avoiding this topic forever."

"Fine," said Yi. He stopped and thought for a moment. "I guess we can't avoid this forever. Hanbing will be learning about the boys, girls, and nan-nu soon. It would be best if it came from us first." He looked over at Ling who smiled awkwardly at him and sighed. "Tell them we will come over for dinner, and we will figure out how to talk about this. At least it is Friday, so we can have the weekend to deal with this if need be," he added as an afterthought as Ling replied to the texts.

Hanbing sat at the dining room table, picking at the small dish in front of her filled with various vegetables and bits of meat. She couldn't figure out why, but she felt very uncomfortable, as if she was in trouble for something that she wasn't sure she did wrong. It was already unusual for her parents to eat at Qiang and Zhuang's house; usually they just picked her up and went home. In addition, everyone was talking in an unusually polite and formal way. It wasn't a holiday or any special event that she knew of, so she couldn't quite understand what was going on. Was this about her talk with Zhuang earlier? She had told him in confidence, and he had assured her that she wouldn't be in trouble. Everyone around her just looked so depressed and scared, and she couldn't figure out why.

Finally, Zhuang spoke up, faking a smile. "If everyone is finished, then why don't Ling and I clean up, and then we'll all go out into the living room.

"I brought some books for you, Hanbing," said Qiang with the same fake smile. "Why don't you and your dad go out to the living room, and we can look at them together. If you want, you can play with Mew Mew first."

"Ok," Hanbing said. She couldn't explain why she felt so worried.

Hanbing was playing on the rug with toy mouse on a rope with Mew Mew when all the adults came out. Her father picked her up, placing her on the sofa. Her father and mother then sat on either side of her, while Qiang stood to the side, and Zhuang sat on the other sofa.

"Ummm…." Hanbing asked nervously. "Am I in trouble?"

None of the four adults knew what to say and merely stared at one another. "No, sweetie," began Yi, "you aren't in trouble."

"Zhuang told us about your talk this afternoon," said Ling. "We need to talk to you about something."

Hanbing glared at Zhuang, surprised. She felt slightly betrayed. Why he would tell her parents so quickly after their secret conversation during the afternoon?

Yi, noticing his daughter's facial expression, interrupted before she could say something or throw a fit. "Don't be angry, Hanbing. Zhuang told us because we are your parents and because we all love you. We aren't angry with you, and you're not in trouble. But there are some things you don't understand. For example…"

"You aren't gay," interrupted Qiang in the background with a slight laugh.

Hanbing was confused, looking up at Qiang. "But I really like boys, like you and Uncle Zhuang like each other. And my teacher, grandfather, and Uncle Zhuang told me that if you are a boy and you like boys, then you are gay."

"Well," chuckled Qiang. "the thing that you don't understand is…"

"You are not a boy," Yi said quietly. The other three adults looked at him and then at Hanbing, speechless and waiting for her reaction.

"What do you mean I am not a boy?" Hanbing asked, confused. "I have a short hair like you, Baba. I have short hair like Uncle Zhuang and Uncle Qiang, so I am a boy."

"The thing you have to understand," began Yi, "is that we told you that you are a boy to protect you. But you are not a boy. You are a girl."

"I don't understand," Hanbing said, even more confused.

Zhuang grabbed the book of human anatomy sitting on the living room table and showed Hanbing, "Hanbing, what makes someone a boy and girl is not the length of their hair. It's a lot more complicated than that." He pointed at the pictures of the nude man and woman, "One of the bigger, more obvious visual ways is the private area. Hanbing, if you look carefully, you might notice you have the same privates as a woman."

"But…but…but…" said Hanbing, glossing over the pictures. "Mama told me that…"

"I lied," Ling interrupted, looking sad. He thought back to the conversation he had with his parents many years ago, when he learned that he would become a nan-nu. He remembered how traumatic it was for him and felt huge empathy for his daughter's pain. All he wanted to do now was protect her from the same trauma and pain. "I lied to protect you, and I am sorry. But you have to understand, I had no choice but to lie."

"Sweetie," Yi said, pleading, "let me try to explain why we lied to you. The truth is…this country no longer has biological girls. Well, that's what we thought anyway before we met you. All the girls in this country start off as boys. They get special surgery, and they become girls. But you are different. You are special. You were never a boy. Because you are a biological girl."

"I don't understand," Hanbing said. "Does that mean my Mama was once a boy?"

"Well…" began Yi, wondering how truthful he should be.

"That's not important," Qiang interrupted once again from

the back. "The thing is, Hanbing, when your parents got you so many years ago, we learned that you are a girl, and that was very special. The problem was…" He hesitated for a moment, looking at Yi and Ling, who merely nodded. "The problem was that, if anyone outside of this group found out you were a girl that would have been very bad for you. Therefore, they—*we*—all lied to protect you."

"Why would that have been bad," asked Hanbing, looking scared, "if people knew I was a girl?"

"Because the government would have taken you away from us, and they would have hurt you," said Ling tenderly, hugging his daughter. "And from the day we got you, we knew we would do anything to protect you."

"But…" stuttered Hanbing. "I thought the government's job was to protect us. Why would they hurt me?"

"Because…" Yi paused. He wasn't sure how to answer.

Qiang spoke up for him. "Because, Hanbing, because you are different. A biological girl hasn't been seen or heard of in this country for many, many years. Girls can do things that boys can't, and that is really important to the government. But the way government wants to solve the problem is different than the way we want to solve it."

"Like clean and cook and watch the children?" asked Hanbing

"No, sweetie," laughed Ling. "Like have children. One day if you want, you will be able to have babies naturally. The rest of us, we came from a factory."

"You mean I didn't come from a factory?" asked Hanbing, holding back her tears. "Where did I come from, Mama?"

"Ummm," Ling began looking around, as if looking for someone to interject. "I found you. I found you in the Yangtze River. I took you home, and your father and I began to raise you."

"You found me? You aren't my real parents?" asked Hanbing. She began to cry. "Where are my real parents?"

"No, Hanbing," said Yi sternly and calmly. "We are your real parents. We are your only parents. We are your dad and mom. We have raised you and loved you since the day you came into our lives, and we will love you for the rest of our lives. But because you are different, we have to take special…precautions."

Hanbing slowly stopped crying. "Like what? Are you going to change my school, do I need to go to a girl school now? I don't want to change schools. I like my school, and I like my friends," she added with a sob.

"Sweetie," Yi said calmly, hugging her. "You aren't going to have to change schools. We spoke to your teacher today, and you are doing very well. We are so proud you. You can be whoever you want to be, and we will support you. But…" Yi stopped looking in his daughter in his eyes. "But this is very important. You can't keep going around asking if you are different. Because you *are* different. You are special. But you can't let anyone know you are.

"Why not?" asked Hanbing.

"Because they will take you away from your parents," Zhuang said before anyone else could speak. "Hanbing, I know you talked to me this afternoon because you trust me. I am going to need you to be brave and trust all of us. What your dad, your mom, me, and your Uncle Qiang are telling you right now is serious, and we all love you and want the best for you. Therefore, we need you to trust us. Be brave and never talk about this with anyone else. If you have questions, you can talk to us, but only one of us. Do you understand?"

Hanbing sank into the sofa, looking around the room. She had never seen her parents so scared and serious. "Yes, Uncle Zhuang," she said faintly. "I understand."

18.
CORRECT DECISIONS IN CHILDHOOD LEAD TO CORRECT DECISIONS IN ADULTHOOD

THE REST OF THE WEEKEND felt rather uncomfortable. Hanbing didn't express much after the conversation on Friday, and both Yi and Ling felt it best to leave her alone and let her play with her toys. They offered to take her out shopping and even offered to take her out to People's Park, but she wasn't interested. Instead, she spent most of the weekend in her room looking through toys, reading her books, and being unnaturally quiet.

On Monday morning, Yi considered taking her out of school for the day, but Hanbing refused, saying she had to study, and she was afraid that she would fall behind if she missed a day. Therefore, after much reluctance and contemplation, he gave Ling permission to take her to school with the Governor's driver. Ling felt helpless as he sat in the car. His daughter wasn't saying much, and all questions and concerns were met with one-word answers or basic grunts. He felt fortunate that Baihe wasn't empathetic or caring enough to ask what was wrong, though Qinghuang looked slightly worried for his cousin.

Hanbing walked into school feeling slightly scared. To be honest, she didn't really understand why the four adults were so serious about her situation, nor was she quite clear what they meant when they said she was not only a girl, but a biological girl. All she knew was that judging by their actions and reactions that this was something serious. Like all children her age, boy or girl, Hanbing knew she wanted to make her parents happy, make them proud. She had noticed how worried they were over the weekend, and she knew she didn't like that. She wished she could be normal. She couldn't stop thinking about how to be normal.

Walking into class, she sat down next to her deskmate and best friend, Nan Zihan. "Look what I got," he said excitedly, pulling out a small packet of cards. "They are from a new cartoon, *Super Chinese Boy and his Monster Friends*. No one has seen it yet, but my daddy showed me a small part. It's so cool. I bet I am only the person who has got cards. My daddy got them from the Capital yesterday. You can't find them here yet," he added. "My daddy says they are airing the first episode tomorrow. You should come over, and we can watch it together. Super Chinese Boy will go fight the Evil Foreign Gremlins."

Hanbing put her bag behind her chair as the other boys came over to see what the fuss was about. "That looks super cool," she said, her mind elsewhere. "Maybe I can ask my Baba if I can go over tomorrow to watch it."

"You don't sound like you think it's cool," said Zihan, frowning and sounding very disappointed.

"I do, I do." Hanbing quickly forced a smile. "Show me more at recess. Teacher Ben is coming. You don't want him to take them away, do you?"

After their usual lunch of two vegetables, a protein, and a bowl of rice, the children ran out to recess to play ball in the courtyard. Hanbing stayed back, cleaning her desk slowly, contemplating.

"What's wrong?" said a voice behind her. She jumped in shock before turning around.

"NAN ZIHAN!" she yelled. "Don't do that! You scared me."

Nan Zihan laughed and giggled like an average seven-year-old boy would before stopping and asking again, "What's wrong?"

"Nothing," she said quickly, turning away.

"Why don't you like my cards?" Zihan asked, sounding hurt.

"I do, I do. I do. I just was tired this morning."

"I don't believe you," Zihan said stubbornly. "Why don't you like my cards? We always talk about cartoons and toys together, and you always like them!"

Hanbing said nothing, leaning on her desk, then she asked quietly, "Zihan, do you think I am weird? Or different?"

"Well right now, I do," Zihan said in surprise, giggling. "Normally I don't. Is that why you are acting weird? Because you think you're weird?"

Hanbing thought for a moment and then nodded.

"You aren't weird," Zihan laughed. Hanbing perked up a little as Zihan continued. "You are cool, you are good at school, you are good at drawing, you are good at math, you are good at so many things."

Hanbing looked at Zihan and smiled. "Thank you."

"And most importantly," Zihan said with pride. "You are my best friend, and I am your best friend."

Hanbing could not figure out the words to express the relief she felt from what Zihan said. "Come on," she said laughing, "I'll race you to the courtyard. Last one there is a fat little pig!" Before Zihan could comprehend what she was saying, she jumped off the table, and ran out the door.

* * *

After dropping off Hanbing, Ling decided he didn't want to go directly home and start on his usual cleaning, cooking, and other chores. It was times like these he really wished Fenghuang was still in town. The two had spoken a few times since she moved out of Xincheng, but it felt awkward and uncomfortable because of the upheaval in her life. He didn't know why, but he could tell that despite Fenghuang's more educated views, she still felt the cultural shame of having her husband sent to a Re-Education Camp. Anyways, he reminded himself, he had never told Fenghuang about Hanbing's true sex. He wasn't sure he wanted to visit Qiang or Zhuang either. It just felt like it was too soon to talk to them again about this topic. It was at moments like this that he felt even more lonely than usual. He wished he could trust someone to talk through what he was going through. It was important that he was in a good mood by the time Yi returned from work.

Finally, after standing in front of the school for an uncomfortable amount of time, he checked his purse to make sure he brought enough money, hopped into a taxi, and headed across town to visit his parents. Usually, he would take the bus to save money, but with so much on his mind, he was worried he would miss their stop. He felt lost and confused, as if the last few days were nothing but a daze.

Raising Hanbing kept him busy; at least, that was the excuse he gave himself and told others. Ling rarely saw his parents more than once or twice every six months. On all those occasions, it was just so Hanbing could maintain a good relationship with her maternal grandparents. On his way, he thought about what he was doing, if going there was even a good idea. He considered telling the taxi driver to take him back home, but by the time he came to that decision, the taxi had already arrived.

The noodle shop was busy as he walked through the door, as it was the start of the lunch rush, and he had to push past the customers in order to reach his parents. His father stood in the back over a hot pot of water pulling noodles, while his mother took orders and helped on the side. Both his parents were surprised to see him, and his father waved from the back. Ling couldn't remember the last time he visited without calling them first.

"What are you doing here?" asked his mother, sounding annoyed. "Where is Hanbing?"

"At school," Ling replied. "I came over because I needed to find something."

"Did you make a major mistake again? Is Yi mad at you?" asked his mother. "Is that why you are here? To think about what you have done before going back to beg for your husband's forgiveness? He is way too patient with you for the number of mistakes you make."

"No, Mother," Ling said, forcing a smile. "Yi and I are great. Hanbing is doing well. I just need to grab something I left here."

"Okay," said his mother indifferently. "All the stuff you left here is still in the trunk on the second floor, in the living room. We have a lamp on it now, so try not to break it. When you are done, come down, and I'll make you a bowl of noodles before you leave."

After he got married to Yi, it was no longer appropriate for Ling to keep many of his own private possessions with him. A good wife gave up her old life to make way for a life of taking care of her husband and potential children. Like many before him, Ling stored a trunk of prized possessions at his parents' house, though it had been years since he looked at them. Stepping into his parents living room, he carefully removed the lamp off of his black wooden trunk and took a look inside. One at a time, he slowly took each item out, the only remnants of the life he had before he was married. A few pictures of him and Yi as children, in the good old days before he switched schools, taken by their teacher during school activities. A few plastic toys of no financial value that Yi had given him as children so that he wouldn't forget him once he entered his new school. The first scarf he had ever made in his knitting class, when they started learning the basic skills all woman should learn. His first training bra, which he wasn't sure why he kept, with fading pamphlets discussing sex change surgery next to them.

While Ling knew what he was looking for, he was in no hurry to find it. Instead, looking to distract himself, he took out his high school yearbook and flipped to his graduating class photo. Out of the thirty or so students, he was the only one who had not gotten his surgery upon graduation. He looked through the pictures of him in his different classes: cooking class, sewing class, cleaning class, child rearing class. Even then he didn't feel like he fit in the duties and the jobs they were training to do. Thinking about it now, though, he realized that his all his classmates were probably in the same boat as him, lost and forced into a role that was not based on personality or identity. They were all taught it was dishonorable and would bring their families shame if they didn't accept the roles that they had been chosen for, and they had no power to speak up.

Ling continued to take out his old clothes and other trinkets before finally reaching the bottom of the trunk. Feeling around, he found a little compartment that most would not have noticed. Inside was his most prized possession, a silk red envelope full of letters that Yi had written to him after elementary school and throughout their different educational journeys. With precision, he slid the letters out of the envelope and unfolded them, careful not to tear the old pieces of paper. The first letter was written one year into middle school.

Hey Ling,

I hope this letter finds you well. My father has forbidden me to contact you, as he finds it inappropriate. He says that our friendship must die in order for both of us to learn our proper place in society and embrace our destinies. But I know he is wrong. You are my best friend, and we will always be best friends.

We are learning a lot in school now, so I am quite busy, but it is not the same without you here. I have started to hang out with Cheng Chen. My father says he is the type of person I should get to know better, and that his family is the type of people we should be associating with. I don't really like him that much though, and we don't have very much in common. I miss making jokes with you.

I hope you are learning a lot also. In the meantime, I will continue talking to my father about you. I know you aren't a woman, and you should be in school with me.

I have asked my trusted nanny to give this letter to you. I will send her back next week to collect the letter that you write back to me.

I hope you are doing well.

         - Yi

Ling shifted through the letters from middle school. During this time, it was the only form of contact between him and Yi. He smiled as he reread the different stories that Yi told him: times he made jokes in class, success in athletics, and watching movies with Cheng Chen, whom Ling felt oddly envious of. He recalled how nervous it made him feel that he and Yi were having this secret form of communication. Perhaps it was why he was still so possessive about these letters.

Upon reaching the letters written when they were high school, Ling noticed how much more serious they had become. It was no longer communication about daily activities or humorous topics, but rather about the future—more specifically, their future. As he thought about it, Ling wasn't sure how he felt about how adamant Yi was, even back during their high school days, that he did not become a nan-nu. He took out the letter written a week before his surgery, right after he had turned seventeen. He remembered he had started to feel awkward, as not only had his body almost fully developed into the body of a man, but he was the only one left in his class who had not received his surgery.

Ling,

I don't understand why aren't listening to me. I have told you before. You are not a woman; you are not a nan-nu. I am extremely disappointed to hear you are considering getting the surgery. I do not care what others say, but this is not happening.

I will figure out a way to solve this problem. Please delay your surgery next week. This isn't you. I will solve this problem. Trust me.

         - Yi

A few days later, he received another letter. Back then, even Ling was impressed by Yi's solution. Though, he had to acknowledge to himself, he didn't really think about what it would mean for their future as friends. As he read the letter, he realized that Yi probably also didn't think about what he was doing, and what his decision actually meant for the both of them.

Hello Ling,

I am super excited to tell you that I have figured out a solution to the whole nan-nu problem and figured a way for you to keep all your parts, as one might put it.

Are you ready for it?

We are getting married!

Ha! I bet you didn't see that coming. This is the perfect solution. This way you 'belong to me,' and I get a say in your future. I wasn't planning to get married in the future anyway, so this is perfect.

Of course, I wouldn't expect you to be 'my wife' and 'provide wifely duties.' Haha. Though if you can cook and help around the house, that would be nice. But we would be roommates; we can hang out, talk, watch movies, just like the good old days, just like when we were kids.

I have already told my father about my decision, and that I am delay-ing your surgery so I can be there for you and this way I can 'choose what parts you get.' He isn't happy, of course. He says I should marry someone better, someone who studied in the Capital. But I was stubborn. Of course, it helped that I recently got accepted into university, and I am studying government just like he asked, so he was happy enough not to argue too much.

Anyway, I guess that is that. The problem is solved. I guess once I grad-uate from university, we will be married. Now isn't that funny to think about?

Your best friend,

-Yi

Ling looked up on the wall. He could see his wedding photo, covered lightly with dust, hanging next to some of his childhood pictures. As promised, a year after Yi graduated from university, he married Ling. Their wedding was full of high-level politicians and prominent people from Yi's side. Ling had invited a few classmates, all of whom jealously congratulated him on marrying the future governor. Ling remembered how handsome Yi looked in his suit. He didn't think he looked half bad in his wedding dress; it had, after all, been specifically tailored for him. He remembered the joke Yi made, that despite trying to expel all dangerous foreign culture and ideology out of the country, they were getting married in a western style suit and a white western style wedding dress, instead of traditional Chinese red robes.

For a few weeks, their life was exactly as Yi stated in the letter. He and Yi were like roommates. Yi slept in the main room while Ling slept in the office. At home, although Ling cleaned and cooked, while Yi worked, he wore boy clothes for the first time since elementary school and had the freedom to just sort of hang out at home all day once his chores were finished. They tried to have many of the same conversations similar to when they were children, but they were both different now, in both age and experience.

Then one night, Yi came home exhausted. Ling didn't know why, perhaps he was feeling guilty or it was the influence of his education, but Ling performed oral sex on him for the first time. Although Yi resisted it at first, soon Ling was doing it every night, sometimes more than once. Not much time after that, Yi asked Ling to stop wearing boy clothing and to sleep in his bed. For his own protection, Yi told him, in case someone came over and visited unexpectantly. A couple months after the oral sex began, Yi came home drunk one day and slightly angry. Unexpectedly, he bent Ling over on the sofa and took his virginity. After that, their relationship as "best friends" and "roommates" was over.

But Ling didn't mind. Although he knew the feelings were

not romantic, and Yi was just using him for his own pleasure, he felt pleased and satisfied, as for the first time he felt he could make Yi happy.

Suddenly, Ling heard someone walking up the stairs. Nervous and embarrassed, he shoved the letters and envelope under his dress so that no one could see them. Turning around, he saw his mother holding a bowl of noodles. "I thought you might be hungry," she said, setting the bowl on the living room table. "What are you looking for?"

Ling debated a moment of telling his mother the truth. About Hanbing and about the conversation they had just two days ago. He wondered for a moment what her reaction would be. But of course, telling her the truth would have been impossible, so he just replied, "Nothing. I was just looking through some stuff. Thinking about how my life has been and how different it could have been. I guess I just wanted to reminisce. I guess I was wondering what my life would be like if I wasn't a woman." He started picking up his stuff and putting them gently back in the trunk.

"You have always been an ungrateful child, you know that?" Wupo said, watching him. "You aren't even a woman yet. More like a fag in drag. Yi has done so much for you, given you opportunities that I never had. Where would you be without him? Probably back in the village, farming every day. Yet, here you are, complaining, wondering about a different life, a life you don't even deserve." She paused for a moment, sounding a bit sad. "You know what I would give to not to have to work every day in this restaurant? To be able to buy nice clothes like you do. I guess it is true, wealth is wasted on the rich," she spat. "When you are done up here reminiscing, spoiled princess, and eating the noodles that I have just made for you with my bare, calloused hands, come down to see what it's like to work for a living."

*   *   *

Yi was staying after school to train his new colleague, Teacher Long's replacement, but it wasn't going well. The new teacher, Teacher Lan, was a lot older than him, even older than Long was, and like with all older people, was stubborn about doing things his way and refusing to communicate in any substantial way. Yi was also distracted, worried about Hanbing and the way she acted the whole weekend. I hope we haven't broken her, he kept thinking to himself. Finally, after listening to Lan ramble on about how if it was good enough for a village, it was good enough for the city, he interrupted. "I am sorry," he said trying not to sound annoyed. "I need to get going, I have to…umm… pick up my son." He tried not to feel too proud of himself for thinking up a lie on the spot.

"I am telling you about my way of teaching. Look, in my village, where I was head teacher, we—"

"Look," said Yi, interrupting in a mocking voice. "I don't care how they do things in the village. Here, in the city, in this school, I am the head teacher. You can listen to me or you can not listen to me. One decision leads to good things, one leads to bad things. It is your choice. I will see you tomorrow." He grabbed his briefcase. Then, thinking up another idea on the spot, this one based on emotions and not logic, he sent a text to Guihua.

> **Hi, I need to talk about something. Can I meet you at the tea shop like when I was a kid? I will be there in about 40 minutes.**

Hen'hao'cha was a little teashop about three blocks from Governor Wang's home, where Guihua used to take Yi after school. Aiming for a certain social class, it was designed with a classic elegance and decorated in a traditional style. As a child, Yi loved the little clay figurines, wooden carvings, and other little antique trinkets that decorated the place. Before his falling out with his mother due to the discomfort of her forced gender, Yi and his mother used to come weekly to just sit and talk together.

He missed those good old days.

Yi found his mother at their usual spot, behind the rock fountain with the little goldfish swimming in the pool. She had already ordered his favorite drink: bubble milk tea with tapioca pearls. She pushed the drink in front of him as he sat down. "How long has it been since we came here?" she asked with a grin.

"Don't know, over a decade." Yi looked around, sucking the tapioca balls out of his drink. "The place still looks the same though."

Guihua smiled fondly. "How is my grandchild doing? I feel like I haven't seen Hanbing in so long. Ever since Ling decided to stop bringing him over and instead started bringing him to see some retired solider." She didn't bother to hide the disgust and disappointment in her voice.

"Hanbing is doing well," Yi said smiling. "But you know the main reason Hanbing keeps visiting my friend's house is because of a cat. If you want Hanbing to visit more, perhaps you should consider getting a cat?"

"Even if I wanted to, your father would never allow it," scowled Guihua. "You know how he believes all animals are disease carrying vermin."

The two shared a small chuckle before taking another sip of their milk tea. "Actually," said Yi putting down his drink, "Hanbing is the reason I wanted to talk to you."

"Is there something wrong with my grandchild?" asked Guihua, concerned.

"No, but we told Hanbing the truth on Friday." Yi tried his best to make his voice sound neutral and project an aura of indifference.

"How did Hanbing react to that?" Guihua replied. She paused looking around, as if suddenly remembering they were in a public forum.

"I am not sure. Hanbing was quiet all weekend. Ling took him to school today. I think we will have to wait and see to understand how Hanbing reacts. I think Hanbing is still processing the information."

"Hanbing is a much tougher child than you give her credit for." Guihua smiled, sipping her tea slowly. "I know Hanbing will do well."

"I am just worried." Yi took a deep breath. "I want to make sure Hanbing has the best future possible. That Hanbing can be whoever Hanbing wants to be. But if the truth ever got out, then Hanbing would lose all opportunity. That's why we raised Hanbing this way. I want society to see Hanbing as an equal and not just a…" He stopped awkwardly, suddenly turning quiet, unable to say the final word.

"And not as a woman," Guihua said. She took another sip of her tea. "It's funny how our attitude towards life changes when it starts affecting someone we truly love, thus affecting us more personally."

"What do you mean by that?"

"If I were to die tomorrow, and someone were to find my body twenty years later, based on my bone structure they would think I were a man. The only thing that would give it away is a pair of silicone breasts that will never rot." Guihua smiled. "If someone were to give me a chromosome test today, they would identify me as male."

"I still don't get it. What does any of this have to do with Hanbing?"

"I don't recall you ever worrying, or even not supporting how society treats women or nan-nu before," Guihua explained. "I don't recall you ever worrying that someone like Ling didn't get the opportunity to reach their full potential. The ironic thing is Ling is still visually a man while the rest of us are simply mutilated men."

"That's…that's different," Yi replied quickly. "Hanbing is innocent. Hanbing is different. Hanbing is getting her choice taken away from her."

"And Ling's choice was given, right? All of us nan-nu, us

womenfolk here, we were given the choice and we were never innocent?" Guihua asked, still continuing to sip her tea. "Do you remember that visit to People's Park, when you must have only been four or five, and you saw that little lizard that got run over by a bicycle? Despite everyone else ignoring it, you tried so hard to save it. I remember you crying, telling me how unfair it was that it had to die. That it wasn't his choice to be hit by that bicycle. Now, that day is very important to me because it showed me how much you were willing to care for another life. But, I think it is also to remember much like that lizard, the women in this country have no choice. Our destiny was decided by an outside force."

Yi felt very awkward again. He hated being put on the spot. It was easier to look out the window, continuing to drink his tea than say anything.

"Of course, you are right," Guihua said nonchalantly. "Hanbing does deserve better. Hanbing deserves to be treated as an equal and not a prop or a means to the end." She smiled thoughtfully. "You have always been a smart and great son. I know you will do your best to protect your child and my grandchild."

19.
REVOLUTIONARY AND TRAITOROUS IDEAS MUST BE STOMPED OUT BEFORE ONE CAN RETURN TO SOCIETY

YI BEGRUDGINGLY GOT OFF THE bus on Monday morning and began walking towards his office. He was not looking forward to work today. His newest coworker, the third replacement after Teacher Long was fired over a year ago, was just as terrible of a teacher as the previous two. Only this one would be a lot harder to fire. Teacher Xiang was the second son of an important government official who had only received this job because Vice Principal Yan wanted to improve his connections to the government. He was young, entitled, incompetent, and—most bothersome for Yi, with his connections—hard to get rid of. The two months he had been there had been marred with complaints from both students and parents, but without support from the upper staff to fire him, there was nothing Yi could do. The previous week had been especially difficult, when the school received complaints that not only had Xiang misunderstood an important lesson on the role and ideals of the ruling party, but also appeared to have been teaching with a hangover. Many parents, being members of the Party themselves, were none too pleased, though Yi wisely suggested they direct their complaints at the vice principal.

Yi walked in the office, set down his stuff, and looked over Teacher Xiang's desk. He was pleasantly surprised to see Xiang was not there. Instead, a new, older teacher had been hired without his knowledge. As he walked over to introduce himself, the new teacher looked up at him, smiling politely. Yi tripped backwards in shock as he recognized the man. It was not someone he had expected to see again. His old colleague and friend: Teacher Long.

Teacher Long looked different than Yi remembered. Some of his teeth were missing, and he appeared to have aged about fifteen years. His eyes were shaggy and weak, as if they had lost the will to live. He stood up and walked over with a slight limp, quivering with each step. Though he wore a long sleeve shirt, Yi could see lines of scars and burns under his white shirt, which turned translucent when under the light.

"Hello, Yi," Long smiled, ignoring Yi's shocked face. "It has been a while. How have you been, my good friend?" he said in a very neutral, polite voice.

Yi opened and closed his mouth in surprise. "It's been good… when—when did you come back?"

"I was released last week from my extended educational training," said Long, continuing in the same neutral polite voice. "On Saturday, our great leaders from our school contacted me and asked if I would like to return to my previous position. Of course, I gladly agreed because it is our duty to serve our great nation and educate the next generation," he finished with a big smile on his face.

"Well…well…" Yi said, still in shock, "welcome back…"

"Thank you," said Long, continuing in the same monotone voice. "It is a great honor to be able to serve my glorious country through this fine institution. I feel very grateful that I have been forgiven for my past crimes and will be able to move on from my past." He reached his hand forward. "I cannot tell you how happy I am to work with you again, and I look forward to learning from your wisdom. I am sorry I didn't listen more to your wise words before about teaching the proper materials. I want to tell you how great and right you were, and I apologize for being disrespectful and disobedient. I wish I could apologize to my many students whom I failed due to my lack of understanding of the wonderfulness of our glorious government."

"Err…" said Yi, reaching forward and shaking Long's hand. "Welcome back."

Teacher Long's return was the source of gossip and a huge class distraction in Xincheng #1 High School that afternoon. Many of the older students were taught by Long just a few years prior and all students, even the new ones who never met him, were well aware of the circumstances behind his expulsion. Naturally, each student had his own opinion about how the high school should handle the situation.

Yi walked in the classroom knowing that his students would wish to talk to him about his colleague's return, though he had decided as he walked through the halls overhearing the discussions, it would be best to avoid it and plow through his lecture as usual. Though he was still shocked by Long's physical changes, what bothered him more were the internal changes. It was as if Long were a different man, and the lack of fluctuation in his voice, how robotic it had become, made him feel queasy and uncomfortable.

"Good afternoon, class," Yi announced as he walked to the front. "Today we will continue our lesson from yesterday. The role of the Central Government in fighting the Sanxia Rebels. Who can tell me where we left off?"

"Excuse me, sir," interrupted one of the students in the back. "Is it true that Teacher Long is back?"

Yi sighed loudly. "Yes. It is true. Teacher Long has indeed been rehired back by the school. But if we could get back to the topic."

There was loud murmuring among the students, who started discussing this information with their desk partners.

Yi coughed loudly. "As I was saying. Continuing from yesterday, the role of the Central Government in fighting the Sanxia Rebels was…"

Another student interrupted again. "If Teacher Long were fired for spreading revolutionary ideas, then why did the school choose to hire him back?"

Yi sighed again. "That decision was not made by me. But, if we could get back on topic."

"Do you, sir," asked another student, "support the school hiring back Teacher Long?"

"That is not important," Yi said, slightly annoyed. "The topic at hand is the Sanxia Rebels."

"The Sanxia Rebels started by spreading revolutionary ideas," said a student. "Couldn't we make a modern connection and say that Teacher Long is a rebel by spreading revolutionary ideas?"

"Teacher Long has spent the last two years in re-education. The school would not hire him back if they thought he were dangerous."

"How can we be assured of that?" asked one student. "Do you think Teacher Long is dangerous?"

"It was not my decision to bring back Teacher Long."

"That does not answer our question," a student in the front called out. "Do you think Teacher Long is dangerous?"

"No," Yi said simply. "I do not think Teacher Long is dangerous. Now if we could get back to the lesson."

"Then," asked another student, "do you think Teacher Long was dangerous before, and do you agree with school's decision to send him off to a Re-Education Labor Camp?"

"These are not my decisions to make," Yi snapped. "Now, if we could please get back to the topic at hand."

"But you are our political ethics teacher," another student cried out, "and Teacher Long teaches in your department, sir. Shouldn't you be the one to reassure us that his being here is safe?"

"Look, I have never believed Teacher Long is a revolutionary, and I do not think he is spreading traitorous ideologies. He is my colleague, and although our teaching styles differ, I have full faith in his ability to provide the students of this school with a good education."

"Does that mean that you disagree with the school and your superiors in this topic, sir?" a student asked in surprise. "Have you ever expressed your personal disagreements? Do you think the school made a mistake by firing Teacher Long in the first place?"

Yi paused, feeling trapped, finally snapping. "The decisions involving the firing and rehiring of Teacher Long have nothing to do with me. I can say that during my reviews of him prior to his arrests, he covered the subjects well. I have nothing more to add. Detention for a week to the next student who asks me about Teacher Long." When no student spoke up, he continued. "Okay. Now class, let's continue our topic from yesterday: the role of the Central Government in fighting the Sanxia Rebels."

Yi and Long were finishing the day in the office by Yi showing Long what had changed with the curriculum during the time he was absent. "Oh, by the way, I must ask," Yi said suddenly and casually, "how is your wife, Fenghuang, and your children, the twins? Ling has been very worried about them."

"They are very well," Long replied in a monotone voice. "Our glorious government generously allowed my wife to move back to the village where she came from, where she continued to uphold the values of a Chinese woman. This weekend, she will move back to our house, where we will live together so that we may serve our glorious nation to the best of our abilities. My children are studying hard to become obedient servants to our glorious nation. I know they will serve us well in the future, with pride and loyalty, just like you always have." He grinned awkwardly at Yi, exposing his missing teeth. "We are lucky to have such honorable and loyal wives who serve both us and our glorious nation to its full potential."

Yi smiled awkwardly back; he wasn't sure how to respond. "Okay, that's good to hear," he said as Long stared at him, grinning.

They were interrupted by a knock on the door, and Yan came

walking in. "Hello, to you both," he said in a cheery voice. "I hope you are having a good first day back, Teacher Long."

"I am, thank you very much. I am happy to be back, happy to have this second honored opportunity to educate our students about the wonderfulness of our glorious nation." Long replied in a monotone voice. Turning to Yi, he smiled and said, "Thank you for your help, Yi, and your gracious welcomes on my return. I will see you tomorrow." Nodding to them both, he walked out of the office.

Yan waited until Long was out of earshot before speaking slyly. "I saw your class this afternoon, Yi. You seemed rather distracted. The students got the best of you from what I saw. Perhaps you should think about how you control your class?"

Yi bit his tongue, refusing to bite the bait. "Yes. It was not my best lesson. Even I have my off days. I guess I was just distracted by my colleague's return."

"I didn't tell you about his return because I didn't know until last night, and I figured by then, you would find out in the morning." Yi said nothing, just continued grading his papers, so Yan continued. "I had no say in his return. Probably would have vetoed it if I could. But, the Board was not too happy with the situation with Teacher Xiang and all the parents' complaints. Despite his traitorous and revolutionary ideology, Teacher Long has always been very popular with the students and teachers."

"He knows how to teach, and he understands the material well," Yi said trying to sound disinterested.

"Yes, he does," sighed Yan. "It's so unfortunate that before he didn't understand the greatness and gloriousness of our country like you and I do. Hopefully, he has learned his lesson better the second time around."

"I am sorry," Yi said, trying to be polite, "but I am a little busy. With Teacher Long's return, there is a lot of paperwork to be filled and filed. I am sorry, but I really don't have time to talk right now. Can we continue this conversation another time?"

"Oh, of course. My apologies, Teacher Yi. I understand how

busy you must be right now." Yan began walking out the door, before stopping at the doorway. "Oh, before I forget, there is something I need you to do…" He grinned wickedly.

"Which is?"

"This Friday, we will be holding a Welcome Back Assembly for Teacher Long," Yan said, now positively brimming. "During which time he will be apologizing to the school for shaming us so many years ago and begging for our forgiveness. I need you to write a speech reminding him of his crimes and shaming him. Be sure to make it clear that the faculty of this school support the re-education and labor that he went through. That he owes us his loyalty for us willing to forgive him for his crimes. Also, you will have your students do a project about his mistakes and why he was punished. The best students will be presenting their project on Friday in front of the school to educate everyone," he added as a matter of fact.

"Teacher Long has gone through nearly two years of re-education and labor. He was a part of the school before you or I were hired. Are we sure we still need to use public humiliation to remind him of his crimes?" Yi asked, trying to control his emotions.

"This assembly is the only way we can be assured that Teacher Long understands his mistakes," Yan replied happily. "It is important that Teacher Long begs us all for forgiveness for humiliating us all those years ago."

"Unfortunately," Yi said, thinking up an excuse, "this week is rather busy for me. You know, as the head teacher of the department and with finals coming up at the end of the month, I need to create all the reviews and tests, and I simply don't have time. As you know, we haven't been able to find the best teachers, recently, and it has been rather uneven in the department for the classes I am not teaching. Plus, with Teacher Xiang leaving and Teacher Long returning, that is a lot of work for me. I appreciate this opportunity, but it would best if another faculty member wrote the speech."

"That is precisely why you must do it. You are the head teacher of this department, and you knew Long best. You saw firsthand Long's revolutionary ideas, and you understand better than anyone how dangerous he used to be." Yan paused, looking thoughtful and grinning. "Although, I don't recall you ever reporting them in an official manner…" He paused again, for a much longer moment this time, as if waiting for his words to sink in. "Anyway, as you know, these are volatile times, and it would be very important for everyone to know that the head teacher and the son of our great Governor supports our policies and not revolutionaries." He grinned sadistically. "I look forward to reading your speech and criticisms, say on Thursday morning? Have a good evening, Teacher Yi," he added as an afterthought as he left the office.

Yi didn't know what to say or to do. Looking over at Long's desk and wondering what choices he had, he took out his cellphone and sent out a text.

Yi walked awkwardly into Qiang's clinic. It had been many years since he had come here to talk to Qiang, as all the recent visits had been at Qiang's apartment, and he never took Hanbing on any of her health examinations. Qiang was standing at the door when he arrived. "So?" Qiang asked. "What are you here to complain about?"

"What makes you so sure I want to complain?" Yi said, following Qiang into his office.

"Because that is the nature of our one-on-one relationship," Qiang smirked, shutting the door behind him. "I am basically your therapist. So, tell me, my patient, what happened today?"

"Yeah, yeah." Yi couldn't think of a clever retort as he sat down on the examination table, and he decided to go straight to the point. "My colleague Teacher Long got rehired today."

"The guy who got sent up to Re-Education Camp?" Qiang asked, surprised. "I didn't realize the school would ever take him back."

"Yeah and…" Yi stuttered as he tried to mask his feelings, "…he is different…"

"Different? How?"

"Hmmm…I guess, well…he looks older, and he is missing teeth, he is crippled, and his arms…" Yi paused thinking about how he felt when he saw Teacher Long in the morning. Suddenly, before he could stop himself, he started tearing up. "They tortured him, Qiang. They tortured my friend. He has scars up and down his arms, like lines. He can't walk properly. Also…he…he is a completely different person now. His eyes, they look dead and soulless. The way he talks, he sounds robotic, and he just says the same thing over and over again. I mean, I know he was sent to a Re-Education Labor Camp, but…"

"But you weren't expecting him to be tortured," Qiang finished his sentence. "Well, what did you expect?"

"I don't know," Yi sniffled. "Don't get me wrong. I know Re-Education Labor Camp is about, you know, hard labor and relearning, and I know it isn't a place you want to be. I guess I never really thought about what it entailed, what those words actually meant."

"Ok…what do you want me to say?" Qiang said harshly. "You want me to act like I am surprised? You want me to lie to you and say your friend will be alright and soon return back to normal?"

"He sounded liked he had been brainwashed!"

"Brainwashing never works. If it did, everything would be much easier for our government," Qiang chuckled before reminding himself of the seriousness of the situation. "Most likely he is just overcompensating because he is afraid. I can't imagine what he has gone though. He probably is afraid everyone is watching him from every corner."

Yi looked around uncomfortably, took a deep breath, and wiped his eyes before speaking in a voice hardly louder than a whisper. "I am scared, Qiang. I am more scared then I am willing to admit." He stopped, his eyes darting, his body shaking as he spoke the truth he never said out loud. "Look how many laws I am breaking: my marriage with Ling, my adoption of Hanbing. Look how many other things could screw me over, my friendship with you and Zhuang, for example." He teared up again, "Today, in school, I nearly told my students I disagreed with the school. Do you know what could happen to me if I did? Any one of those things could put me in the same camp as Teacher Long. I don't think I can do it anymore. Tell me Qiang, what can I do?"

Qiang smiled. "Nothing. This is your life. The decisions you made have led you to this life."

Yi couldn't control his emotions anymore. Falling to the ground, he burst into tears. "Do you know how hard it is? I am sick of hiding; I am sick of feeling scared," he sobbed into his hands. "Hanbing is now eight, you know. Within a few years it's going to be harder and harder to hide the truth. What happens when she hits puberty? At least she appears to be handling herself well. After the conversation we had last year, I felt it was touch and go for a while," he added with half a smile. "But at least she seems happy."

Qiang sat down next to his friend and wrapped his arm around him. "I did offer to Ling to do a sex change on her a few years back, before you told her that she was a girl, but he refused. Guess you will have to deal with having a girl now," he finished with a laugh.

Yi gave a light chuckle and sunk into his friend's arms. "I never understood why you have stood by me after all these years. After all the things I have said or thought about you."

"Look," Qiang said quietly, "the thing you never understood all these years is that no matter how you portray yourself, deep down you are a good man. You are more willing to accept people for who they are than you let on. You saved your friend from a terrible fate when no one else would have. You rescued an abandoned baby and saved her life by adopting her to keep her from hardship. These are actions of a brave and decent man. Also, your family is stronger than you realize. Ling has been hiding this secret for just as long as you have. Hanbing has known she is a girl for about a year and has not told anyone, but as you also noted is still doing as well as before you told her, perhaps even better."

"But as you point out, I use Ling for my physical pleasure and disregard his feelings, and if truth be told, I took in a child because I knew it would get my father off my back," Yi said solemnly. "I hurt the people closest to me because I am afraid and a coward."

"I didn't say you were a perfect man," said Qiang. "You are flawed. But, in your heart, you are indeed a good person. You do care about others. You just need to work on accepting that."

Yi said nothing and slid out of his friend's arms. He stood up. "Thank you for that. I know this has been a short visit, but I should be getting home. I forgot to tell Ling I was swinging by. I am sure he is worried about me."

"Have you thought about a backup plan?" asked Qiang from behind him as he walked out the door.

"A backup plan?"

"In case," Qiang said cautiously, "everything goes wrong. I don't want to see the three of you sent off to some camp and disappear."

"No…" Yi said. He was surprised; such an obvious idea had never occurred to him. "No, we don't have a backup plan. I guess I have been so worried about things going south, that I never thought about what I would do if they *did*."

"Perhaps it would be a good idea to create one," Qiang said sarcastically. Becoming more serious, he said, "This is what I would do. Prepare three suitcases, one for the each of you. Put in some clothing, maybe some important personal items, and valuables. Leave them at my house. This way if things ever reach the point of no return, you can call me, and at least this way, I can try to rescue you."

Yi thought for a moment and nodded. "You know," he said thinking out loud. "I say this a lot, but you really are a much better friend then I give you credit for. Thank you for everything, Qiang."

20.
HIDDEN SECRETS DESTROY FAMILY AND COUNTRY

THE FAMILY GATHERED AROUND THE dinner table at the Governor's House for Hanbing's ninth Arrival Day. Earlier in the day, they had thrown her a grandiose party in People's Park, inviting all her classmates, her maternal grandparents, and a number of government officials for show. Now, they were all settling down, finishing dinner, and eating Arrival cake. Suddenly, Hanbing stood up, rubbing her lower stomach, and whispered to Ling, "Mama, I don't feel so good. I think I am going to be sick."

The Governor looked over with his judging eyes, while Mengqin and Baihe watched carefully, hoping for the Governor to get angry. Before he could say anything, Yi interrupted, "He probably ate too much cake. Ling, why don't you take Hanbing to the bathroom and help him out?"

The Governor watched carefully as Ling and Hanbing left, as if wanting to comment on something. "Thank you for throwing this party," Yi said carefully. "I know Hanbing had a lot of fun."

"A child should enjoy his Arrival Day." The Governor smiled. "My grandson seems very happy."

"He has been, and I know today will be a day he never forgets. Recently, he has been doing very well in school," Yi said proudly. "Top of the class, as usual. This is a nice break and reward for him."

"Qinghuang is doing very well also," Mengqin interjected, patting his son on the head. "His teacher told me he shows huge promise in becoming a politician."

The Governor ignored his younger child's second comment. "In any case, I am glad my grandchildren are doing well. We need smart children to continue our political dynasty."

Suddenly, Ling's voice rang out from the larger bathroom down the hall. "Yi, can you come here from a moment?"

"Excuse me," said Yi, smiling at everyone around the table. "My child needs me. I will be right back."

Yi knocked on the bathroom door. Ling opened it to a crack, confirming it was him, and quickly pulled him in. "Ok?" said Yi, confused by the way Ling was acting. "What is happening here?"

"I think Hanbing got hurt today. I put her in the shower, please take a look," Ling said, tearing up. He shut the door quickly, careful to lock it behind him.

"What?" said Yi rushing over to take a look at his daughter, he pulled open the shower curtain, and gasped in surprise

Hanbing was standing in the middle of the shower. There was blood dripping down the side of her leg. It appeared to be coming out of her vagina. Ling looked over his shoulder. "I don't know how she could have possibly cut herself down there. Maybe she wasn't too careful on one of the slides?"

"Ling…" said Yi in shock. "I don't think Hanbing is hurt. I think Hanbing is menstruating."

"What?"

"You know. When a woman hits puberty…" Yi suddenly realized that there was no way Ling understood what was happening. He would have never been taught this information. The only reason that Yi knew was because he took some basic human biology classes in university. "Let's just say once a month, if I remember from my books correctly, a woman has a cycle, and she starts bleeding."

"What? You mean this will happen again?" said Ling, still too worried to do anything. "What should we do?"

"Are you in pain, Hanbing?" asked Yi calmly.

"A little, Baba," Hanbing said meekly. "But I am scared. What is happening? Why am I bleeding?"

"Baba is trying to work things out," Yi said calmly. "Ling, I need you to wash her up."

"Ok…" stuttered Ling, turning on the water and looking around for towels.

Suddenly, there was a knock on the door. Guihua's voice came from the other side. "Is everything alright in there?"

Ling froze, staring at Yi. Yi took a deep sigh. "Yes, everything is fine."

"Do you need help in there?" asked Guihua out of genuine concern.

Yi thought for a moment, stood up and unlocked the door. "Hanbing is fine, but we have a small unexpected problem. Maybe you can help," he said, gesturing her inside.

Guihua looked at Hanbing in the bathtub. Immediately understanding the situation at hand, she turned hastily to Yi, standing in awe. "Isn't she a little young for this to be happening?"

Yi thought for a moment and whispered, "Yeah, I think so. I don't know. I have only learned about this in biology books. They aren't exactly swarming with details. Any suggestions on what to do?"

"I am not sure what to do either," Guihua said, slightly scared. "I mean, I don't have any experience with this. I don't think anyone in this country still has experience with this. I guess clean her up, maybe use some sort of towel to keep the blood from coming down her legs? But, most importantly, keep her safe and comfortable."

Hanbing looked terrified sitting in the tub as the three adults stood around her whispering. She wasn't sure how to react to all of this, and she had never felt pain like this before. She suddenly started tearing up.

"Tell grandma how you feel," Guihua said, kneeling next to Hanbing and gently wiping her face. "Are you in pain?"

"A little, Grandma," sniffled Hanbing. "I feel like I have a bad stomachache."

"Don't worry, Hanbing," Guihua smiled calmly. "Your daddy, mommy, and I will take care of you. You will be fine. If you want,

Grandma will brew you a special drink that will make you feel better? Do you want that, sweetie?"

"Yes please, Grandma." Hanbing looked up smiling. "Thank you, Grandma."

A loud smash interrupted them. The door behind them burst open. Governor Wang walked in, furious. "What IN THE WORLD is happening here? Why are you all hiding in the bathroom, instead of finishing Hanbing's celebration dinner?"

He looked at the three adults standing there, shell-shocked and speechless. He looked at Hanbing, sitting naked in the pinkish water. He looked downwards noticing her vagina. He gasped in surprise and stumbled backward. "What? WHAT IS GOING ON HERE?"

"I can explain!" Yi said quickly, standing up and trying to push the Governor out of the room.

"You two," Governor Wang said angrily, pointing at Yi and Ling. "Come to my office NOW." He pointed at Guihua. "Take Hanbing upstairs and clean up. Wipe all that blood off of my grandchild. Afterwards, you both come to my office." The Governor looked scared, an emotion Yi had never seen of his father's face. "I don't know what is happening, but I don't like it. I want answers. NOW."

Yi hadn't been in his father's office in a very long time. Even when he was a child, he rarely went in there. It was a rather generic looking room, he thought as he sat down in front of his father's large mahogany desk. He looked around, trying to avoid looking at his father in front of him, or Ling, shivering scared next to him. Behind him, Mengqin and Baihe had followed them in, giggling with glee with the idea of watching the Governor yell at Yi.

The Governor looked at Yi carefully. "Tell me," he said tearfully. "Why do you dislike me so much, that you had to take my first grandson and turn him into a female? Do you faggots want to be women so much that you turned your child into a woman? Explain to me now because I don't understand."

Ling looked at Yi, scared and confused. Yi took a deep breath. "Sir, Hanbing isn't a nan-nu. Hanbing was never even a boy. Hanbing is a biological girl."

"What?" The Governor laughed hollowly. "This has to be some sort of a sick joke. You can't create the X chromosome. That's impossible."

"Technically speaking," Yi said awkwardly, "Hanbing isn't biologically related to me or you."

"WHAT?" the Governor looked at Yi, and then at Ling. He looked as if he was about to vomit as he tried to figure out an explanation. "You mean…you mean…Hanbing is actually…" He looked at Ling, his face disgusted. "ITS CHILD!"

"No, sir," interrupted Ling quietly. "Hanbing isn't related to me either. I found her. I found her in the river."

The Governor looked at Ling blankly and decided to ignore him. He turned back to Yi. "Please explain to me what is going on, and why do you consistently continue to find ways to ruin this family's honor?"

"Nine years ago," Yi began, "Ling found a baby in the river. When we took a look at the baby, we realized it was a girl, and after consulting a doctor, we had reason to believe that it was a Chinese biological female. Although we searched in the national database, we could not find proof of her existence. We decided to keep her and raise her as a son. This way no one could figure out her secret. Our doctor helped register her as our son." He tried to keep his words simple and neutral. There was no reason implicate Qiang or say something to make the Governor angrier that he already was.

"Okay," the Governor said, surprised. "The child is a female. How do you know she is Chinese and not a foreigner?"

"Her DNA matches people who were born around this area, but we have no idea who her parents are. Also, because she was a healthy baby, we could assume she was born slightly upriver around this area."

"Have you ever found her parents?" asked the Governor.

"No, but as you know sir, there are always rumors of biological females in the villages. She could have come from one of those villages," Yi replied casually.

"Basically, you are telling me," the Governor said, "that you found the first biological female in who knows how long, and instead of doing your patriotic duty and turning her into the government, you decided to keep her and raise her as your own." In the background, Mengqin and Baihe were whispering between themselves, equally surprised and shocked by the turn of events.

"Yes, sir."

The Governor smashed his fists on the table. "I don't even know where to begin. You have lied to me; you have lied to your glorious country. What made you think it would be alright to do that? Have I really been this much of a failure as a parent? That my child doesn't even know the difference between right and wrong? Honestly, what made you think this was okay?"

"To be perfectly honest…" Yi said adamantly. He looked over at Ling and reached over to hold his hand. "We were afraid of what would happen to her if the government took her. We all have heard the rumors. Even if they are most likely not true, we didn't want to take the risk. We felt responsible because we found her, and we didn't want her getting hurt."

The Governor paused for a moment, thinking about the data he had learned about the camps that had been set up for biological females. Finally, he said, "That is irrelevant. What is relevant is that my own son broke the law and—"

There was gentle knock on the door. Guihua and Hanbing came walking in. Guihua spoke first. "Excuse me, sir, I am sorry to interrupt, but Hanbing needs rest. I think it would be best for her parents to take her home and let her get some sleep. She has had a long day, and she is in slight shock about what just happened. Maybe you guys can talk tomorrow?" She spoke in a sweet calming voice, careful not to anger the Governor.

The Governor stood for a moment, looking at the clock. It was getting late. "Fine," he scowled. "But I want to continue this tomorrow. You two, take Hanbing home. Yi, I will see you tomorrow. We are not finished here."

"I am sorry, Grandpa, Grandma, Uncle, and Auntie," Hanbing spoke in a quiet voice, sniffling. "I love you. Please don't send me away. I love you all. I love you all so much. I am so sorry about all of this. I love you all so very much."

Ling quickly ran over. "Everything is going to be alright, sweetie," he whispered into her ear.

Governor Wang said nothing as Yi and Ling grabbed Hanbing and walked out. Mengqin and Baihe, still talking between themselves, walked out, followed by Guihua. He stood behind the desk, watching them as they left his office.

The Governor looked out the office window watching Yi, Ling, and Hanbing step into a taxi. He wasn't sure how he felt right now. He loved his grandson, well, as he just learned, his granddaughter. She was so smart, so unlike any woman he had ever met. Then again, he had only met a few biological women before. She was good at school, good at sports, well behaved and well spoken. If it wasn't the problem of her sex, she would be perfect grandchild, the perfect heir in fact. Could he still love her the same way now that he knew his grandson was actually his granddaughter?

Of course, there was another issue. This could be very bad or very good for his career. Should he keep this a secret? What would happen if the public found out? Learning about a new biological female would be good for the country, he reminded himself. Hanbing could be treated as a celebrity, and he could be worshipped for discovering the existence of another biological female in who remembers how long. On the other hand, things could go the other direction, and things could even go badly for Hanbing. As a high member of the government, he had seen some proof of what had happened to the remaining biological females. Even if the government didn't do it on purpose, he knew that there were those in power who would treat Hanbing like a laboratory rat. Did he still love Hanbing enough to protect her if that could happen? He wasn't sure he wanted to let this information go public. Why did such difficult things always happen to his family and potentially ruin his career and their family's political dynasty? First Ling and now this.

"Excuse me," said a voice behind him. Mengqin had come in alone. He shut the door tightly behind him.

"Why do these things always happen to me?" asked the Governor solemnly. "And why does it always involve Yi?"

"I told you before," said Mengqin sadly, "that Yi doesn't understand politics and our family like you and I do. He seems to think himself above the law. He has never been filial to you or respected you. Unlike me. I have always been loyal to you, father."

"What have I said before ABOUT BADMOUTHING YOUR BROTHER!" the Governor snapped. Mengqin winced in pain. "He has always been a good man. Even if he is very confused and lost."

"Yes, sir," Mengqin said submissively, bowing his head. "However, sir, you cannot deny this lie. All his lies, they have gone too far. They are dangerous to us, our family, our legacy, and most importantly, to our glorious nation. What are you going to do now?"

"I…don't…know…" the Governor said truthfully through gritted teeth.

"Sir," Mengqin said, keeping his head bowed so the Governor could not see his slight smile. "I have always valued and respected you for your logic and your loyalty to our glorious nation. I know whatever decision you make will put our glorious country before personal interests as you have always taught us what is right. Something that Yi clearly did not learn, I might add." He stood up and began walking out the door. "I trust you will make the correct decision for all of us, and I respect you for that."

The Governor watched his second son walk out the door, shutting it behind him. He stood behind his desk, struggling with what to do. Contemplating the right decision.

Yi, Ling, and Hanbing didn't talk until they entered the taxi. After telling the driver where they were going. Ling took a big sigh of relief. "That could have gone a lot worse," he said as Hanbing begin to fall asleep on his lap.

Yi didn't say anything. He felt his cellphone vibrate in this pocket and took it out to read to the text.

"For a moment there," Ling continued, "I thought your father would arrest us on the spot. But maybe we were wrong. Maybe your father does care about his family more than we realized. I am sure when you go talk to him tomorrow, you will be able to clear things up and hopefully, everything will return back to normal. Well, as normal as things are in our life. Anyway…" He stopped. Yi was looking as if he were about to vomit. "What's wrong?" Ling asked, surprised. "Are you sick?"

Yi took his cellphone and shoved it into Ling's face. He was white and unable to talk. Ling took a glance at the message. It was from Guihua and was clearly hastily written.

Don't go home police called they are coming don't contact me phone is trackable love you good luck.

Ling looked up, shocked. He didn't know what to say. He tried to process the words from the message in his mind. He suddenly realized he had no idea what they should do…where they could go…

"What are you waiting for?" gasped Yi, yanking the cellphone out Ling's hands. Yi's face was pale and twisted in pain, as he tried to speak properly. "Call Qiang. Call Zhuang. We need to get out of here. As soon as possible." Turning to the driver, he croaked, "We have a change of location. We need to go to…"

21.
PATRIOTISM, OUR MOST IMPORTANT VIRTUE

GOVERNOR WANG STOOD IN THE backstage of the auditorium in the Governor's Manor, rereading his speech and practicing it under his breath. The last week had been some of the most difficult days of his career. The city was filled with rumors. The security he had to send to each of the city's entry and exit points were not helping, nor were the police searches in the street. The city wanted answers, and under the counsel of his advisors, he was to give a speech to the people. He looked out at the picture of the previous governor, his father, hanging on the wall. He wondered how he would have handled it. He knew his father would be disappointed with his grandson. There had been no trace of Yi since he watched them walk out of his house a week ago. He could hear his assistant, Su Xiaoming, talking to the reporters, prepping them. He heard his name called and walked onto the stage. There was only limited clapping.

"My fellow comrades," the Governor began. He coughed; the cough echoed in the silence of the auditorium, and he started anew.

My fellow comrades. I am here to address the rumors currently plaguing and destroying our great city and province and embarrassing our glorious nation. Today, I will officially explain, on the behalf of the city and province, what is happening.

Many of the rumors that have spread recently, though infectious and harmful like a disease, are indeed based partially on facts. A week ago, a biological woman, age nine, named Wang Hanbing, was indeed discovered in Xincheng and has been kidnapped. I can assure you right now that your government and your police force are doing everything in their power to find her and her captors. To ensure your and her safety, the captors must be captured and punished, and Wang Hanbing sent to a specially designed camp for her protection.

Unfortunately, we do not know who her biological parents are. Therefore, at this time, I am unable to report the status of other biological women and men capable of creating the X chromosome. However, we are familiar with her captors, who have taken her from the protection of our glorious government, and I can assure you they will be punished under the full extent of the law when found.

It is with great shame that I report that the captors are indeed my son, Wang Yi, and his wife, Li Ling, both of whom I have officially disowned. They are no longer considered members of my family and should not be treated as such. The captors were last seen a week ago exiting the Governor's Manor and have not been seen since. The police and security on city, provincial, and national levels have been given orders to capture them under any circumstance, dead or alive. We are also investigatng the doctor of the child, Liang Qiang, a surgeon of Shoushu District, to understand his involvement in this case. Unfortunately, he too has disappeared and has not been seen in at least a few days, leading us to believe that he was involved with the captors.

All departments and people involved with this case are currently working around the clock to make sure that the female is found and her captors are brought to justice. We implore any patriotic, responsible citizen to report any sighting of Wang Yi, Li Ling, and Liang Qiang to the police so that this case may be closed, and the government can take Wang Hanbing under its generous care.

Thank you, everyone, for your support. May the heavens bless our glorious nation and keep us prospering.

The Governor finished his speech with an awkward bow. No one in the audience clapped or visually reacted. The reporters appeared confused on how to respond. Xiaoming walked out of the back of the auditorium. "I am sorry. We won't be taking any questions today," he said hastily. "The Governor has a very busy schedule." As they walked into the back, Xiaoming leaned over and whispered in the Governor's ear, "Excuse me, sir, but there are two men in the office. They say wish to speak with you in private."

"I thought I told you," the Governor scowled, "that I don't see anyone unless they have made an appointment. I checked my schedule today, and unless your failed to tell me…"

"They didn't make an appointment, sir," Xiaoming said quickly, "but they come directly from the Capital, from the Office of Supreme President Qin Jiabao. It's not like I could say no."

The Governor paused, surprised. "Okay, tell them I will be there in a moment. I need to use the restroom first."

Governor Wang stood in front of the mirror in his private bathroom looking at himself, thinking. He felt as if he gained many more wrinkles from the stress of the last week. He couldn't tell if was the light or his eyes, but he could swear his hair had turned grayer.

No one had any idea where his son, grandchild, and Ling had disappeared to after they left his house on Hanbing's Arrival Day. Traffic security footage around the city had shown them dropped off on the border of Shoushu District. Unfortunately, due to minimal funding and interest, the Shoushu District lacked the camera security of the other districts, and once they entered, it was as if they disappeared. After their disappearance, they had checked the hospital and residence of the surgeon Liang Qiang, but he too had disappeared without a trace, which in Governor Wang's mind, confirmed his involvement.

He was also concerned with how fast they had disappeared. There were no other men in his office when he called the police to report them, so how could they have known? He had heard

Mengqin talking to his mother outside his office, but it's not as if his son would have warned his brother. It was, after all, his suggestion. Perhaps his office was being bugged, maybe one of his political enemies had snuck in when he wasn't there. He would have to check the security footage when he got back.

He was slightly surprised and worried that the Supreme President had sent representatives over, as he had just spoken with the Supreme President two days ago and had assured him that he had full control of the situation. He knew this issue could be seen as a matter of national security, but he assumed the Supreme President trusted him enough to solve it. Perhaps he was over thinking it. The President could have just sent some extra help or just wanted updates. There was no reason to start worrying now.

The two men were standing around the back of the office talking when the Governor walked in. The Governor was slightly surprised when he saw the first man, Cheng Chen, his now disowned son's best friend and son of one of his political allies. The other man, about the same age, he recognized from numerous meetings but never bothered to learn his name as he never appeared important enough.

"Hello, Governor Wang," Chen began. "I hope we find you doing well?"

"What are you doing here?" asked the Governor suspiciously. There was something about the manner of both men he didn't like.

"We have been sent in from the office of our Supreme President," the man whose name Governor Wang did not know responded. "There are a few issues we need to talk about."

The Governor ignored him and turned to Chen. "Who is he, and why are you both here? I don't usually accept appointments without prior arrangement. As I said to our honorable Supreme President just two days ago, things are under control here. I am sure you have just heard my speech addressing the city and province."

Chen and the unknown man looked at each other. Chen looked

worried as the other man smirked. "My apologies for not introducing myself. I assume you already knew me as we have met in passing, but I guess you never found me enough important to remember. I am Jiandie, and I am the undersecretary to our honorable Supreme President. As for what we are doing here, since you asked so directly," Jiandie paused, enjoying the words coming out of his mouth, "we are here to ask for your resignation."

"My resignation?" asked the Governor, shocked. Then he laughed. "This is some sort of dumb joke, isn't it?"

"Please, don't made this difficult," said Chen, pleading. "I wasn't supposed to be here. I only came here as a family friend to help."

"Chen, you have always been a spineless traitor. Your father would be ashamed," the Governor snapped. "I should have never allowed you to become friends with my..." His voice stopped, drifting off into silence. Turning to Jiandie, he angrily asked, "My resignation. On what grounds do you have to call for my resignation? I have been, my family has been loyal members to the country and the Party since its founding, long before you were born. You have no right to ask for my resignation."

"On the contrary," smiled Jiandie, "you have been illegally hiding a biological female from the government for nearly a decade. That fact alone is seen as treason."

"A fact that I did not know about until last week, when I promptly informed the proper authorities," Governor Wang snapped back.

"Is there any way you can prove you didn't know?" asked Jiandie thoughtfully. "For all we know, you could have known this entire time but never reported it."

"Then why would I report it now?" the Governor asked angrily.

"Don't ask me how the mind of a treasonous governor would work," Jiandie replied, shrugging. "Even if you deny that you knew about the biological female in your household, that doesn't deny the other treasonous skeleton in your closet."

"Which is?"

"That you knowingly supported your homosexual son to get married to another homosexual," Jiandie said simply. He smiled wickedly as he watched the reaction on the Governor's face.

The Governor paused again, shocked. Recovering quickly, he simply stated, "I have no idea what you are talking about."

"There is no need to lie anymore, Governor," Jiandie smirked. "We all know how you helped register Li Ling as a female, despite still being a male, allowing your son to continue in his homosexual ways. That is another count of treason on your record."

"I have no idea what you are talking about," Governor Wang said stubbornly. "I want to talk to my team before I continue. I want to talk to my son, Mengqin."

Chen shook his head sadly in the background. Jiandie laughed. "Talk to your son? Who do you think gave us the information about Wang Yi and Li Ling's illegal homosexual marriage? Who do you think told us everything we now have on you?" He stopped, taking a moment to savor Governor Wang's stunned face. "Never saw that coming, did you?"

The Governor turned slowly to Chen. "Tell me, Chen, as the son of my friend and colleague, and not as a government official, is what this man said true?"

Chen stood there quietly, head down. "It is true, Governor Wang. Your son told us everything yesterday."

"Turns out," Jiandie said, still smirking, "that the need for power is more important than the need for loyalty in the Wang family. The Wangs literally will do anything to get ahead in society." He paused once more to savor the moment. "Once Mengqin realized your career was over, which I think frankly everyone except you saw, he quickly jumped ship and told us everything."

Governor Wang said nothing, just stood there. A look of defeat began to spread about his face as he started to accept the situation.

"The newspapers are already gathering as much information as they can on this new scandal," Jiandie said, smiling. "I expect it will be all over the evening news, if it is not already being broadcast. Apparently, many reporters are already noticing the irony."

"Irony?" the Governor asked meekly.

"About this scandal, and the scandal so many years ago involving a…Judge…Lao?" Jiandie posed the question thoughtfully, but there was clearly an underlying intention. "I am sure you remember the case, when you argued he wasn't fit to be a judge because of his homosexual son. I wonder if back then, did you see the hypocrisy? If so, did you expect it to bite you nearly a decade later?"

The Governor said nothing, fuming. He turned to Chen, with a desperate plea. "I want to talk to you. Alone. Do it as a favor to your father's friend?"

Chen said nothing before nodding slowly.

"Really," laughed Jiandie, "even after he called you a spineless traitor?" He shrugged and started walking out the door. "Whatever. Do what you please." He stopped by the door, and without turning around, he spoke slowly. "You never asked me my family name. That wasn't very polite you know. Maybe now that you are unemployed, you can get a new attitude and learn some manners. But for future reference, it's Lao."

Governor Wang stood there for a moment staring at the door. "Was that Judge Lao's son? I thought…"

"Judge Lao's son is dead. He committed suicide soon after that incident. That was his cousin. Apparently, they were quite close," Chen said honestly and quietly. "Jiandie is quite the skilled politician and has risen up the ranks through keeping things quiet. Supreme President trusts him a lot. He may act like a background figure, but he has always commanded a considerable amount of power. He just isn't one to show it off. Chooses his battles carefully and usually wins," he added as a warning.

The Governor said nothing for a moment, thinking carefully.

"I am not going to go out quietly. You can push me out of office, but I will come back. This is my birthright, and no one can take it from me."

"I didn't think you would take it quietly," Chen said. "That is why I am here. My father asked me to keep you from doing something irrational. And my advice for you is to take your retirement. You had a strong career. Resign and retire gracefully. Take it before things become worse for you."

"You know, Mengqin has always been a coward. I should have seen this coming. I should have known he would betray me," the Governor sneered.

"That doesn't matter now." Chen took a moment, carefully choosing his words. "The simple truth is you made some mistakes, and you have to recognize those mistakes and confess them. Things could be a lot worse if you are not careful."

"HA," laughed the Governor. "I have been pushed out of my job. My sons have both betrayed me. How could things be any worse?"

"You could be tried for treason," Chen said. The Governor paused, shocked at his words. "What happened with this child, with Yi and Ling's marriage. These are high counts of treason, and there are some on the national level who feel you should be charged as such. The only reason you haven't been is no one wants to make this scandal any bigger than it already is and risk dividing the Party. That's why I am asking you—telling you— to prepare your resignation speech. Don't make this into a bigger issue than it already is. Just go quietly, or things could get a lot worse."

Governor Wang thought for a moment, his face turning red with anger. "Fine. I will give a resignation speech. I will step down quietly. But as soon as this is over, when my disowned eldest son is rotting in a cell, when his partner is dead, and my other traitorous son is expelled from government, I will rise again. I will become more powerful than before. This position is my birthright, and I intend to keep it that way."

22.
IN TIMES OF DIFFICULTY, IT IS OUR CHOICES THAT DEFINE US

Yi woke up at 6:00 a.m. again. He had not slept well in the last week or so, and he simply could not fall asleep on a hard-wooden plank bed with straw as a mattress. Next to him, Hanbing and Ling both slept soundly. They didn't seem to have as much of a problem as he did. Quietly, he crawled out of bed and got dressed. He could hear Qiang and Zhuang in the next room, snoring lightly. He looked around the two-room mud hut. There wasn't much here. The straw roof was rotting. Loose wires hung across the wall, connecting to a few electronic appliances. A couple of lights, a small radio. Outside this building was another mud hut with a small kitchen and bathroom. He and Ling had tossed their cellphones the night they escaped as they couldn't risk being tracked, but he no longer thought it mattered. It wasn't like he could get any signal out here. Looking around, he understood why Zhuang joined the army and later moved to the city. There was no way anyone could ever live here and not want to kill themselves.

After scribbling a small note on a piece of paper and grabbing a face filter mask, which had both the benefit of protecting him from the village coal air and hiding his identity, Yi began the couple kilometer trek down to the village. He walked past the inconspicuous van they had left Xincheng in parked at the edge of the property. He looked in it, checking if their luggage was still in there.

It had been a rushed escape, and he was thankful to Qiang for allowing him to leave some stuff at their apartment just a year prior. After receiving the text from Guihua, they had met Qiang and Zhuang on the border of Shoushu District and walked back to their apartment. They couldn't risk spending the night and were gone before midnight. They tossed their cellphones out in a gas station trash can in Shenyi District, opposite the direction they were heading. From there they drove straight to Zhuang's farm, the most private place they could think of, and had been lying low there since.

The walk down to the village was not a pleasant one as there was no proper road. The farms on both sides were sparsely planted, and most of the shrubbery was dead. Years of unsustainable growing techniques, mismanagment of chemicals, and global warming had made it hard for vegetables to grow. Some wild grass and other weeds sprouted here and there, but overall the dusty road and countryside felt very lifeless. There weren't even any birds, rodents, or reptiles about, as starving villagers had eaten them in times of need.

He reached the nearest village after about a thirty-minute walk, stopping at the first local mom-and-pop shop to pick up some supplies. There wasn't much inside, but he found a small dusty bar of chocolate hidden behind a shelf which he knew would make Hanbing happy. She didn't show it much, but he imagined that the last week had been just as difficult for her. Looking around, he was also able to pick up a few drinks and a couple of snacks that were not expired. Finally, he grabbed the morning newspaper, *The PRCC Daily*. A quick glance showed his, Ling's, Qiang's, and Hanbing's faces on the front page, under a large headline. After leaving, he took a quick walk around the thirty or so buildings in the village. The quality of the architecture here was better than Zhuang's farmhouse, but not by much. Living in Xincheng, he often forgot that the areas outside of the city did not receive the same financial support from the provincial and national government. Unable to find what he wanted, he gave up and began his trek home.

Hanbing was already eating breakfast with Qiang by the time Yi got back. Zhuang had managed to buy a few eggs from the neighbors and had brought some food from home on the night of their escape, but they were quickly running out. The farmhouse hadn't been used in years, but they didn't plan to stay long enough to use it anyway. Yi sat down as Ling and Zhuang came out with more food from the kitchen.

"There isn't much food left. I tried to make do with what we have," said Zhuang sadly. "But, I'll go buy some more later."

"I walked down to the village today," Yi said as he took out the newspaper, throwing the snacks he bought on the table. "I couldn't find much food. We are in quite a poor area."

"All areas outside of the Capital and provincial capitals are poor," Qiang interjected.

"I know. That's why I am planning to drive for a bit." Zhuang said. "I would ask one of you to come with me, but you know…" He pointed at the front page of the newspaper that Yi had bought. Large headlines blared across the front page with their pictures underneath.

Homosexual kidnappers and treasonous surgeon still at large

NATIONAL GOVERNMENT OFFERING LARGEST REWARD IN NATION'S HISTORY

"I am the only one who has not been identified," Zhuang finished sadly. "I am sad there isn't much for you guys to do around here but make the best of it." He looked around at all the solemn faces. "I best be getting out of here. I should be back by early afternoon. Be safe and don't do anything stupid or risky."

"Anything in the news worth knowing?" Qiang asked curiously after Zhuang left.

"Yeah," Yi replied. He looked at Ling and Hanbing, who promptly brought her out of the room. They had decided to never discuss the matter at hand in front of Hanbing to spare her the distress. "Looks like my father has finally retired." He passed the page to Qiang:

Traitorous Governor of Zhongjiang Province Finally Retires BY LAN BOKUAI

After pressure from the people and fellow leaders, the traitorous Governor Wang Jiangjun finally gave his retirement speech late yesterday afternoon. Speaking in front of a group of about 300 government officials, he accepted responsibility for the mishandling in the current Wang Hanbing Biological Woman Incident. He also vowed to do everything to help arrest the captors, especially his now-disowned homosexual son, Wang Yi.

Outside of the Governor's Building, many continue to protest the lack of persecution of Governor Wang by the Central Government, with many citing the infamous case involving Judge Lao about a decade earlier, a decision spearheaded directly by the Governor. Judge Lao was not one of the protesters, but sources say he is planning to use this incident to regain political power. In the meantime, many are citing this as another example in which a corrupt individual was not prosecuted due to higher social status and good connections.

"It would be a shame upon society if Wang is not executed," said a young man in the audience. "Wang is the most corrupt Governor we have ever had, and I hope he is shot for it."

When asked, the spokesmen for Supreme President says that they are still currently looking into what Ex-Governor Wang knew and didn't know, but that he is currently cooperating with the National Government, so that the first biological female found in over two decades can be brought under the safety of government control. In the meantime, many government officials wish to assure the public that everything is being done to bring the child to safety.

"Well, we all saw that coming," Qiang said indifferently. "Still, I wonder who outed you to the public. I can't imagine your father doing that." They had all been baffled by the sudden identification of Yi and Ling as a gay couple and the news that Ling was still a man.

"It was my brother," Yi said in disgust, handing Qiang another page in the newspaper. "Take a look at this."

SON OF DISGRACED GOVERNOR PROMOTED TO HEAD OF NEW NATIONAL GOVERNMENT DEPARTMENT

By Su Lantao—Son of Disgraced Governor Wang Jiangjun of Zhongjiang Province, Wang Mengqin, has been selected to lead a new government committee, a spokesman from the Capital announced today. The Anti-Family Corruption Committee has been specially designed to fight corruption within families. Members of the committee state that often traitorous and revolutionary thoughts within families go unreported by other family members and is currently a major problem.

"For many years, I have shamed my country because I ignored the revolutionary ideology from my father and my brother, both of whom I have publicly disowned," Wang Mengqin said, speaking to the press after the announcement. "I am thankful for the undeserved forgiveness given by the honorable leaders of our glorious country. I promise to uphold our nation's values and undo my unwitting mistakes by working hard to fight against corruption within families, which I know from first-hand experience is a plague, weakening us from the inside. Many children, like me, are afraid of their traitorous fathers and other family members and fail to do the right thing. I promise to support each child who realizes that their loyalty must always be to country first and reports anything dishonorable happening at home."

The committee especially promises to encourage younger children to report their parents when they hear them speak about ideas that could be dangerous for the safety of our glorious nation. The committee also promises to start an education program teaching children the kind of dangerous ideology their parents could be spouting without their knowledge.

The choice of Wang Mengqin as department leader has not been without controversy, but sources from behind the scenes claim that Mengqin's loyalty is clear, as it is believed he was the one responsible for not only telling his traitorous father to turn his brother in, but also the man who first told the government and press about his brother's illegal homosexual marriage.

Qiang finished reading, disgusted. "Any other news?" he asked. "How about your mother or Ling's parents?"

"There is another opinion article shaming me, this time by the vice principal of my old school," Yi said casually, skimming an article. "I mean I knew he hated me, but still, this is harsh. Ling's parents haven't been in the news since yesterday, when his mother gave that interview explaining how ashamed she was and what a terrible, rebellious child Ling was." Yi flipped through the rest of the pages. "There hasn't been any news about my mother, so I don't know what's happening with her. But I hope she is alright; I mean we owe our lives to her."

"Guihua is an excellent mother," Qiang said reassuringly. "At the end of the day, she did what all the best mothers do. She was willing to take a great risk to ensure the safety of her son and his family."

Yi, Ling, Qiang, and Hanbing spent the day around the mud house. There wasn't much they could do, and the days of living there were starting to rub on their nerves. As they couldn't risk going too far, they sat around most of the time playing child-appropriate card games to keep Hanbing amused. After making a quick lunch from leftovers, the group moved outside to sit under a tree, once again playing games and awaiting Zhuang's return.

The three adults didn't want to talk about what was on their minds in front of Hanbing, but it was clear that the three of them had the same question in mind: What were they going to do for the future? Yi had put enough money in their luggage to allow them to live for some time, but that would run out sooner or later. They couldn't risk using their bank cards, and more than likely their accounts would have been closed by now. Even with this backup plan of living in Zhuang's house, they had no larger future plans as they were now the most wanted people in the country. They couldn't exactly live as farmers. In addition, Yi and Ling had no interest in living on Qiang and Zhuang's generosity forever.

"Who is watching Mew Mew and You'sun?" asked Hanbing suddenly curious, looking up from a card game. "We have been gone for so many days now. Do they have enough food?"

"Of course they do." Qiang smiled. "We have a good friend watching them while we are gone."

'That's good," Hanbing said dryly. "I don't want to be stressed out on this vacation."

The adults chuckled. At least they could appreciate that an adorable child was there to keep their spirits high.

It was getting close to evening by the time Zhuang returned. Yi smiled as Qiang heaved a huge sigh of relief, hoping that no one would notice. They all walked out to help him carry a surprisingly small amount of groceries.

"This isn't enough stuff," Yi said, feeling slightly annoyed. "This is only like two, three days of food maximum."

"Yes, it is." Zhuang beamed. "You want to know why?" He was too impatient to wait for an answer. "I found our way, well specifically your way, out."

"What do you mean?" asked Yi, surprised. "What do you mean you found our way out?"

Zhuang wrapped his arm around Qiang, kissing him on the cheek. "I didn't want to get your hopes up, but Qiang and I have always discussed a plan of what would happen if, well, this happened."

"Thank you," said Ling in the background. He tried to sound neutral but appreciative, yet his voice was filled with relief.

"What is the plan?" asked Yi. He, too, kept his voice neutral, afraid to get his hopes up. "You are not hoping for us to keep driving until we reach the border, are you? Because we have discussed that, and I maintain we can't risk the security at border control."

"No. But it does involve you leaving the country. As you know," Zhuang said excitedly. "I used to work in the military. But what you might not know is one of my jobs many years ago was working as security at an embassy. I got to know the ambassador quite well. It took me a long time, but I finally managed to get in contact with the ambassador, and I explained your situation. Today, the embassy and its respective country has agreed to help us."

"Really?" asked Yi, surprised. "Which country?"

"Republic of Canada. They are the only western country with an embassy in the Capital," Qiang said. "It won't be easy, though. We need to make it to the Capital and bring you guys to the embassy without being caught. But once we are there, the ambassador has promised to take all of us in as asylum seekers. Then, if possible, they want to send you abroad to their own country, as asylum seekers, so you all are safe."

"If all we have to do is reach the Capital," Ling said hopefully, "then it shouldn't be too bad."

Zhuang frowned. "You three are the most wanted people in the glorious country right now. The reward for your capture is more than most people's yearly salary. Not to mention, the checkpoints. They are everywhere now. Also, even on the best of the days, technically one should show ID when entering the Capital, and it isn't exactly like we can show them yours. Finally, there is the matter of getting there. It's a five-hour drive from here to the Capital and that's if we take the freeway. It would take even longer if we take the side roads. Not to mention, we would have to do it all in one day. This car can't sleep four adults and a child at night and it isn't like we can just find a hotel to crash in overnight."

The adults stood around, thinking. Yi finally spoke up. "I don't see how we have any other choice. It's not like we can stay here forever. Sooner or later they will realize you two are connected, and when they do, they will come searching at this farm."

"Just confirming," Qiang said curiously, "you do realize what would happen if we get caught? Maybe it will be better to rebuild our lives as farmers in a mud hut."

Yi chuckled softly. "Yeah, that won't be happening. But that's not the point. Staying here is just as much of a risk. Sooner or later someone will inspect this village, especially if they can ever figure out the connection between you two. As we all must realize, the only way we can be guaranteed safety at this time is on foreign soil. The easiest way to get on foreign soil is to go to an embassy. Now that there is an embassy willing to help us, there is no excuse for us not to do it."

23.
A CITIZEN'S PRIORITY SHOULD ALWAYS BE THEIR COUNTRY

YI SAT IN THE FRONT passenger seat as Zhuang drove out of his home early in the morning two days later. He could hear Ling, Qiang, and Hanbing snoring in the backseat behind him. They had spent both previous days discussing ideas on how to get to the Capital, but unfortunately, they could not really think of a solid plan. Therefore, they decided to wing it. Zhuang was just going to have to be careful as he drove and hope they avoided any issues. Despite it being barely daybreak, Yi was too nervous to sleep, instead staring out the window half awake. They drove by fields and fields of barren wasteland.

"Why do you think nothing can grow here," asked Yi to Zhuang, "when you are able to grow so much on just your roof in boxes? Is it because of the weather?"

"Because, well…" Zhuang hesitated for a moment, uncomfortable with what he was about to say. "Drought is a minor problem, yes. Pollution and unsustainable development over decades, perhaps centuries, could be identified as another. But I think a big issue that isn't discussed is that the decisions on how to raise crops are not made by scientists. The people who are educated in this field by government officials don't know better but act as if they do."

"That's what I thought," Yi said sadly. "How many problems in this country do you think are made by people with better intentions?"

"I don't know if I would say it was better intentions," Zhuang said, frowning. "I would say ignorance and need for power drove these decisions. Stubbornness and silencing the opposition are what allowed these problems to occur. The intentions no longer matter. The truth is that the decisions made by people in power have caused millions of people in the past and present to suffer. Think about all the suffering that has happened to innocent people due to situations out of their control, situations that they had no say in. Perhaps people should question the government more instead of blind obedience."

"You sound like one of the rebels," Yi said, half joking.

"I am not anti-government. I am pro-society and equal rights for everyone," Zhuang said while concentrating on his driving. "I want to believe there is a world and system that would treat everyone fairly and give everyone equal opportunity, that people can make the choices to live the life that they want, be the people they want to be, and be with the people they want to build their lives with. I don't think the purpose of government should be to silence another person or group of people."

Yi wasn't sure if he agreed or disagreed. Yawning, he closed his eyes and slowly drifted off into a light sleep.

It was late afternoon by the time they reached the Capital, as they had been unwilling to risk taking the freeway or any major roads. Yi felt an uncomfortable helplessness on the road as he looked out the window at the mud-built houses, the children dressed in rags playing in the lifeless fields, and the overall dire state of life around him. Over the course of the last week, he had suddenly realized how privileged he was. There was so much he had been able to get away with or took for granted thanks to his father and his social position. He felt a great deal of sympathy for Ling's and Zhuang's families who he knew grew up in similar areas. He had never asked either of them about their childhoods, he realized. He had no idea what being a scholarship kid must have meant for Ling. For his whole life he had believed that what the government was doing was the best for the nation, and for most of his adult life he had taught the next generation what he believed in. He wondered if he and his family could be seen as personally responsible for the situation around him. As he watched farmers harvest what little vegetables they could grow, only to send it off to support major cities, he realized he never questioned where his food came from. He truly understood for the first time why Ling's family was so thankful that he married Ling and pulled them out of that hardship.

As they reached the main gates of the Capital, there was a long line of vehicles entering the city. They could see military guards all around them, checking everyone's national identification cards and questioning every car entering. The group was silent as they tried to think of a plan on how to enter the city. Zhuang concentrated as an officer checked every car in front of them, coming closer and closer to their van.

"We have to turn back," Qiang said urgently. "There is too much security; we will be caught. Let's try again in a few days."

"Where will we sleep tonight?" asked Ling. "If we can't make it in, we don't have a place to go."

"I am not sure," Qiang said nervously, "but I am sure it will be better than a jail cell or a labor camp."

"Hold it, you two," Zhuang said. He smiled brightly as the officer came closer. "I've got a plan, everyone quickly put on your masks, pretend to sleep, and shut up."

The officer walked up to the car. Zhuang rolled down the window and smiled. "Major Qi, so lovely to see you."

The officer known as Major Qi jumped back in surprise. "Zhuang, this is a surprise! I haven't seen you since you retired. How are you, my old friend?"

"Good, good, just enjoying the farmer's life," Zhuang said. "How are our comrades?"

"They are doing well. Shame you left, Zhuang. You were a

great solider."

"Yeah, I miss it a lot. But you know, after the injury and my father's death," Zhuang said sadly, "I just could no longer serve our glorious nation in the same way. Please tell everyone I say hi. I miss them all dearly."

"What brings you to the Capital?" asked Major Qi.

"I've got bad news," Zhuang said, sadly. "You see, these fellow villagers—they are all pretty sick." In the back seat, Ling and Yi started coughing hard. "I was hoping to take them to Capital Hospital because it is the best."

"I am sorry to hear that," Major Qi said, stepping away from the car. "It's always terrible when people get sick. You are right to bring them to the Capital Hospital. It is the best. Just let me see some identification, and I will let you through."

"Well, that's our problem," Zhang said quickly. "In our hurry, we forgot to bring their ID cards. We were planning to apply for temporary ones in the city, as accordance to the law, but we didn't expect to run into all this security. What is happening, anyway?"

"We are checking for some fugitives. Have you not heard the news?"

Zhuang shook his head. "Hard to get news in the village, I am afraid. I believe I heard something a few days ago though, something about a biological girl?"

"Yeah," said Major Qi. "We are trying to find her and her kidnappers."

"I see," Zhuang chuckled. "They would be pretty foolish to try to get in the Capital with all this excellent security. I am sure nothing can get past with you on the watch, Major Qi."

"Of course not." Major Qi beamed proudly. "We will capture the kidnappers if they are foolish enough to try to come to the Capital."

"I know you will," said Zhuang, "Anyway, I am so happy to have run into you, to see a familiar face, because I have to ask, is there any chance you can let us through? I have my ID card, but as I said before, in our hurry, we forgot to bring theirs. I am really sorry, but as you can see, they are quite ill. I am afraid it's something serious like tuberculosis. They have already been sick for a few days now. If I don't get them treated soon, I am afraid it will become an endemic back in the village, and they won't make it. I promise to get them all temporary identification cards first thing tomorrow morning. I really don't want to drive them all back to our village just to come back tomorrow. It's a five-hour drive, and I fear for their health, not to mention the health of the greater village."

Major Qi hesitated. "I shouldn't, Zhuang. You know the law. Identifications should be brought everywhere."

"I understand, Major Qi. As an ex-military, I would never want to put you in the position to break the law. Nor would I ever consider breaking any laws. If it weren't for their health, I would never have even considered asking for the favor. I promise I will get them temporarily registered in the morning before taking them to the hospital."

Major Qi stared carefully into Zhuang pleading eyes. Finally, he chuckled. "I understand. You are right to be worried about your fellow villagers, and I am glad you still have the military attitude of taking care of the people. I suppose, just this once, as you have your identification, and this is a health emergency, no one would mind that I let such a fine, upstanding military gentleman off the hook. After all, you are not the people we are looking for."

"Thank you so much for your understanding, Major Qi. I owe you so much," Zhuang said, smiling. "Good luck on your search for the fugitives, and I'll be sure to send you a care package when I have free time." Nodding politely, they drove through security and the gates into the Capital.

"That was close," Yi said, sighing in relief.

"I won't lie," Zhuang said, "I am not happy I had to lie to an old comrade of mine. Major Qi is a decent man, and I sincerely hope that no one ever figures out that he was the one who let us in."

The group was quiet. No one knew how to express the relief that they all felt. For the first time in days, things seemed like they could work out, that they could be safe.

"The important thing is we made it in the city. Now, let's head to the embassy," Qiang said loudly, breaking the silence. "I told you my husband is well connected," he added proudly. Looking directly at Zhang, he announced, "I would give you a kiss right now, but I don't want to take any chances."

Zhuang chuckled. "Once we get to the embassy, I can think of so many ways you can show me how much you appreciate and love me."

"Hey, not in front of Hanbing," Yi joked.

Everyone burst out laughing out of relief. Even Hanbing joined in.

Zhuang spoke to security upon reaching the gates of the embassy of the Republic of Canada and was immediately let through. Everyone was exhausted due to the day of traveling. Upon reaching the front doors of the main building, they stepped out of the van. A white-haired Caucasian woman in her mid-70s, dressed in a classy pink dress came walking out of the ornate doors.

"Zhuang," she said walking forward to give him a hug. "Welcome! It's been a long time. Last time we met must have been when I invited you and your husband to dinner, what, almost two years ago? I know it was before I took that long trip home." She turned to Qiang. "How have you been, Dr. Qiang? Is your business doing well?"

"You speak our language," Yi said, surprised that this foreigner shared his common tongue.

"Yes, I have lived and studied in your country for many years now," the woman said, smiling. "My name is Sharon. Welcome to the embassy of the Republic of Canada. I hope you are doing well, and am I glad to see that you made it here safely."

"Thank you," said Yi politely. "Please do me a favor and thank the ambassador for graciously welcoming us to your home and saving our lives."

Sharon, Qiang, and Zhuang stared at Yi for a moment before Sharon broke out laughing. "My dear boy, I guess Zhuang here didn't tell you, but I am the ambassador."

Yi felt his face turning red. "I am so sorry. I guess I was just expecting the ambassador to be…" he was too embarrassed to finish his sentence.

"To be a man," chuckled Sharon. "It's understandable. You aren't the first person in this country to make that mistake." She laughed cheerfully again, pointing at some house staff standing around. "I know you must be exhausted from driving, so I will make this quick. I'll have my staff bring you and your suitcases to your rooms. We have prepared two suite-style guest rooms for you, so there should be enough space. I also had my kitchen prepare a light dinner for you, and once you are settled, they will serve it to you in your respective rooms. I figured this will make things easier and more comfortable for everyone." She gave everyone a hug and handshake. "I know you all must be tired. We will speak in the morning, say around 10:00 a.m.?"

Yi nodded, his face still red, as the embassy staff began unloading their suitcases from the car and bringing them to their respective rooms.

*   *   *

Ex-Governor Wang and Guihua had been living in Yi and Ling's apartment since being ordered to move out the Governor's Manor. Wang figured as it was he who bought the apartment, and it wasn't being used, he should be able to reside in it. Besides, he didn't have any other place to live. He hadn't spoken to his other now-disowned son ever since he schemed against Wang and ruined his career. In addition, he was secretly hoping Yi would try to return, and what better place to trap him than his own apartment?

After cleaning up from the mess done by the police ransacking the apartment, he and Guihua had settled in nicely. For all the problems he had with Yi, he had to admit he had good taste and kept the place comfortable. There were no obvious signs that a homosexual couple and their illegal daughter lived here, he thought to himself. All it needed was an office for him to think in, but alas, that had been transformed years ago into Hanbing's bedroom. Instead, he made himself comfortable on the living room sofa and TV table, trying to figure out his plans now that he was no longer governor. He didn't plan to stay out of office for long, and in his mind, he strategized how to get back into power with what political allies he still had. In the kitchen, he could hear Guihua cleaning up from dinner earlier.

He still needed to know who the traitor in his old home was who warned Yi about his arrest. This question had been bugging him for a long time. In the last few days, he wondered if it was his other son, but he couldn't understand the logic of that decision. He had checked his office, but he couldn't find proof of it being bugged. Perhaps it was security, but how could they? They knew the cameras in the office didn't record sound. The only other logical explanation was that his son had just decided to run off that night. But, if that was the case, wouldn't he have come back to the apartment first? It was obvious after living there that they had not returned after Hanbing's Arrival Day dinner.

His thoughts were interrupted by someone knocking on the door, and he froze in shock. Not only was it quite late, but no one should have known he was here, and he was feeling quite distrustful after the events of the past week. Cautiously, he walked towards the door and looked through the peephole. It was Cheng Chen.

"What are you doing here? And who sent you?" asked Wang suspiciously as he opened the door.

"I needed to speak to you, and I deduced this is where would you be living," Chen said calmly. "Aren't you going to invite me in?"

Wang stared at him for a moment, contemplating slamming the door in his face. "Fine, come on in," he said angrily.

Chen sat down on the sofa, looking around as Wang followed his eyes, watching every move. "This is a nice place," Chen said finally. "Yi has good taste. Guess we should have known he was gay."

"My son, ex-son, isn't a faggot," Wang said angrily. "What are you doing here? What do you want?"

"The Supreme President has decided to give you a second chance," Chen said casually. "Let me tell you first that there were many in the administration who were against it." He hesitated for a moment. "But my father has always said you were a good man, and I believe you deserve a second chance. Plus, it might be a chance to save my friend, Yi, from making the wrong decision."

"What do I have to do?"

"Earlier this evening, we received information that an overseas government is offering Yi, Ling, and Hanbing asylum in their own country. We now know that Yi, Ling, Hanbing, Qiang, and another man are hiding out in an embassy in the Capital. Of course, only a select group of people are privy to this knowledge, and we do not intend to release it publicly, should it stir up the public. In addition, it turns out that this story was leaked into overseas news earlier this week and is receiving, for lack of better word, a lot of sympathy, so the situation internationally has become quite sensitive." Chen paused for a moment. "Now the Supreme President, of course, is against this, but he does not wish angering another country, especially given our limited international diplomatic power right now. Therefore, he has asked me to—"

"What country? When did they arrive?" Wang interrupted. "Also, how did they manage to get into the Capital? I thought all roads were being checked."

"I was getting to that," Chen said calmly. "Remember, Wang, you have no power. Your political allies are gone. I would be more careful with your attitude. For starters, the Republic of Canada took them in. As for when they arrived, we aren't quite sure, but we were contacted by the embassy about two hours ago, so all this information is still relatively new. We still don't have any information concerning how they managed to get into the Capital. We are under the assumption that one of the security guards let them in without doing a thorough check of everyone in the vehicle. Of course, once we find him, he will be properly punished. As for when this happened, we are also not sure, but we will work on it." He ignored Wang who laughed under his breath. "None of that is important. What is important is that Yi and company are currently in international territory, and our Supreme President wishes to have this problem solved quietly."

"What does that have to do with me?" Wang asked indifferently.

"Attitude, Wang," Chen said softly. "Think of this as your redemption for your betrayal to your glorious nation. The Supreme President wishes you to go speak with your son, unofficially of course. Ask him to stop traveling down the wrong road and return to the country. In other words, to reject this offer of asylum. The Supreme President is willing to forgive him and your family, provided you follow through with a few conditions."

"What conditions would those be?"

"Just some general ones," Chen said. "The girl would have to be turned over to the government, of course, for her protection. Yi's wife Ling would have to get sexual reassignment surgery." He paused, understanding Wang's thoughts. "Of course, there would have to be punishments such as light jail time, written and televised confessions, that sort of thing, so the people know what has been done is morally wrong and traitorous. However, it could be a lot worse. The Supreme President is willing to waive things, such as death penalties, for the girl's safe return."

Wang pondered for a moment. "You know as much as I do that Yi is not going to accept this," he said finally.

"That isn't my problem, Ex-Governor Wang." Chen stood up, preparing to leave. "Like I said, this is really your only chance if you want any semblance of your old life back. I'll give you a day or two to think about it as we arrange a chance for you to meet with Yi."

Guihua walked out of the kitchen a few minutes after Chen left. "Are you going to get our son back?" she asked, her voice genuinely concerned.

"What did I tell you about listening to my private conversations, woman!" snapped Wang.

"I am sorry, sir. I am just worried about our son, that is all. Please get him back," Guihua pleaded.

"As I told you a few days ago," sneered Wang, "he is no longer our son. We no longer have children. You are not to worry about him, or his worthless brother for that matter. However, I am sick of no longer living my deserved life. Therefore, I will speak to Yi. I will put him back in his place, this way I can get back mine."

Guihua said nothing. As she felt powerless standing in the doorway, she watched her husband sitting in her son's living room, talking to himself, thinking of a way to return to a position of power.

24.
WHAT MAKES A MAN A MAN ARE THE CHOICES HE MAKES

Yi HEADED TO THE AMBASSADOR'S office around 9:45 the next morning after breakfast. He had slept exceptionally well, happy to be no longer sleeping on a straw mattress in a clay hut. He wasn't quite sure what to expect during this meeting, though. The last week had already begun to feel like a blur to him.

Qiang and Zhuang were already in the office when he arrived, standing around and laughing with Ambassador Sharon. "Good morning," she said cheerfully waving him over. "Should we wait for Ling to arrive so we can get started?"

"Actually," Yi said nervously, "Ling won't be joining us. Hanbing is still eating breakfast, and afterwards Ling was going to take her to walk around your beautiful garden."

"I see," Sharon said frowning slightly. "Then let's get started." Behind her, Qiang and Zhuang looked at each other, aware that Yi didn't want Ling in the room because he didn't think it fit with his role as the woman in the relationship.

Sharon sat down behind her large oak table, beckoning Yi, Qiang, and Zhuang to sit in front of her. She took out a printed news article from one of her drawers. Yi looked at it. It showed some pictures of them and text in a language he didn't understand.

"I know you don't understand it," Sharon smiled. "It's an article from my homeland. As you can guess from the pictures, it is about you guys. Your story is very big news overseas. Many people are curious about the fate of the first biological woman found in the PRCC, the so-called Land of Seahorses." She slid the article off to the side and smiled. "Let's get started, shall we? Last night, we informed your national government that we have taken you in, and our plans for your future. I am not too surprised it isn't being reported by your country's newspaper, as learning about citizens, such as yourself, seeking refugee status in an embassy cannot be good for your country's morale." She stopped for a moment, before smiling again. "Naturally, especially after hearing your story from Zhuang, and given your family's current circumstance, our government is very interested in helping you. We are willing, if that is what your family wants, to move you all to our nation. We believe that it is the only guaranteed way to protect you and your family. Of course, that would mean that there is very little chance you will ever come back. Which is why I want you to think about it and ask questions before we take the next step."

"What would all of this entail?" asked Yi.

"Given the direness of the situation, you, Ling, and Hanbing would be assigned expedited visas that accept you as asylum seekers. Within a few years, you will probably receive citizenship, assuming you follow all of our laws and prove yourself to be good residents."

"But I mean, once we get there," Yi said cautiously, "what will happen to us? I am especially worried about my daughter, given her…sex."

"I am not going to lie," Sharon said smiling. "Many governments, including my own, are curious about Hanbing, given what little we know about your secretive nation and your ethnic background. Hanbing is quite unique, to say the least. However, what happens to Hanbing is up to you and Ling. We are a free country. We give people choices, and naturally, we would not want to harm a young girl. However, for lack of better word, the fate of your "race" does lie partially in your daughter. In addition, given the gender issues globally, though none as extreme as the PRCC, the fact that she is a female alone is important. In the future, if I were you, I would encourage her to do something, like donate her eggs. Voluntarily, of course. To answer your question simply though, I can promise you no harm will come to Hanbing or your family once you arrive abroad."

"What about our living situation?" Yi asked.

"You will be given government housing at least until you get on your feet. I would suggest you start learning our language and culture, as it would probably make life easier. Unfortunately, you will be immigrants facing life in a new land with no friends, and I know that in the beginning your family will struggle. However, I understand there are groups out there who would be willing to help you adjust to your new life. Of course, my husband and I will try to offer as much support as we can," Sharon replied, smiling. "But I would hope once you have gotten settled in that one or both of you get jobs and try to become productive members of society.

"Well, if possible, I intend to find a teaching job. I don't think I will be able to teach politics anymore, but maybe something else. What about the role of both governments in all of this?" Yi asked curiously. "I can't imagine the Supreme President just letting us leave without a fight."

"Behind the scenes," Sharon replied as honestly as she could, "I am sure there will be some form of negotiation, perhaps a removal of an embargo, or a large financial aid package that will benefit the current government. The PRCC leaders have always willingly bowed to money. Right now, the incident involving you is causing a big issue, but for your government in the long run, this might not be worth the fight. Plus, as you are on international territory, they have little jurisdiction over you, and they do not wish to cause an international incident. Now that one biological woman has been found, I am sure that your government is out searching hard for others. For them, if there is the right incentive, it might just be easier to let this one go and create some sort of lie, such as you guys all died in an accident, or that you were captured and taken out of the public eye."

Sharon took a moment to give Yi a chance to talk, but he said nothing, so she continued. "Of course, most importantly, all of this negotiation will be done behind the scenes and out of public knowledge. I guess what I am saying is I think getting you three out of here may be easier than we expect, especially if no one loses face and the right officials feel properly incentivized."

Yi sat there, sinking into the chair to think. "This all seems very fast. Two weeks ago, I was at home…but given the uncertainty of the situation, I suppose we should try to move forward. I guess I have no more questions."

"In that case," Sharon smiled, "unless there are any other issues, why don't we get started then? As the three of you don't have passports, why don't we start with getting you some form of identification? I am going to ask you some personal questions and we will work our way up from there."

Ling sat at one of the tables in the garden, watching Hanbing run around and play. The embassy staff had all been extremely nice and polite, especially to Hanbing, and some of them had provided her with a couple of small toys, which she greatly appreciated. As Ling watched Hanbing sniff some flowers, he couldn't help noticing the other person in the garden, an older black man planting some iris bulbs. He looked to be about sixty, his short hair graying. He glanced up and, noticing Hanbing watching him, smiled.

"Hello!" he called out, waving. He put down his tools and began walking over.

"How are you today?" the man said as he sat down beside Ling.

Ling smiled awkwardly. He had never seen a man with such dark skin before. In addition, in the last twenty-four hours, he had met two foreigners who spoke the same language as him. He felt confused, as it contradicted with what he knew about the world. "Hi," he replied meekly and turned back to Hanbing, ignoring the man.

"You must be Ling. I heard about you from my wife, Sharon, and of course, Qiang and Zhuang." The man smiled. "I am Michael."

"Oh," gasped Ling, "you are Ambassador Sharon's husband? I am sorry, I didn't know." He felt embarrassed for not properly addressing a man with such prestigious background.

"Did you think I was just a gardener?" chuckled Michael. "I am quite used to that reaction, actually. Although, I think you should think about why you feel you should treat me differently when you realized I am a person of power and not just an employee. We are all, after all, human. Whether a person is a gardener or the husband of an ambassador does not mean he shouldn't be respected all the same."

Ling smiled awkwardly as he felt his face turning red. "I am sorry. All of this is so new to me. This is only my second time in the Capital. Everything is so different here. I have never even seen a person like you before."

"I am just making a light comment," Michael said, laughing loudly. "Don't worry, I am not actually offended. I have been here with my wife for a few years now. I understand the complications of your country. However, making people uncomfortable by putting them on the spot is something I like to do. I know it's weird and not culturally correct or sensitive, but that is kind of my style of humor."

Ling stood there for a moment thinking about what to say, before repeating himself. "This is only my second time in the Capital. Everything is so different here…and now, meeting people from other cultures, seeing people that look different from me, and the way people treat me here, it just isn't what I am used to. I don't think I ever expected to be in the position I am in now."

"I understand that," Michael replied kindly. "But as I said earlier, we are all human. Just because of my skin color, or the fact that I grew up in a different place than you, or that I have different interests than you, doesn't mean you and I don't want the same thing. I think everyone in the world, no matter the background, just wants to be treated nicely and with respect."

"That kind of attitude is rare here," Ling replied, half joking.

"Oh, I am aware. I have been here a long time." Michael smiled. "I am happy to have this brief opportunity to meet you. I am not sure if you are aware of this, but Qiang and Zhuang have spoken about you and your husband in the past. Though, they never mentioned Hanbing here, or her gender. Nonetheless, you guys have quite an interesting backstory."

"Have you and your wife known Zhuang for a long time?" Ling asked curiously.

"Quite a few years. He was a very wonderful security guard," Michael said wistfully. "It was a shame when he left. He was always so polite and so different from the other guards. Much more intelligent and open to new ideas. I would love to have him back working for us in some capacity. And that boyfriend of his, I may not understand why he does what he does, but I cannot deny he is talented at doing it."

Ling thought for a moment and decided to take the opportunity to ask the questions he had wanted to ask for a long time, without Yi's judgement. "I have always wanted to know, are foreigners like you familiar with nan-nu culture? Are there even nan-nu overseas?"

"I think foreigners are curious about it. I am fortunate to know a little more than others might, being given the opportunities and years I have lived in your country. But no, nan-nu are very much something unique to the PRCC." Michael thought for a moment. "In other countries there are men who choose to become women, because they identify as women, but I don't think I have ever heard of a case of a man being forced to become a woman overseas."

"Oh, I have a friend who is transgender. Had a friend, I guess I should say," Ling said awkwardly. "She always joked that she was lucky because the situation here worked out to her advantage."

"I can tell you that I am a fan of people having the freedom to embrace who they are without the pressure of being forced to change themselves," Michael said, chuckling.

"Yes, I think that would be nice," Ling said quietly. He suddenly stopped, embarrassed by what he said under his breath. Quickly, he turned his attention to watching Hanbing. "I am sorry," he said loudly, not looking directly at Michael. "I know you are very busy with your gardening. I would hate for Hanbing and me to distract you. I should go now."

"No, no, that's okay. I could use the company. I know you are also curious about life outside of here, so feel free to keep asking me any questions."

Ling nodded but said nothing.

"May I ask *you* a question?" asked Michael casually. He waited for Ling to nod before continuing. "I know this is very direct, but if you don't mind me asking, given your situation, and your daughter's situation, will you continue to embrace the nan-nu lifestyle when you go overseas?"

Ling paused. "What do you mean by that? Has it been made clear that we are leaving?"

"I believe that is what is being discussed right now in the meeting. Anyway, once you go overseas, you no longer have to live your life as a woman if that is not what you choose," Michael said simply. "Will you continue living as a woman?"

"But I am married to a man, so don't I have to register as a woman so we can be together?" questioned Ling.

Michael laughed loudly. "I guess you wouldn't know this, but same sex marriages have been recognized for a long time out in the West."

"Oh." Ling thought for a moment. "Honestly, I guess I haven't thought about it. This all happened so fast. I haven't really thought about what happens when we go overseas."

"If you don't mind me asking? Do you identify as a woman?" Michael asked curiously. "I have spoken to other nan-nu on a personal level, and I know some who do, some who claim they do, and some who don't. But since you still have your male organs, I am sure for you it's more complicated."

"No, I don't identify as a woman," Ling said honestly, "but the problem is I don't know how to be a man."

"What do you mean by that?"

"I mean I have never had a job, I don't really like manly things like sports, I don't have big muscles, and I don't look like a man. I am not really a man, but I am not really a woman either. It's like I am stuck between two different worlds."

"My dear boy," laughed Michael, "being a man does not mean you have to follow society's stereotypes. Being a man just means you identify as being a man. There are no right ways to be a man."

"Meaning?" Ling asked, confused.

"I like to believe being a man is not just about sex and gender roles, but also identification," Michael said. "You are a man not only because you have male sex organs, but because you identify as being a man."

"Oh," Ling thought for a moment. "But I don't have a job, and I am basically a housewife. I am not sure if I am man enough."

"Zhuang and I aren't doing paid work. We help around the house, and you don't see us questioning our masculinity," Michael chuckled. "And for good measure, I am a heterosexual man that has been married to a heterosexual working woman for nearly three decades. We even have children together that I cooked and cleaned for a huge part of their lives."

"When you watched the children, didn't you feel less than a man?" Ling asked, surprised.

"No," Michael said, "and we both did our part in childrearing. It's just that we didn't decide it based on gender roles, mostly financial opportunity. Sharon had much better opportunities than I, and I thought it was best that I support her so she could reach her full potential."

"Wow! You gave up your career to help your wife?" Ling questioned.

"I wouldn't use the words 'gave up,' but essentially, yes,"

Michael replied. "Things are never so black and white, but I support Sharon wholeheartedly. Since becoming a house husband and a stay-at-home dad was needed for our family, I did what was needed."

"And you don't feel emasculated?"

"No. Why would I?" Michael asked. "Sharon and I are partners, not competitors, and we work together to do what is best for our family."

"What you are saying is being a house husband doesn't make you feel inferior then?" asked Ling.

"No," Michael said simply, "and why should it?"

"Because it's a woman's job, and therefore below the jobs of a man," Ling replied as if the answer was obvious.

"I don't think that it is a good way to put it," Michael said casually. "First of all, I don't believe in gender stereotypes about what roles men and women should play in society. I believe a man and a woman can both do any role that they feel comfortable doing. Secondly, even if a job like raising children is more of a woman's role in most cultures, that does not make the job any less important or inferior and, more importantly, does not mean that it should only be done by women. Children should be raised by their parents, and that means one parent might have to do more of the work. I don't think it matters about the gender of the parent, only that the parent loves and cares for the child. Then again, I am more feminist and liberal than most people out there, I suppose."

"What's a feminist?" Ling asked, confounded again.

"I suppose the most basic meaning is that I strongly believe that both men and women are equal in everything," Michael replied, smiling. "We can also say the ideas that I believe in contradict everything that you and everyone in this country has been taught."

"I have never heard someone say that out loud before," Ling said. "I am pretty sure many people, even women or nan-nu, would disagree with you."

"We may live in a patriarchal system, a society controlled by men, but that doesn't mean sexist and ignorant beliefs only come from men. Women in society oftentimes, knowingly or unknowingly, put down other women, continuing and partaking in the system. I am sure some of your biggest pressures to act like a woman not only come from men, but other nan-nu."

Ling didn't say anything. He sat and distracted himself by watching Hanbing play some more.

Michael smiled as Ling bent down and smelled some of the flowers. "Do you believe your daughter should have the equal chance to do whatever she wants to do?"

"Of course," said Ling. "That was one of the benefits of raising her as a man. By hiding her true sexual identity, she would be able to do whatever she wants."

"I would say," Michael said thoughtfully, "that she should be able to do whatever, not because society thinks she is a man, but because she is human, and all humans are equal no matter the gender or sex, or even race for that matter. Don't you agree?"

"I don't think things are that simple," Ling said truthfully. "And since it's not the reality, it doesn't really matter what I think."

"Of course, it isn't the reality yet," Michael said, shrugging his shoulders. "But that doesn't change what I believe in, and it doesn't mean I shouldn't fight for it. As I said earlier, I am a bigger proponent in equality for all humans, no matter their background or identification. I think we should all support that idea, and we should fight for that."

Ling went silent again. He really had no idea what he thought about the issue. But he had to admit, all the people he respected the most—Qiang, Zhuang, and Fenghuang—all told him similar things at one time or another.

"Anyway," said Michael, "we kind of went in a circle, but you never answered my question. When you leave this country, will you continue living as a woman?"

Ling thought for a moment. "I think I need to speak to Yi

about this, and I know he won't be happy, but I don't think I want to. I want something more equal in our relationship. I want to be able to be who I want to be. I don't identify as a woman. I never have. I think I need to embrace my identity as a man, whatever that means." As Michael nodded approvingly, he paused again, thinking. "And more importantly, I want my child, my daughter, to be able to be the person she wants to be."

Sharon finished the final touches on the asylum applications for Yi and Hanbing and began working on Ling's application. "What should we put for Ling's gender?" She asked, typing on her computer.

Yi thought for a second, unsure how he should answer. Finally, he said, "Well, since we are married, and I am the man, shouldn't Ling be the woman?"

Sharon chuckled. "I guess you don't realize this, but two men can get married in my country. We can put Ling as a man, and you two could still be married, if that is what you wish."

Yi laughed nervously. "In that case, I am not really sure, but I think you should put…"

Qiang interrupted him, speaking for the first time since they sat down. "Ling identifies as a male. He has male organs. He is only female because society has forced him to be. Put him as male." Next to him, Zhuang nodded silently.

Sharon turned to Yi, awaiting his answer. Yi felt all eyes watching him. "Fine, I guess, let's put Ling's gender as male."

25.

ALL FILIAL SONS RESPECT THEIR FATHER. ALL LOYAL WIVES OBEY THEIR HUSBAND.

LING LAY IN BED, LISTENING to the radio station. Next to him, Hanbing lay there still asleep. He could hear Yi taking a shower in the bathroom. On the radio, there was a discussion between two people about him and Ling.

Radio Host: It has been over a week now. Why do you think that the general public has not been given a status update on the fate of the kidnappers? Do you believe that they are still out there? Hiding in villages?

Interviewee: Of course they are still out there. Our honorable and glorious government would inform us ignorant public if they were caught, to celebrate the life of this young woman, and punish those who kidnapped her. But I think that it is unlikely they are out hiding in the villages. Our glorious government would have found them by now. They have done so much for the villagers, improved lives in ways these peasants could never have imagined, so they are very appreciative and patriotic. Clearly, these people have the connections to know the people who could keep them hidden. I believe that it must be some corrupt government official that is hosting them illegally. I just hope the traitors that hid them will be caught soon, and these kidnappers properly punished so we can rescue the poor girl.

Radio Host: One of the things that keeps confusing the audience is who these kidnappers are and their motivations.

I think most audiences are extremely baffled, especially by Wang Yi. He came from an excellent background, had a strong political understanding, and from most who knew him, was extremely patriotic. Even his so-called wife, Li Ling, seemed to have been very well-liked and loyal. What do you think would drive these two people to such traitorous actions?

Interviewee: I think Yi's story is the proof of the dangers of homosexuality. We can assume, based on his superior background, Yi caught this disease from his so-called wife, Ling, and it poisoned his mind. As for Ling, his homosexuality probably came from the fact that he grew up with an outspoken female in the household. His refusal to become a proper woman while being with a man clearly shows that Ling had caught a dangerous disease.

Radio Host: I think everyone in the audience understands the dangers of homosexuality, but can you elaborate on where you think Ling caught the disease? His family appears to be very loyal to our glorious country. As I said earlier, our audience is surprised that two people from such good backgrounds could turn out to be traitors.

Interviewee: I am surprised that so few have pointed this out, but in interviews concerning Ling's family, we always hear from the mother, not the father.

Radio Host: That is because the mother has been very vocal about disowning Ling and supporting the authorities in his capture. I believe she even has called out for the death penalty on her child. This woman's patriotism is not to be doubted.

Interviewee: You miss my point. It's not what the woman believes in that is the issue. She is a woman with all the right views and understands them. The problem is she is so comfortable expressing them in public, and in addition, she is talking more openly than her husband. Having such an unnatural atmosphere in which a woman can speak her mind so openly is very dangerous to a child and probably was what caused him to develop the disease of homosexuality. It can come from any place when proper values and roles are not strictly enforced. Something that seems harmless can grow to something very dangerous. For example, families need to be aware of the dangers of women with opinions and women who aren't subservient to their husbands.

Radio Host: I guess I have never thought about it that way, then—

"What are you listening to?" snapped Yi, as he walked back into the room from the shower. "Why in the world would you listen to that garbage? Turn it off." Ling quickly obeyed, feeling uncomfortable and embarrassed.

"You already read about the bullshit they say about you, me, and our daughter," Yi said angrily, "so why do you need to listen to it also?"

"I don't know," Ling said truthfully. "I guess I haven't heard about my mother recently, and I worry about her."

Yi frowned. "Your mother has already made it clear before, and now, how she feels about you," he said harshly. "You should not waste your time and energy thinking about her."

Ling recoiled as if he had been slapped. "I know, but she is still my mother. Despite her faults, she still raised me."

"I know," Yi said, sitting on the bed beside him. "But we already have so much to worry about. We might be leaving the country in a few days. You should be focusing on that, not on what has already happened."

"I understand," said Ling. "But I never even had the chance to say goodbye to her and my father, and now we are leaving. Who knows if I will see them again?"

Yi didn't know what to say. He was slightly surprised that Ling would feel this way, especially after how his mother treated him, but decided it would be insensitive to comment on the subject. "Come on," he said, wrapping his arms around Ling. "Go take a shower. I will wake up Hanbing, and we can go have breakfast."

Yi was having a discussion with Qiang around the breakfast table when Sharon walked in looking crestfallen. Zhuang and Ling, who had been playing with Hanbing, went silent upon looking at her face. Sharon stood for a moment. "I am sorry, Yi, but my hands are tied on this one. There is someone who wishes to speak to you, and I have been commanded by my government, that unless you adamantly refuse, it would be better for all our sakes if you met up with him."

"Who am I supposed to meet up with?" asked Yi suspiciously.

"A government official who has fallen from grace. He wishes to talk with you about your future options," Sharon said grimly. "But I suppose you would better know him as your father."

Yi was led by Sharon into the door of a small conference room. "Now before you go in," said Sharon casually, "I should inform you, although this is a one-on-one conversation, it is being recorded, and representatives from both governments will be watching."

"I would expect as much," said Yi calmly.

"Right now, you are on embassy soil, which means there is very little your government can do without causing an international incident, which I am sure they are not willing to risk," Sharon said. "But we can only protect you as long as you stay in the embassy."

"I understand. Thank you."

Sharon gave him an awkward smile. "Good luck."

Yi walked into conference room. His father was already sitting there, wearing a simple sweatshirt and pants. Yi had never seen him dressed this casually before, and he immediately recognized the sweatshirt as one of his own. Despite it only being two weeks since they had seen each other, he had lost a lot of weight. His face was a mixture of stress and anger.

"Hello," said Yi calmly, as he pulled out a chair and sat down. "How have you been?"

"How do you think I have been?" Wang said angrily, grinding his teeth. "You ruined my career. You ruined my life. You ruined this family. Do you know what your brother has done? Do you know how distraught your mother has become?"

"You were the one who decided to call the cops on us." Yi shrugged. "You could have kept this between you and me. It could have been solved differently."

"You were breaking the law," Wang snapped. "How could I live with myself knowing my son was breaking the law?"

"You live with yourself doing a lot worse," Yi said, shrugging. "I see you are living at my apartment now, and wearing my clothes."

"I bought the place; why shouldn't I be able to live there?" Wang replied angrily, smashing his fists on the table. "Besides, once I was forced to retire, there wasn't anywhere else for me to go."

Yi and Wang stared at each other, as if daring one another to say the next thing. Wang decided to speak first. "It's time to end this bullshit, surrender Hanbing, and come home. The Supreme President has offered a very good deal if you do."

"What deal is that?" Yi asked casually. He crossed his arms to make his indifference obvious.

"Assuming you follow all his demands: Ling gets his surgery, you admit your wrongs, and you give up Hanbing," Wang said the last part rather quickly. "He is willing to pardon you after a short sentence. You will be able to get your old job back, perhaps even get a better one, if you are willing."

"I don't see how this offer benefits me," scoffed Yi. "You know I would never give up my child. You should have told the Supreme President that before you came. You are wasting your time."

"It's not like I had a choice," Wang snapped, before slumping back into his chair. "You and your worthless brother have ruined everything. My job. Our family name. I have nothing now. This is my last chance to return things back to normal. Help me out here."

"You mean you want me to help you get back your normal— your job, your house, your power."

"Yes."

Yi laughed. "Why would I help you? You don't care about me. I was always just a prop in your legacy. I am sorry, but no. I am not going to give up my child to help you get back into power."

"I AM YOUR FATHER!" Wang stood up, bellowing. "IT IS YOUR DUTY TO LISTEN TO ME! NOW I AM COMMANDING YOU TO DROP THIS BULLSHIT AND COME HOME!"

"You have no power here! You are the one with everything to lose, not me!" laughed Yi. "Tell your friends, tell the government, or they can just listen to us right now, that I am not going back to Xincheng until I have guaranteed safety for my child. That she can continue living with me."

Wang ground his teeth. "I don't think they will negotiate that."

"Then I have nothing more to say."

Wang stared at him for a moment. "Fine. I will talk to them. Let's arrange to meet again in a few days." His eyes started to twitch, and he pleaded, "Please don't do anything rash or stupid. We can still fix this; we can return to our rightful positions. You can still be governor one day, as is your birthright."

Yi couldn't believe the arrogance and stupidity of his father. Having nothing else to say, he stood up and began to leave. He was about to open the door, when Wang called out to him, "I need to know."

"Need to know what?" Yi asked calmly.

"How did you know that the police coming were after you? I assume you knew, which is how you left so fast."

"What do you mean?" Yi asked, genuinely surprised.

"Which man warned you? Was it your brother, did someone in security tell you? I have been thinking about this everyday, and it's driving me insane. How did you know that the police were coming? Did you bug the office? Maybe you didn't know, and you just played it safe?" Wang asked frantically.

"No, someone told me." Yi said. "You really can't figure it out?"

"No, who?" asked Wang angrily. "Tell me which man it was so I can punish them."

"Goodbye, sir," Yi said sadly as he walked out the door. He could still hear his father screaming "tell me, tell me" as he walked away.

Sharon greeted Yi outside of conference room. "I know you probably don't want to talk about what just went on, and I respect that." She gave him a supportive smile. "That being said, you should know that your asylum application has been approved. We have temporarily arranged a flight for the day after tomorrow."

"Wow," Yi said distractedly. "That was fast."

"We felt it was better to get this over with as soon as possible," Sharon replied. "I think you have a lot to talk about with Ling. I'll let you get going. Good luck."

Even though he knew that Ling and others would want to know how things went with his father, he decided to delay telling Ling until after dinner, and perhaps he would tell Qiang and Zhuang tomorrow. He needed time to think about things.

Perhaps, he thought, they should delay their trip out of the country. Wang was going to go back and talk to the national government, and as long as he could guarantee their assurances, then perhaps it was time to go home. He had thought about it, and he felt he could be comfortable with Hanbing being used as symbol of hope of some sort, as long as she was treated fairly. He hadn't really been thinking about it, but maybe it was time for him to enter government. Maybe he could create a new committee or be offered a position that protected biological women better. Of course, if he was going to fill this position, Ling would have to be a proper woman. Ling hadn't offered to get the surgery in many years, but he didn't see how that would be a problem for him. Isn't it what he had always wanted? To properly serve Yi and make him happy?

The three of them walked quietly into their suite. After Ling put Hanbing in the bed, the two of them walked into the small living room and sat down opposite each other.

"How did it go today? I hope your father wasn't too harsh,"

Ling asked, breaking the ice. "Sharon told me she has arranged for us to leave the day after tomorrow. Soon all this will be over."

"I think I am going to ask Sharon to delay our flight a few days," Yi said after a moment of thinking.

"What?" Ling perked up in shock. "Why would you do that?"

"My father has offered to negotiate for our safe return. I want to hear him out. See if we can go back to Xincheng," Yi said casually.

"What about Hanbing? What will happen to her?"

"Of course, I would not accept any deal that doesn't give us full control of Hanbing," Yi said, scoffing. "Hanbing would have to live with us and stay as our child. I suppose I would be comfortable and understanding if they wanted to use her a symbol of hope or something similar, as long as they don't hurt her."

Ling didn't really know what to say, so he just sat there as Yi continued. "We could continue our old life. You could go back to your ladies' group, hang out with Fenghuang. I think I might change my job though. Maybe it is time for me to enter government."

"Yi." Ling's voice sounded scared, yet oddly confident. "I don't want to go back to Xincheng. I don't want our old life back. I don't think it is what is best for us."

"How is it not what is best for us?" asked Yi, slightly raising his voice. "What makes you think leaving is what is best for us?"

"Because we wouldn't have to hide anymore. We wouldn't have to pretend we are something we are not. We wouldn't have to worry about not being safe," Ling replied. He was starting to get emotional.

"That point is moot. I wouldn't go back unless they promise not to hurt Hanbing."

"What about promising not to hurt me?" Ling asked. "You promised me to protect me. As children, at your house."

"What do you mean?" Yi asked, "How is that even relevant?"

"What do you mean, how is that even relevant? Someone is going to have to take the blame for all of this. You know it is going to be me." Ling sounded worried.

"Look, we can worry about that later," Yi said, perhaps slightly too indifferently. "I am sure things will be fine. Right now, we need to think of what is best for Hanbing."

"You mean what is easiest for you, Yi," Ling said harshly. "This is about you being scared. About you being unwilling to try new things. About your unwillingness to stand up to your father."

"My father has nothing to do with this. We have a life in Xincheng. If we can go back to that life, shouldn't we take it?" Yi asked incredulously.

"You had a life in Xincheng, Yi. Going back to Xincheng is what is best for you, not us. Stop pretending it is about us," Ling snapped back.

Yi stopped for a moment. "I don't see you why you are making such a big deal out of this."

"Because, Yi." Ling paused, taking a huge breath. "Do you not remember? Do you remember what you said to me when we were children? Let me remind you Yi. You said to me, 'I will protect you. From now to forever. I will protect you, so don't you cry.' I will never forget those words! That has been the basis of this friendship, relationship, marriage, whatever you want to call it. Yi, you have promised to protect me and protect Hanbing. This decision you are making does not protect me, and only if we are super lucky would it be protecting Hanbing."

"The only thing that would affect you directly," Yi said indifferently, "is that you will probably have to get your sex change surgery. But haven't you been begging me to give you that for years?'

Ling thought for a moment. It was now or never. "That's the other issue. I don't want to lie anymore. Yi, I want Hanbing and I to be able to have the freedom to be who we are." Ling took a deep breath. "I don't want to pretend I am a woman anymore. I want to live my life based on my sex, as a man."

Yi laughed. "That's ridiculous. You've got to be joking."

"No, I am not joking."

"But," Yi chuckled, "you are my wife. Like I just said, it wasn't so long ago when you were begging me for sex change surgery, and now you tell me you want to be a man?"

"I asked because I thought it would make you happy. I asked because I thought that is what you needed from me," Ling said emotionally. "I didn't ask because that is what I wanted. I want to be able to live freely as who I want to be."

Yi stopped laughing. "I don't understand what is happening here."

"These past few years, I have lived this life to make you happy, but I haven't always been happy," Ling said. "I am not a woman. I will never be a woman. I am sick of doing things because society tells me I should do them, and I want to do what *I* want."

"If you are so sick of this life, then why didn't you mention it to me?" Yi snapped.

"Because I thought that's what you wanted from me, and I wanted to make you happy," Ling simply.

"If you are so miserable, then do something about it."

Ling took another deep breath. "Look, Yi, you don't get it. I did it all because I love you. I have loved you for a long time now. I loved you for protecting me and never forcing to me to change my sex. I just never said it."

"You love me? What, you think you are gay now, also?" Yi said incredulously. "Aren't you full of all these fun surprises tonight?"

"Yi, we have been having sex for the last ten years. Yes, I know you deny it by saying it is not sex, but guess what? It is. Guess what, I enjoy it most of the time, and based on what the ladies say, I enjoy it a lot more than they do. So yes, I'm still a man, and I like having sex with you, who is also a man. So yeah, probably gay," Ling said obviously and sarcastically.

"No need to be all sarcastic," Yi snapped again. "I am just surprised, that's all. Guess what? I am not gay, and if I had a woman, I wouldn't need you."

Ling grimaced, tearing up. "I know you aren't gay, Yi. I never said you were. I really wish you could be with the person you loved. I am sorry that I can't give you what you truly want. These last ten years, I have really tried to make you happy. If we leave tomorrow, that will give you a chance to choose to be with someone you actually love, so why stay here and have us both suffer?"

Yi sighed, feeling guilty. "Look, I didn't really mean that. That was harsh. Like I have always said, it is not you; it is me. I know you love me. Thank you for everything you have done for me." He paused again. "However, that doesn't mean I support you becoming a man. What will Hanbing say when suddenly she wakes up and realizes she had two dads?"

"I don't think she will care as much as you," Ling said. "Hanbing already knows that Qiang and Zhuang are gay. The only person who has a problem with this is you."

Suddenly, Hanbing walked out of the bedroom. "Baba, Mama, don't fight. I can hear you next door. Baba, I don't care if Mama wants to be a boy. Mama should be able to do what he wants to be happy. Baba, if leaving here will make Mama happy, we should leave. Also, this way Baba, I can live as a girl. I don't want to pretend that I am a boy anymore."

Yi looked at Hanbing who looked at Ling and forced a smile. "Fine. We will leave. If that's what you both want." He looked at them both again. "Hanbing, you should be sleeping right now. Ling, can you put her to bed? I need to go for a walk."

Yi sat outside on the steps of the embassy, annoyed and confused. Though he never smoked, some days he wished he had. He had heard it could be quite relaxing. This was one of those days. He needed something to calm his anger.

The doors behind him opened. "I don't want to talk right now, Ling," Yi said bitterly.

"Actually," Sharon's gentle voice echoed in the dark. "It's me. I brought you a cup of hot chocolate."

"A cup of what?" asked Yi.

"Hot chocolate." Sharon sat down beside him. "I figure you

could use a warm beverage and someone to speak to. You had a rough day."

"How did you know I was out here?" asked Yi surprised.

"Your room is actually right below mine. Plus, there are security cameras in the hallway," Sharon said, smiling.

"Thanks for the drink," Yi said. "I am fine, really. Just a small fight."

Sharon took a sip of her own beverage. "Did you know I only had a long conversation with Qiang once before this?"

Yi looked as Sharon, slightly confused.

"But even during that conversation," Sharon continued, "he spoke of you. He told me about your unique history, how you met Ling and married him so he wouldn't have to get that invasive surgery. He told me about Hanbing and how you guys were raising her to protect her. He made it clear what great people the three of you are. He asked me then—if you three ever needed help, if I would help."

"Well," Yi said solemnly, "he is wrong about one thing. I am not a great man."

"I disagree. I may have only known you for a couple of days, but I know enough about you to see what Qiang meant," Sharon said. "True, you are a flawed man. But I think there is a nobility inside of you. I think your actions, not your words, have expressed who you are. I think you need to work on your words."

Yi didn't say anything. He looked out into the darkness. He could hear crickets chirping in the inky night.

"What is on your mind?" Sharon asked gently.

"I don't know. That fight," Yi said quietly. "It was different than any other fight before. Ling has never said those things to me. It's like he is making me out to be the bad man, who is out to hurt him. It's like he doesn't recognize the sacrifices I have made for Hanbing, or for him."

"I don think Ling thinks you are a bad man at all. He was just standing up for what he believes in."

"I know that, but I don't like it," Yi replied. He laughed loudly and uncomfortably. "I just don't know what to do."

"Then let's approach it from another direction. Ling loves you a lot," Sharon said. "He would do anything for you."

"I know."

"In that case, do you love Ling?"

Yi thought for a moment. No one had ever asked him that the question before. "No—yes—I don't know. Honestly, I don't think I know what love is. I mean, the romantic kind. The only person I know I love is my daughter, and that isn't the same thing."

"Let's make it simple, then. I know you care about Ling. I know when you were children, he was your best friend. I know you made this decision to protect him," Sharon said as she took another sip of tea. "Therefore, by that logic, if you still truly care about him, you would support him in doing what he needs to be happy and healthy. You wouldn't make any decision that would physically or emotionally harm him."

"I know. But it isn't that simple." Yi thought for a moment. "I don't think I could stay with Ling if he is a man."

"How is that different than before? It's not as if he was a woman before," Sharon chuckled. "Or are you more afraid of facing the reality of the situation once it is out in the open?"

"You know," Yi said randomly, dismissing her comment, "I suddenly realize, that outside of Hanbing, you are the only biological female I have ever spoken to."

"I don't think my biological sex matters," Sharon said, "unless society or people make it an issue. I didn't become an ambassador because I am a woman. I became an ambassador because I worked hard, and I am good at what I do. It would be beneficial for you to look past people's appearances, especially something as stereotypical as gender roles. Every person, no matter their background, deserves to be treated respectfully."

"I know," Yi said. "It's just hard for me."

"It's hard to treat people with respect?" Sharon questioned. "I think excluding some awkward comments you say here and there, you do treat people well, except for Ling. Why do you think that is?"

"I don't know. Some might say I blame him for my problems and frustrations. Perhaps that is true, but I made those choices, not him," Yi said, reflecting. "Everything feels so different now. So much has happened in the past few days, the past two weeks, and in the last ten years. My world and my ideas keep changing. I guess I don't like not being in control of the situation."

"You were never in control of the situation," Sharon said, taking another sip out of her mug. "Because life is not controllable. Ling and Hanbing are not objects for you to manipulate. If you truly cared about them as people who care about you, you would let them be who they want to be. You need to learn to let go."

"But I am the man of the household. I need to take care of them," Yi explained.

"Taking care of them is not the same as controlling them." Sharon stood up, picking up her empty mug. "It is getting late, and I need to head to bed. This is my advice for you. Let go of the cultural views you were taught in this country, this extreme version of a patriarchy. Let go of everything you ever learned about what men and women are supposed to be, and what men and women are supposed to do. See Ling as someone who is equal to you and ask yourself how you would feel in his situation." She paused, looking him in the eyes. "It's time for you to make a choice about what you believe is right. Life is all about choices and it is our actions that define who we are."

Yi looked back at her. "I don't know how to do that. I don't know how I am supposed to treat Ling."

"Then, let me make it simple." Sharon smiled as she walked to the doors. "Treat Ling like someone you respect. Treat Ling like you would treat Qiang."

26.
A FAMILY IS HOW YOU CHOOSE TO DEFINE IT

"Are you sure you want to do this?" asked Zhuang. "I mean, once I do it, there is no going back."

Ling thought for a moment. "Yeah. I think so. I just want to know what it is like."

"Ok," said Zhuang, "but just so you know, I haven't done this in many years. So, if I mess up, I take no responsibility."

"I am sure it will be fine." Ling smiled. "I don't have any big expectations."

"Then let us begin." Zhuang took out a pair of scissors and an electric razor and began cutting off long strands of black hair. "This hair can be donated, so I am going to try to keep it intact. You have really good hair."

"Thank you," Ling said awkwardly as the pile of hair on the ground began to grow.

"What do you think?" asked Zhuang about twenty-five minutes later.

"I...I am not sure. I guess I am surprised. I haven't had short hair since I was like, ten," said Ling, staring at the mirror in shock. He rubbed his hand through the few centimeters of hair he had left. He could barely recognize himself in the mirror. "Do I look okay?"

"You look fine," Zhuang chuckled. "Actually, you look better than fine. Qiang always said you made a pretty woman, but you appear to make an even more handsome man." Zhuang grabbed a paper bag next to him. "Now that you decided you want to look like a man, Qiang and I decided to get you a present. I picked it up yesterday in the Capital. Just something small."

Ling opened up the paper bag. Inside was a white shirt, a simple brown belt, and a nice pair of jeans. "Now that you have embraced your manhood," laughed Zhuang, "you need to dress like a man, too. Go on, try them on."

Zhuang averted his eyes as Ling slowly tried to put on the new clothes. "What do you think?" Zhuang asked as Ling slid on his belt.

"I am not sure," Ling said truthfully. "I haven't worn pants in over a decade. They feel very different."

Zhuang chuckled. "In any case, you should know you look very handsome."

"Thanks. I know...I know Yi is not going to be happy," Ling said uncomfortably. "But I had to do this. I don't want to continue being someone I am not, especially in a new country, when I don't have to."

"We could hear your argument last night," Zhuang hesitantly said. "Are things going to be alright?"

"I don't know. I hope so." Ling grimaced internally. "We leave tomorrow, so I don't think there is much of a choice in this matter."

"Are you going to talk to him about it?"

"I think we have done enough talking," Ling said sadly. "I told him what I want. I told him what I need." He paused. "I know I should do everything to make him happy, but I want to be happy, too. I don't want to keep pretending to be someone I am not to please him. I know this makes me a bad wife, but I don't want to keep doing things just for him."

"Qiang and I have told you and Yi many times. A relationship cannot be healthy if both parties are not equal and don't treat each other with love and respect," Zhuang said sternly.

"But Yi doesn't love me."

"Since he appears unwilling to let you go," Zhuang began simply, "he needs to learn to treat you as his equal. He needs to respect you. You are not his object to control and mold. Qiang and I like Yi a lot, but we have never approved of the way he treats you. Qiang is actually quite vocal about it, but I am not sure you knew that."

Ling didn't know what to say. He hesitated for a moment. He had been thinking about an idea for a few days now. He had thought about it before but now it actually seemed plausible. "Zhuang," Ling said suddenly. "There is another favor I need to ask. I want to get a gift for Yi. I think you can help me get it. I know you won't approve, but I have been thinking about it for a while now. So, please hear me out."

Like Ling suspected, Zhuang was not supportive of the gift he wanted to give Yi. However, Zhuang was respectful enough understand that Ling was determined, and didn't try to convince him otherwise. Instead, he told Ling he would help him only after he got the ambassador's permission. Ling thanked him profusely and ran off to Ambassador Sharon's office. Time was of the essence as this was their last day.

Ling stood outside of Ambassador Sharon's door, going over the plan and conversation in his head. There was so much that could go wrong. He was asking for too much, especially after everything she had done for them in the last few days. Trying to summon all his courage, he gently knocked on door.

Sharon answered, slightly surprised. "Ling! Wow! You look so different! I almost didn't recognize you. Great haircut! Nice clothes. What are you doing here? Is everything alright?

"Yes. I am sorry to bother you." Ling looked around nervously. "I need to ask you a favor, and I know it's a big favor. Can I come in?"

"I am kind of in the middle of something." Sharon began, but upon looking at Ling's determined face, she relented. "Sure, come on in, but make it fast."

Qiang and Yi sat in the downstairs dining room talking as Hanbing tried some new western style cuisine. Yi was shocked and surprised at her willingness to try new things. Though the emba sy served a mixture of local food and food from their own country, Yi and Ling had both been uncomfortable in trying new dishes and accepting the new flavors. Secretly, what they were going to eat was one of his biggest concerns when they moved abroad, but it didn't seem acceptable to ask. He realized that sooner or later his diet would have to evolve, but it made him happy to see that his daughter wouldn't have the same struggles.

"I understand why you guys won't go with us when we leave tomorrow," Yi said sadly. "It still sucks though. Have you guys thought about what is going to happen next?"

"I guess we move to the Capital. Now that Ambassador Sharon has offered Zhuang a new position as head of security, it's my turn to play the role of, what do you call it, the housewife?" chuckled Qiang. "Besides, we could never leave as long as our babies, in this case Mew Mew and You'sun, are still alive."

"Now, now," laughed Yi, "I believe Zhuang told us, you were always the woman in the bedroom. I guess you can be the woman in other aspects now as well."

"Hey," chuckled Qiang, feigning embarrassment, "as I told you before, we take turns in the bedroom!"

The two men laughed for a moment, reflecting on their own friendship. "I remember when I first went to your house, and saw all the pictures on wall, of you with all the celebrities, whose wives you had created or operated on," Yi said finally, awkwardly making small talk. "Suddenly, I realized how skilled and connected you were. Now this week, I found out that Zhuang is as equally skilled and connected as you. I would have never guessed he knew people from the embassy."

"You didn't expect me to be with someone who was not equal or greater in greatness, did you?" Qiang said smiling. "I'll let you know. It wasn't easy finding him. I am pretty great. Few people can match that."

Yi laughed again. There was no avoiding it. He had to say what he wanted to say. "I am going to miss you a lot, you know, and Zhuang, and the cat and the bird, I guess. You saved my life. Our lives. More times than you realize. You have changed me so much." He tried hard to not show too much emotion. "I am sorry I am getting emotional, but I know I am a better person because of you."

"You would have done the same for me," Qiang said encouragingly. "Maybe not in the same way, but you have always been a good guy. I have never doubted that fact. Now go out, be free, and show the world who you really are."

"Are you sure you guys will be alright?" Yi sniffed, wiping away his tears. "Perhaps we can figure out a way for you to come with us. Hanbing would love that. Especially if you brought the cat."

"What about You'sun? He is in no state to travel. Although Zhuang would never admit it, I know he would choose the bird over me any day," he added with a laugh. "But that is not the point. This is your opportunity, Ling's opportunity, and Hanbing's opportunity. Go out, and be true to yourselves. Embrace your destiny."

Yi smiled, wiping his continuous tears.

"I will be fine. Don't worry about me," Qiang said reassuringly. "Ambassador Sharon has managed to negotiate a pardon with the central government as long as I keep my head down. Who knows how much that will cost them financially, but I appreciate it. With Zhuang working, we will be able to keep a quiet life. I can stay home and play with the cat and bird all day. Perhaps one day I will cook and clean as well as he can."

Ling silently walked into the room. It took a moment for Yi and Qiang to recognize him. Qiang's mouth dropped in shock. "Wow, Ling. You look handsome. Seriously. You look good!

Zhuang did a great job."

"Thanks, and yes, I think Zhuang did a good job. Thanks for the clothes." Ling turned to Yi. "Can I speak to you, please? Alone?"

"Sure," Yi said, confused and slightly surprised. He stood up and the two of them walked into the hallway. "What's going on? I like that short hair on you by the way. Your clothes look nice; you look handsome. Is this about last night because—"

"Thanks. No, don't worry, I don't want to talk about last night," Ling interrupted nervously as he paced around a bit. "Look, I wanted to get you a present. A thank you present, before we leave. For dealing with all this. For everything you have done me, for Hanbing, in the last ten years."

"It's really no big deal. Look, I realized last night…" Yi said, slightly worried by Ling's behavior. "As long as you are happy, I am happy."

"I want you to be happy too," Ling said rather quickly. "That's why I got you this present." He took a deep breath. "Right now, in our room. There is a biological girl waiting for you. She is willing to have sex with you."

"What?" asked Yi, shocked.

"She is Asian. Korean, I believe. I know you like Asian girls, like the ones in your dreams. She is very pretty," Ling continued, talking very fast. "I want you to have sex with her. See if you like it. Then you can decide what happens to us when we leave tomorrow. If you want to be with a woman, I understand. I just want you to be happy, and if being with a woman is what makes you happy, then so be it. You will still be a part of Hanbing's and my life. We can work out an arrangement. But before all that happens, I want to give you this opportunity to try this out, no strings attached."

"Wait a moment here," Yi said. "What is going on? Why are you doing this? How did you arrange this?"

"I asked Zhuang. Turns out military men are not all as pure as they are portrayed. I got permission from Sharon, also. She knows she is here, so you aren't breaking any rules or anything." Ling stared at Yi's surprised face for a moment, before continuing, "I know you would never go out and do this by yourself. You would probably think it's cheating or something and talk yourself out of it." Ling's voice began to sound pleading. "But I think you need to try it out. I just want you to be happy. So, like I said, she is waiting in our room. She has a few hours of free time. Also, I have told her about you, shown her a picture. She says you are handsome, and she is interested. So, it isn't like I am forcing her to do this, I think. But when you are done, I'll be in the garden with Hanbing, waiting. I know she wants to play with Qiang and Zhuang for a while. She is going to miss them a lot."

"Look…" Yi began awkwardly.

"Just go." Ling smiled uncomfortably. "I will see you in a few hours. Come find us in the garden when you are finished."

Waving a small goodbye, Ling began walking slowly back into the dining room to grab Hanbing.

Ling struggled uncomfortably in his seat while sitting in the garden. It was difficult for him wearing pants. He didn't really enjoy the tightness up front, and combined with the sweat and his nervousness, he couldn't stop scratching there. He wasn't sure how he felt about his short hair. He wondered how long it would take before he would be comfortable with this new look. He still did a double take every time he looked in the mirror.

He could see the sun setting in the distance as he watched Hanbing play with Qiang and Zhuang. This would probably be the last time she ever saw her uncles, and he watched her laugh as she chased them. Her hair was the longest it had ever been, and though the immediate reaction made him slightly nervous; he realized that after tomorrow, this was not something he would ever have to fear again. He was so thankful to the many people who had helped them in the past few weeks and given them this opportunity to go overseas. He decided he would honor them by living his life accepting himself as he was.

He tried so hard not to think of Yi and the woman in the bedroom. He didn't like it, but this was about Yi's happiness, not his own. For so long, he longed to please Yi and make him happy. Finally, he was doing that, he told himself. He had finally accomplished what so many nan-nu tried to accomplish; he had pleased his husband. If he loved him, he needed to love him enough to let him go.

He wondered how long it had been since Yi went in the bedroom. He looked at his watch. It had only been slightly over fifteen minutes. Time was going by much too slowly.

His silent pondering was interrupted by footsteps behind him. Michael, Ambassador Sharon, or some member of the embassy staff must have come out to watch Hanbing play in the garden. He jumped as a hand touched his shoulder and squeezed it. It was Yi.

Yi watched Qiang and Zhuang chase Hanbing around the garden. "I think the hardest part for her will be the fact that they aren't coming. Do you think we will ever see Qiang and Zhuang again?"

"What are you doing out here? I wasn't expecting you out so quickly. I mean, that was fast," gasped Ling in surprise. "You usually take longer than this, I mean, I know from experience. Were you just nervous because it was your first time with a woman? Did you not want a second round? You have pretty fast recovery, you know?"

Hanbing looked up, seeing her father out in the garden and began running towards him. Yi put up his hand to say no.

"I didn't have sex with her. I couldn't do it," Yi said calmly. "I walked into the bedroom, and I saw her. We talked for five minutes, and I told her I couldn't have sex with her."

"Why not?" asked Ling, confused. "She is beautiful, she is your type, she is everything you would want for your first time."

Yi took a deep breath. "You just don't get it do you? Look,

you may not be what I was hoping to marry, and you may not be what my body craves, but I married you. I could never cheat on you, even if you gave me permission. That is not the man I am."

Ling sat there; he wasn't quite sure what he was supposed to say. He began to speak, but Yi put his finger over his lip, shushing him.

"Please, let me continue," said Yi, pleading. "I have been thinking about this a long time. Even before our fight, I thought about this. I thought about it again last night after our fight. I thought about what you said. At the end of the day, I would rather be in a relationship than not at all." He paused to take a deep breath. "You are right, I made a promise as a child to protect you, and although back then I didn't know what that meant, I meant every word of that promise when I made it. We are starting a new life in another country tomorrow, and I will continue to protect you and Hanbing."

Yi paused again, thinking hard, and contemplating on how to form his words. "You talk about how I am not gay, and I should have the freedom to be with whoever I want, and you tell me you are gay, and know you are in love with me. Guess what—you are right. I am not gay; I know men are not what I am attracted to. But, I don't think that matters. As you said, I can choose who I want to be with, and you know what, I am choosing to be with you. Ten years ago, I chose to marry you, and in our vows, I said we are together for life. In my mind, that has not changed. Even if you decide to live your life as a man, I will still stay by your side. I guess what I am saying is…that I am willing to live a gay lifestyle to be with you. I am willing to make that sacrifice for you."

Yi raised up his hand, beckoning Hanbing, Qiang, and Zhuang over. He got down on one knee upon their arrival and held Ling's hand in his.

"I want everyone here to see this. I want you to all to be here," he began. "Li Ling, I am doing this in front of our daughter and our closest friends. I know I can be the man that you want me to be and I will strive to be that man. I want to continue raising Hanbing with you. I promise I will treat you with the care you deserve and work to make sure you are happy and satisfied in every aspect of our lives. I promise I will treat you as my equal in everything. I promise to love you both to the best of my ability. Will you let me continue being a part of your life, by becoming not my wife, but my husband?" He stood up, and before Ling could react, leaned over and kissed him.

Ling stood there, stunned. He could feel Yi's tongue thrust into his mouth. This was unlike any kiss they had in the past, and he felt slightly dizzy. As Yi let him go, he took a moment and thought about what Yi was saying. He wasn't quite sure how he felt about what he said. Yet, he couldn't stop the tears flowing from his eyes and the words from his mouth.

"Of course I will."

Epilogue
9 YEARS LATER

Eighteen-year-old Wang Hanbing slowly packed her suitcase. On her bed, her calico cat, Mew Two, lay half asleep, watching her as she moved about the room, grabbing the things that she needed or thought were important for the next step of her journey. Her waist-length hair flowed behind her. She hadn't cut it since the day she started growing it out nine years ago, and it was a huge part of her self-identity.

She grabbed a small binder off her shelf in which she kept some old, important pictures. Memorabilia from a past she was no longer a part of, yet had determined so much about her. Contacting her old family and friends from her birth country was impossible, and these pictures represented the only connection she had. Slowly opening it, she flipped through some of the old pages. A picture of her grandfather, the once-famed Governor Wang, cut out of a newspaper, was on the first page. He had been executed on charges of treason about two years after they had left the PRCC. She didn't have any other pictures of her grandparents, but she still thought about them fondly, despite everything she knew about them. She had also heard that her paternal grandmother, Guihua, had committed suicide, as was culturally appropriate, soon after her grandfather's death. Her parents didn't really know how to react to the news, and they never spoke about it. As far as she knew, her maternal grandparents were still alive and running a little noodle shop. She often wished she could have another bowl of her grandfather's noodles.

She didn't have any pictures of her uncle, her aunt, or her cousin, Qinghuang, either. She missed her cousin a lot, as he was one of her childhood best friends, and she had fond memories of them playing together in the Governor's Manor. Her parents had heard from rumors that her uncle continued to work in the government. He had never been able to successfully escape the family name. As he always lacked the proper skills and natural leadership ability, he had been demoted to lower governmental positions after his father's execution.

On the second page was a picture of a different calico cat than the one currently sleeping on her bed. The first cat she ever met, Mew Mew. The picture had been given to her by Ambassador Sharon, who had received it from Zhuang about one year after they arrived. Below were pictures of a rooftop garden and a large falcon. You'sun had died soon after the picture was taken, and Mew Mew a few years after that.

The next few pages were pictures that her parents kept from her childhood, which were kept in the suitcase the day they ran away from home. They were wrinkled from years of travel, but she still looked at them fondly, laughing at the pictures of her with short hair, and the pictures of her daddy with long hair. She knew she would never get a chance to return to her birth country, and she understood why, but that didn't keep her from reminiscing.

There were also pictures of her arrival in her adoptive country. She had been a bit of celebrity upon of her arrival in the Republic of Canada, with many politicians and talk show hosts wishing to meet her and her family to discuss her life. But her parents had always wished to give her a normal life and canceled these interviews as soon as she stopped being headline news.

On the last page was picture of her family with Qiang and Zhuang at the airport. They had left under asylum status about three years prior. After the animals died, they said they felt no reason to stay behind. Today, they lived in another city which was a three-hour drive away, but she still managed to see them about once every month.

There was a small knock on the door. Turning around she saw her father, who she once knew as her mother, standing in the doorway. He kept his hair short now, and was still very skinny and young looking, despite now being in his early forties. The only thing odd about him was his decision to wear kilts. He had never gotten use to the idea of wearing pants and had embraced the traditional Scottish garb wholeheartedly.

"Your father is almost done packing downstairs," he said, tears gleaming in his eyes. "I can't believe my daughter is leaving home and going off to university."

"It's only a three-hour drive, Mama." Hanbing said laughing. "Besides, I am only a twenty-minute drive from Uncle Qiang and Uncle Zhuang. I am sure I will see them often. I heard Uncle Zhuang is learning falconry professionally now."

"I know," Ling said tearfully, "but it's just this is going to be your first time away. I have been at your side ever since we took you in. What am I going to do without my baby girl around?"

"You can always go back to school," laughed Hanbing. "Besides, someone needs to take care of Baba."

"Excuse me," interrupted a gruff voice. "I don't need anyone to take care of me." Yi walked in. He had a gained some belly fat since arriving in their adopted country, acquiring a taste for cheese. Recently he had been busy trying to work some of it off. He still worked as a teacher, but instead of teaching politics, he now taught his native language.

During her teenage years, Hanbing had wondered to herself if her parents would stay together. They never fought or anything, but as she got older and understood the background of their relationship, she wondered if she was the glue to their relationship. But both her parents always seemed content, if not happy. They cuddled together on the couch when they watched movies in the living room, and often did little things like hold each other hands when they thought no one was looking. A few times, she even saw them kiss.

"Are you ready?" Yi asked, looking at the opened suitcase on the floor. Mew Two meowed loudly at him.

"Almost, Baba," Hanbing said, quickly throwing the binder and a few other things in the suitcase. "Now I am ready," she beamed.

"Oh, before I forget," Yi said, helping her lock the suitcase, "the Alliance called. They wanted me to tell you good luck."

The Alliance was a small group of around fifty people who were from PRCC or allies of the refugees. Since arriving, they had met a few other biological Chinese females, but they were all older, in their late forties to sixties. They knew, however, that there had to be more in the larger Oversea Chinese diaspora and perhaps one day they would have a chance to meet them. Hanbing had been thinking about the possibility of donating her eggs one day when the time was right. For now, it was just a chance for people to meet and discuss the old days.

"Anyway," Yi continued, "why don't you head downstairs and put your luggage in the car. Your daddy and I will take a last look around. Make sure you didn't forget anything."

"Bye, Mew Two," Hanbing said, reaching down to pick up her cat. "I know I will miss you most of all." She chuckled as she handed her cat to Ling. "Don't forget to feed her twice a day when I am gone."

"Aww, we could never forget Mew Two," Ling said, giggling as he cuddled the cat.

Yi and Ling stood around in Hanbing's empty room. They heard the front door slam as Hanbing walked out. Yi walked behind Ling, putting his arms around him. "She is going to be alright you know; we did a good job."

"I know," Ling said, leaning back into him. "She just has never left the nest before. What if something goes wrong?"

Yi smiled. "You worry too much." He leaned over and kissed Ling. "It's one of the things I love about you."

"So, you do love me?" said Ling, half serious.

"I think I always have. I was just too concerned with labels—gay or straight—stuff that didn't matter. It's just taken me longer to realize and accept it," Yi said, smiling. "The day I spoke to you on the playground was the smartest thing I could have ever done. Second, being the day I asked you to be my husband. You and Hanbing are truly the best things that could have ever happened to me."

"So, no more dreams about women then?" joked Ling.

"Please, for the last few years, the only woman in my dreams is you. You still wear the long skirt and everything," laughed Yi as Ling gently punched him on the shoulder. "Besides, I know you can please me better than any woman ever will." He leaned down, giving Ling another kiss. Looking Ling directly in the eyes, he whispered, "I love you, Li Ling. I wish I had started telling you sooner."

The two stood there for a moment, looking around the bedroom as Ling leaned contently against Yi. Mew Two purred in Ling's arms and Yi smiled brightly. In their hearts, they both knew things would always be alright, as long as they both had each other.

ACKNOWLEDGEMENTS

Every story is a collection and reflection of experience, even a story such as this one, which first came to me in a dream, as cliché as that sounds.

There are so many people who have been part of my life journey, all of whom in their own little way, influenced and shaped my ideas. Although most of these people I am no longer in contact with, I would like to take a moment to acknowledge and thank everyone whom I had the fortune to meet and talk to, thus in some small way, influencing my first novel, and many of my other writings.

To my childhood friends and classmates in Taiwan, the first people I lost contact with, for hanging out with me when it wasn't popular to be friends with the Eurasian kid.

To my friends and classmates in Auburn, Washington, who introduced me to pop American nerdy culture, which I still engage in today.

To my high school friends and classmates in Olympia, Washington, who hung out with the new student in the last two years of high school.

To my friends and coworkers from Toys"R"Us, who taught me the value of hard work and service with a smile.

To my friends and classmates from The Evergreen State College who debated with me and forced me to defend my ideas.

To my friends and colleagues in the film industry, which gave me a unique experience in the world of entertainment.

To all my friends and coworkers from my other career pathways, who have challenged me professionally and taught me new skills.

To all my teachers, ranging from kindergarten to university, who taught me new ideas and inspired my career in education.

To all the students I have had the pleasure of teaching and gave me the experience to be better at my job.

To all the people involved in helping me get this book out to the world, every step of the way, thank you for helping me make one of my goals come true.

To my family, for bringing me into this world and giving me a place to grow.

And of course, to all the others that I have met along the way in my adventure so far.

I could not have written and published this story without learning from each of you.